A matter of Truth

by

Heather Lyons

Cerulean
Books

To my mom,
who taught to me to read
and to love books at such a young age,
this one is for you.

Chapter One

I lift my hand up, shading my eyes as I peer at the loud and heavy surf crashing onto the pristine white shoreline. Overhead, gulls scream in a painfully bright blue sky, but even they are nearly drowned out by the ocean's anger. "You can't be serious about going out there today."

An inscrutable smile spreads across Jonah's lips as he pulls up the rest of his dark wetsuit. He reaches for the zipper, but I step around him so I can slowly tug the tab upward. "I think a storm is coming in," I tell him, trailing my other hand up the metal path.

When his head tilts back to survey the cloudless sky, black hair brushes against my fingers; a delicious shiver shakes my spine. I lean forward, my arms going around his chest, so I can press my face against his neck. His arms crisscross to wrap around mine, and we stand like this, watching the waves continue their furious pounding of the shore for long minutes of hushed unease. All too soon, he pulls away so he can pick up his surfboard.

Anxiety spreads throughout my belly; I reach out and trace the length of his arm, aching to chase my fears away. "Promise me you'll be careful?"

His cerulean eyes are so sad when he studies me, a mute accusation that asks me why I don't trust him enough.

I do, though. Probably more than I trust any other person in the entire universe.

His free hand cups the back of my head, drawing me in close. I savor how my heart slams around in my chest when our lips meet, how my world tilts when his tongue touches mine. I let myself drown in this kiss, and in him.

I love this man, I think to myself.

It's over too soon; he's off into those wild, terrifying waters. I trail him to the exact line where water fades to sand, holding my breath as he duck dives under the blackening foam of a monstrous wave. I count in my head to ten, then twenty . . . I get to fifty, one hundred, but Jonah has yet to surface. I scan the horizon for his profile, but no one else is out amongst these waves today. And then I scream his name until it becomes a second heartbeat, yet my voice is alone on this beach.

In desperation, I tear away the waves until all that lies before me is a dripping, sloped shelf riddled with gasping sea life. Jonah is nowhere to be seen.

I race into the dying coastline, bare feet shredding against sunken rocks and broken shells, but I can't find him anywhere. Hours are spent searching, but there's nothing, no one. Just a silent, dead former ocean I've created in my panic.

I've lost him.

In my agony, I let the world around me explode.

Dammit, I missed the bus.

As I hurry down the nearly empty street, I attempt to shake the lingering aftereffects of yet another nightmare that pulled me so far under I only awoke when a neighbor pounded against our shared wall, shouting for me to turn off my alarm clock. It wasn't the first time this has happened, and I doubt it'll be the last. Nowadays, my dreams are never kind to me, and along with all-too frequent blackouts, they wreak havoc upon my work schedule.

I'm an hour late for my shift at the Moose on the Loose, and although the owner loves me like I'm his kid sister and won't fire me (let alone write me up), I hate abusing his generosity. Being late to work is something I'm not okay with. Most days, I'm painfully early; routine, even that of a job, proves to be a healing balm. I allow myself to sink into the lull of going through the motions of working in a diner, perfecting them until I feel comfortable in my skin.

Elusive as those moments are, and as brief as they can be, I chase after them with everything in me.

Waiting for me outside the Moose, coatless despite the bitter weather and holding a steaming cup of coffee in his hands, is a welcome sight. Or, maybe not, since Will's glaring at me with the equivalent of an unwelcome *I told you so.*

I kiss my hand and pat my butt.

"Why you are so insistent on taking the bus instead of letting me drive you to work continues to boggle my mind," he tells me, his sexy Glaswegian accent diluted by a mere five years in Alaska. And then, in an awful facsimile of an American accent, a good octave above mine, *"What kind of girl am I if I can't get to work on my own, Will?"* He tsks-tsks. "I have an answer for you—a tardy one."

I brush past him, wrenching the door to the diner open. "Smart-assery is not your most attractive quality."

He laughs, and even though laughing is not something I can easily do anymore, I adore listening to his. It's like somebody bottled up happiness, and it's hooked up inside him, so whenever he wants, he can just let some loose to infect the people around him. "I beg to differ. In any case, as you've missed most of your shift already, we decided to best utilize your talents at the bowling alley rather than servicing patrons."

Even though I know he's kidding, I still wince. "I'm an hour late. I hardly call that missing most my shift."

Inside the diner, Paul—the owner-slash-dishwasher of the Moose—is leaning against the counter, flipping through a motocross magazine. He looks up when the bell over the door sings. "There's our girl." I'm gifted with one of his earnest smiles. "You had us

3

worried. Everything okay?"

I wonder what he'd think of me if I were to ever answer that question honestly.

I glance around the diner—it's a ghost town. Not a single customer is to be seen. I'm taken aback, as I've never witnessed the Moose so empty. "I am so sorry, Paul. My alarm clock sucks. I'll buy a new one tomorrow. I promise this won't be a problem again."

Acting like my missing an hour of work is nothing of consequence, he comes over and hugs me. Paul Neakok gives the best bear hugs, ones that can nourish even a soul like mine, especially when everything in me feels like it's being sucked down into a black hole.

Like today. Like every day nowadays. Four months' worth of black hole days.

"I believe you. Don't worry about it, Zoe-girl. Did I ever tell you how I was late to my sister's wedding? By something like forty minutes. Worse yet, I had the rings with me. I thought my *aaga* was going to skin me alive, but—maybe it was all the pre-celebration champagne, she just laughed. Mothers, right?" His grin spreads all the way to his nearly black eyes. "If I can get away with that, you can get away with oversleeping a little."

See? Way too generous. "But—"

"Ginny was loads happy you were late." Will stuffs wrapped straws into an old-fashioned glass dispenser. "She's itching to buy a new phone, so she could use the extra cash."

It's not like I'm exactly hurting for money myself right now, but the money I've got hidden in my room back at the boarding house is coated in guilt and hard to keep using.

I guess theft can do that to a girl.

I sigh and unwrap my scarf, only to have Will reach over and press his hand against mine. "No need. Like I said. Bowling. Us. Now."

Paul flips his baseball cap backwards and rubs his closely cropped beard. "We sent Gin ahead to pick up Frieda so they can get

4

us a lane at the alley."

I suck at bowling. SUCK. Which is why they probably love playing with me—I'm the guaranteed loser. "Not to be a whiner or anything, but I kind of need the tips, guys." And pride. I'd love to keep what's left of my pride tonight, thank you very much.

Paul opens the cash register and takes out several twenties. "Ask and ye shall receive."

I refuse to take them. "Paul. C'mon."

"Who're you expecting to get tips from?" Will steps in front of me, straightening my scarf. "Ghosts? Zo, the diner is closed, lest you haven't noticed."

I sigh. The Moose on the Loose Diner actually does pretty well on most days. Tonight is clearly dead, yes, but Paul certainly isn't hurting. But I like earning my money, so even though he hands the bills off to Will, who slips them into his pocket to pawn off on me later, I resolve to work overtime on my next shift and not clock in for it.

While Paul is locking up, Will shoves a cup of java into my hands, already prepared the way I like it. A small smile breaks free before I sip the warm brew; the motion feels foreign, but good.

I wish I could smile more often. Real smiles are so hard to come about anymore; I'd give my left foot to be able to feel pleasure without it being extraordinary or alcohol-induced. But if I'm going to smile, it's usually because Will coaxes one out of me.

"This is good," I tell him.

He's affronted. "Of course it is. I made it."

It's a moment in which I want to laugh. Really laugh. Because that's so Will: egotistical, generous, and hot-hot-hot all rolled into one. Instead, I smile a bit more, relishing the sensations these small muscle movements incur.

"I know I probably say it too much, but you should smile more often, Zoe." One of his fingers touches the corner of my mouth, but before I can say anything, he pulls it away and shows me excess foam from my latte. "Because, you're lovely when you do."

Not because he's telling me I'm beautiful or anything, but I love this guy. Seriously, flat-out adore him. Fate has nothing to do with me and Will, and I like it that way. Even still, I can't dismiss the guilty twinge that plucks through me whenever he calls me Zoe. But then, Will Dane doesn't know me by any other name than Zoe White, which is the worst alias ever. Four months ago, when I fled everything I knew and who I was, it wasn't like my brain was firing on all cylinders. I have a slew of paperwork I created for myself with various pseudonyms, but when it came time to fill out the job application for the Moose, I ended up using the one that sounds too much like my real name. I was terrified that if I chose one of the others, I might never get used to acknowledging people when they spoke to me. Zoe White seemed doable after nearly twenty years of being Chloe Lilywhite.

"I'm working on it," I say, despite knowing it'll take a miracle for what he wants to happen.

A miracle or giving up. Due to heavy stakes, and more importantly, the well being of those I love most in all the worlds, I'd rather attempt a miracle.

He loops an arm around my shoulders and walks me out to where his truck is parked in the back; Paul stays behind to finish locking up, saying he'll meet us in twenty. I fiddle with the heat once we're on the road, turning it up full blast. "Do we have to go bowling tonight?"

There's that laughter of his again. I pray I can get a contact high from it. "If we don't, Frieda will concoct some kind of story about how we ran off to get married."

My heart constricts painfully, but I manage to keep my face calm. "Why does she have such a hard time accepting our friendship?"

He reaches over and pats my knee. "Because she's Frieda."

Another moment I wish I could laugh. A tiny exhale escapes me, which is the closest I've gotten in awhile; I revel in the simplicity of this release. Leaning back into the heated leather seats of his truck, I stare at the sign Will taped on the dashboard a couple of weeks ago as a joke, when Ginny kept complaining she never got to ride shotgun anymore. *Zoe's spot. Not for sale.*

He flips through the radio stations until he finds a country song he likes. "Stay over tonight?"

Relief fills me up. It's exactly what I hoped he'd ask, even though I've been the one stubborn about moving in already. "OK."

His lopsided grin flashes at me as he sings along to the song playing. I join in, and the urge to laugh has never been so strong in months. We sound ridiculous—neither of us are naturally talented singers. But together? We take awful to a whole new level, and it's glorious.

Will is my drug of choice nowadays. I'm utterly addicted.

Ginny has pitchers of soda and beer already waiting for us, plus a stack of plastic cups. She's also got enough chili cheese fries to feed a small army. "Zooooeee!" I'm tackled into a hug. "Tonight's the night! I just know it!"

Poor, hopeful yet deluded girl. Ginny Swanson is the eternal optimist of this group, ever smiling, ever bubbly, kind of ditzy, yet in possession of the biggest heart I've ever come across. I can't help but always feel grateful for meeting her; had I not, I never would've gotten the job I did. Having this job, meeting these people, is what saves me every single day from throwing the towel in.

I sit down and shuck my shoes off. "Gin, the day I get a strike is the day I win the lottery."

"Could happen." Paul reaches across me to grab a cheese covered fry. He somehow miraculously beat us to the bowling alley. "You just have to play."

Frieda Carthage slaps at my hands the moment I grab one of my rental shoes. "Put that gross thing down." She smiles, her lips blood red against pale skin, a perfect cross between her namesake and a vampire. "We got you a gift, girlfriend."

Ginny bounces up and down, clapping her hands. Maybe I did win the lottery after all.

Will slides into the plastic seat next to me, slinging an arm around the back of my chair as Frieda pulls a box out from underneath the scoring table.

"For you," she says. It's wrapped in newsprint, tied with twine, but rather than looking shoddy, it comes across as retro and kitschy. It's a true talent of hers. "From all of us."

I take my time unwrapping it, which elicits a number of groans and laughs from my friends. Inside is a pair of my very own bowling shoes: lavender with bright turquoise stripes. On the backs, in glittery rhinestones, are matching Zs, no doubt products of Frieda's latest arts and crafts stage to bedazzle nearly everything she owns.

Like I said, kitsch.

For the first time in months, a smile overtakes me. A big one. A big, fat, genuine smile that almost hurts, it's so wide.

"I told you she'd like the Zs," Frieda says to Paul. They used to date and now . . . well, I'm not sure what they are now. Ginny claims they're friends with benefits, but I don't like to pry. Whatever they are or aren't, they're still close and love to bait each other as often as they can.

"There's no accounting for taste," he says, but he's smiling, too. We all are. Finally, I'm smiling right along with my friends, and I'm not faking it.

As Will drives me to his house that night, I finger the raised letters on the back of my new shoes. A small sound of disgust precedes, "Paul's right, you know. Those things are bloody hideous." He shakes his head in exasperation.

I clutch one to my chest. "Hush. I love them." And I do. Not because they're pretty—which, admittedly, had I picked out my own, these would not have been the ones, but because they're symbolic of my life right now. My friends chose to get me bowling shoes because they like having me around. Not because they have to have me around, or because Fate made them, or because they've got some skewed perception that I'm somebody important, but because they *want* me around. And that makes these shoes more precious to me than gold.

His cell phone rings, a special tone that alerts the both of us to just who is calling. I chew my bottom lip, sneaking a look his way. His focus remains on the road. Eventually, the phone goes quiet. He turns the volume up on the radio; a sad country song fills the cab, which is fitting for the rest of the drive back to his house.

Chapter Two

I pad toward the kitchen sometimes around three a.m., in search of a glass of water after awaking in a cold sweat from another nightmare in which I lost Jonah. Months after leaving Annar, I still dream about him nearly nightly—not the lucid dreams we shared for so long, but the kind where I have no control over what happens. Tonight we'd been in a forest, and when the dream died, all that'd been left behind was blackened bits of trees upon charred ground.

I was the one to leave, and yet, every single time I lose him in a dream, it cuts me to the core.

My hands are still shaking when I flip on the kitchen light, and then I jump when Will's still form at the table comes into view. He jumps, too, his chair clattering loudly in the night's silence. "Jesus, Zoe! You scared the shite out of me."

"I'm not the one sitting in the dark!"

He smiles sadly, and it's then I see his cell phone on the table. I drop into one of the chairs as he rights his fallen one. "Want to talk about it?"

He shakes his head, just like I knew he would. He and I, we're excellent at avoiding the big issues in our lives, which is probably why we gravitated toward each other so quickly. I resisted getting to know him all of a week before I couldn't help myself. I needed a friend and Will seemed like he'd fit the bill nicely. And I was right—I'd heard the term kindred spirits before, but never had it applied like it does now with this guy. It sounds awful, but one of the biggest draws toward Will is that, like me, he puts on a good front. Inside, he's just as much damaged goods as I am.

Helpless that there's nothing else I can do but be here for him, I motion to the stove. "Want some warm milk?"

"Shouldn't I be asking you that?" He stands up before I can protest and digs a pan out of the cupboard.

"The better question is, why are the two of you up at three-bloody-o'clock in the morning?"

I turn around to find Cameron Dane shuffling into the kitchen on well-loved slippers. His barely graying, sandy blonde hair is wild, his thin robe riddled with holes, but his handsome face is one of kindness. Acceptance. And, at the moment, paternal amusement. My eyes go wide in guilt. "Did we wake you up? I'm so sorry!"

He drops a kiss on my forehead before sliding into the chair next to me. "Just worried about you two, that's all."

Will pours milk into the pan, adding a few ingredients that make it his special recipe. As he stirs it, I stare at his phone and wonder how long he was in here. How long the call was tonight. How much heartache he's in.

"Want some, Dad?" he asks without looking up from the stove.

"Don't mind if I do." It's then that Cameron also spies the phone. His dark eyes are troubled but unsurprised. Like me, he knows better than to push, though. "What's got you up at this god awful hour, hen? Everything alright?"

As I cannot tell him the truth, I smile weakly. "Just thirsty."

Will looks up from the pan. "Coming right up."

"Learned this from his mum," Cameron tells me, arranging the mugs down in a straight row, handles aligned nicely. I already knew this, but I love hearing stories about Molly Dane, so I gladly listen anytime Will and Cameron reminisce about the woman whose influence on their lives still runs strong.

And yet, despite their happy memories, there's so much

heartbreak in this kitchen, it's nearly dripping off the walls and ceilings, into our hair and skin. I try not to think of my own mother, who never made me anything to help me sleep. Or my father, who never asked what was wrong, let alone spent time with me in the dark of night to ease my worries.

The chair creaks when Cameron sits back down. "I heard there was a mugging not far from your boarding house this week."

I'm not surprised by the crime or by Cameron's gentle disapproval. He's letting me off the hook for why I'm up in the middle of the night, but he won't let me off for where I live.

The Dane boys have been after me for weeks to just move in with them already. Both object to where I live, citing "shifty characters" in an "unsavory neighborhood" filled with "transient workers" that apparently think of nothing but "accosting innocent women" after being at sea for weeks or months.

The guys have a point. It's not like I think of where I live as home anyway. The boarding house is cramped; I share a bathroom with some old dude who smells like the Preparation-H he must buy in bulk, and there's some other guy missing teeth who's always on the stairs, ready to pummel me with his requests for a date, or, worse yet, a night of "raging, unencumbered sexual gratification."

But living here? With Will and Cameron? That'd be the same as putting down roots, which doesn't seem fair to them, or me no matter how much I want to. Because, sooner or later, somebody is going to come looking for me. And when they do, I'll have to run. And yet . . . I feel safe with the Dane boys. Their house has been my sanctuary. The love they've shown me, the utter acceptance into their lives and home, have been a lifeline. For nearly twenty years, I've been starved for what they offer so freely. Security. Acceptance. Love. Honesty.

And most importantly: *family*.

"Having a girl around full-time will cramp your bachelor style," is what I finally say, even though I know it's a lie.

This amuses Will. "You spend the night at least five times a week anyway. You're over here every day as it is. There hasn't been a single dinner we haven't had together as a family—except when any of us work—since the week I met you. You have a toothbrush in the bathroom. Deodorant. Your clothes hang in the closet. You picked out our Christmas tree. You buy Nell food. Hell, I even heard you call her *your* 'good girl' the other day."

I glance down at Nell, who's curled up underneath the table. She snorts in her sleep and kicks a leg; unlike the rest of us, Nell only dreams of good things, or so I hope. But he's right. This old girl is the dog I'd always wanted growing up but was denied due to my parents' beliefs that pets were irrelevant and burdensome to their crafts.

"I mean, I found one of your bras in the hamper this past weekend."

My cheeks burn. I'd wondered where I'd put that one.

Cameron chuckles at my shame. "Nothing either of us hasn't seen before, lass."

Could this get any worse? What's next? Did I leave behind stray tampons, too?

Will turns away from the pan to face me, hip propped against the counter. "We can even go over to your place right now and box everything up. It'll take, what—a half hour at the most, between the three of us?"

I study his dark eyes, gauging his seriousness. It's three in the morning, after all. And he's just gotten off what was, no doubt, a hellishly difficult phone call with his technically ex-girlfriend, even after all that's happened between them. "I would never ask you to do such a thing in the middle of the night."

Cameron rubs at his neat beard. "You need not to ask. We're more than happy to go and pack you up and bring you home."

Home.

After resisting it for so long, I finally allow the word to sink into me and spread out. *This* place is home to me, has been for weeks. Months, if I'm being honest with myself.

Cameron must see the sheen of tears in my eyes—they won't fall, I refuse to let anyone see me cry anymore—but he must see them, because his large hand covers mine. "I cannot stand the thought of you being alone in that place when you have a room here to call your own."

I should say no. It's the smart move. I'll only hurt them in the long run when I have to disappear. But the truth is, I love Cameron Dane like a father. More than my actual father, which sounds awful yet liberating to admit, if even just to myself. And I love Will, too. In these short months, these two have truly become more of a family to me than anyone I share blood and genetics with. So I take a deep breath, count to ten in my head, and say the only thing that I can and be completely true to myself. Something expands in the hollow of my chest, something warm and comforting, when I murmur, "Okay."

They both blink, startled, like they can't believe I finally caved in.

I exhale another fragile laugh. Two in one night. I'm on a roll. "This will be fuel to Frieda's fire, you know. Did you hear her earlier at the bowling alley? She was egging Ginny into a bet over when we'll seal the deal."

Will fills our mugs with the milk; more importantly, he fills the kitchen with his addictive laughter. "How much?"

I'm smiling. Oh, gods, I'm smiling and almost laughing and it's amazing. "Twenty bucks. Paul collected the bills from both girls."

Both men are amused. Will asks before sipping his drink, "What were the conditions?"

"I think Frieda thought we'd last a week at most. Ginny says we'll wait until we're married." And . . . the smile drops right off my face. Because I should've been married by now. My last name, my real one, would've no longer been Lilywhite. I should be a Whitecomb, but I'm not.

And that hurts more than I can articulate.

"You two are too young to even contemplate marriage," Cameron grumbles.

14

If he only knew.

Will joins us at the table. "Hypocrite, thy name is Cameron Dane. Didn't you get married at twenty-two? Sired me at twenty-three?"

I mouth, *sired*? He winks in return, the corners of his lips tilted upward.

"Times were different." Cameron wipes at lingering milk on the edges of his moustache. "You two have your whole lives ahead of you."

Will's long fingers curl around his mug. "Luckily, Zoe and I have no intention of ever marrying one another. Or shagging, despite all of Frieda's urgings."

I stretch my mug out to clink his in agreement. It relieves me to no end that he and I are on the same page about that. But I need to shift the conversation to something less likely to drown me in what-ifs and what-could-have-beens. "Think we can figure out a way to collect the money instead?"

His dark brown eyes, so similar to his father's, light up. "Listen to you, wanting to encourage our friends' gambling tendencies. I've finally corrupted you, haven't I?"

I swat at his arm and he laughs all the more.

Fifteen minutes later, while we nurse our milk and eat slices of homemade banana bread, Cameron raises his mug. "Zoe White, we officially welcome you home."

The urge to cry this time doesn't stem from the overwhelming anguish I drown in daily. Instead, I'm swaddled in relief. And a belief that maybe, just maybe, I can do this after all.

Cameron is upstairs in the boarding house, taping up the last two boxes of my meager possessions, while Will and I slide the pair we've brought with us into the back of his truck.

"Earlier, in the kitchen, we were joking around about that ridiculous bet of Frieda's. You were happy, and then . . ." His head tilts toward me. "It was like someone punched you in the gut. What happened?"

He knows me, knows how easily I can go from being okay to being decimated within seconds, because he's the same. But even still, I shake my head, hating the pain that spreads at the thought of what could have been. I ask, whisper soft and white in the frigid January air, "How do you know whether you made the right choice?"

He knows what I mean. He knows I'm asking about Becca.

"I don't." Another cloud forms between us from his deep sigh. "I fucking kick myself nightly, wondering if I have."

I wipe a dirty slush off the tailgate and think how I reevaluate my decision on an hourly basis.

"My parents were this grand love story. I grew up knowing nothing differently." He kicks his boot against one of the large tires. I know this story, and yet, I love to repeatedly hear it. It gives me hope that there are true love stories out there filled with people who make it work. "I thought I had it and . . ." He stares into the distance.

Part of me wishes I could fall in love with Will, how this could solve so many problems for all of us. But even considering such a betrayal leaves me rotting in guilt, an emotion I try desperately to outrace on a daily basis. Because, the fact is, my heart belongs elsewhere. It always will, which makes accepting harsh truths a bitter pill.

"Sometimes I drown in the What Ifs," he tells me quietly.

"Love isn't always enough," I whisper into air. My words lift up and dissipate before my eyes. I wish it were. I wish love were easy. Gods, I wish that so very much.

"No matter what you do, love never fails to kick you in the arse," he agrees, but there's no vehemence behind his words. "Look at Dad. Happy as can be until his wife dies, leaving him to be a single parent to a teenage boy. It eats him up every day, wondering if there was something he could have done to change the outcome." He slips off his beanie, runs a hand through his sandy hair before tugging on his ear. I can practically hear the words running through his head, the ones he won't say out loud, even to me: *Just like I do*.

Words I consider every single day myself.

I lean into him, tugging my own beanie down around my ears. The silence that surrounds us at nearly four o'clock in the morning is dense and sleepy. "For what it's worth," I murmur, "I think you're doing the best you can for yourself."

Like me, though, he's not able to talk about his choices easily. His arms circle me for a brief moment in a hug that leaves my heart hurting for him. "We should help Dad get those last two boxes down before he kicks both our arses."

Because I love him, I do not push any further. Not this morning, at least.

Chapter Three

The first time I ate at the Moose on the Loose, I was reminded of the diner I used to frequent with my friends back in high school. Called The Hollow Deer, there were dusty stuffed animal heads on the wall. It used to turn me off of meat when I was there, simply because those poor animals would stare at me balefully, like they were saying, "*Et tu*, Chloe?" Well, the Moose is similar in that there are animals everywhere—moose, obviously—but rather than stuffed heads, it's more in décor: moose curtains, moose statues, moose pictures on the walls, and moose etchings on the tables. If you like moose, this is definitely the place for you. If you don't, well, you're definitely in the wrong diner.

I like it here, though. Kitschy as it is, it's also very welcoming, and locals flock to this place for comfort food and easy camaraderie. Well, mostly easy. There's still Frieda to contend with, especially when she's in a gloat-y mood like right now. "Imagine my surprise when I saw a change of address form in Paul's office."

The yin to Frieda's yang, Ginny bumps hips with me. "I can't believe you and Will are living together!"

I roll my eyes. "Roommates," I stress. "We're roommates."

"Riiiggghhhht," Frieda drawls. She scoots until her hip is also against mine; I'm trapped in a gossip sandwich. One of the locals who comes on a daily basis chuckles from his spot at the counter. I try not to glare at him. "Like anyone could be just roommates with someone as tasty as Will."

Ginny giggles. Frieda chortles. The words are on the tip of my tongue, but I never can get them out, no matter how much I wish I could unburden myself, even to friends. Because if I were to let it out, it'd break me even more than it already has. And I'm a Class A, prime example of a broken girl. You're wrong, I want to tell them. Will is nothing more than my best friend. He will never be anything more than my best friend, because I already am in love with somebody else. Two somebody elses, actually. And that will never change, no matter how much I wished differently.

I tell them instead, "You realize my bedroom is next to his dad's, right?"

"I bet old Cameron snores," Frieda says. "And sleeps like the dead."

I wrap another set of silverware with a napkin. "He's forty-five, Frieda. That's hardly old."

"I think it's great!" Gum snaps between Ginny's super white teeth. "You're the best thing to happen to Will in ages."

I scratch the back my neck, uncomfortable with this turn in the conversation. I hope Will doesn't come out of the kitchen. He's incredibly uneasy about anybody discussing what he considers to be no one's business but his.

"Right?" Frieda puts a new liner in the coffee pot. "We thought he'd given monkhood a go until you entered his orbit, thanks to some bitch he couldn't seem to get over."

I don't have the heart to tell them that Will isn't entirely over that *bitch* just yet; just this morning, there was another traumatizing phone call that had Will in nearly a zombie state for the better part of an hour. I don't know what's worse—the lingering tie he and Becca, his ex-girlfriend, can't seem to unknot, despite the vast physical distance and history between them, or the forced separation and radio silence I've enforced between me and my fiancé. And his twin.

But I can't let myself think about them right now. I grab my pad and pen, ready to let myself fall into my work routine.

Frieda's not done with me, though. "You cannot honestly tell me that you haven't hit that yet." She purses her red lips together.

I look her straight in the eyes and say slowly, but clearly, "I haven't hit that."

"Are you asexual?"

I level a long look at her. She's only asked me this about, oh, a hundred times since we've met.

"Because, honey, Will is what we call USDA Prime beef."

"Well, thank you. Nothing makes a man feel manlier than being compared to actual cow flesh. Shall I lift my shirt so you can check my marbling as well?"

Ginny gasps, fire engine red, as Will sets a rag down on the counter next to us. Several customers nearby laugh loudly. Another smile curves my lips. It's an epidemic.

But Frieda is not shamed in the least. She pats Will's rock hard abs, still hidden behind his shirt and apron, before sauntering away. Ginny flees shortly afterwards.

"You're evil," I tell him, but he knows I'm joking.

"Bullocks. I am the epitome of angelic fortitude. Besides, they clearly don't know Dad. He wakes at the drop of a pin. Any shagging we'd ever do would have to be out of the house. I'm extremely loud when aroused, and I have a feeling you are, too. Some things just cannot be helped. Dad could never sleep through us."

I hush him, mortified. Frieda is at the end of the counter, taking an order while slyly watching us. I'm positive she just heard every word he said, as did much of the Moose's clientele in our vicinity. "Seriously. You're oiling the gossip machine."

He chuckles. "Perhaps I am a wee bit evil after all. But it's hard to resist. She's utterly tenacious with this insanity."

Most girls might be insulted, not to mention disheartened, if an extremely hot and charismatic guy chose to describe the thought of them being a couple as insanity, but I'm not most girls. Every time he reaffirms what I already know, that we're family and the closest of friends, sweet relief washes over me. I don't know what I'd do if I had to push Will away, if his feelings toward me were to change.

I poke at his chest with a spoon. "*Try.*"

His laughter is positively charming beyond words. "For you, I will try. No guarantees, though."

"Man, can you believe what's going on in Tibet?"

My head whips around to find a man seated at the counter, holding his smartphone out to the woman he's with. "So, crazy," she murmurs. "I cannot believe the riots going on over the occupation. It's like that part of the world has gone mad."

Suddenly, it's hard to stand, thanks to my knees giving out. Will grabs me before I fall. His eyes are filled with worry. "Are you okay?"

I nod my head, gripping the counter behind us. I silently curse myself for once more not being able to get myself under control. Anytime I hear about something like this, where emotions are high, a flood of memories threatens to pull me under.

Because I have a pretty good notion as to why Tibet is in chaos.

An acrid taste fills my mouth as I consider how Jonah must have been so close to Nepal, where he's always wanted to go—claiming it'd be good for his soul—only to end up doing something I know must be salt against the wounds such actions cause his conscience. And I can't help but wish I were there with him, reminding him how good of a person he is, how he's helped more people in the last year and a half than hurt, and that it'll be okay.

But I'm not. He's in Annar, and I'm in Alaska, and it'd been my choice to leave. I left my fiancé, hoping to give him a chance at a better life. I can only hope somebody is there helping him get through this, even if it's his ex-girlfriend Callie Lotus.

And that thought there crushes me, not to mention makes me want to destroy the entire diner.

I force myself to calm down. To focus. I cannot let my grief control me like this.

"Zoe. Talk to me," Will says quietly. His fingers brush against my cheek. When he pulls his hand back, I marvel at the wetness reflecting on his skin.

I'm crying, and I didn't even know it. It pisses me off that I let myself get this far in public.

"I'm fine," I tell him, but whom am I kidding? My heart has been gone for months now. How can anyone be fine when there's a cavity in her chest?

"Let's play Tell Me," Will says as he cooks me dinner later that night. It's a game we've been playing since the day I decided to let him in. *Tell me a secret. Tell me the truth. Tell me something you've never told anyone else before.* Tell Me has been both a challenge and a relief for a girl with too many secrets.

"Alright." I sit down and butter the pancakes he's set out for me. Cameron is at work, managing a large warehouse down in the port, leaving us to fend for ourselves. "Shall I go first?"

His shaggy, sandy hair goes flying as he shakes his head. "Tell me what made you cry today. I've never seen you cry, Zo. I'll admit it's got me worried."

I focus on pouring syrup rather than the concern that surely shows on his handsome face, struggling to find some kind of truth to tell him. Finally, carefully yet purposefully nonchalantly, "I'd overhead somebody talking about what's going on in Tibet."

He's silent for so long I eventually look up, only to find him staring at me like I've lost my mind.

"It's a horrible situation," I add quietly.

That snaps him back into form. "No—right. Of course. It's awful, no doubt. But, Zo—you were crying. Was it—"

"My turn." I answered his question; he knows the rules. He can only ask for clarification on his next turn. "Tell me about this morning's phone call."

His annoyance makes me regret the question—but only a little

22

bit. As concerned as he is about me, I'm just as worried about him. "She . . ." He clears his throat. "Becca somehow got ahold of a phone again and rang me to see why I hadn't been over today."

Gods. I try to hold back the slam of pity that crashes into me, but it's impossible. "Will—"

But he gives as good as he gets. "Tell me why you're so upset about Tibet. Be honest."

I sigh and set my fork down. I practically have to tear the words out of my throat. "Tibet reminds me of Nepal, since they're neighboring regions." Confusion fills his eyes, so I quickly counter with, "Tell me how you felt when you talked to her."

"How do you think I felt? Like I was fucking living through all of that shite once more." He doesn't have to clarify, but miraculously, he does. "The Becca I was talking to this morning was the one I stupidly planned on spending my life with. She was *lucid*. Confused, unsure of what happened over the last year, but she . . ." He shakes his head. "I very nearly bought a ticket to Glasgow on the spot."

I reclaim my fork back up and try to pretend that Will isn't baring his soul to me, because I know that's the only way he'll get through the next hour, let alone night. But I'm worried about him, so I gently press on. "Why didn't you?"

"Tell me why Nepal, via Tibet, upsets you."

I cut my pancakes into neat little triangles. "Nepal reminds me of somebody."

His eyebrows lift and then drop lower into a vee. "Somebody."

"Tell me what stopped you from flying to Glasgow."

He yanks the griddle off the burner. "Other than the money it would cost? Because, no matter how lucid Becca was this morning, it will never be permanent. The girl I loved is gone forever. Was gone even before . . ." He turns away from me and busies himself with piling pancakes on his plate. And then he laughs, so very bitterly. "Jesus. You think after a year and a half I'd be able to let it all go, right? She fucking shagged my best mate behind my back, even as she was planning on moving out here to be with me. Was going to have his *baby*, possibly even pass it off as mine. And then they got in that bloody car crash, and I had to learn about everything they've done afterward from his and her parents, when apologies and explanations mean shite." He tosses his spatula on the counter.

I get up and go over to where he is, laying a hand against his shoulder. His breath is shallow as he continues softly, tugging on his ear, "That wanker got off easy when he died."

But Becca didn't. Becca has severe brain damage and is confined to a wheelchair and a ventilator for the rest of her life back in Scotland. Most days she doesn't know who she is or where she is, and others . . . others she remembers Will and what they had, and always finds ways to bring that ghost home to him. He struggles so hard to forgive her, to let go of what could have been, but even for somebody as strong as him, it's asking a lot.

Although my natural inclination is to clam up, I know it must have been tough for Will to just let that all out. So I lean my head against his back and admit to him something I haven't done before. "Nepal reminds me of somebody I love." I swallow the growing lump in my throat. Even now, four months in, it's incredibly difficult to talk about Jonah. "I was sad today because when I heard some people talking in the diner about Tibet, I thought of this person, and of what Nepal means to him." I take a deep breath and count to ten, because saying this next part is like stabbing myself in the gut. "I miss him so much it makes it hard to breathe. Sometimes it's hard to move on, when memories refuse to let you go."

Will's voice reverberates through me when he quietly asks, "Did he die?"

I tell Will a lot—but I cannot talk anymore about Jonah with him. With anyone, really. All he knows is that love has broken me, too, and that I'm in no place to even contemplate a relationship. So much of me wants to open the floodgates, though, let Will into the dark parts of my heart like he's slowly been letting me in, and someday I will do just that. It's just . . . I need more time.

I shake my head against his back. There is no more Tell Me for the rest of the night.

Chapter Four

Over the last five months, I've learned to live in constant pain. It's similar to a perpetual migraine, only it affects my entire body. My chest aches, my lungs are tight, my joints throb, and I'm continuously light-headed. It has nothing to do with my workload, which, in the beginning kicked my ass but now only leaves my feet tired at the end of a shift.

No—this pain has everything to do with the fact that I'm separated from my Connection. Scratch that—*Connections*.

Being a Magical has its perks; most of my kind might believe they've hit the jackpot if Fate deems them lucky enough to have a Connection, which probably only three-to-five percent of our population has. It's a permanent bond that ties two people, two soul mates together. A Connection is your best friend, your lover, your confidant, and your comfort. You feel things, both physically and emotionally, that cannot ever be felt towards another person. But with the good comes the bad, because when you fight or are separated, your body and soul wither into a half-existence, filled with pain and sorrow. Which doesn't make it sound so desirable after all, does it?

Now, because I purposely left my Connections behind, I'm a mess. I'll be forever a mess. But it's for the best, and because of that, I'll work my butt off to ensure that it wasn't done in vain. Jonah and

Kellan have a chance to rebuild their relationship. I have a chance to live without feeling like I'm being torn in two every time I pull air into my lungs. I hurt, and I miss Jonah—and Kellan—more than I can articulate, but it's something I can live with if it means we all get a chance at having a normal life.

The bell above the door jingles, letting me know Frieda's surprisingly on time. Today, she looks like a cross between a Goth and some kind of tragic heroine out of a Regency novel. I can't help but admire how fiercely she refuses to conform to be anybody else but exactly who she is. This is one of my goals lately—be who I want to be, not who I'm expected to be or who I'm told to be. I've spent most of my life trying to be a Creator. And I am one, there's no doubt about that. It's just . . . I don't want to be only a Creator. I want to be Chloe. Or, rather, Zoe, who must surely be an improvement upon my old self.

"Keep Gin away from me today." Frieda grimaces as she ties on her half apron. "I'm hung over and not ready for her brand of sunshine this early in the day. As a matter of fact, keep everybody away—but most especially Paul and Gin."

It's four o'clock in the afternoon. Amused, I say, "Paul isn't here yet."

She mimics back my words, but it's not done in a cruel way. Just a typical, mocking Frieda way. "I left him at his house. He wants us to get back together. Can you believe that? Asshole."

I don't even know how to respond to that, especially since there's no way in hell I could ever label Paul an asshole.

"Hey you two!" Ginny sing-songs, bouncing toward us like the pogo stick she is. Her shift is over, and she's ready to leave, purse in hand. "Isn't today glorious?"

"Glorious?" Frieda snorts. "Jesus Christ. This girl in love is nauseating. Zoe. You're fired. You didn't even try to stop her."

Normally, comments like this wound Ginny, even though she's known Frieda and her bristly personality her whole life. But today, she's adding clapping to the bouncing. "Can't bring me down, Miss

Sourpuss!"

"Fine." Frieda glances around the diner; half the tables are filled, but all the meals are out. "Tell us what has you acting like a ray of mother-effing sunshine on this snowy day."

Ginny clasps her hands together and presses them against her heart. "I met someone."

Ginny meets a different true love on nearly a daily basis, so this is nothing new. Even still, I ask kindly, "What's his name?"

Her eyes are practically glowing, she's so excited. "Brent! He's so handsome, girls. He's just the best. The very best. We've been talking for a couple of weeks—"

Whoa. Now this is different, because normally Ginny tells me and Frieda every small detail of every guy.

"And I decided last night to give my heart to him. After I came home from our date, I found three-dozen roses in my bedroom. Can you imagine how dreamy my room smelled?" She sighs. "It smelled like love."

Seven months ago, my bedroom was filled with roses. So was a street in Annar after Jonah found his ring. I couldn't help myself. It was one of those rare moments in my life where I was so blissfully happy that I lost control of my craft in the best of ways.

Ginny is right, though. Love—at least that night, at least to me—smelled just like roses.

"And here I thought love smelled like sweaty sex and vodka," Frieda snarls.

I cough and scratch the back of my neck. Ginny merely wags a finger. "Uh-uh! Not even your sexual innuendos can ruin this for me!"

Frieda's affronted. "What innuendo? I'm pretty sure that was a straight-forward comment."

"I think that's great, Gin. I'm really happy for you," I tell our friend. I'm pleased my voice is steady, even though inside, I'm dissolving into a blubbery mess. I miss him. Gods, I miss Jonah so much that it's hard to even see straight.

Her feet come back to earth and stay steady against the floor. "I was thinking . . . is it okay if Brent comes bowling with us? I want him to meet you guys."

"What?" Frieda nearly screeches. Patrons look up from their meals and stare. She raises her hand, no doubt ready to flip them all off, but I smack it back down. Then she says, lowering her voice, "We don't bring temps to the bowling team. What if you two break up? What then?"

"But I'm the fifth wheel," Ginny says, and I swear, she deflates right in front of us. "You guys are all couples, and then I'm—"

"Will and I are not a couple." I'm a broken record, but c'mon.

Ginny sniffs. And then sniffs some more, her lower lip tremulous. Frieda backs down off of the Bitch High Horse, like she always does when she goes too far with our sweet friend, and digs out a lace handkerchief from one of her pockets to pass over. It's bedazzled with an F and then a U. "Calm down, will you? Fine. He can come and bowl with us. There. Stop this shit now. No crying in the diner."

The image of Frieda becoming a mother someday and soothing one of her children in just such a way makes me want to laugh, but it also sobers me, too, because I've got one of the worst moms on record. She and my dad informed me last year that they wanted nothing more to do with me.

Well, they got that wish.

I wonder if they even know I'm gone. Or care.

"Tell me what high school was like for you," Will says as we cheat on the Moose during our break at a nearby coffee shop.

"High school sucked." I groan, thinking about it before picking up my cappuccino. "I was a cheerleader."

He hoots in laughter. "Are we talking about the kind of cheerleader with pom-poms and teeny skirt?" He mimics a rah-rah, go team motion.

Shoot me now. I nod, tugging on my knit hat until it lowers past my ears.

"That's fantastic." He tears off a corner of his scone.

I cock an eyebrow up. "Should I be offended?"

"It's just, I've always seen you as the girl sulking in the back of the cafeteria, writing morose poetry."

"For your information, I never wrote a single poem outside of English class."

His grin is lazy.

As I do often with him, I roll my eyes. "Your turn. Tell me what it was like for you."

He stretches his long legs out in front of him; they tangle with mine under the table. "I was rubbish at school, especially in Glasgow. Barely graduated, and only then because once we moved here, I was able to pick my grades up a wee bit."

"Really?" I'm surprised. Will is one of the smartest people I've ever met.

"Yeah." He sips his espresso. "I ditched a lot, pre-America and all." He's thoughtful. "Often with Grant, but mostly Becca."

He seems okay talking about them today—no anger, no sadness. So I say lightly, "Don't tell me. Did you and Becca ditch so you could have sex in the janitor's closet?"

He laughs and then blushes, prompting me to squeal too loudly for the small joint, "SERIOUSLY? At *school*?"

The nearby barista shoots us a warning look. She's a taskmaster at keeping voices below stereo levels.

Will pays her no mind. "Once even," he adds, "in the head master's office."

Oh, I'm laughing now. Real laughter, the kind that feels like flat-out chortling. In fact, I'm laughing so hard I'm actually crying. It's taken five long months, but I'm finally, really, truly laughing. "No. Way. You're lying to me."

"I wish I were. We got caught, mid-coitus. Jesus, was that embarrassing."

I crack up even harder; now my sides hurt. And he laughs, too. For once, a Becca memory makes him lighter, not heavier.

Chapter Five

For the third time in ten minutes, I turn around and leave the bustling office only to come back in. What am I doing here? Am I really this big of an idiot?

"Can I help you?" the guy behind the desk asks. He's been eyeing me ever since I walked in, no doubt wondering if I'm already a student or just some stalker who likes to hang out in admission offices of public universities.

"Um . . .?"

A couple of girls wearing sorority gear laugh loudly nearby. Clearly, I am an idiot. I have no idea what inspired me to come down here on my day off.

No, that's a lie. I know exactly why I'm here. I was denied a true college experience in Annar, and I'm here to rectify it. Only, I'm low on cash (okay, not exactly low, because I still have a ridiculous amount that I'd stolen from my fiancé before I ran last year hidden away in my bedroom, but using it makes me feel like shit, so I don't) and without transcripts. Moving in with Will and Cameron was bad enough for somebody who's terrified to put down too many roots in one area; enrolling in college? It'd be even more of a reason to stay.

"Are you . . ." He gives me a look over. "A student here?"

I nearly beam. He thinks I look like a college student. Not a

Creator, but a *college student*. I take a few steps closer. "No. But I thought . . ." Deep breath. "Maybe I could be?"

He's surprised a bit, I think, as most colleges accept online applications. But here I am, in an admissions office, asking for actual paper. "Oh. Of course." He opens a drawer nearby. "Are you transferring?"

When I went to the University of Annar last year, I'd been allowed all of one class. It was worse than a joke. The so-called professor spent more time telling his students—admittedly, there weren't many of us, but STILL—that we weren't required to do much work for his class as we obviously already knew our crafts well than actually teaching. All of my friends, save Jonah and Kellan, were in multiple classes that went in depth over the best practices for their crafts, and how to wield them on the various planes effectively. They were slammed by paperwork and research. I got to write all of two papers, and they were five pages apiece.

Obviously, I will not be requesting a transcript from the U.

I shake my head, and the admissions guy reaches down into the already opened drawer and pulls out a different packet. "Okay. Here is the University of Alaska's enrollment application, along with some pamphlets about our school." He lays the papers on the counter between us and highlights a section for me. "As the next semester is just about to start, you'll be best off trying for Fall admission. Or maybe Summer, if you like."

I stare down at the papers, my eyes tracking across photos of happy undergrads. My twentieth birthday is next week. Am I too old to be a freshman?

"Do you know what you want to study?" the guy asks.

My cheeks warm considerably when I shake my head no again.

He's sympathetic. "I went in undeclared, too. And now I'm a junior and I'm still undecided. But I figure, I'm young, and I have plenty of time to figure it out, right?"

I like that. No pressure to figure out exactly what it is that I want to be, or learn, or do. Plus, he looks a bit older than me, so maybe I'm not past my prime for college just yet.

He slips the papers into a folder and hands it over. Then he passes me a business card. "Feel free to call us anytime if you have any questions. College is a great place. We'd love to have you here."

The folder sits on my dresser for days. There are highlighted deadlines in there that I need to meet, if I'm going to go through with this plan of mine. But to do so, I'm going to have to use my craft for the first time in five months.

When I left Annar, I made a conscious choice not to use my Magic anymore. According to Etienne Miscanthus, a Council friend of mine, the worlds can function properly as long as a Creator continues living whether or not they're working. Truth be told, I have no idea if Magic can be traced or not—I think not, but Trackers, the Magical equivalent of bloodhounds, are extremely good at hunting down people and things. I have no doubt that a horde of Trackers is out searching for me. The Council will want me and my skills back; not only am I first tier, but I'm also the only Creator in existence. The Guard will want me back, thanks to a number of friends who are no doubt in a panic over my disappearance. And of course, Jonah and Kellan may want me back: Jonah, being an influential second tier Council member, and his brother, a high-ranking Guard with a lot of pull, probably put the screws on both the Council and Guard to find me.

Unless they hate me for leaving them in the first place.

But my choice to cease Magic was more than just a fear of being found. It was because I wanted a chance to figure out who I am without Fate sticking its fingers in every one of my pies. So, as tough as it's been at times, I'm glad that I'm learning to do things the hard way. It's refreshing to actually earn things rather than simply create them at will. Except, now I'm going to have to create myself some documents if I plan on going to college. I need a high school diploma and transcripts that don't have *Chloe Lilywhite* on them. I need references that don't exactly exist. And yet . . .

Using Magic makes me feel like I'm failing somehow.

"Whatcha doing?"

I jerk away from the folder to find Cameron standing in my doorway, Nell at his feet. "Nothing," I say, even though I must've looked like a weirdo, staring at the admissions packet as if it were Pandora's Box.

He makes a motion, asking for entrance, and I wave him in. "College, hmm?" he asks once he joins me on the edge of my bed.

I tuck short blonde strands behind my ears. I miss my long hair. People say shorter hair is easier to style, but it's a total lie. "Been thinking about it."

He reaches over for the folder and flips through it. "Personally, I think it's a brilliant idea."

I don't know why, but this surprises me. "You do?"

"Well, sure." He shuts the folder. "Please don't tell me you want to work at the Moose for the rest of your life. It's a great place and all, but there's got to be more for you than that. You're a smart girl, Zoe."

Not once in all my years, did my biological father say something like this to me. I don't know why Cameron's kindness always startles me. I wish it didn't. People ought to be kind to those they love.

I pick up the packet and stare at the words on the front. It all seems so easy, so attainable—and yet impossible at the same time. I tell him lamely, "It's expensive."

"That it is. But there are loans and grants you can apply for." He studies me for a long moment; I know what's coming, because I know Cameron, and I scramble to think of the right words to counter his offer. "I could help—"

"I can't take your money." I grab one of his hands and squeeze. "You've already done so much for me already."

He won't back down, since he's a pit bull about things that matter to him, but for now, he concedes to me with a small nod.

"I've been trying to talk Will into Culinary school. He's . . ." Cameron scratches at his beard. "I'm afraid my boy is adrift. By twenty-two, I'd already been in and out of the military. Married his mum. Got a good job. Not that I'm saying he must follow my trajectory, because the Lord knows I don't feel he's ready for marriage and what not, it's just . . ."

"You worry about him." I lean over and kiss his grizzled cheek. "That's what good dads do."

Does my father worry about me? Wonder where I am? Or is he relieved that I'm gone, that I'm no longer causing him embarrassment?

Will appears in the doorway, the seam of his pillowcase fading on his cheek from his nap. "My ears are burning. Want to tell me why?"

I like Cameron's smile. I like how it's on his face more often than not. "Zoe was telling me about her plans to apply to the University of Alaska."

This seems to please Will as much as it had his father. "Yeah? That's brilliant, Zo."

"What about you?" I ask innocently. "While I was searching online, I saw some great culinary schools here in Anchorage."

He shakes a finger at his dad. "Getting Zoe to do your dirty work?"

Cameron isn't apologetic.

"Personally, I think it's a great idea," I tell Will. He's amazing with food. Even still, I have to tease, "The world always needs more Scottish cuisine."

He laughs as his father mocks outrage. "Ah yes," Will murmurs. "Fast food haggis. I can see my future franchise now." He joins us on edge of my bed. "In all seriousness, you two. Enough with the poorly concealed hinting. Fine. I had a bit of a look around recently. Found a place that might be a good fit."

I swear his father whispers, "Thank you, Lord."

"But just because I looked doesn't mean I'm going," Will

warns. "It was just for research. And I certainly haven't applied or anything."

"Of course," Cameron murmurs. But I see the light in his eyes. He knows it's only a matter of time before Will gives in and goes, because Will is one of the most cautious people I know. Will wouldn't say something like this without thinking about every last in and out of the situation. He's probably got a pro and con checklist in his back pocket.

Unlike me, who makes rash decisions on the spur of the moment. Only this time, I'm resolved to think things through.

They leave a few minutes later, Will to go play poker with Paul and a few friends, Cameron to work. I clean the house, do the dishes, take Nell for a walk, play ball with her, take a shower, yet all the while, the folder burning a hole in my every thought.

But when I go to bed that night, no additional papers are added.

Chapter Six

I resisted getting a cell phone for the first two months I lived in Anchorage, but Ginny and Frieda browbeat me into ownership after one night that had me trekking home alone in the dark and snow due to a broken down bus. Will railed at me, going over every excuse in the book about how important a cell phone is nowadays, how women on their own in big cities is not a good idea, especially at night (for which I accused him of blatant sexism), but it was Ginny and Frieda who dragged me to the store and practically pinned me down to a kiosk until I selected one.

My old phone, the one I left behind, was a top-of-the-line Dwarven smartphone. I loved that thing. But I left it behind, like I did with everything else, knowing that if I had it, it would be too much of a temptation for me to give up.

My new phone is a pay-and-go model. It's not fancy by any means. It serves its purpose and I guess that's what counts. Only, sometimes, it taunts me, like it's doing now. I've been clutching the phone for the better part of an hour, repeatedly typing a certain number I know by heart, only to delete it each time my finger even contemplates hitting send.

Some days are harder than others. Today is a really, really tough day. It's my birthday (not that I've admitted it to anyone, though—Will and Cameron think it's still another month away), and I miss

Jonah so much that I'd give every last cent I have to hear his voice. Magically, it'd be easy, really. I could make myself a little machine and see him. Or hear him. Even easier, I could simply call and hang up, wrong number-like. Or disguise my voice and then hang up. He'd never be able to trace me to a random phone call from Alaska, because he has no idea I'd ever wanted to come here. It'd be nothing more than a three second call to him.

There's a strong fear that if I see him, though, let alone hear his voice, all my resolves would crumble and I'd be once more begging for forgiveness. And where would that get me? Us? For all I know, he's doing great nowadays. Every time I turn on the news, I search him out. Is that protest march in Washington due to him? That rebellion in Tibet? The fundraising efforts going around to help rebuild the East Coast, so recently devastated by a storm? The community rallying around the little girl with a bucket list and less than a year to live? Pride swells in my chest, as bittersweet as it is, whenever I visualize him out there doing his job and doing it well.

I think about Kellan, too—gods, everyday. But in these last five months I've noticed something. I love Kellan. I miss him so much I physically ache . . . but it's nothing compared to the withdrawal Jonah's absence is putting me through. I don't dream about Kellan the way I do with his brother, don't wake up with his name on my lips and tears in my eyes because the crushing agony of his absence in my life overwhelms me.

I don't get it. I really don't. I share Connections to both of them. Love both of them desperately. Is it because Jonah and I shared dreams for so many years? Or were living together before I left? Is it because I'd gotten used to not having Kellan in my life?

But I tore my life apart over Kellan, didn't I? Destroyed everything I had with Jonah? And yet, for five months now, I've drowned in just how hard it's been to let Jonah go.

Minutes later, functioning on autopilot, I'm on a bus across town, until, nearly an hour later, I find myself on the outskirts of Anchorage. It takes another hour before I locate a payphone. Thanks to cell phones, they're hard to find in the wild. I'm an idiot, because this is the stupidest, riskiest thing I could possibly do, but I keep telling myself it'll be just this one call. I just need to hear him say one thing. Just hello. It'll be enough to help me get through the coming months. Maybe it'll recharge me and my resolves rather than weaken me—because I'll know I did the right thing if he sounds happy, that everything I've done and gone through will be worth it.

My hands tremble when I pick up the receiver. I force myself to take a breath before I clean the black plastic with an alcohol wipe. I drop my coins twice before I get them into the phone. My heart jackhammers in my chest, but, as nervous as I am, I'm bursting with excitement, too.

One word. I'll take just one word. He'll say hello, maybe once, at the most twice, and then he'll hang up. I won't say anything in return. Better yet, if I'm lucky, I'll get his voice mail. I'll get a whole bunch of words then.

Each button is pressed slowly. The call will go fast; it needs to tide me over for months. The ringing in my ear competes with the thundering in my chest. His phone is ringing. Gods, I'm going to pass out. My breathing, my heart—everything is fast and hard right now. I've got to get myself under control. Can't have him think I'm some deep breathing stalker or anything. Can't raise any of his flags.

Two rings.

Three.

"Hello?"

The butterflies in my chest break free. My ribs open up, my skin parts, and that muscle in my chest flies right on out. Jonah! Jonah's answered and he's said hello! He sounds . . . well, not happy, but tired. Which could be work or—

Elation morphs into searing pain. *I miss him.* I ache for him so much right now that it takes me physically biting my tongue until it bleeds so I don't answer him back.

If I could, I'd say: *I love you I'm sorry I miss you I want you I made a mistake I wish you nothing but happiness are you happy please tell me you're happy that everything I've put us through is worth it you deserve so much more than a broken girl like me are you happy Jonah do you miss me have you moved on is your life good please tell me that this has all been worth it please please please—*

"Hello?"

Everything around me hazes. I can't see my surroundings. Why is it I always break down in payphone booths?

A dial tone fills my ear.

"Zoe! What in the hell do you think you're doing?"

Will yanks the bottle out of my hand. I swipe at it, but he's so fast right now, he's blurry.

"Mine," I tell him. Only, I think it was his whiskey, or his dad's, but he did say, when I moved in, "What's mine is yours." Or maybe he said, "What's mine is mostly yours. Hands off the whiskey," but I can't remember if he actually said that one or not. So technically, that's my bottle of whiskey and I need it back.

"How many shots did you have?" He shakes the bottle in front of my face. "Because it looks like you drank NEARLY A THIRD OF A BRAND NEW BOTTLE OF WHISKEY!"

"YES I DID." I can give as good as I get.

"That's it. We need to go to the hospital. Get your damn coat on!"

I drop back onto the couch. "Not sick. No need." I kick my feet up on the coffee table, knocking over a glass. Oops. "Hospitals can't piece together Humpty Dumptys, Will-eeee-am!" I laugh, because I sound like Cameron when I say it like that.

"What?" One of his hands yanks through his hair before tugging on his ear. His blonde is nice. Pretty. Doesn't look trashy like my fake blonde.

"I like your hair," I tell him. "It's pretty."

"Fuck my hair!" He disappears and reappears, my coat replacing the whiskey in his hand. Where's the booze? "Get up. We're going."

"Not sick," I remind him, struggling to stand up. "Healthy as a .
. ." Huh. "What's healthy? Apple?" I snap my fingers. Ew, they're a
little sticky. "Hog. No! Horse. I'm a horse. I keep on running, like
the Pony Express." I pat my chest. Jog in place. "See? Not sick. It'd
be easier if I were. Sick, I mean. If I could only get sick." I pick up
speed. "I tried to break one of the Connections tonight, you know.
Thought it could help me be whole." I stop jogging; it shames me
I'm winded. "Didn't work. Isn't that ironic? A Connection makes me
whole and broken all at the same time." I jab at his chest. "It.
Bloody. SUCKS."

And then I laugh, because now I sound like him. *Bloody,
bloody, bloody.* And then I'm sad again because of what I did.

"What the fuck are you prattling on about? You think you're
fine? Think again! You bloody well won't be after they pump your
stomach at the hospital!" He grabs me and shoves my arms into the
coat. "Whatever possessed you to drink so much alcohol?"

I stumble as he drags me out the door. "I called him. Thought I
could handle it, but I can't." There's no way to swallow the burning
lump in my throat. "Thought it'd help. Just wanted to hear
something, especially today. Just—it's hard. So hard. I'm trying."

He waits until he's got us in the car and on the road before he
asks, quieter now, "Whom did you call?"

"Doesn't matter," I whisper. "Was a mistake. Tried to break the
Connections—at least one, you know? Only made it worse. Hurts
more now." It does. So. Much.

He digs around, like he's looking for my phone. I don't have my
phone. It's back home. No, wait, he's got my purse and my phone,
and he's got the phone out and—

"Cell phones and driving do not mix," I inform him haughtily.

Will doesn't answer me. He does something with my phone and
then tosses it back into my purse. I grab the bag and hold it close to
my chest. I think I'm going to puke. Something burns in my throat.
"Who'd you call?" he barks. "Who fucking did this to you?"

42

Yep. Vomit. So gross, it's all over my legs. Worse yet, it's warm and smells bad.

I close my eyes and let my head sink back against that thingy at the top of car seats. I swear I'm floating. Floating is so much better than sinking.

"Zoe White, you keep your goddamn eyes open right now! You will not pass out on me in this car, do you hear me?"

I let myself float away.

Chapter Seven

Will is pissed off. That much is certain, as evidenced by the door slamming behind us, not to mention the string of curses in addition to the biting lecture he'd unleashed on me on the way home from the hospital. Plus, there was the blistering lecture I received from an increasingly difficult to understand Cameron Dane in the early hours of the morning. I guess it's a thing for both him and Will. The more upset they are, the harder they are to understand with their Glaswegian accents. But, the point is, if I'd ever doubted Cameron's fatherly inclinations toward me, they were illuminated in stark detail this morning. I'd scared him. Hurt myself. Hurt him. Hurt Will. Hadn't thought of others. What if something had happened? Most importantly, I wasn't allowed to do it again.

I've got to say, disappointing a caring parent is brutal on the heart. I actually broke down and sobbed for the first time in nearly six months after he strode out of my little curtained cubby of a room, certain I'd failed him in every way. And then I had to listen to him yell at Will in the hallway, and Will yell back, and it amazed me to realize that they weren't shouting because they blamed or were mad at one another or were mad, but because they were worried. And upset. And it was because of me.

Which made me sob all the more. *They care about me.*

Would my parents have done the same? No—my parents didn't

even come to see me in the hospital after I'd nearly died after an Elders' attack. They'd been too busy with their careers. If they knew I'd had alcohol poisoning, and of course were still speaking to me, there's no doubt I would've only received a lecture via phone. Except, instead of the one in which Cameron practically grounded me (an adult) until I'm thirty, I would've heard something along the lines of, "Stop embarrassing us."

Cameron and Will, though—they'd stayed with me all night. When the nurses tried to kick them out, Cameron told them I was his daughter and he had every right to be with me if I wanted him there. He immediately demanded that a friend of his who worked in the hospital come see me personally. In my weakened, vomit-y state, I could swear the dude was part-Elf, but I figured I was just imagining things. Will filled out my admission paperwork. They took turns holding back my hair as I threw up everything in my stomach, and then some. Cameron listened to his friend's diagnosis and after-care like my very life depended on it, and, shaking with rage and worry, vowed I would follow each instruction to the letter.

He's at work right now. He didn't want to go, but Will eventually convinced him to go, insisting my butt wouldn't leave the couch longer than to go the bathroom the entire day.

The moment we're through the door, Will barks, "Alcohol poisoning is not funny!"

I'm not laughing, but as he's on edge, I decide to wade carefully into this mess of my own making. "I know, Will." My smile is weak. "At least they didn't have to pump my stomach. Thank goodness for small favors, right?"

This was the wrong thing to say, because his eyes go so wide I fear they'll pop right out. "Oh yes. Thank goodness! You only had to spend the night hooked up to IVs whilst vomiting up the contents of your stomach. How lucky you were."

I bite my lip, unsure as what to say. But I do know this: he deserves an explanation. "Can we sit down?"

He nods and stalks over to the couch; I perch on the coffee table so we face one another. "First off, thank you for what you did for me. What both you and your dad did."

Some of the anger eases off his handsome face. "Zoe." He takes my hands. "In the last half year, we've become family. Screw blood." He squeezes my hands gently despite the vehemence in his voice. "We are *family*. Which means you're daft if you think I'm going to just sit back and watch you try to drown yourself, even if it's what you think you want."

Bits of my hair stick to my face when I nod, but I don't want to let go of his hands long enough to wipe them away. "I know. And I thank you for that, because I love you, too."

He scoffs, but I know it pleases him. He loves me just as much as I love him, even if he's not one to say those three words out loud.

"Last night . . ." I shake my head. "Yesterday. I did something stupid yesterday."

"You called someone."

I blink in surprise.

He rolls his eyes. "You told me that last night." He sobers. "I checked your phone, but the last call in your log was to me. Zo, what's going on? I know you're unhappy, that somebody broke your heart, but I figured I'd wait until you felt safe telling me. But now . . . Fuck this. I'm not tiptoeing around you anymore. Tell me what drove you to nearly kill yourself last night."

Oh, it hurts so much to realize this is what he and his dad must've thought I'd done. "I didn't try to kill myself. It was more . . . I wanted to forget. To stop hurting." I take a deep breath, only to find Will watching me with immense concern. "I . . ." The words are hard to get out, especially as there's no way I can tell him about how, in desperation, I'd actually attempted to break the Connections I have. I'd figured . . . I'd closed the door between me and my Conscience. Why couldn't I do so with a Connection? It seemed simple at first—I visualized erasing those ties, but I ended up basically stabbing my heart about a hundred times before ripping it right out of my chest.

In the end, the Connections remained, and I had to find myself something to drink because I hated myself even all the more.

"You can trust me," Will is saying, bringing my attention back to him.

"I know. It's just . . ." Another deep breath. Time to open up a bit about what I can, even if it'll hurt. Even if all of this changes how he feels about me. I can't keep lying to all the people I care about in my life, or shutting down and pretending everything is fine when it's not. "I called my . . ." Connection. Soul mate. The person I've loved since I was four. "Fiancé."

Will rears back. "Your *what*?"

I feel myself weaken, but I need to be honest with him. Will's been so good to me, and I've hidden so much in return. There have got to be pieces of truth I can tell him without putting his life in danger. "Probably ex, considering I'm here and he's . . . where he is, but . . ." Viper tight, pain constricts my breathing. "I needed to hear his voice yesterday."

What a way to celebrate my twentieth birthday.

I stand up and pace the room. Then I go on to tell Will that I drove across town to find a payphone and that all I heard was the one word, twice, and it broke me. I don't tell him why Jonah and I aren't together, other than to say things were complicated (which is truly an understatement) and that us being apart was for the best all around, since he deserved better than me.

"You love him."

Another understatement. I nod, chewing on the inside of my lip.

"Does he know where you are?"

I shake my head. I've drawn blood.

Will's quiet for a long moment. "Did he physically hurt you?"

"OH MY GODS, WILL! NO!"

I try not to smack my forehead, realizing my slip of tongue. Gods, I'm a mess.

He tugs my hands until I sit next to him on his couch. Then he folds me in his arms until I'm surrounded by his safety and warmth.

It feels really good, being held like this. Like he really is my brother, and he loves me, and wants to protect me. I haven't been held by anyone in a long time. I want to cry, want to rail about the injustices of it all, of how Fate sucks and how I hate it, but in the end, I take the remote control Will hands me and turn on the television. We watch the hockey game he taped last night in silence, his arms around me, my heart aching.

When I was younger, and resentful, and scared of what I am, I used to fantasize about running away. I imagined hundreds of places to go to, and of who I'd become once arriving. But I always believed it was done in vain, because I'd never be allowed to escape being a Creator.

And yet, here I am. Gone from everything I know.

It's so cold out here that parts of me are numb. Rather than being bothered by this sensation, I revel in it. Numb is good. When I'm numb, I'm not in agony. And the pain that follows numbness— the kind of prickling hotness from being too cold—is preferable to the kind I live with on a daily basis.

Kellan was right after all. All those times he tried to literally break his bones, go into shock so he could escape our Connection—I thought he was crazy. But he was right. Anything is better than the pain that an unfulfilled Connection can wreak upon a Magical's soul. Even still, I can't believe I was desperate enough to try to break the bonds I have with him or Jonah.

I've borrowed Will's truck and driven as far as I can get outside of Anchorage until all I see is dark skies and stars and cold. This is part of the beauty of Alaska; so much of it is still wild, still free and untouched by human and Magical hands. I like this area, like how it makes me feel. I've been constantly chasing the Northern Lights; sometimes I thought if I could see them just once, it'd be a sign.

I'm finally rewarded, nearly half a year after moving to Alaska. The Aurora Borealis is streaked across the sky tonight, yellow and green ribbons that dance across my vision. They're so unbelievably dazzling that when I lay back in the snow, arms and legs out in angel formation, my breath is wicked away. Ice crystals cling to the fringe of hair sticking out from underneath my beanie cap and to the nape of my scarfless neck.

I am small.

I am irrelevant.

I am not even a speck of sand in a vast beach of worlds, no matter what anyone says.

The next morning, I make a decision.

I'm going to college.

Chapter Eight

Using Magic is the same as, say gambling. Or alcohol. Or drugs. Detox is hard, abstinence becomes easier over time, but if you give into it, man, the hit is too strong to resist.

I fabricated myself all the transcripts I need. And then, even though it'd been suggested I hold off for Fall admission, I go for Summer. Flush with my decision and subsequent action on that resolution, I can't help myself. I make myself a new pair of boots and a new coat and take Nell out on a walk with a brand new, fancy leash that says her name on it.

Maybe I can do Magic and still be Chloe. Er, Zoe.

As I walk through the neighborhood for one of me and Nell's ten-minute-max walks, I spot Mr. McGillicuddy kicking his ancient Oldsmobile. The thing is notorious for breaking down on him on a daily basis. He's a nice old man. He's helped me out several times when Will and Cameron weren't around. So I decide to help him by giving him a new engine. And it feels awesome, just incredibly awesome to help somebody out and know that I didn't kill anyone or destroy anything.

I gave an old man the means to go visit his Alzheimer-afflicted wife in a nearby nursing home without having to pay for a taxi.

Maybe I can do this after all.

Will tosses a pack of paper towels into our shopping cart with the enthusiasm of a shot putter. He's in a mood; Becca called twenty minutes before we were supposed to leave to run errands and broke down once more, weeping about she might be pregnant—except, she lost the baby in the accident and that was over a year ago. It's a conversation they've had a dozen times, when snatches of memory crawl their way back to the surface of her broken brain. Poor Will suffers through hearing about how his girlfriend and best friend cheated on him more times than is fair. And yet, he listens to her, offers forgiveness, but like always, she and the memories tie him down in ways he can't escape.

As I can only imagine the horrors I would feel, let alone act upon if the same were true about Jonah (or Kellan), I've decided to try my best to distract him. "Did you know that houseflies taste with their feet?"

He regards me as if I've turned into a fly myself. I nod vigorously—interesting facts! I gots them! But he shakes his head and grabs the wrong toilet paper, chucking it next to the paper towels. I quietly put it back on the shelf and pick the right kind. Cameron is quite particular.

A little girl nearby wails; her sibling dances around the cart she's strapped in, clutching a dolly's head. Sure enough, the little girl is holding a decapitated, naked baby.

My heart goes out to her. As the mother ignores the two, I zap the doll's head back on. The children go quiet—the boy stunned, the girl increasingly delighted. I debate giving the poor thing clothes but figure the kid must have a reason why her dolly is naked. I hide the small smile creeping on my lips when she clutches the doll to her chest.

"Jesus. I've prattled on so much that I've lost you. Sorry, Zo."

I jerk my attention back to Will. He looks so sad, so . . . lost. "No! Don't be silly." I nudge his arm with my shoulder. "Maybe it's time to change your number."

"You don't think I want to?" He tugs on his earlobe. "Becca's mum begged me not to. Says the connection to me is the only thing that gets her through some of her better days." He sighs heavily. "She cheated on me. Broke my heart. But . . . I've also known her my whole life, Zo. I stupidly can't let go of her or Grant. I just . . . I wish I knew how."

It's because he's a good person. He puts Becca's fragile mental welfare at times above his own. As for me? I just abandon those whose hearts I shatter.

When the mother pushes the cart past me, the little girl grins and holds up her doll for me to see. "Pretty," I tell her.

"My baby," she proudly tells me in return.

Her brother scowls, trailing slowly after his mother and victorious sibling.

Four—no five—uses of Magic in less than two days. I need to get myself under control, especially since there's this rotting undercurrent in my brain that my craft is being wasted on things like dog leashes and boots rather than the betterment of civilizations.

My mother's words, crafted from caution and disgust, weigh heavily upon my conscience. She turned away from me first. Why should I care about what she thinks? I grab a box of tissues. The good kind, with lotion, which I have a sneaking suspicion I might just need in the dark hours of tonight.

"Grant's mum called last night, too."

I look up from the cart. "What did she want?"

He won't look at me when he says, "The fuck if I know. She cried. Tried to remind me of how we played together in our nappies. That this was all Becca's fault. I don't know. She—I guess she needed to reach out to somebody who loved him, too."

I wish I could personally call the woman right now and tell her to back the hell off.

For the rest of the shopping trip, Will is on autopilot, leaving me to wonder what I would do if I were in his shoes. What if I found out that Jonah was expecting a baby with someone else—somebody like his ex-girlfriend Callie, whom I called a good friend? For the last five hundred years or so, Magicals have been able to produce one pregnancy, so if in my absence they have sex and he's so taken away with the moment he forgets a condom and she's fertile or some crap like that—

Ka-BOOM!

Five seconds later, Will grabs my arm, asking me if I'm okay. He's absolutely soaked, covered head to toe with laundry detergent. As am I. As are the three other people in this unfortunate aisle of the store. Because every single bottle of detergent just exploded, sending down a rainstorms of scented, slimy cleaners down upon us.

I'm shamed to my core. Some things never change. Even now, even after I've tried to deny myself Magic, I still can't control it when my feelings get too intense.

The store manager grovels at our feet, which is horrible and humiliating for him, since I'm to blame. All our bills for that day are paid. But when we go home, Will won't let the subject go. He's curious. Of course he's curious.

In the end, I lie to him, as I've done since the day I met him. Because what would he think he if he knew his best friend was the kind of person who destroys things when she gets upset?

"May I help you?"

The man sitting at the counter is fairly nondescript: tall and lean, with mousy brown hair and matching eyes. His face is pockmarked and aged by sunlight. Head tilted slightly to the side, he's studying me.

He may be nondescript, but he's also an Elf, which sends my freak-out-sensor into high gear.

Rationally, I'm aware that there are Elves living on the Human plane, including non-Magical Elves who know nothing about Magicals. Or Creators. Especially Creators who, just a week before, destroyed the laundry aisle of a big box store. It'd been in the news, which left me stumbling on uneven ground.

When the Elf doesn't answer, I'm tempted to turn around and get the hell out of here. But then his head snaps back to normal position and he smiles, teeth crooked on the bottom row. "Sh-sure. Do you h-have coffee?"

Seriously. He says this in a diner, with a coffee pot brewing right behind me. "Decaf? Regular?"

"Decaf is f-fine," he says. "Got to keep my senses f-focused, you know?"

Like the junkie I apparently am nowadays, I use Magic to will the shield I built around me all those months ago to become tighter, stronger so that, even if this Elf is a Magical, he'll have no clue who I am. Excepting, of course, if he's carrying a picture of me; blonde hair and blue eyes aside, it's not like I had plastic surgery. "What is it that you do?"

He blinks a few times, like he's shocked I would question him.

"Your job," I clarify, leaning against the counter. I tuck a strand of my hair behind an ear. "That requires you to be alert?"

"Oh." He fingers the menu I've handed over. "It's, hmm . . ." He rubs at his forehead, flipping his lanky, greasy hair to the side. "C-complicated."

I don't recognize the guy, but then, Annar is a large place, and even a first tier Council member doesn't know all the main players, even ones who stutter. But if I had to guess, this guy, this Elf, is a Tracker for the Guard.

Part of me wants to run, like *now*. Hit the road, rework all my shields, and find a new place to hide. But another part insists I've done good work. I've got roots growing. I can't leave Cameron and Will behind—not yet, at least.

I burned a lot of bridges to get to where I'm standing. There isn't a lot left of Chloe Lilywhite that exists outside of Annar. But if I run right now, he'd be at my heels within seconds. I wonder if he carries handcuffs. Would he arrest me? Exactly how would he drag me back to Annar?

Worse yet, what if he *tells* somebody?

My heartbeat is deafening. I give the Elf what I think is a smile and ask, "You're not from around here, are you?"

He takes a couple of deep breaths, nostrils flaring. He's breathing my scent in which leaves me no longer in doubt—he's a Tracker. I've seen enough Trackers in my time to know they do this. "No."

No kidding. "What brings you to Anchorage?"

He clears his throat. "I'm here for a j-job."

Is he testing me? "The so-called complicated job?"

He nods, his fingers tracing over the rim of the cup I've slid over.

I'd been told, a year or so back, that the Guard's Trackers can assume roles easily, become whoever and whatever it takes to find their quarry. I'd be willing to bet my life savings that this nervousness and that stutter are fake.

So, as freaked out as I am, I'm also pissed off. I issue my own challenge. "How long are you in town?"

If he senses my anger, he doesn't show his hand. "Oh, not . . . uh . . . well, as l-long as it t-takes, I guess. I mean, as long as the job t-takes."

I bet. "Have you found what you're looking for?"

His eyes narrow for the briefest of moments before resembling a lost puppy dog's. "Huh?"

Asshole. I tap his menu. "Do you know what you'd like to order?"

"Oh! What's g-good here?"

"The pancakes," I tell him truthfully.

"It's n-nine o'clock at n-n-night!"

I fake grin. "There's always time for pancakes." Like the bastard deserves Will's pancakes.

He orders them, though. I force myself to go about my normal duties. I hang the order up at the kitchen window. I fill a few other customers' cups with coffee. I take another order. Hang that one up. Get the pancakes. Give them to the Tracker. Tell him to let me know if he needs anything else. Watch him the entire time out of the corner of my eye.

The nervousness fades away when he doesn't think I'm watching. He fingers the menu, the silverware I placed in front of him, the mug I held. His fingers slide across the plate in the exact spot mine laid.

How did he find me? Was it the grocery store mishap? The flurry of Magic usages I did over the last couple weeks? Or was I just not good enough with covering my tracks?

I wrack my brain for what his name could be. Someone Karl might've mentioned as being good. Or Kellan. Lon—no—Larry? No. *Lee.* That's it. Lee Acacia. An Elf named Lee Acacia was considered to be royalty when it came to tracking difficult quarries. He was one of the guys who made the most progress with the Elders.

Lee Acacia is sitting in my diner. Eating Will's pancakes. Watching me. And sending text messages.

"Yo. Space cadet."

I nearly jump out of my skin. But it's only Will, taking a break from the kitchen.

"You look like you're a million miles away," he says to me.

"Just thinking about whether or not I'll get into college." It's not a lie. I'd been fixated on that before the Elf walked into the diner.

"Why wouldn't you? You're brilliant. They'd be daft to not accept you."

Bless his heart. "You're biased."

He leans his hip against the counter and grins. "Nah. I'm nothing if not a brutal realist."

The Tracker's cell phone rings. I jerk at the sound.

"I know we're supposed to go bowling tonight, and you've got your tricked out trainers, ready to lift you out of the gutter, straight on the path to victory, but I was wondering if we could just go home instead. I'm knackered," Will is saying.

Yes, yes, go home. Lock the doors behind us. I nod vigorously. "I'm beat, too."

The Tracker appears annoyed. He's talking quietly, and I can't hear his words, but I see his face. He's angry and clearly arguing with whoever is on the other end of the line.

"I DVRed a hockey game." Will tosses a straw wrapper at me.

"You're so Americanized," I murmur, but my attention remains riveted at the end of the counter.

Lee Acacia is now in that weird defeated yet pissed off stage. He's shaking his head, drumming his fingers against the counter, rattling his cup and silverware balancing on the edge of his plate.

Will leans down and says quietly, "Want to explain why you've been ogling that bloke?"

He can't think . . . *No.* I visibly shudder and tell him the truth. "He's been staring at *me.* It's kind of creepy."

Will straightens and then, without warning, heads down to where the Tracker is sitting. "Can I get you anything else?" he asks. "Dunno if you noticed or not, but we're closing in five."

The Elf rips the phone away from his ear, apparently startled to find Will hulking over him. Only one other couple is left in the diner, but they're digging out their money. Paul is in his office, probably searching the Internet for motocross videos. "Uh . . ."

Will is apparently enough to scare the Elf away, at least for tonight. After the last person leaves, I drop into a chair, my hands trembling.

Howhowhow did he find me?

"Is that your ex?" Will asks after a long moment.

"What? EW! No!"

"Alright then. Want to tell me why he has you in knots?"

We used to not push each other much. Lately, living together, especially since the alcohol-poisoning incident . . . we push all the time. The deeper our friendship gets, the more we care. The less we're able to ignore. "Will, I—" I shake my head. I can't put him at risk. I can't.

"Don't shut me out. Something is going on, and I've been a prick for too long, letting you get away with it. Whatever it is, you know you can trust me to help, right?"

They'd come and take him away, if they found out he knew. Annar would swallow him whole or erase his memory, and I don't know if I could stand Will Dane being punished because he made the mistake of caring for me. I've hurt too many people I love already.

"Zoe." He grabs my hands. He's so steady. "I hope you're not thinking I'm going to judge you. Or . . . I don't know. Stop talking to you. Or caring. Or do anything other than be your best friend. No matter what it is, let me in. Let me help you."

I should wait until he goes to sleep tonight and leave. He'd be safe then. Cameron, too. I'd miss them, but I could do it. I let the two most important people in my life go, the ones that I love more than my own life. I can let the Dane boys go, too, if it meant they'd be okay, especially now that Annar's come sniffing around.

He sighs and lets my hands go. "What can I do to convince you to trust me?"

He shouldn't trust *me*. "I do, it's just . . ."

"Just what?"

The truth. "I'm scared."

"Of me?"

I shake my head. No. Never him.

"Of . . .?"

More truth. "Hurting you."

His eyes widen before he laughs. "You're kidding, right? You weigh, what, a hundred—"

I cut him off. "There's stuff about me that you don't know. Stuff that could possibly change how you see me."

"Impossible."

"And yet true."

He sits down on the red vinyl seat next to me, swiveling until we face. "Well, here's what I think I know about you. You ran away from wherever you really came from, which I never believed was Hollywood."

I can't help the eye roll. That was all Ginny. I just never denied it.

"Are you in some kind of trouble?"

I rub my temples. More like *I'm* trouble.

"Am I wrong?" Will's concern brings my attention back in focus.

"No," is my answer.

Chapter Nine

Later that night, I change my mind and decide to tell Will and Cameron everything. Or, at least, everything I can without outright signing them up for matching lobotomies. I spring it on them as they nurse a pair of Guinnesses, shouting at the hockey game on TV.

"You were right about everything, Will. I did run away."

Both heads snap toward me. It takes approximately two seconds before Cameron shuts the television set off.

"Bloody hell, lass," he murmurs.

I swallow and mentally cross my fingers that they'll still be here when I'm done. Or, rather, I'll still be here. "I was in . . . a bad situation where I used to live. I had a very stressful job that . . ." I flash back to Jens Belladonna's claims of how I'd been responsible for a couple of nons' deaths during a mission I oversaw. Even thinking about it now steals the air straight out of my lungs. "I had to do things I didn't necessarily agree with. Things I wouldn't choose to do if I had a choice."

Will's eyes are so dark, and yet, probably the most expressive I've ever seen. Right now, he's staring at me with an uncomfortable mix of pity and *I knew it!* "What kind of job?"

Admitting I'm a Creator would go over well, I'm sure. Magicals have too often been thought of as monsters by nons who know nothing of our kind. "I can't tell you that. Can you trust me enough to—"

"Of course I trust you." His smile is small but genuine. "And, Zo, more importantly—you can trust me."

"Us," Cameron clarifies. He motions to the recliner near the couch, and I sit down on the edge, Nell hopping up behind me. I don't want to rock. I'm too nervous to do anything but perch on the edge and await my fate.

But hearing Will call me that name, that nickname that's just his to use, is too much. I need to correct it immediately, even if I might as well be signing my death warrant. "About that. My name isn't Zoe."

I worry I've frozen time again, because both men still completely—Cameron with his beer halfway to his mouth, Will while reaching for his own drink.

I want to whisper, but I force my voice to carry across the living room. "Zoe is the name I chose when I came to Anchorage."

They're regarding me like I'm the fraud I am. And I hate it. But if they're gonna despise me, they're gonna do it with all the info I can give. I touch my hair. "This isn't my real hair color." My index finger traces my lower lash line. "My eyes aren't really blue." I scrub my face tiredly. "My parents aren't . . . they're not dead. But they've pretty much disowned me, so it sort of feels like I'm orphaned. I'm from California, but not Hollywood. I lived near San Francisco." I press my hand over my heart. I think it's breaking again. It's a thing, my heart and breaking. It happens way too often. "Please believe me when I tell you I've never lied about how I feel about you two."

Will reaches out and lightly presses his fingers against my hair, like it's brittle and he's afraid it will clump off if there's too much pressure.

I have to keep going, though. I owe it to them. To me. "The job . . . it was hard, yes. But I was also . . ." My lower lip trembles. "I am . . . maybe *was* engaged." I nod once. "And it was . . . amazing, really, but also complicated, because I cheated on him."

Will's hand falls away from my hair as he drops back onto the couch.

I fight to keep my voice above a whisper when I admit the crime I rarely let myself acknowledge. "I hate myself for it. I'm not . . . I've made a lot of mistakes, and I don't know what to do anymore." Or, worse yet, who I am.

There's surprise in Will's eyes. Pity, too. And more than a wee bit of scorn, because the wound Becca and Grant's cheating inflicted hasn't healed fully, and he knows just how much that can gut a soul. Cameron, though—he's all pity, and it slays me to see him look at me like that. Like he wants to give me a hug and tell me it's all going to be all right.

Like a dad should, even when his daughter makes the wrong choices. Even when she's breaking his heart.

I draw in another shuddery breath. "So, here I am. Zoe White, in Anchorage, Alaska. That guy at the Moose—I think he's from my work. I think they're looking for me."

So much of me wants to ramble on right now, justify what I did and why, but fear smothers me in its grip. I was going to lose the Dane boys anyway once I ran again, but this might be worse. They might willingly choose to kick me out of their lives—especially Will, whose trust has been broken too many times to count, too.

He ends up chugging his beer before staring at the ceiling. Then he gets up, paces the room a few times, all the while looking lost and pissed at the same time while I remain statue still on the recliner.

Cameron says quietly, "What is your real name, hen?"

I tell him the truth. Will snorts a laugh from across the room; it's small, barely a breath, but it's a laugh all the same.

"Obviously, you're not a runaway spy like I thought at first," he says. "Your hiding skills are shite. Your name is Chloe Lilywhite, and you chose *Zoe White*?"

If only it was as simple as me being an ex-spy.

"Chloe is a beautiful name," Cameron says. "It suits you better."

Will takes a few steps closer. "Promise me your ex wasn't

abusive."

Cameron's eyebrows shoot up and then down. Both pairs of dark eyes pin me further into the recliner.

I don't hesitate. "He's . . ." *Swallow. Breathe. Swallow. Breathe.* "He's the best person I know. The very best. He would never hurt me. Ever." Not like I hurt him, anyway.

"If he was all those things, why would you cheat? Why would you do that to him?" Will looms over me, his arms crossed, his back rigid.

Any explanation but the truth is only going to make me sound awful, but how can I explain a Connection without spilling the entire mess? I chew on my lip and stare at my hands, laced tightly in my lap. "It's complicated."

"Bollocks."

Cameron counters with, "Son, let her explain before you pass judgments."

"When somebody cheats, they do it purposely," Will continues heatedly, as if his father hadn't spoken. He glares down, and it hurts so much to see the distrust in his eyes. But I deserve it. I did something awful. Unforgiveable. "It's not like your lips accidentally fell onto someone else's."

I blink back the sadness threatening to spill over my lash line.

"Son." Cameron stands up, his large hand going straight to his son's shoulder. "*Chloe* did not cheat on you. She is not Becca." His fingers curl gently around the base of Will's neck. "We do not know what drove her to do what she did. Don't go getting furious with her for something that has nothing to do with you."

Will closes his eyes and nods. "I know. I'm . . . I'm a prat. I'm sorry, Zo—*Chloe*. It's just—"

"It's an unforgiveable thing." I clear my throat; and then, because it's hard to hold it in any longer, tears snake down my face. "I get why you're mad at me."

"Yeah. No—" He gives me a sad smile. "Not unforgiveable. At least, not to me." He squats down in front of me. "I'm . . . I'm not going to lie to you. To hear that you've done this stuff, yeah, I'm disappointed—because you know how I feel about cheating, how it tore me apart."

A heavy stone slowly sinks to the pit of my stomach.

"I personally can't ever see a time in which this is acceptable, but I also haven't walked in your shoes. You can tell me to bugger off, that it's none of my business. But I'm calling bollocks on your excuse." His smile grows a fraction of an inch. "Family doesn't let you get away with that kind of crap excuse."

Cameron slaps Will's shoulder blades and sits back onto the couch. "Hen, it does my heart good to know you trust us enough with the truth, as painful as it may be." His smile starts strong but fades. "But Will's right. If you're going to be honest with us, be honest."

My left hand's felt wrong the entire time I've been in Alaska. The ring that I used to wear, the special Dwarven gold one that Jonah and I found that proved our Connection, is back in Annar in a hidden compartment in a jewelry box. I wonder if Jonah's found it. If he's gone through my apartment, if he's thrown everything away. If he's taken the matching ring off his finger.

I stare at the smooth bit of skin that no longer shows the absence of a ring. There'd been a pale line when I left, but I used makeup to hide it until it eventually faded away. And now, now that I'm staring at that spot and having Will call me out on everything, I can't help the regret that threatens to pull me under.

"You're right." I hate that my voice shakes. "I knew what I was doing when I cheated. And I did it anyway." My nails curve to dig into my palms in an effort to stave off extra tears. "It wasn't—we didn't have sex, if that's what you're thinking." Which is a humiliating admission in front of a man you consider to be a father figure and another man who's your best friend. And I don't know if it was a lucky thing I didn't have sex or not, but there are times I wish so badly I could have had just that one experience with Jonah to help carry me through the years.

"So you two broke up?" Will asks. He's staring at me like I'm a stranger, which I probably am to him, now that I've shown him the real me. "And you didn't end up with the other bloke?"

I draw both lips inward, biting down hard before I slowly shake my head no.

"No to . . .?"

I am truly an awful, awful person. It'll be a miracle if either Dane can even hear my words, my voice drops so low. "We didn't break up."

Silence. These two are excellent at waiting a girl out.

"I . . ." Am a coward. Selfish. "I left. Just left. No note, not . . . nothing."

Will's eyes widen. "You just fucking left? No goodbye? No, 'We're done?' No *nothing*?"

I wouldn't blame them if they're judging me now, Cameron included.

"That's fucked up, Zo—*Chloe*." Will's frustration is tangible. "How long were you two together?"

Officially? Nearly two years. Unofficially? "I've known and loved him my entire life."

Cameron lets out a melancholy sigh. Because he is another person who found true love at a young age, and he'd give anything to have his wife back. Here I am, admitting I'm a total whore who cheated on her lifelong love and then left him without a word.

Will's long, slow whistle fills the living room. "You cheated on this bloke that you claim you loved your entire life, and then just . . . left. Without the decency of a goodbye. Jesus, Chloe. I don't even know what to say to that."

I can't even look at Cameron. There's got to be more disappointment there than I know I can handle.

And yet, I've dug my grave, I might as well lie down in it. "It was with his brother," I tell my best friend. Tell the man who has treated me better than my own biological father. "I cheated on my fiancé with his own twin brother. And they . . . they fought a lot.

Because of me. I hated it, couldn't stand being the reason they weren't close, so . . . I thought the best thing to do was just leave."

I think I've stunned them both into an even more horrified silence. I can't look up. I can't.

"I don't expect you to understand," I ramble on. I'm so nervous I feel like my limbs, my hair, my eyelashes—everything is just going to drop off with the next breath. "But I made the best choice I could at the time. Work was unbearable. They were fighting. I . . . I got sick. I didn't know how to handle the mess I'd made. I lost a lot of weight from the stress. Got a bleeding ulcer that kept coming back. Had constant headaches. Couldn't sleep. Couldn't eat. They fought, and stopped talking to each other, and I hated hurting them, hated knowing I was the reason they were unhappy, and all I could think was—was—if I weren't there, they wouldn't have a reason to fight. And work was—I couldn't deal with what I was being asked to do, so I left, and I did it in a way that they can't find me, or work, or anyone from my old life, and I've tried to build myself a life that has more to do with what I want to do than what other people tell me I have to do. And . . . yes. I miss him. *Them.* I miss a lot of things, and it eats me up inside, and I break sometimes, and I want to give up or give in, and that's why I called Jonah. But right now, I'm not sorry I left. I'm sorry that I hurt them, and I'm sorry if I hurt anybody else, but I'm not going to apologize for doing what I thought was best. Because I will do anything in my power to make sure that their lives are better. I'm not—"

Will grabs my face between his large hands. "It's okay. Jesus. I'm sorry. It's okay. *It's okay.*" He wipes away tears I didn't know I was still crying with his thumbs.

Cameron leans down next to me, too, and we do a three-way hug, and while it feels good—their love and acceptance are more than I deserve—I can't help but think Will's wrong. Because, it's not okay. And I'm a fool for ever thinking it could be.

66

Chapter Ten

After spilling my guts to the Dane boys and crying until I blacked out, the Tracker appears at the diner during my shifts for three days straight. He orders pancakes, inhaling them like he's starving, swearing I'm a goddess for serving him the best things he's ever eaten. I don't doubt his honesty; once, while he raved about them, he lost his stutter.

Being constantly on edge, waiting for the anvil to drop, or at least the Guard appearing and literally dragging me back to Annar at any moment, though, is too much for my rapidly unraveling nerves. I'm not lying when I finally break down and tell Paul I'm sick and need to go home. Once I'm there, standing in my small bedroom in a small house that has felt more like a home than the one I shared with my parents most of my life ever had, I debate whether or not to cut my losses and leave like I did before, with nothing but a handful of doctored paperwork and cash.

It'd be simpler, that's for sure. Cameron and Will don't deserve this. My baggage is too much for me to carry, let alone burden others with.

At the door, I'm just about to leave my keys behind when I spot an envelope bearing my assumed name. Hands trembling, I rip it open.

I've been accepted to the University of Alaska Anchorage.

Part of me is elated, another is furious, yet another is incredibly saddened. I fudged my transcripts, but I ensured they reflected my true grades. To know that I got into a school of my choosing is fantastic—but to what end? It's not like I'll be able to go anyway. Not with Annar breathing down my neck.

I was so naïve, thinking I could ever be something other than what I've been told to be.

I shred the letter into tiny pieces. Then I shred the envelope. I collapse down into the ring of tattered, unrealistic dreams below me.

So it only makes sense that this is when the screaming I haven't heard for over eight months fills my ears.

I'm on my feet and at the large bay window in the living room, searching the white neighborhood for any sign of the Elders. They've gone silent; it was more of a burst rather than the continual siren I'd grown accustomed to over the years. Although, come to think of it, the last time I was attacked, by a singular Elder no less, it was silent.

If they've found me in Alaska . . .

I snap the blinds shut and slide over to one of the walls, willing the house to become impenetrable. A massive earthquake could strike Anchorage and this would be the only building left standing, I've made it so sturdy. The windows melt into something better than bulletproof. The roof is hardened into a tough shell. If they're going to get me, it isn't going to be in this house.

I weigh my options. If the Elders are here, and the Tracker knows it—well, the Guard is probably on their way. When I was last in the loop, capturing Elders was a high priority for both the Guard and the Council. Which means . . . maybe the Tracker isn't here for me. Maybe he was scouting the region for Elders and stumbled upon me in some twisted sick joke of Fate's. But if the Guard are coming, there's an excellent chance Kellan will be with them, or even Jonah; the Guard had long believed the twins to be more effective working in tandem against the Elders. As much as I want them, miss them, need them, there's no doubt in my mind that their lives have vastly improved in my absence. Letting anyone find me would be setting them back.

I could run. It'd be the safest thing, especially since I refuse to let the Dane boys get caught in the crosshairs of whatever war the Elders are fighting against Magicals. The nons I love are painfully fragile, and I'm not exactly simpatico with any Shamans at the moment.

But, if I leave the house, it'd be me against who knows how many Elders. I could maybe hold my own against a couple, but against a large group?

Etienne's words swarm my memories: as long as a Creator lives, the worlds will be okay. It's the vacuum that will cause havoc. The last time there wasn't a living Creator, the worlds fell into chaos.

I need to stay alive.

A strangled gasp of a scream sounds nearby. I jump, and then double jump when the backdoor slams shut.

HOLY HELL. I made this place Fort Knox and then forgot to actually lock the doors.

I refuse to go down without a fight, though. Two glowing balls of blazing energy materialize in my palms. The best defense is offense, or so I'd heard from all those sportscasters Jonah used to watch.

Something bangs in the mud porch.

I calculate my odds. I've got a wall behind me. The front door to my right. The hallway to the bedrooms to the left. The kitchen to my front. Another hallway to the laundry room and back door. I erase the entryway to the hallway and kitchen and bolt the front door. They can only get me from the one point of entry now.

Goosebumps race up and down my arms, but they're not from the frigid February Alaskan weather. My heart hammers in my chest. I can do this. I can *do* this.

My eyes narrow on the entryway. My hands clench the balls. A controlled burst of a scream sounds somewhere behind me, outside, followed by a shadow leaking out of the hall. I hurl the ball in my right hand as hard as I can at the doorway, switching its properties mid throw to act like a gun silencer. No need to freak the neighbors out, after all. Plaster and wood explode in an eerily silent shower leaving the room hazy in dust and smoke.

Something slams against the front door.

And then, "WHAT. THE. FUCK?!"

Will stumbles out from the gaping maw I'd just created, his clothes covered in plaster, his hair disheveled, his hands clutching a partially singed, white to-go bag from the Moose on the Loose. He's white as a sheet, his eyes saucer wide, and it's no wonder, because here I am, standing with glowing fireballs in my hands after destroying part of his house in an assassination attempt.

I literally have NO IDEA WHAT TO SAY.

Something slams into the door once more, nearly ripping me out of my skin. The Elders are right outside, and if they didn't know I was here before, they do now. The situation has officially hit the fan now that Will's trapped in here with me. Thank all the gods that Cameron is at work.

We have to get out of here, stat. I collapse the remaining energy ball into my fist. "Where's your truck?"

His mouth falls open.

"Your truck, Will! Where is it?" I stand on my tiptoes and peer out of the peek hole in the door. I swear, something smiles back at me. Smoky black shapeshifter? Present and accounted for. Just one as far as I can see, but one is too many when there's a Human involved.

But Will isn't talking. He's just gaping at me like I'm a monster. Fine. He can hate me and fear me, but I'm still getting his ass out of here.

I grab his arm and drag him back from where he came from. From the back door, I can see the truck. It's maybe two hundred feet from the door. A hopeful, quick scan leads me to believe the Elder is still at the front of the house.

"Do you have your keys?" I whisper. When Will doesn't answer, I do something that I'd never done to anyone before. I smack him straight across the face so hard fingerprints are left behind. I try not to cringe. "Keys, Will!"

It must've been enough to snap him out of whatever stupor I'd driven him into, because he recoils, flushes bright red, and hisses right back, "In my pocket."

"Get them out." I scan the area again. Another thump sounds from the front door. Once I hear the jingle of keys, I grab the doorknob.

A hand drops on my shoulder "Wait."

"There's no time," I tell him in return. Realizing that the back door is creaky, I end up erasing it instead. Will's breath draws in sharply, but I grab his arm anyway. "Don't. Make. A. Sound."

His nod is quick and jerky.

"On the count of three, we're going to run to your truck. We're going to get in and we're going to drive as fast as we can. Do you understand?"

Another jerky nod. "I'm driving, though."

Fair enough. I match his nod and hold out one finger. Two fingers. Three. We scramble down the steps, slipping on the icy path, but we make it to the truck in seconds. "GO GO GO!" I yell, and the truck swerves, sliding in an arc, but it shoots out the back of the driveway. I redesign the wheels so ice and snow are nothing to them.

The Elder's off the porch in a blink of an eye, slamming into the driver's side. I immediately reinforce the metal and glass surrounding us. "Drive, Will!"

"WHAT IS THAT THING?"

Death, is what I want to tell him. His worst nightmare. How does one even begin to coherently explain what's going on? As we speed away, the Elder hot on our trail, I notice the white to-go bag, sitting in between us. "What's in the bag?"

"ARE YOU KIDDING ME? YOU CAN MAKE DOORS DISAPPEAR AND SHOOT FIREBALLS FROM YOUR HANDS AND THERE'S SOME KIND OF MONSTER AFTER US AND YOU WANT TO TALK ABOUT THE SOUP I BROUGHT YOU? ARE YOU OUT OF YOUR FUCKING MIND?!"

He has a point. Still, "You brought me soup?"

"Chloe!" His eyes don't leave the road, but they narrow into slits. "Priorities!"

I eye the Elder in the side mirror. It's fallen behind. "You need to take us out of town. I can't fight it out in the open all by myself. We have to go somewhere where we'll be isolated. Where there won't be collateral damage." Or, at least, I can hope. I snap my fingers. "Take us to Chugach."

The state park outside of Anchorage would be the perfect place. Plenty of wildernesses to hide in. Plus, as it's February, it's not like the park will be filled with hikers.

"Fight it? Are you mad?"

"Should we just let it kill us?"

He guns the truck around a corner; we skid for two heart-stopping seconds before he manages to right us. Huh. I redesign the wheels once more. "Start talking, Chloe Lilywhite. Who in the hell are you?"

"This isn't the time—"

"Really? Because I'm thinking it's the bloody perfect time. TALK."

I sigh, my eyes never leaving the twisting black shape behind us, even though it's fading from sight. He's not going to let this go, and it's not like I have the ability to make him do so, so I do the unthinkable. "Fine. I'm . . ."—oh Gods I'm really telling him—"not quite Human. Not like you, anyway. I'm part of a race of beings called Magicals. More specifically, I'm a Creator, and that thing back there is what we call an Elder, which just so happens to be one of the first of my kind, if legends are to be believed. My ancestors went to war against them and sucked out all their essences. Since escaping from where they've been imprisoned for thousands of years, they make it a point to hunt us down and kill us out of revenge. I'm sort of a big get. I stupidly didn't think about the Elders tracking me down when I ran away, because I'm clearly an idiot and really only thought about things like my broken heart, but here one is, and it won't stop unless it gets me or I manage to get it first. Chances are, though, that guy who's been stalking me at the diner has already called back home and a team is on their way to take care of it. Which means, if I don't take care of it first, they'll most likely find me, too, and I'm not ready to go back. *Capiche?*"

I'd barely taken a breath, spitting all that out. I don't think Will took one while listening, either.

"I didn't tell you before because telling non-Magicals about us is forbidden. Chances are, if they find me, they'll find you, too, and they'll punish you by erasing your memory. Which maybe you want after what's going on. But I hope you can believe me when I say I was trying to protect you and your dad from my past."

The truck spins around another corner. We're miraculously on the outskirts of town without more outright attacks by any Elders.

He's silent for a full minute before asking, "Are you an alien?"

I nearly choke. My laughter borders on hysteria. "What?! NO. I am most certainly *not an alien!*"

The truck slides across a lane. Why can't I get these tires right?

Another minute ticks off between us. "Was it all a joke then? Playing . . . what. Friends? With a lowly little peon who works at a diner in Alaska and his dad?"

"Gods, no, Will!" I tentatively reach out a hand, but his arm jerks just out of reach. "When I left home, I thought I'd screwed myself out of any happiness in life. But I met you, and your dad, and Frieda and Ginny and Paul, and I realized . . ." I swallow. "You're my best friend. You're my *family*. No matter what else happens, I want you to know I will never regret meeting you."

He sucks in his bottom lip, eyes glued on the road. I can't tell if he's angry, disgusted, scared, or bored, and that worries me almost as much as the thing following us.

"If we make it out of this," I tell him quietly, "and you want to talk about who I am and what I'm capable of, then we will. Absolutely. I'll tell you everything you want to know. But right now, we need to get this thing out into a less populated area so I can try to take it down."

This finally earns me a quick glance. "Have you ever done so before?"

His question surprises me. "Uh . . . I've imprisoned some before. None of us have ever been able to kill them, though. They're pretty much immortal."

"Are you?" When I don't answer, he clarifies, "Immortal?"

I shake my head. "These things . . . they've hurt me before. Last time, it took me by surprise. Broke a bunch of bones in my arm and one of my knees."

His head whips to face mine, eyes wide in horror.

"Eyes on the road, Will." I wait until he refocuses. "We . . . my kind. We have people who can heal others, like doctors. But you and I don't have a Shaman with us today." A quick scan shows we've lost the Elder for now, but I can't find any optimism in the cab of this truck. "Whatever happens, if I tell you to leave me behind and drive away, I need you to do that, okay?"

The horror in his eyes transitions to incredulity.

"They've gone after people I cared about before. Nearly killed my cousin. Hurt—they hurt my fiancé. More than once." I'm trembling all over. "It was—I can't . . . ." I slam my palms against the dashboard. "I don't know what I'd do if you got hurt because of me, too."

His eyes refocus on the road. "You're saying I'm a liability to you."

Yes. In more ways than he knows.

He swears softly under his breath. "It doesn't feel right,

agreeing to that. I don't leave my friends behind."

I nearly melt in relief. Angry as he is, he still calls me a *friend*. "I know." He lets me touch him now, my fingers cool against his arm. "And that's one of the things I love best about you. But you'll need to do it anyway."

And yet, I get no promise from him in the end.

Chapter Eleven

After nearly an hour of driving, Will calls his dad and tells him not to go home, because there's a problem at the house that needs to be fixed—if by problem, he means part of the house being destroyed and all. I'll repair the damage if I make it through the next several hours, and then most likely pack Cameron and Will up in their trucks and insist they get as far away from me and Anchorage as possible.

"So. These things." Will cups the back of his neck and angles his head toward me. "What's the game plan?"

Yes, Chloe. What IS the game plan? I've spent much of the hour wondering that exact thing myself. "I guess imprisonment. I've done it before." I shift; my butt has gone numb. I've never been one for road trips, even tiny ones that barely constitute the label.

"When you say it's immortal, do you really mean it?"

I twist my neck until it cracks. "I'm pretty sure that immortal means immortal, Will."

He's frustrated with my responses. "I'm just saying, how can we fight it?"

"*We* can't fight it at all. *I* will fight it."

He's quiet for a long moment. And then—"Is that bloke you were engaged to like you?"

"Yeah." I want to lean my head back, but I won't have a good view of the side mirror anymore. I haven't seen the Elder in a long time, but I know better. They always come back. "I mean, not exactly like me—but he's a Magical."

"You said you're a Creator. I'm assuming it means you can create stuff."

I exhale a breathy laugh. "That's the gist of it."

"What does he do?"

I twist my hair up in a faux bun and then let it drop back down. "He's an Emotional. He can . . ." It hurts to just think about Jonah, let alone speak about him. "He can make anybody feel whatever he wants them to feel."

Both of Will's eyebrows shoot up. "That's . . . incredibly fucked up, Chloe."

Now that I've opened the floodgates, worry and love and concern come crashing through. What is Jonah doing right now? Is he in Annar? Here on the Human plane?

"And the brother?"

Another pang, right against the tender valves that hold my heart in my chest as I snap my attention back to Will. "The same."

He pauses before he asks, "They make you fall in love with them?"

A glance out the window shows trees and snow all around us. I give in and let my head fall back, staring up at the cab's roof. "No. I mean—not like you're thinking." My finger touches the spot where my ring used to lay. I twist my head until I'm facing Will. "They rarely ever used their crafts on me, and when they did, it was usually with my full knowledge."

One of his long arms drapes across the steering wheel. "I sense a *but*."

By now, I have little left to lose. Will knows what I am. I've dug our graves. So I give him the Cliff's Notes version of Connections, about how I have two, and how it's torn *me* in two. About how I met Jonah. How I met Kellan. How I planned on marrying Jonah. Cheated on him with Kellan.

When I'm done, he's quiet. I pick at a popped stitch in the

leather below me. "True love isn't so shiny and desirable now, is it?"

He smacks my hand away from destroying his seat any further. "Let me get this right. You are incapable of falling in love with anyone else?"

I nod and resume my watch for Elders. "Well, I mean—I can love people. I love you and your dad, for example. I just can't *romantically* fall in love with anyone else."

"What made you decide to pick one over the other?"

I look away from the side mirror. "Huh?"

"Despite how you felt about both guys—you picked one. You told Jonah you'd marry him. If I'm not mistaken, you were actually willing to elope. Why did you decide on him instead of Kellan?"

I groan, rubbing the spot in between my eyes. "Ask the easy questions, why don't you?"

"Were you with him because of a sense of obligation?" Will asks. Both hands are back on the wheel.

I shift to fully face him. "Whaaaat?"

"You said you thought Fate or whatever meant you two to have a Connection. You guys met in your dreams. Grew up together. Did you decide to stick with him because you *thought* you should? Because it was *expected* of you?"

I can actually feel my eyes grow so wide I fear my eyeballs are going to pop straight out. Pop right out and smack him straight in the face. If they do, I hope they explode and ooze gross eye juice all over him. It would serve him right.

"No!" My voice rings in the cab.

"He shows up at your school, and you had the perfect chance to reconnect with him. What do you do? You ignore him and fall in love with his brother. You hooked up with this other bloke multiple times. Pined for him. That's very telling, Chloe."

"I . . . I! I EXPLAINED THAT! It was because we're Connected!"

"And yet, if I understand this correctly, you have a Connection to Jonah, too. One you were more than willing to ignore for the sake of being with his brother. Were you ever pining for this Jonah when you were with his brother?"

Hell yes, I did. My fingers curl into fists, jagged nails digging into my palms. "You don't understand."

"I disagree. I think I understand better than you think."

One of the tires explodes. Will jerks the wheel and limps us over to the side of the road. I don't bother telling him that it was because of me. Or that I can make him a new one. Because, Jonah was never an obligation. I was never with him because I had to. I love him. He's the best person I know. I've always loved him.

He's not an obligation.

What I feel for him isn't an obligation.

It isn't.

Is it?

The more I think about it, the angrier I get. The more frustrated. And feel all the more helpless.

"Well, isn't this just the perfect time for a tire to crap out on us," Will mutters, getting out of the truck.

Wait—is he planning on changing the tire? Does he not remember what I am? Or that we have a monster chasing us? I wrench open the door and throw myself out of the cab. I round the front of the truck, my fists still tight balls, ready to argue and fix the truck all at the same time. "You don't know the first thing about how I feel about Jonah."

Will pulls a red beanie out of his pocket and tugs it over his now wavy, wet hair as he gets out the tools needed to change the tire from the back of the truck. "I know what you feel for him isn't real."

Excuse me? I'm seething now. "*Yes.* It is."

He pulls out a wrench and bends down next to the tire. "Magic made you believe you love him. It's not real."

That's it. The wheel he's working on disappears; a fuchsia one appears in its place with flowers, hearts, and rainbows swirling through the tread. When the wrench in Will's hands freezes, I stomp closer. "Really? Is that tire real? Because I just made that with my so-called *Magic*."

He slowly stands up to face me. "Tires are not the same as feelings, Chloe."

"Why? Because you can't touch them?" I shove a mittened finger against his chest. "Because you can't see them?"

"Because feelings ought to be organic," he stresses, knocking my hand away. "People should fall in love because they want to. Not because something *makes* them."

Caleb, my Conscience, used to force me to count to ten before I said something I may regret. I try this now and find myself needing to count to fifteen instead. "The joke's on you then. Most of the so-called *organic* stuff you're referring to has been either altered or created by Magicals. It's what we do."

"Emotions are different. They're personal. Nobody has a right to mess with somebody else like that."

My teeth grind together. "How do you know that my feelings for him aren't"—I flash air quotes—"*organic*?"

He crosses his arms. It's brutally cold outside, but we're both too stubborn to actually get back into the truck at the moment. If the Elder comes along now, we'll be easy pickings. "Because you just told me that you have some shite voodoo called a Connection that ties you to him."

"Yes," I stress, "but I also told you that I grew up with him. I *know* him. I fell in love with him. *Me*. With *him*. Not because Fate said I had to, but because I. Fell. In love. With *him*." We're toe-to-toe now. "He's the best person I know. The best." I poke Will in the chest again. "If I didn't have a Connection with him, I'd still love him."

He scoffs. "Then why are you here instead of there?"

I shove him until he stumbles back, not enough to fall, but just enough to skid on the salted roads. "I told you."

"Yeah, but that's a load of rubbish. If you really loved him, you would've stayed and tried to work it out."

A tree falls down nearby, sending an explosion of snow to cover us. Will jumps, but I know it's not due to the Elder. This is all me. And I've got to get myself under control. I count to twenty this time. "Did you not hear anything I've said?"

"I heard you. I also heard what sounded like you two grew apart, and you were more attracted to his brother than him. And it was only when the shite hit the fan and got real that you ran back to what you thought was safe."

Another tree bites the dust. "That is *not* what happened."

Will stares at the shrinking grove of trees near us.

I throw a hand out and the trees float back up, trunks stitching back together. "Look. I won't deny I love Kellan. That I haven't thought about what it'd be like to be with him. That I miss him still. But—"

But that's the thing. For the last several months, I've drowned in how much I miss Jonah. I've thought about Kellan, yes, but the pain of losing him has never cut me quite so deeply as Jonah's. I love Kellan, I've thought about what it'd be like to be with him, but I never pulled that trigger. And I think I finally know why.

It's Will's turn to look like a cartoon character with eyes ready to explode as the trees right themselves. Some of my anger eases, but not much.

I let out a groan of frustration. "Yes, Will. The trees are me."

He snaps his fingers. "The laundry detergent! That was you, as well!"

Now I'm flat out humiliated.

A chuckle precedes his finger wagging. "My, my. Somebody has a temper."

A scream fills the quiet distance. I whirl around and peer through the white behind us. "You better hope I can keep it up."

He's instantly by my side. "That thing—the Elder. It's coming?"

I nod. Still no sighting, though. "Get in your truck and go, Will."

"Fuck that. I'm staying. Besides, you think I'm going anywhere with a tire a four year old would've designed?"

"This isn't a game!"

"Obviously." He steps in front of me. "I'm not leaving, so you might as well make me as useful as I can be. What can I do to help? Can you make me anything to fight this thing with?"

Fight? Like . . . hand-to-hand combat? I shudder. Is he forgetting the whole immortal thing?

Will's hands clamp down on my shoulders. "Whatever it is, it used to be like you. Living, breathing, whatnot. Living things can be hurt. Give me something to work with. If it can smash into my truck, it can hurt if I shoot it or stab it."

Is he joking? "No. I won't risk you."

Another scream fills the air, closer still.

His dark eyes bore down into mine. "I'm not asking. I'm telling. If I have to go get a branch from the woods to beat it, I will. No matter what, I'm staying."

I close my eyes and take a deep breath. This goes against my instincts, but . . . "Fine. Fine!" I open my eyes and whip up my favorite bow and arrow set and pass them over to him. And then I make another for me.

He's amused. "Are we hunting?"

"Big game, my friend," I tell him. My smile is vicious. "The biggest you'll ever see."

Fighting on the open road isn't going to happen. Not that many vehicles have passed us in the last fifteen minutes, but I can't risk nons reporting anything going down. I'm already risking enough as it is; I'll be damned if I leave Will out in the open. I convert our clothes to a waterproof, cold-proof fabric of my own making, plus switch out our footwear for sturdy snow boots and then take off into the woods with Will hot at my heels.

"Do you think it'll follow?" Will asks. Bastard is barely winded, but the stitch in my side reminds me that months of bowling and hanging out in a diner have done little to keep me in shape.

The screaming swells sporadically, each burst like nails against the chalkboard lining the inside of my skin. But I need the advantage. I need to be the one to take a stand first. And I need to do it in the right spot. So I keep running, the bow bouncing on my back, until we get to a large clearing.

Will stands next to me, surveying our location as I lean over, hands against knees, searching desperately for my breath. "Seems awfully open." He squints, peering through the trees. A controlled shriek in the distance answers.

"Better open than trapped," I gasp.

"I've been thinking." He taps his fingers against his thigh. Why is he so calm? He ought to be freaking out. Sane people would be, especially nons who've just learned monsters are real. Is that it, though? Is Will truly insane and I just never caught on until now? "I need a sword."

Yep. Full on INSANE. I straighten, my eyes widening. "Oh, you do, huh?"

"Paul tried to take me hunting once. I was shite at it."

"And yet, you're a master swordsman?" I let disbelief coat my words.

He grins. "I'm Scottish. Highlanders have been wielding swords for centuries."

"You're from *Glasgow*. Isn't that like, sacrilegious or something to call yourself a Highlander when you're a Lowlander?"

"You're just being picky now. Would it help if you made me a kilt or something to go along with the sword? Also, why is this taking so long? Do you need to create a forge as well?"

I sigh and hand over a lightweight yet indestructible sword. "Be careful. It's sharp—"

"Swords normally are."

I consider it a victory that I don't bop him on the head with the butt of the sword. "Just keep it away from me."

"No stabbing Chloe. Note taken." His grin diminishes some.

"What's the plan?"

I wipe sweaty loose strands away from my face; they've begun to develop ice crystals. And then I make myself a super warm white beanie. Upon consideration, I switch all of our clothes to white to match our surroundings. Will jerks in his boots, like the color change shocked him. "Don't be a baby. All I did was camouflage your clothes. Keep it up and I really will make you a kilt. Didn't they wear those without underwear?" I leer. "Gosh, can you imagine that in this weather?" He protests, so I talk right over him. "I'm kidding. The plan is simple: take the Elder down before it kills us."

"Oh, yes, that sounds quite simple," Will mocks. He pats his pants, clearly making sure I didn't switch them out for a kilt after all.

A scream fills the clearing. My knees spasm, but I know that I can't let Will down. I must stay calm for him.

He slides an arrow out of the black leather quiver I made. "What kind of arrows are these?"

His voice is still calm, filled with a hint of amusement. Seriously. What's wrong with him? Any sane person, Magicals included now, ought to be scared shitless in a situation like this. "They're like little suns," I say, pointing to the glowing arrow tip.

He jerks his fingers away from the shaft. *"The fuck . . . ?"*

This freaks him out more than the monster coming to hunt us down? "Well, I took away the gravitational pull, and altered the properties so it doesn't, you know, blow up the planet or anything, but technically it's a concentrated bit of hydrogen." He stares at me with growing horror, so I add, "It's not like I'm a scientist or anything. They're probably not even technically suns. It's just what I call them. I made them up. They're effective. Unless you get shot with one, you ought to be fine handling them."

He's still horrified.

"Oh, gods," I groan. "Just give me the damn thing. Stick with the sword." I probably shouldn't tell him that I made the blade out of a metal found only on the Goblin plane that can cut through anything, including stone, like it's a sheet of paper. I take the bow away from him. I keep the arrows, adding them to my quiver, but erase the rest.

"You're a wee bit terrifying," he finally says.

A shriek follows, the closest one since the house. I will my courage to not fail me. "Let's hope I stay that way. Get ready." I slide an arrow into the bow.

Will holds his sword up, looking for a brief, snowy moment like the warrior from the past he'd joked about. Like metal in his hands was second nature. If I were truly smart, I'd knock him out and hide him, but the truth is, it's sort of nice to know I'm not alone right now.

Because . . . there it is. Right at the opposite edge of the clearing. It's found us.

Chapter Twelve

I nearly started screaming in terror. This Elder looks, for the first time ever, *humanish*. Still smoky, still distorting, but damn if it doesn't actually mold its shape into a person with eyes—glowing ones that can't seem to decide on a color. I don't know which is worse—the shape-shifting creature, or the choice to look like it does now. No, wait. I do. This one. This one looks far more frightening than any of the others.

"Bloody hell," Will whispers.

What he said.

A concave hole opens where a mouth ought to be and . . . it laughs. LAUGHS. Not screams, but *laughs*. And it's an awful laugh, all evil and angry and . . . female. This thing here, it's a *female*.

"Found you, little Creator," it hisses, voice distorted and hollow.

Oh. My. EFFING. GODS. It spoke to me. It spoke! THEY SPEAK.

Furthermore, its arms extend and twist until they resemble fists curling around twin sais. WHAT IS HAPPENING HERE? This— Elders don't do this! Do they? Have they changed in the last six months?

I fight to reclaim my voice. "What *are* you?"

It tsk-tsks, black smoke trailing out of its cavernous hole of a mouth. "Rude little piglet. Not what. *Who*."

My own mouth snaps shut. I pull the bowstring in my hands so tight my arms ache. Finally, "Alright. *Who* are you?"

It swings the sai-like extensions in whip-fast circles that lead my heart in a matching rhythm. "I am feeling generous right now, so I will answer you. I am Cailleache, little Creator. And I am here to collect you."

Cailleache. Cailleache—the wheels in my mind spin as my arms slowly liquefy under the strain of keeping the bowstring taut. And then it hits me, why this name is so familiar. This is the first Creator's wife. The second Elder/Magical in existence. The one who controls all four elements: earth, air, wind, fire.

The first Elemental ever.

"Oh, shit," I whisper.

Cailleache glides forward, like some kind of nightmare from a horror film. "Come with me, and I won't kill your pet."

Will beats me to the punch, his sword out, two fingers pressed against the blade. He slowly circles to the side, so we've got two angles on this thing. "I'm no bloody pet."

Cailleache laughs again, the sound so awful that snow dumps down around us from the surrounding trees.

Even still—she doesn't want to kill me? She wants me to *go* with her? Go where? Elder Headquarters? "You want me?" I tell it. *Her*. "Then you're going to have to take me."

I let the arrow loose and it whizzes lightning fast toward Cailleache. She dodges it, but just barely, howling in fury. I reload, but now she's charging us, so fast she's a black, wispy blur. *Thwang.* Reload. *Thwang.*

She manages to dodge everything.

The next thing I know, my shooting arm is bleeding heavily. Bitch cut me with one of her smoky sai through my coat. Why didn't I think of making Elder-proof clothing? When will I learn?

That awful mouth twists into a distorted grin. "We can do this all day."

I draw another arrow out, arm shaky. Bandages snake around

my arm. The snow below me is stained red. Will barks something about moving, but I position myself so I'm standing in Cailleache's direct line toward him. "Is that all you've got?" I ask her, glad my voice is even despite me wanting to barf everywhere.

"Oh, little Creator. The things we've got in store for you," it hisses in return.

The next strike, I manage to sideswipe her with one of my arrows. Her scream is an explosion, followed by heavy snow raining down on us. Will comes at her while she twists to the side, slashing at what resembles a leg; the scream turns atomic. Trees splinter around us, but she's back on her—well, not her feet, because she's floating, but definitely ready for another round, fresh with a new set of stereotypical villain *wait 'till I get ahold of you* threats.

Both Will and I are bleeding profusely. I triage us with bandages as quickly I can, but if this is her game—cut us down, piece by piece—I'm truly scared for our chances as we go round after round. She cuts us, we barely nick her. If I'm not careful, we'll bleed out in the snow. What can I do? What can I make?

I . . . I walled the last one in. That's it! I drop a heavy, but clear wall behind her just as she slices at my leg, and then two more on the sides. A roof curves over us, blocking out the snow. It's enough to momentarily distract Cailleache; one of my arrows finally lands a clean target. Bits of smoke surge out of her in disturbing waves as the arrow tip explodes in her torso. Her mass regroups quickly, but as her anguished shrieks rattle the impenetrable material surrounding us, I drop another wall behind me and Will, effectively caging us all in. And it's enough for Will to leap forward, looking like he's in a movie to my blurry eyes—all lithe, slow motion as he first goes up and then down, driving his blade straight through what appears to be her upper back and into the snowy, hard ground below.

He's pinned her.

And she stays where she is. She's struggling, fighting against the blade, but somehow, Will found some tangible part of her existence and trapped her to the floor.

"I'll destroy you." Black smoke pours from the maw on her face. "Piece by tiny piece!"

"Big words coming from the shish kebab," Will says to me. He's panting, sweat swirling with blood on his face.

I'm stunned. There is an Elder effectively pinned and captive, right in front of me. Terrified she'll somehow break free, I drop a secondary cage around Cailleache's body, boxing her into position.

Okay. Okay. She's not going anywhere. At least, I hope not.

"Chloe," Will murmurs, limping closer. He's bleeding heavily in at least five or six different places. I'm the same. I get to work on bandaging him, but he grabs my face with one hand, forcing me to look at him. "What are we going to do with her?"

"She's . . . she's contained."

"I know." He winces as one of my bandages tightens on his leg. "But we can't leave her like this. What if somebody stumbled upon her?"

I press my palms against my temples. "Normally, we imprison them underground. A team comes and helps. The—the Guard decides what to do."

"Whatever the Guard is, they aren't here." He grunts quietly, flexing a wounded arm. "I am. I'm your team. So again, I ask—what are *we* going to do?"

I stare at Cailleache; she stares right back, her head twisting up, those semi-lips distorting in pure hatred and anger.

"Back at the house," Will continues, "you erased the back door. You made us new clothes. You changed my tire after making the first one disappear. You—hell, you made these bandages appear out of thin air."

I switch my focus to him. "Yes, but—"

"You can make a door disappear," he says quietly. Firmly. "Why can't you make that thing disappear?"

What?

All of a sudden, Cailleache thrashes in the box, her efforts to get out redoubling. And the weird thing is, little drops of dark red—

more blackish than ruby—splatter around the sword pinning her intangible body. Is she bleeding?

"You're asking me to kill her." My voice is hollow.

He doesn't answer, simply squeezes my shoulder.

I've made lots of things disappear over the years. I'm a Destroyer, after all. But in all this time, it's never occurred to me to erase a living being. I don't know if I can, let alone want to.

And then I remember Oliver Crocus, an Elvin Storyteller on the Council, telling me a couple years back that, once upon a time, an Elder who was a Creator asked another Creator, one of his own making, to will him out of existence. What was his name? Oh. Rudshivar—the son of the same being now bleeding out in a box in front of me, the Creator who stood up to the rest of the Elders. The one who created all of the races that exist today. The one who made Magicals who they are. He was an Elder, and he no longer exists.

He had another Creator will him out of existence.

"If you do this," she spats, like she can read my mind, "the others will never stop hunting you. They will destroy everyone you value."

So, she knows. She knows what I'm capable of.

"How many of my kind have you killed?" I squat down next to the box. I'm impossibly sad all of a sudden. This creature, this thing—this woman, the first woman of our kind—she a killer. She's hunted Magicals and sucked their lives right out of them. Nons as collateral damage have been killed, too.

She's nothing more than a monster. No reason she can give, no excuse, can ever explain why she's been privy to the serial killings going on.

Instead of answering me, she smiles that terrifying sneer instead.

I really have no right to serve as judge and jury, let alone executioner, but Will is right. Nobody else is going to come in and clean up this mess. It's just me. I count to ten, just like Caleb taught me. And then I say in clear, crisp words, "I can't let you hurt anybody else. I'm sorry. I can't."

Cailleache stops moving. "If you think this is the end, think again, little Creator. This is only the beginning."

Images flash through my mind, reminding me of the damage the Elders have done to those I love. Even if it takes my dying breath, I refuse to let that happen again. *You've caused too much pain over the years*, I think in my mind. *It's time to rest. You are no more.*

And yet, here she still is. I lean back on my heels, stunned. Maybe I can't do this after all.

As if she knows I've failed, Cailleache laughs. Billows of twisting smoke pour from her mouth as she cackles at my incompetence.

Why didn't it work? If another Creator could do this to Rudshivar, why can't I?

I lean forward against the box; the moment my palms flatten against the plastic, Cailleache's laughter ceases. Thrashing replaces it, alongside threats even more frenzied than before.

I slowly rock back on my heels, my palms dropping to my lap. The thrashing slows considerably.

Could she . . . is she scared of my *hands*?

I stare down at my bloody mittens. Prior to today, I've only ever had to think about destroying something for it to happen. But then, I've never stolen life from a sentient being before. Maybe . . . maybe Fate wants something more than my thoughts when it comes to physical life. Maybe Fate requires a risk from me.

I strip off a tattered glove and make a small hole in the box, just large enough for my hand to reach in and press against her shifting shape. She flinches sharply when my skin touches whatever it is that makes her her, but then she calms once more, like she knows what's coming.

I whisper, "I'm sorry," and then I do the unthinkable.

I will her out of existence.

And I'm left leaning against an empty box surrounding a sword.

Chapter Thirteen

"You're shaking," the master of the obvious says to me as we limp back to the truck.

I erased both boxes, the sword (much to Will's displeasure), and my bow and arrows just as easily as I erased an Elder before we left the clearing. Truth is, I feel a bit numb. "Just cold."

"Liar." He peers up into the sky. It's no longer snowing now that the first Elemental is dead. "We need to get going. The temperature is dropping."

I simply make us warmer clothes.

When we get to the truck, Will digs out his cell phone and calls Cameron. He tells his father we've been in a car accident and that we need to go to the hospital because we've both lost a fair amount of blood. While I'm rearranging the car's appearance to match Will's claims, I hear him say, "What? Dad—we both need stitches. I need to get Chloe—"

I switch his phone to speaker function without even touching it. "Son, trust me," Cameron's saying. "Just come to my work and I'll make sure the two of you are taken care of. Hurry. I'm worried about you both losing more blood than you already have."

Will and I exchange uneasy glances after his father hangs up. "D'ya think Dad has lost his mind?"

"I killed somebody," is what I say in return.

92

"*We* killed somebody." He smashes his hand against the steering wheel. "Lest you forget, that thing tried to kill *us*. And probably killed loads of other people before today. I'm not mourning its loss, Chloe. I beg you don't, either."

I pull in a breath, but it stings. My ribs ache from being knocked over by Cailleache one too many times. "How moronic am I that I never thought about willing any of the Elders out of existence before today?"

He grins, even though there is a nasty cut above his upper lip. "You're welcome."

Hollow laughter fills the cab. "Just my luck, right? I have to get up close and personal with serial killers in order to take them out."

He grunts, wincing. He's holding himself strangely, like it's painful to breathe.

I lean my head against the cold window. It feels good. "They've killed a lot of people," I whisper. "They've tried to kill the people I love most too many times. So why do I feel so awful right now?"

His large hand falls against my knee and gently squeezes. "Because you've got a good heart."

The rest of the trip back into Anchorage is spent in silence. And even though it seems like I ought to be focusing on what just went down, my mind keeps going back to the argument Will and I had right before the Elder showed up. About how he accused me of only being with Jonah out of some weird sense of obligation.

The more I think about it, the surer I become of what I said. I love Jonah. Not because of our Connection—well, okay, yes, I guess the Connection is responsible for at least us meeting—but because I. Love. Him. He's smart, and loyal, and thoughtful, and kind, and so many other things that make him one of the best people I know. We grew up together. He was my first kiss. And I stayed with him, even though I was confused over my feelings toward Kellan, because Jonah has always been my safety. In a weird way, he's also been my most constant source of stability and reliability, two things I've craved my entire life. And even though consistency, stability, safety, and reliability sound like boring things on paper, with him, they weren't. They were what I needed. What I still need.

I have enough excitement in life. I am capable of earth shattering deeds. I need steadiness and acceptance. I need love that can be just as gentle as it can be passionate. The kicker is—I had that, and I foolishly threw it away.

People are wrong about Connections. Connections don't define you. Having a partner doesn't define you. Love doesn't define you. You have to do that yourself. You have to decide who you are, what you want, and where you want to go. But when you do find somebody you want to share your life with, it needs to be for the right reasons.

I don't want Jonah because of our Connection. I know what Connections do to people. I refuse to let that define me, or, more importantly, *us* any further. I want to be with Jonah because of who he is. I've learned too late to appreciate what he brought to my life. The truth is, I stayed with him, despite feeling like I was being torn in two because I always knew, deep down, who was best for me. And I ran because I thought it was best for him.

I love him.

And it's time I let him know that.

Cameron hovers over me, arms crossed. Some middle-aged dude who's supposedly a nurse practitioner that he knows is stitching up my numerous cuts in Cameron's small, neat managerial office in the back of a fishing warehouse.

Wait. I know him. He's the guy Cameron insisted on helping me in the hospital during my embarrassing alcohol-poisoning episode. And my assumed feverish thoughts about him were right, because here in the harsh florescent lights of Cameron's office, I know for sure he's an Elf—or, at least, part-Elf. Tall, aloof, and classically handsome, Erik Hernandez works quietly and efficiently, with precious little chitchat with anyone other than Cameron. He's given both Will and I something to numb the pain, hooks us up to IVs to help with the blood loss, and forms neat rows on all our injuries.

He didn't question our story about the supposed car accident, even though it's obvious to everyone in the room that we're lying through our teeth. He doesn't question our blood types, even though I know mine doesn't rate on a normal Human scale. And Cameron doesn't push either, until Erik leaves, taking his old-fashioned black doctor bag and empty blood bags with him.

"I want the truth, and I want it now," is what he says to us.

Will eases himself onto the couch in the office, wincing with the effort. The pain meds Erik gave us have yet to fully kick in. According to the nurse practitioner, Will has two bruised ribs that could very well be broken, but the best he could offer was a tight wrapping that restricted movement and breath. "We got in a car acci—"

This doesn't fly with Cameron. *"The truth."*

I shrink back in his swiveling desk chair; like the idiot I am, I bump my freshly stitched arm against the armrest. I bite back the scream that attempts to escape. Holy schnikes, stitches *hurt*.

But . . . not quite as much as parental disappointment.

Will takes a deep breath. "If you'd only have a look at the truck, you'd see—"

He's a horrible liar. Furthermore, I can't believe he's willing to do this for me. Even now, even after he almost died to help protect me. I love him for it, but I refuse to let him wade into the murky waters of deceit in my name. I cradle my throbbing arm and hold my chin up. "Cameron, there's something I need to tell you."

Will wisely shuts up, gratitude flashing in his eyes.

I pray inwardly that in the next few minutes, the father will be as accepting of the truth as the son. So I tell him exactly what I am, what I'm capable of, and what happened with the Elder out there in the woods. I leave nothing out.

When I'm done, he sinks down next to Will on the couch, staring at me with one of his patented inscrutable expressions. It's one thing to accept a girl into your heart and your family, even one who ran away and has baggage that would make any sane soul run screaming into the distance; it's an entirely different matter accepting somebody who could be defined as unnatural and possibly evil by those who don't understand my kind.

But as a friend of mine once said, love requires risk. How sad is it that I'm only now beginning to realize that love comes in many forms, and that the risks involved need not necessarily be romantic in nature.

Love is a gift. Love is often given freely, sometimes by people unexpected. And as generous and wonderful as it can be, it also sometimes needs to be deserved and should never be based upon lies.

It's a lesson I hope I haven't learned too late.

Cameron finally comes to stand in front of me after several minutes of forever silence, in which I contemplate a dozen different reactions from him, a hand scrubbing over his face. He's tired. And surprisingly not raging. Or fearful. Which sprouts tiny, tender shoots of hope within the walls of my chest. "I have a confession to make as well."

Okay. Maybe I jumped the gun there. Maybe he's gonna kick me right out of here after all. Maybe he's—

"I already knew you were a Magical. I've known for quite some time."

—gonna call the police or the military, and they're going to cut me open and—wait. *What?*

"I'm sorry," Will says for me, since my mouth is dangling open in an unattractive and fly-luring fashion, "but did you just say you knew Chloe was a . . ." He shoots me a guilty look, like he was going to dub me a monster or freak and then thought better of it out of fear of me zapping him into oblivion, too.

"A Magical." Cameron pats his son on the back, a long sigh escaping his lips. "Indeed I did. I suspected she was the missing Creator, but I didn't know for sure of her Magical heritage until the night she was in the hospital." He stands up and wanders over to his desk. Both Will and I watch him in a fragile stillness as he picks up a framed photo of him, Will, and Will's mom, Molly.

He knew? He KNEW?

"And now, a confession for you, son." Cameron gently touches a finger to his wife's smiling face. "The reason I am familiar with Magicals is because your mother was one."

Had the sky ripped apart and rained furious wombats down upon us, I would not have been more surprised, because, *hello*. I SO DID NOT SEE THIS ONE COMING.

My mouth flops open again, my eyes widening. As if we were genuine blood and bone siblings, Will's features match mine.

"Furthermore," Cameron continues, voice hoarse, "Molliaria Hellebore was not Human—not like I am. Your mother was an Elf. She immigrated to our plane of existence for her father's job when she was a teenager."

Will's mouth snaps shut, a sound suspiciously like the love child of a gurgle and old-fashioned choking emitting from his thinning lips.

Will, an Elf? Or—half Elf? I can't help but stare at him as his version of reality collapses down around him in grand, movie disaster fashion. He's always been insanely good-looking, but Elvin? How could I have missed that? Was it because I didn't want him to be anything other than what I had hoped for—a normal boy who fit into what I hoped to be a normal life?

Because studying him now, I can finally see those features. The exotic slant of his eyes. His swan-like neck. His graceful, elongated fingers. All of them are faint, hidden within the influence of his father's Human genetics. He's a far cry from Callie Lotus, who radiates her Elvin heritage. Her Human features are the ones that take a back seat. Or even Erik, who I could tell was Elvin even as I was drowning in vomit. But Will—Will's the opposite. And I feel stupid for being so blind, and annoyed at my astonishment, because why ought one species naturally outshine the other in all cases?

Cameron sets the photo down. "I know this is a lot to take in, son, but—"

Adrenaline supersedes pain, because Will shoots off the couch. He's shaking—and I'm not sure if it's in rage or shock. "Is this a bloody joke?"

His father solemnly shakes his head.

Will turns to me, the plea in his dark eyes tugging on my heartstrings, but I have no answers to give. Or explanations. Or anything other than my support, which I attempt to offer in an awkward hug after an equally awkward extraction from my chair.

Even his voice shakes against my ear. "Did you know?"

I tighten my hold against him as much as I can, given our matching Frankenstein monster-like wounds. But he pulls away, adrift in his new existence. "No. But, Will, it's not—"

It's not what, Chloe? Bad? Shocking? Reality destroying? The worst thing? Because in this moment, I can see how all of these things could be truth to him.

He waits for me to finish, but I can't.

So Cameron tells us his story. How he met Molly, how they fell in love, how he knew early on what she was and what she was capable of. Of how they were met with stark disapproval from her parents, kept his in the dark, and tried living within Annar's society and boundaries until the strain of their frowned-upon union got to be too much. How, after careful discussion and consideration, they agreed that Molly would make a break from Magical society and try to live life without Magic since she didn't want her son to be stigmatized as a half-breed like other children born of Magical and non unions. How she and Cameron decided to keep all of this from Will during his childhood and raise him simply as Human. How they eventually found an outpost of such couples and children in Glasgow, and of how there are some, like Erik the nurse practitioner, who've gravitated to Anchorage.

Upon his own admission, Cameron assumed there'd never be a time in which he had to reveal Will's heritage unless absolutely necessary. Will rarely got sick over the years, yet when he did, Molly always sought out people within these surprisingly large networks of so-called half-breeds, which is why Cameron was so insistent on neither of us being treated at a regular hospital. He knew Will's Elvin genetics and blood type would send up red flags. How mine—even though I'm technically Human—would do the same. He admits that, when I was in the hospital for alcohol poisoning and the doctors pulled him aside, telling him they'd found abnormalities in my blood work that I don't remember giving (thanks to puking my guts out), his suspicions about me were confirmed. He paid off somebody, another half-breed here in Anchorage, to go and destroy my records, then poked around until he got the lowdown on a missing Creator. From there, it wasn't too difficult to put the pieces together, especially since it was second nature for him to want to protect me just as surely as he does his son.

He tells us, his voice quiet and steady, that this is what his wife would've wanted. Molly didn't want to be involved in Annar society, yet desperately wanted to make sure anyone and everyone who felt they didn't have a place there *did* have a place somewhere. We learn that there are numerous children and adults running around Anchorage right now not knowing they're the products of Magical parents.

The entire time he tells us this, time ceases. I don't even think the clock on the wall ticks. There's nothing, no one but Cameron and his truths. And when he's done, his heart on his sleeve and his good intentions laid out, ready for bruising and judgments, I find that there is no way I can deliver anything but love for this man. He knew what I was and still chose to love me. Protect me. Give me a home and a family. Support me as I got back on my feet.

"I'm bloody furious at you for this," Will eventually says, his voice as hoarse as his father's.

Cameron accepts this.

Will's good hand, the one untouched by Cailleache's fury, shoots through his sandy hair in carefully controlled bursts. "You've lied to me. My whole life. You and Mum."

There's no argument. No defensive comebacks or further rationalizations. Nothing but Cameron accepting his son's anguish in the same calm, steady manner that marks his character.

"Can I do what Chloe does?" There's a wild desperation in his eyes. "Magic, I mean?"

Cameron slowly, but surely, shakes his head, his focus never leaving his son's face.

"Will," I say quietly, "to have a craft, a Magical must have two full-blooded Magical parents."

He closes his eyes, and I can't help but wonder—is it relief he feels, knowing this? Or disappointment? Callie Lotus carries her bitterness over what she perceives as a poorly dealt hand that Fate passed to her on her sleeve for all to see. But then, she's grown up with Magicals, has watched Magic practiced by everyone she knows, respects, and loves. Will never had that. Will's only ever known life as a non.

Finally—"We need to get Chloe home."

Which reminds me, I have work to do when we get there. I blew a huge hole in that house this afternoon. The skies above know the poor place is probably drowning in snow by now.

When we leave, it's done in silence. But while Will storms ahead of us, his fury allowing him to overcome his pain, I reach out and grab Cameron's hand and squeeze it.

And he squeezes mine back.

Chapter Fourteen

Constant, brutal winds have ensured that the plateau I now find myself precariously standing upon remains barren of anything but scraped, raw rock. Even still, I inch closer to the uneven edge before me so I can peer out into the yawning expanse of canyons, rivers, and creeping tendrils of darkness that stretch as far as the eye can see.

Something wails from somewhere within the alcoves in the distance, something mournful and yet angry all at once. Unease skitters across my skin; the wind does me no favors by refusing to blow it away.

I shade my eyes from sharp rays of dying, orange sunlight and peer down, scanning row after row of jagged, twisting tunnels. Nothing. Another round of keening sounds, closer still, followed by such a gust of wind that I'm knocked down to my knees. I reach out to grip the surprisingly soft edge I'd just been standing on, only to find chunks of rock crumbling beneath my palms.

"It seems impossible." I hold up handfuls of bleak, gray shards of rocks and watch the remnants float away in the wind. "And truth be told, I'm terrified."

Jonah simply stares at me in return, dark hair cutting across his face, as he approaches the edge.

A new wail drifts up to the plateau, circling us before floating higher and away.

The tips of Jonah's toes dangle over the edge as he surveys what I've been studying for hours. "You shouldn't stand too close." I brush my hands on my jeans. "The wind's pretty strong up here."

This sigh that escapes him drifts directly into the wind.

He never understands. "You can't blame me for caring. For wanting to keep you safe."

Another sigh, but at least he backs away from the edge. But then, just as I'm about to push myself up, he reclaims the steps he'd lost in a run and then flings himself right off the plateau.

I scream his name, but my only answer is another round of keening that transitions into full-fledge shrieking. Back-to-back gusts of wind drown my words out while driving fear even deeper into my pitted bones. Just as I'm about to jump myself, a hand grabs my arm.

I whirl around to find Kellan. Dirt smudges his face and arms, exhaustion nearly drips off his body.

Thank gods. "Jonah—"

Kellan holds up his index finger and presses it against his mouth. The look in his eyes is so sad that my heart crumbles just as easily as the rocks below me.

He lets my arm go. Before I can even complete a full blink, he follows his brother's lead right over the edge.

The screaming in the wind is deafening.

I wake up from my dream, shaking so hard that I break down sobbing in the comfort of my bed and darkness.

Will didn't speak to his father the rest of the night. Other than to ask me how I was doing and whether I was hungry—his need to take care of loved ones via cooking overriding even his rage—we didn't speak that much, either. Once the house was repaired and put to order, he went into his bedroom and hasn't reemerged.

"Give him time, hen," Cameron says to me as we drink coffee in the early morning. "Will's always been the sort who is slow to change. But he's a good boy, and a logical one despite his hotheaded Scottish heritage. He'll come around."

I find it ridiculously endearing that Cameron strives to comfort me when I've been trying to do the same for him for the last half hour. "I never thanked you last night for saving me at the hospital," I tell him. "And for everything else you've done for me."

He ruffles my hair. "I would do it again—no questions asked." His dark eyes flick towards the hallway. "You know, Molly would've adored you. She loved her son—was the fiercest mama bear you could imagine—but part of her wanted a girl, too. We thought about adopting at one point, but . . ." His smile turns bittersweet. "But life goes the way it does, and the next thing you know, you're saying goodbye, and there's a box full of unfulfilled plans." He sips his coffee. "It's truly serendipitous you came about just when we needed you most. When I deduced who you were, I figured Molly sent you to us."

Tears for a woman I've never known, but who must've been incredibly special, prick my eyes. I'm just a weepy mess today, aren't I?

"Of anyone, my Molly knew what it was like to fight for what you want out of life. She was never one to sit back and let this so-called Fate bulldoze her future. She may've walked away from the life she knew as a Magical, but she did it on her own terms. There are a lot of people out there—more than you could possible imagine, hen—who've done the same. But I have a feeling, even though that may be what you've thought is your best choice, maybe it's not after all."

And . . . he's right. I barely slept last night thanks to that horrible nightmare that led me to two conclusions: 1) as scared as I am, I need to take care of the Elders, and 2) I need to make things right with Jonah (and Kellan). In order to do both, one thing is certain . . .

It's time I go back to Annar and finally take responsibility for my actions.

"I'm afraid," I tell Cameron, and it's an incredible feeling, knowing it's safe for me to open myself up to him, without fear of besmirching the family name. To know that he's here for me. "I'm afraid that if I go back, I'll be right back on the hamster wheel I'd been on before."

He nods slowly, rubbing his closely cropped beard. "It is a possibility, true. But the thing Molly always stressed to me was that Magicals are just like everyone else. They've only tricked themselves into believing they have no choices. You have a choice, lass. You can go back and get right back onto that hamster wheel, or you can go back, chuck the bloody thing into the trash, and make your own way on your own terms."

He makes it sound so simple.

"We'll go with you. You won't have to go alone."

Will's standing in the doorway, his shirt and hair rumpled, his eyes ringed in dark smudges which tell me he didn't sleep much last night, either.

I simply stare at him, sure that what I just heard come from his lips was wrong.

But Cameron gives his son a nod, his smile transforming again. This time, pride curves his lips upward.

"Look. I've thought about this—I guess . . . I guess I can see where you and Mum were coming from," Will says to his father. "You guys thought you were doing best, protecting me from what you perceived as an injustice done to so-called"—he shudders slightly when he says this—"half-breeds. But I'd like the same choice you claimed is available to Chloe. I want to see all of this for myself."

Cameron's smile grows even more satisfied.

My heart threatens to swell to unnatural proportions. "Are you sure?"

"Yeah," Will tells me. "I think maybe this is a journey we all need to go on." He lets out the sound of rue turned into a burst of breath. "That's if you want us to go with you, I mean. There's always the possibility you'll tell us to bugger off, but—"

"Yes." Yep. My heart's ready to burst out in ishy, squishy goo made of pure love.

Will's still tired, still . . . shell-shocked. His world has been rocked. But here he is, smiling that crooked smile at me, and suddenly things don't feel so undoable anymore. "Family sticks together, you know?"

"Yeah," I whisper back.

Cameron' arm loops around my shoulders and I lean into his familiar, nurturing comfort. "Then it's settled. While you two go to work, I'll start making plans for us to return to Annar."

"What the hell happened to you two? You look like you got ran over by a bulldozer made of barbed wire."

I ignore Frieda while attempting to tie on my apron. She takes surprising pity on me and gently knocks my hands away so she can tie it. "Car accident," I mumble, and I wonder—even now, even after I've bared my soul to Cameron and Will—when will the lies stop rolling off my tongue so easily?

All of her natural hostility fades as she turns to Will. "Your truck?"

It makes me want to laugh, the way she says this, like his truck is sacred and his life is changed forever by its destruction. Only, the truck will be fine as soon as I get the okay to fix it. Will's life, though?

He's refused to talk about it with me so far. No questions about the Elves I know, no voiced curiosities about what life in Annar is like—nothing. Just a resigned sense of weary acceptance that hurts to see on his face. I left him and Cameron alone after they decided to move to Annar with me so they could talk, but mere minutes after

105

my door shut, so did Will's bedroom door.

Will does laugh here with Frieda, though. It's normal sounding, the kind he'd do on any other day than the morning after his world was turned upside down. Maybe Will's as good of an actor as I am. "Truck's fine. The important thing is Zoe and I are okay."

Zoe. When just ten minutes before he called me Chloe.

"Obviously, you jackass." Frieda goes to swat his arm, but pulls back with only millimeters to spare.

"I'm not fragile," he teases her.

There's a bit of envy in me, hearing him say that with such conviction.

Throughout the day, I allow myself to contemplate how I'm going to make my way back home. On paper, it seems easy enough: get myself to Juneau and go through the portal back to Annar. And yet, like everything else in my life, my return cannot be this simple, as there are so many factors I need to consider that it makes my head spin. Aside from the truly shitty way I treated my fiancé and friends by abandoning them without a word, I'm also a first tier Council member, and I fled my job and responsibilities. I have no idea what the repercussions are for that. It's not like there's another Creator to fall back on, so they're stuck with me until a new one is born and Ascends. But what if they put me under arrest? Do they even do that? Maybe something like house arrest? For all anyone knows, I could've been captured and/or killed by the Elders. Are they out there searching for me, like they did for my team, missing now for over a year? I let myself imagine, for the briefest of moments, that Nividita, Harou, and Earle were found, safe and sound, and all three are in Annar right now, exactly where they should be. It's a lovely feeling, until the reality of my abandoning of my responsibilities weighs down on me once more. Countless beings on seven different planes count on Creators.

I failed them.

I thought only of myself, and I left.

I glance around the Moose, at all the customers I've come to

106

know in these six months, of the people I call friends who I work with, and I think—could I have abandoned my responsibilities to them so easily? Because, even on my darkest, most self-loathing day, I still put on my apron and came to work. And this job—this job I love, this job I made mine—isn't the one I really ought to be doing. Not because I'm above it, not because it's not worthy of a Creator, but . . . *I'm a Creator*. It's the simple truth. I need to start acting like one.

I have a lot of *mea culpas*, I think. And a hell of a lot of growing up to do.

"Cut them some slack," Paul is saying. "I'm sure both Zoe and Will would much prefer going home and relaxing than going to the bowling alley tonight."

"Losers," is Frieda's endearing reply to us. She kisses me quickly on the cheek, slaps Will on his ass, and then saunters out of the diner.

Paul scratches his head. "Ginny's bringing her new boyfriend around. I think it makes Frieda a bit—"

"Bitchy?" Will offers. He's grinning, though.

Paul sighs. "I was going to say insecure. You sure you two are up for closing, being banged up the way you are and all?"

We assure him we are, and then he leaves. Will heads back into the kitchen; I trail after him minutes later, a cleaning bottle and a rag in my hands. "Want to talk about it?"

Several pans bang together as he puts them away. "What's there to talk about?"

"Oh, I don't know. You finding out who I am? What you are? That your parents have kept secrets from you your whole life? I have some experience with that myself."

The look he gives me nearly shrinks my spine, but I remind myself, he's been through a lot over the last forty hours.

The bell over the door chimes, and we both roll our eyes. Paul must've forgotten to flip the closed sign on his way out. "We're closed," Will yells, and then winces as his lungs press against his ribs.

"Well that sucks, as there are a couple customers waiting out here for some orders," comes Frieda's response.

Well, crap. There goes going home early and sleeping. And also, what is she doing back?

Will bends down to put another pot away. "Give us a moment, yeah?"

Her voice drifts closer. "Ooh, is that a grunt I hear, William? Is there some sexual healing going on in the kitchen tonight?"

She just doesn't give up. I don't even bother arguing the point. Why should I? It's likely to go in one ear and out the other. "You know it," I call out. "We're attempting to break health codes left and right."

Will laughs, but puts a hand on his wrapped chest, wincing.

Frieda appears in the doorway. "Well, this is a disappointment. Why are your clothes still on?"

"What are you doing here?" Will leans back against the sink, crossing his arms around his waist, like he's trying to hold the pain in.

She disappears into Paul's office and reemerges seconds later, jingling keys in her fingers. "Somebody forgot his house keys. I'm being generous and fetching them."

"Miracles never cease," Will mutters. But he's smiling.

Frieda grimaces. "Honestly, I had to get away from Ginny and her boy toy in the car. Jesus. They're disgusting. They're slobbering all over one another. I won't be surprised if she's already knocked up."

This comment cuts a little too close to home for Will, who turns back toward the sink.

Frieda swirls the keys in a circles. "Now, you two . . . mama wouldn't mind seeing some action there."

I sigh. "You said there are customers?"

"One is that greasy dude who has been stalking Zo here lately," Frieda says. "The pancake obsessed one?"

Great. Just . . . great. Like I need another go around with the Tracker.

Will's pissed. "I'll go tell him to bugger off. I'm not reopening the kitchen tonight."

"No, I'll do it." I rub the spot in between my eyes.

Frieda smiles sweetly, like she's just enjoyed stirring the hornet's nest. "On that note, I'll leave you two,"—she walks out of the room, raising her voice—"to that sweet, sweet love making you were just starting in on."

I wait until the doorbell jingles before saying, "She's tenacious."

"That's a kind way of putting it," Will muses. "Now, let's go get rid of that bloke, shall we?"

We enter the dining room together, only to be met with, "WHAT THE HELL IS GOING ON HERE?"

Chapter Fifteen

When you haven't seen someone in a long time, it's rather easy for a mind to assume they're a ghost. Or a figment of a very overactive imagination. But I don't think I can pawn off this incredibly uncomfortable moment, in which I'm standing with an extremely handsome man whose arm instinctively goes around my shoulders, while facing one of the most important people from my past.

Honestly? I have no idea what to do. Not one. Single. Idea.

Will snaps, "Pardon?"

Karl Graystone removes his burning hot eyes that have been cooking me inside out to laser in on Will. And then Will's arm. His hands curl into fists and I legitimately begin to worry about this situation, already rapidly spiraling out of control, going nuclear. The weasel of a Tracker sits down at the counter and lazily smiles at me, like he knows he's the cat who caught the canary.

Bastard.

I finally find my voice. "This—this isn't what it looks like."

Karl's focus whips back to me, nearly cutting me off at the knees. "Really? REALLY? Then maybe you can explain this all to me in explicit detail. Starting with WHY THIS SONOFABITCH HAS HIS ARM AROUND YOU. And then move on to how you're apparently trying to break health code violations by making, and I quote, '*sweet, sweet, love!*' Wrap it all up why you look like you've been in a car accident!"

He makes a good point.

Most people would drop their arm and move away when faced with a furious giant of a man. But not Will. If anything, he moves a bit closer to me and says, "Look, I don't know who the hell you think you are, but you do not get to just come in here and start throwing around orders. You can either calm down on your own, or I'll help you do so."

The Tracker, who's been watching in fascination, actually sniggers. Karl, on the other hand, flushes scarlet, he's so pissed. But it's not his words that scare me. No—I'm more afraid of his hands and what they could do to Will. So I take a deep breath and say as evenly as I can, "I will gladly tell you everything, but you have to first promise me you won't hurt Will."

Will protests at the same time Karl barks, "Why should I?"

I can do this, I think. It's going to sound prima donna-y and awful, especially in light of what I've done, but it's necessary. "Because I'm ordering you to."

The Tracker stops laughing. Karl stands there, staring at me like I'm a stranger, and it hurts. Just flat out hurts to see this disappointment in his eyes. But then, I'm good at disappointing people. You'd think I'd be used to it by now.

"Lee," he bites out after a long moment, "go outside and keep watch."

So I was right about his name. The Tracker gets up and exits the door without another word.

Will waits until the door's firmly closed before rounding on Karl. "Have you been siccing that prat on Chloe?"

I slide out from underneath his arm and move myself in between the two men. "Will, stop. Just—just let me—"

"Is this wanker your fiancé?" Will growls. "Because if he is, I can totally see why you got the hell out of Dodge."

This takes both Karl and me by surprise. My Guard friend yelps,

"What?!" as I throw out, "Oh my gods, NO!" And then, realizing how I might have come off as inappropriately disgusted with my vehement denial, I quickly add, "I mean, no—this is Karl. Um, Karl Graystone. He's . . ."

One of my closest friends. My mentor. My protector. My goddaughter's father. One of the few people in Annar that I felt was family. And I'd left him just as easily as I left everyone else.

I can't even begin to imagine what he thinks of me.

But I try for optimism. "He's my friend." I thank all the gods when Karl doesn't contradict this. "And Will, you know—" I wave my hands between us, like it somehow tells my story again, "you know why I left."

Will tugs on my arm until I face him. "Promise me right now that this person isn't here to hurt you."

Out of the corner of my eye, I watch Karl's outrage bloom into epic proportions. But it isn't lying when I easily make that promise. To Karl, I say, "This is Will Dane."

To my relief, Karl does not accept Will's outstretched hand. Will's got enough ailments going on right now—he doesn't need a broken hand to add to the litany of injuries he's racking up. Instead, he nods his head, just barely, but it's enough of an acknowledgement for me to continue on.

Only, I really don't know how to approach everything I need to say to Karl. So I ask weakly, "Was it the Tracker that gave me away?"

Karl's head drops slightly to the side in amazement at the same time his forehead furrows. Okay, he's right. That was incredibly asinine for me to start with.

So I say the thing that I've said far too often in my life. I offer an all-encompassing, "I'm sorry."

Another uncomfortable moment passes before Will breaks it. "I suppose I should make some coffee, as you two apparently only utter sentences to one another after minutes have passed. At this rate, we will be here all night. Why don't you two go have a seat in one of the booths? D'ya like pancakes, Karl? Chloe hasn't had dinner yet and she needs something to eat with her pain meds."

Karl grunts, which Will takes as an assent before heading back to the kitchen. And then my Guard friend stalks over to one of the booths and crams himself in. I follow, sliding in across from him.

"You're blonde," he spits out. "With a horrible haircut and—are those contacts? Which is ridiculous, because it makes it seem like you're in hiding, but Chloe Lilywhite, lead Creator and first tier Councilwoman, would not run away like a coward."

Something bangs in the kitchen, and I jump in my seat. My nerves are completely frayed. But this is a situation of my own making, so I inhale slowly to center myself. "I did run away."

He sucks in a breath, like this surprises him, despite us sitting in a restaurant a zillion miles away from Annar, with me wearing a nametag that says, *Hi! I'm Zoe*, while in disguise. "Why? Why would you do such a thing?"

I straighten my wrapped silverware so it aligns perfectly on the table. "It's—"

But he cuts me off. "Did you know that there have been people searching for you for months? That there are people worried out of their mind back in Annar, not knowing where you are or how you are? Did that even matter to you when you left? Did you ever stop to think, 'Oh, hey, maybe me running away without even a note was, I don't know, a HORRIBLE IDEA?"

His anger is fully warranted. I nod slowly. Yes, I did know those things—or at least suspected them.

He jerks back in the booth, like I'd slapped him in the face.

"Karl, I . . ." I shake my head. But then I decide to lay it all out there. No more hiding. "I guess I should start at the beginning. I'll answer your first concern you voiced. You asked what I was doing here with Will. Well, I work here with him. Obviously, he knows who I am, but to everyone else, I'm Zoe. Whatever you heard us saying about,"—I swallow hard—"us being together or whatnot, well . . . that was a joke. The other waitress likes to tease us. But he and I are only friends. He's . . ." I smile sadly. "He's my best friend. And I'd prefer if you didn't beat the crap out of him simply because he chose to be friends with me."

Karl's lips flatten. "You hooked up with an Elf."

Was it so obvious to everyone but me? "Half," I clarify. "His mother was a Magical." I lower my voice. "He only just learned about that, so I'd appreciate it if you didn't poke that bear with a stick."

Karl's eyebrows shoot up.

I count to ten and pray I get this right. "You're right, though. I was a coward. I ran away, and I didn't leave a note, and here I am, in Alaska, working at a cheesy moose themed diner, hanging out with a half-Elf, all while in disguise, but Karl—I honestly didn't feel like I had a choice." I close my eyes and try not to cry. I count to ten again before opening them, only to see the confusion on his dear face. "There's something I should've told you a long time ago, but I never could. Part of why I left is because I couldn't live with . . ." Attempting to swallow the huge lump in my throat is futile, but I have to own this. Have to take these steps toward making things right. "What was happening with Jonah . . . and with Kellan . . . it was breaking me. Breaking them."

Karl briefly closes his own eyes, sighing through his nose, in a way that shows his belief that I'm just over reacting. "Chloe, I appreciate that you worry about whether or not you're hurting Kellan, but the fact is, you're Connected to Jonah. Case closed."

I bite my lip and stare up at him. I wish it were so simple. And then I shake my head slowly. I can barely get the words out. "Not just Jonah."

He stares at me hard. Another bang comes from the kitchen, startling us both.

"What does that mean?"

So I tell him the truth. He listens to me fall apart without a single word until Will appears with a tray filled with pancakes and coffee.

114

"Ah," Will says quietly, setting the tray on a stand next to the table. "She told you."

Karl's wide eyes go even wider before Will's words snap him back to attention. "Uh . . ."

I pass Karl a plate of pancakes, eggs and bacon. He takes it, still staring at me like I've got two heads.

I sip my coffee, wishing I had some of Cameron's whiskey to strengthen my nerves.

Karl clears his throat as Will slides into the booth next to me. "Let me see if I've gotten this right. You—you claim that you're not only Connected to Jonah, but to Kellan, too?"

Hearing their names from a shared friend is so, so bittersweetly difficult.

Will answers for me when it's obvious I'm about three seconds away from going either catatonic or hysterical. It's a toss-up, really. "That's the gist of it."

"Nobody has two Connections," is what comes out of Karl's mouth.

Will sets his coffee cup down. "She told me that these blokes do, too—to each other. Is that correct?"

"Well, yes, but—they're twins. It makes sense why they'd have a Connection to one another, albeit not a romantic one." Karl's not touching his food. He's still staring at me, confused as all hell.

"I'm no expert in the matter," Will says smoothly, "but one could assume that since identical twins share DNA and whatnot, they just might share one of these Connection things."

Karl's features soften into something I despise. His anger, so tangible fifteen minutes ago, has been replaced by pity. I think I prefer his anger, especially now. "Is this true, Chloe?"

I viciously tear apart my pancakes with my fork. "Confirmed by several Seers."

He's still confused. "But you—you and Jonah. You guys are like me and Moira. You had a doorway. You shared dreams."

I've begun sniffling. *Dammit.* I do not want to break down

crying tonight. Will passes his napkin over but I ignore it. "Exactly. Can you now see why things were a little difficult between the three of us?" I hate that my voice just cracked while saying that. I focus on the plate below me. Do not break down, Chloe. Not now. Not in front of them. I close my eyes and count to twenty. When I open them, I say, thankful my voice is more even, "You've got a Connection, Karl. You know how overwhelming it is. Just imagine having two. Imagine being torn between two people. Imagine knowing that you're constantly causing somebody you love more than life unbearable pain at all times. And it wasn't just Kellan I was hurting. Jonah suffered from my actions, too." I allow myself a sad smile. "Did you know that, by the end, the only talking they'd do with one another was during fighting?"

"Chloe, I—I can't believe all of this," is what Karl says.

"You knew them growing up. They were best friends. When I came into the picture, all of that changed." I force myself to breath in and out. In and out. "What would you have done? What if it'd been you and Moira and,"—it's a low blow, but I say it anyway—"Kiah? You'd have done the same. Had I left a note, they would have still come after me. They'd have tried, like they always did, to rationalize things. Offer more promises that they'd find ways to fix everything, even when those and others couldn't be kept and they'd beat themselves up over it. So, yeah. I'm selfish. I left. I left without a note, and I know I've hurt them, but it was the best I could do."

He rubs his forehead and shakes his head slowly.

I'm indignant, which is so much better in this moment than weepy. "I'm not lying about the double Connections."

"I know," he says quietly. Then he laughs under his breath. "I'm a really shitty friend, aren't I? For never noticing any of this before?"

What? There is no way he has any reason to feel guilty right now. That's all on me. "That's ridiculous! How could you—"

"Moira would every so often ask me if things were okay with Kellan. She'd say he was . . ." Karl shakes his head again. "Those of us who knew you two used to date knew your breakup was hard on him. But, I just figured . . ." He sighs. "Moira knew. She was worried about him, and Jonah, saying they were acting weird, but they refused to talk to her about it. Always said they were fine."

My pancakes are now in tiny pieces.

"Jonah and Kellan—they're good at hiding their feelings," Karl continues quietly. "They always have been. I think the few of us who ever saw anything just assumed that they were stressed from work. Eighteen is a really young age to have so many responsibilities laid on your shoulders, even when you're as talented as they are. And the better they did their jobs, the more the Council and Guard expected of them."

I'm pretty sure the diner just lost most of its oxygen from me sucking it all in at once.

Will clears his throat meaningfully, which prompts Karl's eyes to widen. "Shit. Sorry, Chloe. Obviously you would know that best."

An uncomfortable silence encloses the table until Karl's phone rings. Six months of actions crowd my mouth and send panic shooting through each and every vein in my body. When he pulls it out of his coat pocket, time slows down until all I see is that phone, in his hand.

"It's Zthane," he tells me, his voice tilting upward at the end in silent question.

Time to face the music, Chloe. And yet, he doesn't answer it, making the moment I wait for the ax to come down on my head stretch out for eternity.

"What bloody kind of name is *Zthane*?" Will asks during the third ring.

Karl's hazel eyes hold mine until the phone goes silent. "It's a fairly common name from a particular country on the Goblin plane." He mercifully looks away so he can regard Will. "Sort of like John here."

"Zthane is . . ." I swallow and force myself to sound business-like. "He's on the Guard."

"Head of the Guard now."

My focus flies back to Karl. "Since when?"

He rubs at his chin. "Since Paavo Battletracker couldn't find you and the Council deemed him incompetent. Zthane is on his last legs right now for the same reason."

Well, hell. "Is it Jonah who's threatening to fire him?"

Karl laughs a little, but there's no humor in it. "He was certainly one of the people behind Battletracker's ouster; there was no love lost between the two of them. But the truth is, as much as Jonah respects Zthane, he's also frustrated that you . . ." He motions towards me and Will. "Let's just say that Jonah's legendary patience isn't so legendary anymore."

Double hell. I have so many bridges I need to mend that I don't even know where to begin. "Surely Kellan is defending Zthane?" I mean, Zthane is Kellan's mentor and been outwardly vocal for some time about wanting Nightstorm to head the Guard.

"If you think that Kellan has taken any other position than his brother's in the last six months regarding the issue of finding you, then you truly are delusional, Chloe." While his words sting, his voice is surprisingly gentle. "But let's not talk about that right now. Why don't you tell me instead why the two of you look like you do."

As if this is an easier conversation. I sigh and shove my plate away. "Last night, we had a . . ." I slide a glance toward Will; he's stone-faced, arms crossed. "Let's just call it a skirmish with one of the Elders."

Karl actually spews his recent sip of coffee all over the table. "WHAT?"

I grab a napkin and mop the mess up.

He reaches across the table and stills my hand. "Chloe— seriously. What happened to you two?"

"It's as she said," Will says flatly. "One of those beasties tried to kill us, so we killed it first. As it did not want to die, it made sure it did its damndest to tear us to shreds. It's not a complicated story, mate."

Karl's eyes grow so wide that I fear he's going to have a stroke.

So I take another deep breath and I tell him everything that happened yesterday, down to the littlest detail.

And he listens.

Chapter Sixteen

"So how is this going to play?" Will sets a bottle of wine down on the table. We've retreated back home so we could bring Cameron into the loop and introduce him to Karl. And now here we all are, drinking wine when all of our lives are once more being turned upside down. "What are the ramifications of Chloe going back to Annar after running off like she did?"

Talk about a buzz kill. I draw my hand back from reaching the wine and lean back in my chair, sighing. How is this going to play, indeed.

Karl takes the bottle instead, unscrewing the cork with a bottle opener Cameron passes over. "I honestly don't know. Being a first tier Creator is certainly in her favor, though." His hazel eyes pin me to my chair. "I've put off talking about this with Zthane for the time being, saying I'm still searching Anchorage, but Chloe—I need to talk to him sooner rather than later. Especially in light of what you guys have told me about what went down with the Elders." He sets the cork down on the table. "There are people searching for you as we speak. It's not fair to let them keep spinning their wheels, possibly putting themselves in danger, when you're safe."

I scratch the back of my neck as he fills the glasses on the table. "Yeah, of course you're right. It's just . . . ." I hold my empty hands out in front of me; Nell nuzzles me from underneath the table. "I need to be the one to talk to Jonah first. I can't just show back up in Annar and blindside him again. It's not fair."

Karl pushes a half-filled glass toward me. I nearly laugh at the irony, except—right now, right here, I get to choose whether or not it's half full or half empty. His voice is quiet when he tells me, "For courage."

My hands shake when I take the glass from him.

"We'll be there with you, hen," Cameron murmurs. "You won't have to do any of this alone."

"Are you sure about this, you guys? Because—as Will just pointed out, who knows what's going to happen to me when I go back? As far as I know, they might throw me in jail. Or house arrest. Or, I don't know—put an ankle monitor on me."

Karl snorts, like I'm being overly melodramatic.

"If they do," Cameron says steadily, "then it will happen with you knowing your family has your back and will be there to support you every step of the way."

Although I think he'd guessed I was close to Cameron and Will, Karl's eyebrows still lift high into his forehead at the use of *family*.

And I don't blame him. What did I do to deserve such love, given so freely? "You guys will have to leave behind Anchorage and everybody in it. Your jobs."

"There are portals," Cameron says. "And cars and airplanes, not to mention telephones. Plus, I happen to know lots of places in Annar hire nons. Hen, we already discussed this."

Even still, nagging, latent fear taunts me that all of this might be too good to be true. Surely somebody like me, after everything I've done, doesn't deserve such generosity and loyalty. "What about the Moose?" I say to Will.

"They will most likely go under without my stellar cooking," he says with a straight face.

More quietly, "And Becca?"

That strikes a nerve. "What about her?"

I bite my lip, sneaking a glance at Cameron. He looks . . .

desolate, like he fears his son will change his mind over this reminder of what once was. "It's just," I tell my best friend, "Annar is obviously not . . ." I tap on the table. "Here."

"Did you fail geography?" He pats my shoulder sympathetically. "Because frankly, I'm concerned. Anchorage is quite a distance from Glasgow, too. Separate continents and all. Maybe you should make us a map so I can—"

I shove his hand off. "Smartass." And then, more gently, "I just . . . I don't want you to do something that you'll regret."

He laughs bitterly before he sips his wine. "That ship sailed long before you ever entered the picture." He sets his glass down. "What will it matter if I am in Annar or Alaska? My phone will ring just the same."

Karl sends me another silent question, but this is not my story to tell. So I say instead, "I can't ask you to give up everything for me. You two have a rich life here in Anchorage, especially with . . ."—I glance back at Cameron again—"the community here."

"We are not giving up anything for you," Cameron says. "This is not only your chance to make amends back in Annar, but mine and Will's, too."

Will frowns before finishing the rest of his wine. "In case you aren't up to speed," he says to Karl, "my mum was apparently not only an Elf, but a Magical, too." He stands up and wanders over to the sink with his glass. "Yesterday was a fun day, mate. Found out my best friend is a superhero and that I'm not even human, that I never knew who my mum really was. Good times were had by all."

Karl clears his throat as he lays his iPad down on the table. "On the car ride over, I was able to access your mother's file, Will." He coughs uncomfortably. "I . . . well, I needed to background check you and . . ." Another uncomfortable cough. "The point is, it's standard procedure. If you want, you're . . ." I nearly laugh, because Karl looks like he'd rather be anywhere than here at the moment, in the midst of this drama, "free to look at it, if you like."

Will's eyes widen before zooming on his father. "Why in the

world would my mum have a file?"

Cameron says, voice calm as ever, "Molly was on the Guard like Karl here. I'm assuming she has one due to that. Unless there are files kept on every Magical?"

This makes Karl even uneasier, like he's revealing state secrets. But he tells Cameron, "Every Magical has a file. Some are more detailed than others, though."

Will sucks in his bottom lip while he gazes at the iPad. It doesn't take a rocket scientist to know he's pissed at learning this new bit about his mom, not so much that she was a Guard, but because it was something that wasn't expressed earlier.

I try to fill the void. "What was her craft?"

"She was a Smith," Cameron says. I envy how he always sounds so steady. So composed. So in control, even though he must be nervous about revealing all his secrets after decades of building and hiding them.

"A good one, too." Karl's smile is small but genuine. "According to the file, the Guard tried on several occasions to change her mind about leaving."

"Wait." I shove my glass away. I need to be clearheaded here. Because if he's saying what I think . . .? "The Guard *knew* she was leaving and was okay about it?"

Karl taps on the iPad. "Obviously not, as they tried to convince her to stay."

"But she left." I can hardly believe this. Since Cameron told us the truth about Molly, I'd just assumed they'd snuck off like I had. But she left, and they knew, and she still did it.

There's hope I can get out of this alive after all.

"Before you go too far with this line of thinking," Karl says quietly, "neither the Guard nor the Council knew you were leaving. Molliaria Hellebore wasn't a first tier Council member, nor was she the only Smith around."

Well, there goes that bit of hope.

"What's a Smith?" Will finally asks.

Cameron's the one to answers. "She was ace with metals, son. Could make anything she wanted with any kind of metal. Could even make metal appear out of thin air." He holds up his left hand, where a slim silver band laces his ring finger. "Made me this." His voice is soft. "She was so bloody talented."

Will stalks back over to the table and asks to view the file. When Karl passes over his iPad, I get up and leave the room. It's not that I don't feel welcome while Cameron and Will share this bit of family past, it's just—this is something father and son need to do alone.

"Not thinking of bolting while I'm not looking, are you?" Karl's followed me into the living room.

I let out an exasperated laugh. "Believe me, I've learned that running away isn't always the answer." I bite my lip. "Will you be honest with me?"

His answer is pointed. "I've *always* been honest with you."

Ouch. I try not to wring my hands like some stupid damsel in distress, but my palms are sweaty and adrenaline is making me woozy. This answer—I need this answer like I need air to breathe. "How is he?"

He crosses his arm. "Which *he* are we talking about?"

Double ouch. I sink onto the couch and stare at the framed picture on the mantle over the fireplace. It's Cameron and Molly and Will, maybe three years ago? And they all look happy, like they belong with one another.

I have some pictures of me happy with somebody back in Annar.

Connections are all about whom you belong with. But I'm tired of Fate thinking it can dictate that to me. If I belong to someone, and that person, in turn, belongs to me, it's going to be because we choose to give ourselves like that, not because some nebulous universal concept deems it so.

It's funny, but I think I finally, *finally* understand that concept. I'm not lying when I say, "It's always been Jonah, Karl."

He lowers himself down on the couch next to me and studies me, lacing his hands around his knees.

Might as well lay myself bare, since he already knows most of the truth anyway. "Do you know how many times I considered leaving Jonah so I could be with Kellan?" I shake my head slowly. "A lot. I was so, so tempted. Kellan is . . . he's exciting. With him, there's always a sense of urgency and heightened emotions. And I don't know if that's because it seemed like every time we were together it felt like it could be the last or . . ." I trail off, not knowing exactly how to verbalize what I was thinking or feeling during that year. "Whatever the reason, the damage was done. I was drowning in guilt. He's my Connection, yes. But Jonah . . ." My hands curl around my sides as I hug myself. "I think this time away has allowed me to realize that, Connection or no, he's the one for me. The one I need. I dream about him almost every night. I think about him constantly. I worry all day about how he is." I lay it all out there. "I love him, Karl. Even though I probably don't have the right to ask, I'm going to anyway. Please tell me how he is."

Karl chooses his words carefully, but his disappointment in me is obvious. It hurts—but I totally understand it. "How do you think he's doing? His Connection—his fiancée, to boot—disappeared without a trace. He's trying his hardest to keep it together and do his increasingly more difficult and time consuming job like the Council expects, and to his credit, he has, but he's clearly having a hard time with you being gone."

I want to ask what that means—*having a hard time*. But Karl beats me to the punch by pulling out his cell phone. "A lot of his free time has been spent pointlessly searching for you. If you mean what you've just told me, I think it's time you call him and set his mind at ease, at least on that front."

I stare at the cell phone he's offering. "What if he never forgives me?"

"That's a chance you took the moment you left." He motions at me with the phone again. "I just want to warn you he's out on a mission right now on the Elvin plane and might not answer. Normally, I'd advise you to wait until he's done, especially as this is an extremely . . . difficult assignment, but as I know he'd want to hear this right away, I'm going to give you the go ahead to call."

Everything in me turns to frail glass as old insecurities and guilt rear their ugly heads. But he's right. This has been a hard truth to uncover, and I've possibly risked everything, but it's been my own doing. And it's got to be my doing that makes amends.

I take the phone from him. Then I try to keep down the dinner I'd barely managed to get in my stomach.

Karl stands up and heads over to the door. "I'm going to go check the perimeter. Lee's supposed to come over and give me a report on Elder activity in the area. I'll be outside if you need me" And then he's gone, leaving me alone with his phone.

Chapter Seventeen

I can do this, I tell myself. I can press the numbers and say the words: *I'm sorry, I love you, I'm coming home.* I can do this.

I can't do this.

And yet . . .

I *have* to do this.

I close my eyes and press the phone against my forehead. This is excruciating. I abandoned him. I loved him and abandoned him after he found me when I thought I'd lost him forever. He came for me, and I love him, still love him so much, maybe more now than before—and I have to do this. No matter what, I have to make this call.

I let out a long breath and lower the phone. And then I punch his numbers in and wait.

Three rings, and then, "Whitecomb here."

My words dissipate and fly away. My tongue goes asleep. My brain flat lines. Because, gods, I love his voice. But I do not love hearing what sounds like gunshots in the background. Karl mentioned a difficult mission, but—

"Karl?"

Chloe, I want to say. It's Chloe.

There's an exasperated sigh and then a dial tone.

With trembling fingers, I redial the number. Why are there

gunshots going off where he is? Two rings this time before he answer with, "Don't waste my time, Karl. I'm already late to the rendezvous point thanks to Rosemary's incompetency at reading maps."

Somebody screams in the background, a blood-curdling shriek that vocalizes pain and terror. My stomach twists until I'm breathless. I search frantically for my voice. And then, barely vocalized, "It's me."

Silence.

I clear my throat. Louder now, "Jonah, it's—it's Chloe."

There's an intake of breath over the line, one loud enough to act like defibrillators on my light speed racing, aching heart. But he still doesn't say anything.

"I'm . . . Karl's with me. He, uh, I'm on his phone, and I wanted to call you and let you know . . ." Do not cry, Chloe. He does not need to listen to you have a breakdown, especially if he's in a warzone. "I'm okay."

His words are just as broken as mine. "Where are you?"

I clench my eyes shut and lower my head. "Alaska. We're in . . ." A futile attempt at swallowing the water balloon in my throat is attempted only to fail. "Anchorage."

What sounds like an explosion goes off at his end, sending me off the couch in alarm. It takes Jonah a good five seconds before he answers. "I . . . Anchorage? Is that near a portal? I'm—fuck. I'm in Kuergal right now. But I can get there in—"

An inner dam breaks and the only thing holding back the deluge is my self-imposed blindness in the moment. "No. You—you just said you're late for your rendezvous. I don't—don't just drop that because I'm . . ." I grapple for my coherency. "You don't need to come here. You need—it sounds like you need to find somewhere safe. Don't risk—I'm not . . ." Why can't I get out the right words? My nails dig into my palm in my free hand. "I'll be back in Annar soon with Karl. I just . . . I wanted to let you know I'm okay. To tell you I—" I'm flat out flailing. "Just . . . stay safe. Please just . . . stay safe." Oh, gods, this is awful. I'm doing a horrible job at this. I might as well rip my heart out and stab it to the ground right now, it hurts so much. Plus, I apparently cannot string together cohesive sentences and now I sound like a total fool. The last thing he needs when guns and bombs are going off around him in fricking Kuergal, a country on the Elvin plane renown for its violence, is dealing with me on the phone. "Can you . . . when I get back, can I see you? Can you—" Another explosion goes off, leaving my ears ringing. Jesus, how can I do this? "Can you and your brother come to see me? There are a lot of things,"—another fruitless attempt at swallowing—"I, uh, *we* need to talk about."

There's a pause in which I debate a thousand times whether or not I just made another massive mistake. Finally, like he's saying the hardest thing he's ever had to admit, "You don't want me to come get you?"

More gunshots fill the background. Angry voices yelling a language I don't know punctuate the tiny bursts of silence between explosions. My fingers tighten around the phone.

I don't know how I'm going to do this. Misery and shame and love and a dozen other messy emotions bloom and threaten to cripple me. "It's not that I don't," I choke out. "But, you've got a job, and . . . It's . . . I'm so sorry. I need to do this. I need—I need to come back to Annar and I need some time to think." Gods, how selfish does that sound? Time to *think*? Like I haven't already spent six months thinking? I'm butchering this. Flat-out hacking to pieces this lousy first contact between us in months.

Somebody on his end shouts at him, this time in English; I can only pick a few words out, but they're terrifying ones: *hide, protect you, get the fuck out of here, anarchy.* He ignores them to ask me, "You swear you're okay?"

My crystalline heart shatters as it drops to my feet. He sounds like I'm the one with the gun, and I've shot him right in the chest while grinning. "I swear," I tell him, even though at the moment, I'm not even close to fine. And then, because I am the worst kind of girl,

I put my foot on top of his bleeding chest, like a hunter with a smoking rifle downing my trophy and posing for a victory photo, because I say next, "I'll text you the address I'll be staying at when I get back to Annar."

Getting air into my lungs is becoming increasingly difficult.

I love you, I want to shout. I miss you. I choose you. YOU. I love you. I'm so sorry.

But my lips don't move. His do, though. "That's . . . that's what you want? To *text* me an address where you'll be staying when you get back to Annar?" He says it like he can't believe he's saying it. Like it's a jumble of foreign words he's merely regurgitating.

My voice shatters entirely when I tell him it is.

Another explosion fills the phone, and then there's silence. Our connection is broken.

I've never felt more panicked in my entire life.

Kuergal is in chaos.

I'm staring in horror at the small television set I've just created, as it runs cellphone videos of anarchy at its worst. Whoever was yelling at Jonah wasn't kidding about that. Cars and buildings are burning, people are dying, and guns and bombs are going off.

I'm two seconds close to creating a portal in the Dane's living room to get myself to the Elvin plane when Karl comes back inside from his perimeter check. "Ah," he says quietly. "You got through to Jonah."

All I'm capable of is a number of gurgling sounds. I decide right then and there that I need to make sure Jonah's okay. I need to see it for myself. I make myself a screen, but Karl snatches it away from me the moment a picture flickers to life.

He crushes it between his hands. "Things have gotten really bad in Kuergal lately," he says, sitting next to me on the couch. I stare at the mangled screen, still dangling from his fingers. "That's why Jonah's there. He's trying to get the conflict to end." Karl drops the mess on the coffee table and scrubs at his hair. "Funny thing is, the civil war didn't even start due to any of our missions. Took the Council totally by surprise; things had been quiet there for a good few years now." He pauses. "Well, quiet for them, at least."

It's a weird relief, knowing Jonah wasn't the cause behind this madness. Still, since I can't see how he's doing and the line I just called him at seems to be dead, I drill Karl for information. "Does he have a team with him?"

"Yes. He brought four additional Emotionals with him, including Kellan. This is a really tough gig, though. There are a lot of deep-seated prejudices and hatreds in that area that need more than a quickie Emotional hit."

So, Kellan is there, too. I . . . I don't even . . .

"That's all he has? Emotionals? Nobody else to back him up?"

"There are some other Magicals working in Kuergal right now, but Jonah felt it best that, for what he was going to do, he work with Emotionals." Karl taps a finger against his knee. "According to mission specs, they were supposed to separate today to work in different quadrants of the city. I can't promise you right now he has anyone with him."

But he did. Somebody was trying to get him out of wherever he was, so at least there's that. Even still, it's nearly impossible to just continue sitting here and do nothing. What if he gets hurt before I have the chance to try to make things right between us? "He wanted to come here. Come get me. I told him no. To stay there and find somewhere safe."

A heavy hand curls around my shoulder. "Which was the right thing to say, Chloe. As much as I know this has been . . . tough on the two of you, he's desperately needed there."

There is so much blood on the TV. So much pain and suffering. "What if—"

"He'll be fine." Coming from Karl, it sounds like it's the promised truth. "You think he's going to let somebody take him down now that he knows you're coming home? Please. He's got a fire under his ass now. Kuergal is going to turn into the happiest place in all the worlds. Just you wait and see."

Jonah's in a warzone. A freaking *warzone,* risking his life so he can help people. And here I am, like a coward, in Alaska, with blonde hair and a fake name, shirking her duties, and I have never, ever felt more worthless in my life.

Something in me hardens. That girl? That stupid, pointless, coward of a girl? She's gone. Dead.

I will never, ever be her again.

Chapter Eighteen

I'm seconds out of the bathroom, towel around my wet hair, when Will comes to tell me I need to come out to the living room. Cameron and Karl are already out there, talking to the Elvin nurse practitioner that patched me up the other day.

Thank goodness I've been wearing sweats to bed.

"It's bad," Erik is saying. "People are scared. Nobody knows what to do. There's talk of splitting up the colonies, at least until things die down. We thought this was over, but it's starting anew."

Karl's brows are drawn down, like he's caught between being pissed and worried. Cameron's obviously concerned, too, but his frown attempts to hide behind his beard. "There's safety in numbers, Erik. I think it's best to stay put."

I pull the towel off and comb my fingers through my hair. "What are you guys talking about? What colonies?"

There's a strange look in Erik's eyes when he regards me. When he was sewing me up, or helping me through alcohol poisoning, he'd been cool and professional. Now, there's a bit of fear and distrust mixed in with concern. "Can we truly trust her?" he asks Cameron. And then, motioning toward Karl, "Them? Their sort isn't known for being sympathetic to us, after all."

Both Karl and I bristle. "Look," Karl bites out. "You can't hold any of this against Chloe or me. It's not like we were aware of the situation."

This angers Erik, who flushes red under his brown skin. "Your people chose to ignore our plights for years. Pardon me if I'm not too eager to lay my faith in a group of people who believe I'm an abomination and treat me worse than the dirt on their shoes."

Whoa. "I don't think—" I begin, but Karl's already on this.

"If Annar knew and ignored it, then that's definitely something that needs to be addressed." He's obviously trying to keep his temper in check, but his hands have curled into fists. "And I vow to you, it will be. But instead of bitching about hurt feelings, know you've got two high-ranking Council members who happen to also be on the Guard listening *now*. Neither of us will turn our backs on you."

It's an overly generous thing of Karl to say about me, considering I'd done just that on Annar and my loved ones back home six months prior. This promise of his only steels my resolve to be a better person.

A better Creator.

A better *Chloe*.

"You're here to take the Creator home." Erik's sneer is ugly. "Which is all well and good, considering she's most likely the reason this is happening!"

"What's going on?" I try again. I mean, if the dude's going to blame me for something, I at least deserve to know the reason why.

Will snaps his fingers. "Everyone, just shut up for a moment." His hands form a tee for time-out. "Cheers. Let's catch Chloe up."

Cameron gives me a small, tired smile. "Hen, the shape shifting monsters—"

"Elders," Karl quickly corrects.

Cameron nods. "The Elders have attacked and killed several Métis recently, including one on the outskirts of Anchorage earlier tonight. People are scared."

Uh . . . "Métis?"

The sneer Erik gave me moments before has nothing on the one he's angling toward me now.

"Erik," Cameron says quietly, "do not take your anger toward Annar out on Chloe. As Karl has just explained, she is ignorant of all of this, which shouldn't come as a surprise as our communities have made supreme efforts to keep Magical-kind just so."

Erik gives a tight nod, and then another to me in reluctant apology.

"Hen, the Métis are what the people and families I told you about earlier—the ones like me and Molly and now Will—are called, where there is Magical blood but no powers in children from mixed unions. Many of our kind have either married into the Métis or are children of Magicals."

Jesus. I have truly been ignorant and blind for years. Apparently Karl has, too, because he's just as surprised as me. "You said there are multiple colonies of Métis? How many?"

Erik's answer is less hostile than before. "It varies on each plane, but on ours, there are six, including Anchorage. Comparatively, this is one of the larger groups; at last census, we totaled seventy-three."

Karl's eyes widen. "All with Magical bloodlines?"

"Yes," Cameron answers. "But remember, a lot of the Métis might be several generations removed from their Magical forbearer."

"But—Magicals can only produce one pregnancy," I say. This is unreal.

"True. But Métis like Will or myself," Erik says, "are no longer bound by such genetics. Many Métis families have multiple children in them."

Will's pissed. "Is everyone else kept in the dark, or was that just me?"

Cameron sighs. "Son—"

"No, I'm curious," Will retorts. "If there are so many of these so-called colonies, and they even have a fancy name for us half-breeds, then one would assume that it's public knowledge, at least amongst the citizens. Right?"

Erik looks at Will like he's nothing more than an annoying

toddler. "Many Métis children are not told until they're older for the safety of the colonies."

"Because children are blabbermouths, right?" Will asks darkly. "That would have been my first impulse. Tell everyone in Glasgow so they could come after us with pitchforks and torches. But let's not forget I am no longer a child—or is twenty-two still considered infancy amongst you wise, elderly folk?"

I lay a hand on his arm. His sarcasm, so easily accessed when he's in defense mode, isn't going to help any of us right now. "People fear what they don't understand. I know it seems hard to believe, but your parents were looking out for you."

"Don't do that," he snaps. "You railed about how your parents kept you in the dark. Don't go excusing why mine were just as guilty."

His anger is painful to see. "It's true I grew up knowing I was a Magical. But I also had the ability to protect myself if somebody ever tried to hurt me. Your mom and dad—they didn't want you to get hurt."

He clearly doesn't believe me.

"Look. I have a friend back in Annar who is like you. A Métis. She grew up knowing what she was, surrounded by Magicals, and . . . it was hard for her. She's struggled with self-esteem issues her whole life." I squeeze his arm gently. "You mom and dad cared enough about you to take you out of Annar when you were little. You grew up never thinking you were any different from anybody else. That you were any less than them. That was a gift, Will. I know it's hard to see that now, but it really was."

His face is blank when he asks, "Is that the case now? That you think I'm less of a person because I'm only half of a Magical with no powers to show for?"

I can't help but smile a little. "Do you think less of me, knowing what I am, what I'm capable of? After all, you've seen me destroy things. Some would call me a monster."

"No." His words are hushed. "You're just Chloe to me."

"And you're just Will to me." The corners of my lips lift higher. "Plus, Magical or not, you would have made your mom proud with the way you handled a sword and helped take down an Elder. Maybe you do have a bit of Smith in you after all."

He kisses the back of my hand and then turns back to the rest of the group. "Fine. I'm being a bloody prat. There are obviously loads more important issues to be dealt with than me kicking my feet and fists against the floor. Shall we commence on figuring out what to do about people dying?"

"Have the Elders attacked the Métis before?" Karl asks. He's got his phone out, typing in notes like he does at mission briefings. I love that he's doing it, that he sees this here—these people I've grown to love—equally as worthy of his time as the Magicals back home.

There's a tense silence that has Erik and Cameron debating whether or not to answer his question. It hurts to see Cameron hesitating, but I guess old habits prefer slow deaths. Finally, Erik says, "Yes. I don't have specifics, but I think they've murdered a few dozen of our kind over the last ten years."

My eyes fly to Karl's. He's uncharacteristically grim, and that's saying something. Because I think we both realized something at the same time.

In their quest for vengeance, the Elders are killing more than just Magicals. They're killing the Métis, too.

The situation just got a thousand times more serious.

Chapter Nineteen

"How long have you known Will was a Métis?"

I turn away from the few dozen people mingling nearby to face Karl. "Believe it or not, only a couple of days. I know it sounds stupid, but I didn't even know he was part Elf."

It was decided an hour ago that a Métis meeting was needed to help address what was going on with the Elders. A telephone tree was enacted, and now here we are in the warehouse Cameron manages surrounded by dozens of terrified people and children. Looking around, I'm shocked to see just how many of the species are present. Human, Elvin, even Gnomish and Dwarven traits pop up in the faces before me.

"This is crazy." Karl's voice drops so only I can hear it. "I mean, I obviously knew that there were half-breeds out there, but . . . whole communities? How is it that Annar isn't aware of this?"

I counter with something that I know will upset him. "What if they are?"

Bingo. He bristles big time. "Wouldn't they have done something if that was the case?"

"Karl, you've been friends with Callie for a long time. C'mon. Look at how she feels people still treat her at times, and she's the daughter of an extremely influential and powerful Seer. Wouldn't it make sense if she still gets treated like she's a second class citizen that others would, too?"

His answer is a grunt.

I stuff my hands into my coat's pockets. "If the Elders are attacking the Métis, then we need to do something to help. We can't turn a blind eye now that we know."

Karl reaches out and fingers the lapel of my coat. "Did you make this?"

Uh, subject changer, thy name is Karl. "Yes. Why?" I'd made the coat during my binge of Magical creations after I caved into my craft.

Karl's smile is slight buy sly. "It's a replica of Jonah's coat, right down to the button sewn on with red thread instead of gray. The only thing different is this coat is white."

I start, staring down at the button he's mentioned. I'd stolen Jonah's well-worn and well-loved gray pea coat to wear numerous times in the past. It was comfy and smelled just like him, all minty and warm. This one, though . . . "Huh," I murmur. "I guess I didn't realize I did that."

"That seems improbable."

"No, I mean—I'd needed a new coat." I guess I was unconsciously searching for comfort.

Talk of Jonah reminds me of where he is and what's going on around him. Karl must see the panic on my face because he says, "I got an update on the mission while you were in the shower tonight. He and Kellan both checked in with Zthane on time. The Guard is requiring them to check in every two hours."

I want to press for more about the mission, but Erik is asking everyone to quiet down. Once they do, he recaps the situation for the crowd. After eight months of quiet, the Elders have reappeared and managed to catch a thirty-something Métis named Burt Eversgreen unaware. His body was been found on the outskirts of Anchorage; apparently, according to Erik, it looked like he aged a hundred years in death.

In all the time I've dealt with the Elders, I've never seen a victim before. Or even thought to ask what happened to them. "Is that normal?" I whisper to Karl.

He nods gravely.

For nearly fifteen minutes, debates rage on about whether or not people should flee Anchorage and find a new city to colonize or even go underground. Will eventually joins us at the far edge of the room; we are the three outsiders in a group of outsiders.

"What are we going to do about this?" Will whispers to us.

Karl's eyes don't leave the trio of Métis debating the merits of joining Oklahoma City's colony. "Meaning?"

"They said that there were a handful of these beasties. I suggest we go find them and kick their arses. That way, nobody will have to leave."

"Are you serious?" Karl asks, voice low. "We need to call in a team to scout for them."

It's obvious this displeases Will. "What, like one of your Magical Guard teams?"

I take a deep breath and remind myself that I no longer have the luxury of being a coward, even when I'm scared at the mere thought of what I'm about to say. "Between the three of us, I think we can do it."

I briefly debate if I just lost my mind, especially with how Karl is glowering at me.

But no—this is the right thing to do. "Lee is still in town, right?" He nods, so I continue, "If need be, we can get him to track their location. But Karl, let's be honest. No team is going to effectively neutralize the Elders. Now that we know I can do it—"

He leans in and practically hisses, "From what you two told me, you two very nearly didn't come out the victors. Look at you. You're a mess and will probably take a Shaman at least an hour to fix apiece. I shudder to think just how much blood you lost. Or what that guy over there even replaced it with." I open my mouth to counter him, but he steamrolls over me. "Have you forgotten in this last half year that we must have a living Creator?"

My spine straightens. "No. But I'm not going to stand by while these things hurt people. I can . . ." I can't say it, can't willingly admit how easy it is for me to murder beings, even ones as evil as these. So I compromise with, "Take care of the Elders. None of the rest of you can. Somebody died here in Anchorage, and chances are, it was because of me."

"Don't you think that's going a bit too far?" Will murmurs.

"Not at all. The Elders have left Anchorage alone for awhile. You heard what Cailleache said. They want *me*. They're looking for *me*. Burt is dead because he happened to be in the city where they're hunting *me*. I am not okay with anybody risking their lives because they happen to be caught in the crosshairs of the Elders' efforts to get to me." I look up at Karl. "I hope you don't make me issue an order, because I'd hate to pull rank on you like that again. But the simple fact is, several Elders have been sighted in town. You know they're looking for me—and now possibly you, since you're here, too. It is imperative that we take care of this matter *now*."

Karl studies me for a long, uncomfortable moment. It's then I notice that the room has hushed and all eyes are on us.

But then an amazing thing happens. He smiles. It's not a big one, nor is it snarky. He's proud of me, and that means the worlds right now. "Tell me what you need from me."

Relief whooshes out in a surprised breath. I tap his hand. "This."

He makes the call to Lee Acacia.

While Lee scouts the area for the Elders so he can lure them towards us, I'm taken to a few of the larger Métis homes nearby to reinforce their walls. Cameron and Erik organized everyone into groups for safety and have warned them to only leave these houses when absolute necessary until Karl and I have had a chance to deal with the Elders.

Even still, the Métis regard us suspiciously; their distrust burns, but I can logically get where it comes from. Whispers always follow us—our crafts rather than names are thrown around—but I force myself to ignore their fears and instead focus on my own.

Because, yes. Obviously I have fears. A ton of them are filling me up, like sand in the proverbial hourglass. The last time I faced a single Elder, she nearly killed me before I figured out what I was doing. Before that, one shattered my kneecap and arm. It's not like I haven't risked my life with these things before. And now? I'm purposely seeking a group of them out in an effort to take a stand.

Only a fool wouldn't be scared. Or Will, who practically radiates his boredom as he drives me around Anchorage. I wish I had his nerves.

At the last house, right before I leave, the owner, a pretty thirty-something named Kathryn comes up to me. Her voice is quiet and sweet as she tells me her story. "I was born in Annar, but left with my mom when I was eight because people were really mean to us. I was called a freak by the kids I went to school with. My mom was made to feel like the only reason my dad was with her was because they got pregnant while dating. Which—it was true, but I genuinely believed my parents loved each other, despite their fighting." Her smile is shaky. "Shows what I know. My dad is still there, said he couldn't give up being a Magical, not even for his family. I haven't seen him since the day he closed the door behind us. He doesn't know my children. He didn't see me graduate high school or college. I have to admit, I've hated Annar for a long time, believing it took so much away from me. But tonight . . ." She sucks in her lower lip as she studies me. "You don't have to do this. You're willingly going to go stop these things, and . . ." Her slim hand grabs mine. "Thank you. I'll be praying for your safety."

Will's phone beeps; it's a message from Karl. **Lee says 4 incoming. Get ready to get back to warehouse.**

We hug goodbye; when Kathryn closes the door, I alter the wood until nothing can bust it down. And I vow that the she's not going to have to fear door closures anymore. Not from me, and not from Annar.

142

Because the Elders aren't the only thing that needs to be taken down.

"This is stupid," Will says. "You two need to be with the others. After all, aren't you leader-y types?"

Cameron merely smiles indulgently at his son. Erik motions at Karl and me like we're idiots. "What if you bleed out? What then? I'll be damned if Annar comes blaming the Métis for the loss of two of their more powerful Council members. You two need me and my skills here."

Karl says, "I can call in a Shaman—"

"The closest portal is in Juneau," Erik counters. "That's a twenty-two hour drive; even by airplane it'd take too long. When you're losing blood, even an hour is too long to wait." He motions to a small cooler on the floor that holds bags of blood. None of them are specific to Magicals, but he claimed, since they came from first generation Métis donors, they'd do in a pinch until Shamans can check us out.

"Well, then you two are staying in the office." Will peers out of the window; according to Lee, now lounging on Cameron's old couch while flipping through a fishing magazine like he hasn't got a care in the worlds, the Elders were last spotted a mile and a half away from the warehouse.

"Don't worry, hot stuff," Lee drawls, without looking up from an article on the best flies to use. "I won't let anything happen to dear old Papa and his friend."

I think I preferred his stutter.

Will snatches the magazine out of his hands and tosses it on the table. "If I'm not mistaken, you're a Tracker."

Lee snatches it right back. "That's right. Since you're new to the Annar scene, let me illuminate you. Not only am I brilliant at finding tangible items and people, I am also quite adept at locating hard to find exits and hiding places." He flips the magazine open to the page he'd last been on. "Therefore, let me once more reassure you that if things go south for you all out there, I will ensure that these two make it to safety."

As the two of them jockey for who can outsnark the other, I pull Karl to the side of the room. "Can I borrow your phone?"

There's no hesitation. "No."

I sigh through my nose. "Look. I totally butchered the last call. I don't want Jonah not knowing how much I love him if I go and die tonight or something."

Karl leans back against the wood paneled wall. "Then don't die."

Did he just really say that? "One call—"

"Last I heard, he's working the riots; his position is precarious, at best. As it's not likely that Jonah has a team of bodyguards around him to protect him from bullets, there'll be no distracting him from his mission simply because you're finally willing to step up to the plate after abandoning him."

His kick to the gut lands exactly where he wants it.

The hard angles of his face soften a tiny bit when he leans forward. "As somebody who has a Connection, I can safely say that, no matter what he thinks and feels about you right now, Jonah is aware that you love him."

He doesn't understand. I try again. "He also knows I love his brother. It's—he needs to know that I—"

Karl's not having any of my rationalizations, though. "I guess that gives you incentive to get us out of this alive tonight, huh?"

I'm not the one to answer him, though. Screaming in the distance does it for me.

Chapter Twenty

"Ready?"

I can't help but smile at Karl's whispered word, because, honestly. What a ridiculous question. Is anyone ever ready to go to battle? Take a chance and know it could be your last? Die? Granted, I have the upper hand—I can actually kill these things. Only, I apparently need to be up close and personal to do so, which means, while I can kill them, they can kill me just as easily. My Frankenstein monster-like stitched up body is a living reminder of that.

But I tell him yes anyway. I have to be ready. I have too much to lose right now if I'm not.

We're barricaded inside the office, just waiting for the proverbial hammer to come down. Will lets out a long, quiet breath, his focus on the ceiling, the sword he fought with before now remade and tight in his grip. I think even Karl is nervous—not that he'd show us, but he's quieter than normal. And it just serves to remind me that it's my duty to protect these men that I love, that even though there are four Elders out there and we're outnumbered, I'm going to make sure Karl gets home safely to Moira and Emily, Will escapes unscathed (well, at least not adding copious amounts to his laundry list of current injuries, anyway), Cameron and Erik are untouched, and the Métis in Anchorage are safe once more.

"You should have a weapon," Will tells Karl. Naturally, Karl holds up his fist. "Yes, fine, you're badass with the earthquakes and all, but are you really ready to send Alaska into the Dark Ages because of these arseholes?"

Karl's smile is vicious. "I don't need to hit the ground to have an impact. You guys said they bleed. If they can bleed and be staked to the ground, my fist can connect with their matter. I might not be able to kill these things, but I should be able to knock their asses out long enough for Chloe to do her thing."

Will's impressed.

I whip up a multi-view screen on one of Cameron's office walls that shows us the activity outside the door. These things have once more molded themselves into humanoid shapes, and in the dark, their nebulous forms, floating a good couple of inches off the ground, are the creepiest things I've ever seen. Plus, there's the whole bit where, like Cailleache, they've all extended their limbs with weapons.

Frankly, I want to shriek in terror like some chick in a horror film. Turn and run and hide. One was bad enough. Four? Four is flat-out petrifying. What was I thinking, luring them here?

Courage, I tell myself. *Think of everybody who's counting on what you're about to do.* I force myself to take a deep breath and count to ten. Then twenty, as Karl begins to detail our plan of attack.

When he's done, he asks me once more if I'm ready.

I nod and place my palms down against the stained concrete. Within a second, I'm kneeling in dirt. Cameron and Erik both gasp quietly in the background, but I can't let myself be distracted by them.

"Lee?"

He's somewhere right behind me. "Yeah?"

"Remember what you promised. Any signs of trouble, and you get these two out of here."

He lightly touches my shoulder before backing away. I count to ten once more and then reach out and grab an arm of the two men

146

insane enough to willingly fight with me. "You don't have to do this—"

"Not this fucking speech again," Will mutters.

"Chloe." Karl's eyes bore into my own. "If you think I'm going to ever send you out in a situation without my protection, then you don't know me at all. I made that mistake once; I won't fail you again."

What is he talking about? "You've never failed me!"

"I did. Last year, when I left you alone in a house and one of these bastards came and used you as target practice. I should have been in there with you."

My insides go a bit gooey. "You have nothing to feel guilty about. *Nothing.*"

"Funny. Kellan and Jonah both felt quite differently." He pulls me in for a brief hug, before shoving me away. "Behind me at all times. Got it?"

I nod.

Will positions himself at the rear of our line. I'm sandwiched in between the two men that have become more family to me over the years than my own biological one. I don't care what anybody says. These two are my brothers. And like good big brothers, they think they're protecting me from the boogeymen outside.

The truth is, I'm the one who'll be protecting them. Because I'll lay down my life today to make sure they get out of here alive.

The door and surrounding walls disintegrate when Karl kicks it, shards exploding out into the warehouse. It's enough to both alert the Elders and stun them, because for some dumbass reason, they don't charge us immediately in the bottleneck.

I cock an arrow in my bow as I reconstruct the door behind me, reinforcing it until I know nothing can get in there that I don't want to be there.

Whispered words echo through the room until it surrounds us, filling the air from ceiling to floor: *Earthmover. Creator. Half-breed who reeks of metal.*

It's Karl's first time hearing them talk, let alone see those gaping maws that serve as mouths, but he only falters a single step. "Well, well," he says, voice loud and clear, knuckles cracking as he flexes his fingers, "there's a party going on and I didn't get an invite. That makes me sad."

The whispering transitions to hissing.

"Perhaps it's a party of stray cats," Will says. He taps the blade against an open palm. "It's one's duty to neuter such creatures, lest there be hordes roaming the streets."

I choke back my laughter even as the Elders approach us from four sides. But we're now standing in the close triangle Karl wanted us in.

"You killed Mother." The one closing in on me says this, black smoke trailing from its mouth. It's male, that much is clear. And pissed.

Will's blade swishes in the air until he's standing in position, blade out. "Let's not give our friend here all the glory. I made sure your mum was stuck like a pig on a spit before Chloe killed her. It was a team effort."

Karl wants us to get them mad. Anger allows confusion and poor judgment. So I add as nonchalantly as I can sound, even though my knees are knocking and my palms sweating, "She bled. It was nasty looking, though, all dark and steamy in the snow. Sort of like . . ." I'd snap my fingers if I weren't holding the bow so tight. "Acid. Will? Would you say that it looked like she had acid dripping out of her? It would make sense, as she was a monster and all."

I'm pretty sure the hissing and screaming just burst at least one of my eardrums, not to mention every window in the warehouse.

"Was she maybe a Gorgon?" Will muses. I'm still amazed at how calm he portrays himself. "Oh, wait. We didn't turn to stone when she looked at us. Pity, as she was an ugly thing."

Apparently insulting one's mama serves as their breaking point, because all four charge us, lightning fast. Karl swings an arm out, his fist colliding hard with an Elder. What I can only describe as a sonic boom detonates in the warehouse, breaking the last bits of glass that hadn't already shattered from their screaming. Will and I both stumble to our knees, but we're right back on our feet in time for what's coming at us.

Thwang. Reload. *Thwang.* Reload. Two are charging me, which, I get. Big catch apparently and all, but they're lithe like Cailleache and able to dodge most of my shots. Out of the corner of my eye I see Will kick an Elder right in the middle of its so-called chest, sending it sprawling.

Karl shouts, "Ten seconds!"

I fire another arrow. It streaks against an Elder's arm; the monster streaks high into the air above us, momentarily losing its shape as it howls in mixed rage and agony.

Ten seconds. Karl unleashes a sonic boom against these things and they're only down for ten effing seconds.

Thwang. Thwang. I want to check in on Will and Karl, but I have to trust they're holding their own. The two hunting me charge at once, and the next thing I know, I'm on my ass in the dirt, my shooting arm bleeding like a geyser set free.

I bandage it up immediately. But the attack served its purpose—our triangle has widened.

A shriek comes from my right—Will's blade made contact. I scramble over to where he's got the Elder pinned to the ground. "Do it!" he yells. The Elder thrashes against the sword, ready to rip its body right off.

One of its knife-hands slashes me as I approach. My breath sucks in at the pain, but I've got to get close.

"DO IT!"

Two sonic booms go off behind us, rattling me down on my hands in the dirt. But it's enough of a jolt to get me close enough. I stretch out my fingers and make contact, even as it slashes frantically at both Will and me.

It feels cold and hot at the same time. Like . . . cotton balls with splinters. It's a disgusting sensation. I want to jerk my hand back, but Will yells once more, as another sonic boom sounds, "FUCKING KILL THE THING, WILL YOU?"

When I will it out of existence, I collapse, my chin hitting dirt. Will immediately yanks his sword out of the ground and hauls me up. "Karl's got one down. Go!"

His blade swings out in an arc at an approaching Elder. *Boom.* It's hard to stay on my feet, but I dart over to where an Elder lies, unconscious. And . . . I spoke too soon, because its pseudo-eyes open the moment my hand touches its chest.

I go flying through the air, landing right on my quiver, sending a sharp spike of pain straight up behind my eyelids. *Holy effing hell.*

BOOM.

"Chloe!" Karl yells. His swinging fist makes no contact this time. He's bleeding heavily, his dominant arm slashed to ribbons. "They're adapting! Eight seconds!"

I scramble over to where the Elder who just fell is, trying desperately to ignore that lightning pain threatening to consume me. For insurance's sake, I ram an arrow straight through its chest, pinning it to the ground just as surely as Will's sword can. It's surprisingly difficult, considering I can see the floor through its body. It comes to, but—for the first time, even with the stars dancing in my eyes, I see something other than hate reflected back to me.

I see fear.

Good. It fights desperately, driving one of its dagger-like hands right into my shoulder and the other into my upper thigh. The pain is so intense I nearly black out, but then I remember that there is a bunch of people out there counting on me to get this job done. Plus, there's Jonah—I need to get back to Jonah and apologize and let him know how much I love and need him. So I gather everything in me and pray it's enough before willing this monstrosity out of existence. Within a split second, its body disappears; I collapse once more into the dirt. My chin hits the ground hard, making my already spinning head whirl even faster.

Piercing howls fills the warehouse and then, the next thing I know, Karl, Will and I are left alone in stunned silence.

We're all bleeding. We're filthy. But more importantly, we're all alive while two of the Elders aren't.

Karl's arm dangles uselessly next to his side. Will's having a tough time standing, which makes sense as both legs are cut up pretty bad. As for me, I'm still in the dirt with no doubt huge holes in my shoulder and leg.

"Open the office door, Chloe," Karl grunts. He wipes his good arm across his forehead, streaking dirt through blood and sweat. I've never seen him more exhausted.

I give up trying to stand up and simply lay my cheek in the dirt. Dammit, I forgot to make us some Elder-proof clothing ahead of time again. It takes a few seconds, but I manage to focus long enough to open the door. Cameron and Erik bolt out like they'd been leaning against the wood just waiting for the moment they could be freed.

"Lee." Karl's voice is hoarse as he addresses the Tracker, now sauntering out of the office, picking at his teeth with the corner of a magazine. "Follow those bastards and report back to me in an hour. We need to know if they're still in the area."

As Erik drops down next to me, a medical bag in one hand, the cooler full of blood in the other, I watch Lee Acacia drop both the magazine and the jaded act and sprint out of the warehouse. He moves so fast he's nearly a blur. Is that how Trackers work? That they're faster than normal people?

"Cameron?" Erik touches the arm that got the worst of it from the Elders; pain lances through me like lightning. I jolt, but it only intensifies my agony. "We need to get her out of the dirt. Too much risk of infection with these—Jesus. There's a hole in her shoulder about three and a half inches wide."

Ha. Hahaha. I've been saying for months, even if just to myself, that there's a hole in me. Now there really is.

"Christ. There's—it got her leg, too."

Karl murmurs an answer, his voice soaked with weary concern, but something stabs my butt. Pathetically, I don't have the energy to cry out, so I—

Chapter Twenty-One

There are no more Elders in Anchorage, at least for the time being. Lee was able to track them as far as Vancouver, but as they seemed to be consistently heading south, Karl felt the Métis were safe enough to come out of hiding.

Which means I need to get out of town as soon as possible so the Elders don't have a reason to come back. Technically, it's an easy enough decision. I'd already planned on going back to Annar to begin the long road toward atonement. But now that it's a stark reality, I'm a bundle of confused, jittery nerves. Cameron insists that all of this is due to Human medications Erik has me on, but I'm thinking it's more likely because taking responsibility for a whole slew of mistakes can make a person nauseated.

Karl's phone goes off for what must be the thirtieth time in less than twenty-four hours. When we finally got home last night, he was too exhausted to answer any calls—even Moira's. All communication was done via text, including an admission to his wife that he'd found me and was with me at that very moment—although, first thing this morning, he called her right away to elaborate. But now that we've had nearly a day's worth of rest (albeit mostly under the influence of Erik's drugs), I'm informed when the phone goes silent, "I need to tell him, Chloe. It's time."

He's talking about Zthane Nightstorm, his best friend and

apparently the only other person in the Guard more senior than he. That surprise was dropped on me just a few minutes ago, when he admitted he was second in command.

I certainly don't want Zthane to lose his job—or Karl. "Okay," I tell my friend. Nell comes over and jumps on the couch to sit next to me. I love how she instinctively knows when I need some good old-fashioned support.

Karl dials Zthane with his good hand and then puts it on speaker. He and I are alone in the living room; everybody else is going through the motions necessary for moving. Cameron's gone down to turn in his resignation at the warehouse; Will's in his bedroom packing. I stroke Nell's satiny head when Zthane growls, "You better have a damn good reason why you haven't checked in with me in nearly a day, Graystone."

Ugh, not a good sign. I've never heard Zthane call Karl by his surname before.

Karl leans forward, wincing as his wounded arm, cradled in a sling, jostles against his leg. "As a matter of fact, I do."

Nell licks my hand and looks up at me, her dark eyes shiny with unconditional love and acceptance. I take this small bit of encouragement and cut Karl off as he's about to speak. "Hi, Zthane."

Something sounds on the other end, like a chair falling over. "Chloe? Is that you?"

Karl gives me a small, reassuring nod to continue. "Yeah." I clear my throat. "It's me. We're—Karl's here with me in Alaska."

A small, protracted silence precedes, "Pardon my language, but thank the effing gods. Karl, is she okay?"

I love how Zthane thinks that he's swearing.

Karl bites his lip as he surveys me. According to Erik, the sooner I see a Shaman, the better. The same goes for him. We're in pretty bad shape. But Karl knows as well as I that that isn't the best thing to start out with. "We'll be heading back to Annar within the next thirty-six hours."

"I can have a team sent out—"

But Karl insists that a team isn't necessary since we'll be on our way shortly. I get the feeling Zthane is grossly unhappy with this, but after I swear to him that I'll be back in Annar with Karl as soon as possible, he relents. And then he asks Karl to take him off the speakerphone.

It doesn't take a genius to know that Karl's getting his ass chewed out big time. Yet another thing for me to feel crummy about.

Minutes later, when he hangs up, I realize he didn't tell Zthane about the Métis or what went down with the Elders. When I question him why, he says tiredly, "Some things are better discussed face-to-face."

His point is not lost on me.

Saying goodbye sucks. It flat-out, unequivocally sucks.

Despite my reservations (and fears, if I'm being honest with myself), I insist on saying goodbye to the Moose and its inhabitants in person. I'd insisted on walking on my own two feet despite Erik wanting to push me in a wheelchair. So Will and I, we were like the walking wounded hobbling through the front door, and when the bell above it jingled, tears sprang to my eyes.

The Moose was a haven to me. It was safety when I had nowhere else to go and needed a place to lick my wounds and grow up some. And now, as I glance around the cheesy décor, I worry that I might have taken it for granted like so many other things in my life. I can't help but wonder if I'll get to come back here, if I'll ever get to go bowling with these people again. If there'll be moments when I roll my eyes at Frieda's snark, encourage Ginny to follow her dreams, or feel one of Paul's nourishing hugs again.

Gods, I hope so.

Paul took the news of our leaving—well, not exactly well, but I guess better than we expected. I let Will do the bulk of the talking, because it just hurt. Every time I went to open my mouth, something inside me quivered and strained and I feared just flat-out ugly bawling, so I stayed silent, nodding at appropriate times. When it was all done and said, Paul mentioned he was disappointed and would miss us, but ultimately, he understood. Then he stupidly offered us severance pay, like he laid us off rather than us up and quitting on him with little-to-no notice.

In other news, Frieda raged. Ginny cried softly.

And now, the girls are here with me, hugging Will and me like we're porcelain dolls, thanks to our injuries, and they're not acting like themselves. They're holding back, and I get it, but part of me resents it, too. These girls helped me in ways they'll never know. Their honesty was one of the things I valued the most.

But I can't hold this against them. Because, when Paul asks Will, "You'll call us when you get there?" he's referring to how we've told him we're moving to Glasgow so Cameron can be close to a sick relative. And that stings, because while I value their honesty, I've never reciprocated in kind—not even here in the end.

"Yeah, yeah, of course," Will says. He's moving slowly today; Erik says he's got three broken ribs for sure. The sooner he can see a Shaman, the better I'll feel.

"Told you they're shacking up." Frieda knocks her shoulder into Ginny's. She's a strong girl—she'll never let me see her tears. But I know she's upset we're leaving.

I'll miss her. Miss them all.

I just give them a small, sad smile in response. There is more gentle hugging, more promises made to keep the ties we've created between all of us meaningful even though distance will spread us apart. And then we walk out of the Moose and into Lee Acacia's nondescript rental waiting at the curb.

"Everything taken care of?" Karl asks. He insisted on coming with us, despite needing to rest, giving some bullshit excuse about needing to talk with Lee about a mission. I'm positive the real reason was that he doesn't trust me anymore. He wanted to make sure I didn't run again.

I don't blame him.

I lean my head against Will's good shoulder and stare out of the window as Lee pulls away from the curb. Anchorage is beautiful. It was home, if even for a tiny moment. "Yeah," I tell him.

I'm holding onto Nell's leash as Erik pushes me across the tarmac in a wheelchair. He got his way, saying there was no good enough reason on this green earth for me to walk to a plane when I can be pushed. Will and Cameron are already on the small bush plane Erik owns; he's flying us to Juneau and then coming into Annar for the first time in nearly fifteen years, thanks to Karl's suggestion that it might be helpful to have a Métis with us when we discuss the situation with the Council. At first, Erik and a number of other Métis were reluctant, saying they'd worked hard for years to distance themselves from Annar. But I think they also understand that we're all interconnected—and that people stand more firmly on the ground when they have others to stand with them.

It's a lesson I'm learning myself.

Erik rationalized his addition to our little party by claiming he needed to stick with us, at least until we got to the hospital in Annar, to oversee our injuries. I think he's nervous, though. He left Annar much in the same way so many Métis do—in anger while filled with justifiable hurt. His mother, a prominent Elvin Shaman who'd had an affair with an army doctor she'd met on the Human plane during the Vietnam War, refused to leave Annar and her work. Despite her obvious distaste for him and what he represented, Erik had stuck it out for years, shuttled back and forth between his parents (who, according to what he'd told us last night, still refuse to speak to one another; worse yet, his father doesn't even know his mother is a Magical and believes she lives in Europe). But when he realized his mother basically saw him as merely an obligation rather than her son, he left and didn't look back until today. He moved in with his dad, thought about attending medical school, but eventually chose to pursue being a nurse practitioner because he knew it'd piss his mother off.

And now we're asking him to go back to Annar, possibly face his mother (who would probably be swell friends with my own mom, what with the stories I heard of her yesterday) and all the memories of people and places that tried to make him feel less than he was. I didn't say it to him, because I don't think Erik is the sort to be reassured by words, but I made a mental promise to him that I was going to do everything in my power to end the struggle Métis face in our community.

Because I'm going to do this Creator thing my way. I'm going to own it. I'm not going to sit back and be a passive participant in the Council who waits for her marching orders. It's the only way I can survive it all.

I glance at the snow-covered mountain range in the distance, and their majestic beauty strikes me. I make myself another promise. *I'll be back.*

And then we go up the ramp, Nell's nails clicking on the non-skid strips next to me. "You okay?" Erik asks quietly. Him talking to me directly is so rare I jerk in the chair.

But his eyes are kind and filled with concern. If anyone knows what it's like to fight for what you want for your life, it's him. So I don't resent his question, which everyone and their brother keeps asking me lately. "Yeah," I tell him.

Because I think I finally, truly am.

Chapter Twenty-Two

When the first flash goes off, I dismiss it as nothing. When the subsequent dozen nearly blind me, I realize there's a problem as I gingerly step out of Transit Station and onto the streets of Annar for the first time in over half a year. There's what seems to be a handful of photographers shouting at me, questions about where I've been and who the people I'm with are, as well as a rapidly growing crowd of rubberneckers that form a living wall difficult to breech.

It's like a nightmare come to life. How did they know I'd be here?

Karl yells at everyone to back up, but as he's suffering from a few bruised (and possibly broken) ribs, his voice doesn't boom like it normally does. Will loops his arm around my shoulder and pulls me in closer, one of his arms coming up to block my face from all of the critical eyes around us. Erik hovers behind us, hands pressed against our backs like he's trying to keep us upright in this madness. From behind us, I can hear Nell barking her warnings, and Cameron's stern voice trying to keep her from attacking anyone who comes too close to us.

Chloe, the people around us yell, Councilwoman Lilywhite, is that you, you look so different, where were you, what happened, did the Elders get you like we all feared? Who are these people? Why are you blonde? Who is the guy? Why is his arm around you? What happened to you? Why do you look like you've fallen off a ten-story building and barely made it out alive?

Chloe, they keep asking, why won't you answer us?

But the truth is, I don't think I could get the words out right now if I even tried. Pain twists and blooms through every breath, every step, making any chance at grabbing my breath damn near impossible. These people, they're reaching out, trying to touch me, but their touches are needles against my injuries.

More shouts circle us; only these aren't from the crowd, now edging into the hundreds. I spot Giuliana Arancionestella, a friend from the Guard who protected Jonah and Kellan several years ago against the Elders, pushing her way through the crowd while ordering people to back away. And then I see Kiah Redrock, Kopano Melesi-Yellowbird, and Iolani Popolohua doing the same. Somebody's called in the cavalry.

"Get us the hell out of here," Erik snarls at Karl. "If any of these people were to smash hard into the three of you . . ." He doesn't have to finish, though. We already know what hell we'd suffer through, since it's already started to happen.

I've been bumped into at least a dozen times already, and each jostle makes my already shallow breath harder to find. The effects of my pain pills are coming to a close, making each uneven step one I'd rather not take. The agony in my thigh threatens to completely overtake me. As curling into a ball and crying until I pass out on the street below us isn't an option, I push myself forward, alongside Will and Karl who are in similar boats as I am.

Only, a hundred feet take five, grueling minutes to traverse. My head swims in sharpening agony. I stumble on the sidewalk, and my wounded leg buckles under me. Nell barks furiously. Will and Erik grapple to catch me, but the jerking motions steal the air right out of my head.

And then I do something incredibly, pathetically embarrassing. I collapse right there in front of hundreds of Magicals and flashing cameras and cellphone videos. Worse yet, when I look up, I see a nightmare from the past—gorgeous Sophie Greenfield standing just a few feet away, malicious anger flashing in her eyes.

What is *she* doing here?

She turns on her heels and disappears back into the crowd. As I track her departure, a flash of white hair catches my eyes. Is that—

"I've got you," Will grunts, his voice echo-y but still solid. But he's hurting, too, and stumbles just as surely as I did as he tries to pick me up.

"The hell you do," Erik says above me. "Pick her up and we'll be having to carry your sorry ass out of here, too. Cameron?"

"I've got her, son." Cameron materializes to rest a hand on his son's tender shoulder. "Erik's right. Karl's on his last wind, too. We need to get out of here as fast as we can. Here, take Nell." And then the man I see as my father picks me up and carries me the rest of the way to the hospital.

Kate Blackthorn, Shaman extraordinaire, is not currently in Annar at present. Zthane Nightstorm, who met us in the lobby, informs our small group that she's currently on assignment back on the Human plane. I try not to think about what she's doing—Kate's renown for her work with debilitating, nasty viruses. Instead, Sjharn Thunderbridge, the Guard's lead Shaman, is the one to meet us in the room Zthane had reserved. He looks exactly as I remember him: stern, with a craggy face and skin so dark green it's nearly black.

"I'm going to go out on a limb and say there was a leak about Councilwoman Lilywhite's return," he says to Zthane in a deeply accented voice as he washes his hands in the nearby sink.

Will, who is sitting on the couch next to Karl, is outright staring at Sjharn like he doesn't know what to think or say. I'd told him about Goblins, and of all the other races, but I know it's got to be a shock for him. Cameron and Erik are sitting on an adjacent couch, quietly talking to one another, not bothered in the least by who's joined us in the room. But then, both have lived in Annar before, leaving Will the odd man out.

Zthane leans out of the door, shouting orders at somebody outside about the consequences if anybody he hasn't approved first comes within three hundred feet of the room. Then, once the door is firmly shut behind him, he says to Sjharn, "No kidding. Heads are going to roll when I get back to the office. What a mess." He sighs, then focuses on me. "Hello, Chloe. I cannot tell you how happy I am to have you back in Annar in one piece."

Sjharn blocks my view when I wheeze a greeting in return. "Leave the girl alone, Nightstorm. You can talk to her when I'm done."

Karl lets out a laugh from where he's sitting when Zthane sputters in indignation, but it's short. He winces, his good hand automatically going to his chest. "Remind me to never go on a mission without a Shaman again."

Sjharn says nothing as he presses his large but thin hands against my thigh. I jolt from the initial pain, but it melts away as he starts to work on me.

No offense to Erik, but I've got to agree with Karl here.

"It's funny," Zthane says evenly, "but you never mentioned until two hours ago that you all were going to need to come to the hospital. I wonder why that is? Especially since the three of you look like you've been put through meat grinders."

There's a beat of silence in the room before Karl says, "I figured—"

But I cut him off. Technically, I outrank every single person in this room. And the truth is, Will and Karl wouldn't be as injured as they are had it not been for me. "We were in a skirmish with some Elders."

His hands don't leave my body, but I can hear Sjharn's breath suck in in surprise. Zthane's does, too.

Will finally speaks up. He scoffs, "Skirmish? Is that what that was? Funny, I thought it more like a bloody life or death battle."

Zthane whips around to face Will. Karl sighs, but then winces as his lungs expand. His mouth opens, but Zthane lets loose a string of biting reprimands.

"These stitches are good," Sjharn says, cutting Zthane's rant off. He glances over at Erik. "Your work?"

Erik stands up and comes over to where we are. "Yes."

The Shaman's eyes narrow as he takes Erik in. "You look familiar."

"As I tend to look more like my mother than father," Erik says flatly, "I am not surprised."

Zthane throws his hands up. "Somebody better start talking, and they better do it soon." He rounds on Karl. "You do not get into *skirmishes* with the Elders without telling me about them! Gods, Karl! You helped me write the most recent sets of Guard protocol, and now you're choosing to only selectively follow them?" He switches over to Erik. "You obviously know about our kind—and I want to know why!" To Will and Cameron, "The same for you two! Why a non is fighting Elders with two Council members . . ." His fists clench. To me, "And for the gods' sakes, where the hell have you been for the last half year, Chloe?" He snaps his fingers. "I want answers, people! NOW."

So we give them to him. I tell him everything, including the truth about my Connections to both Whitecombs. We tell him about the Métis, their colonies, and how the Elders are attacking them, too. We explain how Cailleache tracked me down in Anchorage, how I discovered I could destroy her kind. Of what happened in the warehouse just days ago. Hours pass, people are healed, and Zthane finally gets all his answers.

"Holy hell," is what the head of the Guard says when the truth is laid bare for him to see. And then, to Karl, "Well, this is a game changer, isn't it?"

Karl laughs quietly, but any mirth is replaced with exhaustion.

Zthane rubs at this hair, pacing the room for a good ten seconds before coming back over to where I'm sitting with Will. "This has been an official debriefing, Councilwoman Lilywhite. I will send you the paperwork concerning just such to review and sign tomorrow. Until then, I advise you not to talk to anybody else about what you've just told me." His dark eyes flick over toward Karl. "I know you are tired, friend, but we have much to discuss tonight. You might as well call Moira and tell her you won't be home until late."

Karl nods and pulls out his phone.

"Will you be heading to your old address?" Zthane's question is quiet in the already sterile room.

Is my old address even still mine? I shake my head. "I'll be staying with . . ." I turn toward Cameron, who smiles and finishes for me, "Us. Let me give you our address, in case you have need for further clarification."

While Cameron types in his address in Zthane's proffered phone, the Goblin says, "I've heard tales of Molliaria Hellebore's work before. She could do things to metal that many Smiths only dream about. There's still a plaque in the front of HQ that she fashioned."

Will stands up and goes over to one of the windows to peer out into the fading sun. "Too bad she had to go and have me, right?"

"Son," Cameron warns softly, but Will is already issuing a bitter apology of his own.

Awkwardness fills the room; Zthane's feet shuffle uneasily against the parquet floors. My next question only adds to the unease. "The team that went missing while protecting me from the Elder attack in the Elvin forest . . . were they ever found?"

Zthane's lips thin. "Unfortunately, no."

I swallow back the rising guilt. "What about Jens Belladonna? Was he ever found?"

Zthane slowly shakes his head.

As much as I disliked Belladonna, my heart sinks over his continued disappearance just as strongly as that of my team. "Are you guys still looking for them?"

A sigh precedes, "No. We don't have the resources or the time to spend searching anymore."

Not when they were searching for a runaway Creator, is what he isn't saying to me.

I ask quietly, "When will Jonah be back?"

"If all goes as planned, tomorrow morning." Zthane steps forward and hugs me; I sink into his familiarity, grateful for his willingness to not treat me like the pariah I deserve to be. "Go easy on him, Chloe. Go easy on them both." He smiles sadly. "That said, don't be mad at the escort I'm sending with you to the Danes' apartment. I don't want a repeat of that melee outside of the Transit Station."

He's worried I'll run again. I bite back my own sadness and nod. I really have no one to blame but myself for the doubt that's replaced years of hard-earned trust.

165

Chapter Twenty-Three

Cameron and Molly's apartment is nice—homey, albeit dusty and mostly knickknack free, which makes sense since they left it behind years ago. It's a four-bedroom, so there's more than enough room for us all, including Erik. And since we came with a duffle bag each of clothes and personal items, I get to work right away with replacing key items, not to mention clean sheets, bath towels, and toilet paper.

"You're quite handy to have around," Will tells me after he requests a hand duster. Nell snuffs at my new creation. "Although we still need to go to the store soon for food and the like." I laugh at this, but then he says, more seriously, "Don't you have a phone call you need to go make?"

It's pathetic to admit, but, despite my overwhelming need to hear his voice, see his face, I've so far avoided texting Jonah. There's this fear that I'll only distract him during a mission that requires him focusing on his safety, but if I'm being honest, I'm also terrified of finally standing trial for the choices I've made over the last year.

No, that's not fair. Jonah isn't the sort who'd judge me, but he certainly has every right to have the opportunity to hear what I have to say and have his say in return. And Kellan deserves that chance, too. I haven't been fair to either of them.

I haven't been fair to myself.

"Look," Will says, setting the newly made duster down on a nearby kitchen counter, "if you aren't ready, you don't need to make the phone call." He props his hip against the granite. "This Jonah of yours deserves a proper apology and explanation. If you're not in the right frame of mind to do so, then I suggest you wait until you know you'll be able to do a bang-up job."

I don't take offense at what he's saying. If anything, I'm excruciatingly grateful that Will's brutal honesty acts as a firmly yet lovingly placed reality check. "I appreciate that, but I've waited long enough." I twist my hair up and tie it back with a rubber band I create. Then I bend down and scratch Nell's belly. She flops over, kicking a leg. "I wish you could have this talk, too."

He knows what I mean. A long breath escapes him as he plants both hands against the counter. "You know what? I wish I could, too." His head tilts toward me, a low, bitter laugh passing through his full lips as he tugs on his ear. "As tough as it will be for you, at least you have the comfort of knowing, good or bad, when you guys talk, it'll be . . ." I watch his eyes close, his shaggy hair swing side-to-side as he groans. "If I were to confront Becca, tell her how I felt—still feel about what she did—it'd be pointless, you know? Within a few hours, she'd forget, and we'd be back at square one the next day."

I could fix this, I think. Cora could fix this for me. I could send her to Glasgow and nobody would ever know that I've called in a personal favor. She could heal Becca, and maybe Will would finally have his closure.

Only, Cora and I aren't exactly on speaking terms at the moment since I abandoned her, too. Dammit.

Will pushes my cheap Alaskan cell phone toward me. I say his name, load that one word with love and questions, but he picks the duster back up. I watch him leave the kitchen, his shoulders stiff and weighted down.

Someday, I promise him silently, I will help you like you've helped me.

In my new bedroom, as I turn my new phone over in my hands, I wonder if my old phone is still in my old apartment. Wonder if that apartment is even mine anymore, and what happened to all of my stuff. Did Jonah leave everything there, hoping someday I'd come back? Box it all up and put it in storage, not knowing what else to do? Sell it in a fit of anger and betrayal? Surely my parents don't have my things, as they made it clear that I was out of their lives.

But all that stuff? They're just things. Whether or not I get them back . . . I've made my peace with letting them go, except for possibly the ring I took off my finger before running. Jonah's what matters. Jonah and Kellan and all the people I love whom I left behind.

Zthane says Jonah ought to be en route back to Annar sometime in the morning, which means I can't let this go on any longer. As Will pointed out, good or bad, I need to explain to him what I did, and how I feel. Starting with: **Hi, it's Chloe. I'm back in Annar. If you have time, can I see you and Kellan tomorrow?**

It's lame and fairly ambiguous, but texting my feelings to him isn't going to solve anything. I chew my lip until it's bloody during the three minutes it takes for Jonah to answer, consoling myself but petting Nell. **We'll be in Annar in 16 hrs. Where are you?**

This is the part I dread—admitting I'm staying with someone else. But I do. I tell him I'm at a friend's, including the address. And I don't know why it surprises me when he's clinical with his answer, but it does.

10am okay?

It's just so—I don't know. Normal. Like I haven't been away for half a year after abandoning him. But he's extremely guarded with his emotions, meaning there's no way he's going to show any of his hands to me right now, especially in a text.

I know him well enough to know this.

So I tell him ten o'clock is fine, even though it's only 2 hours after he's supposed to return. And then I prepare myself for a long night of nervous waiting.

The bedsprings creak as Will slides under the covers next to me, shoving Nell to the side. I quickly wipe at my eyes, even though I know there's no way he can see me in this darkness.

"Dad's snoring sounds like a buzz saw," he tells me quietly. "Erik's fighting him on that front, matching snore for snore. Would it be too much to ask you for a pair of sound-cancelling headphones?"

I let out a gurgly laugh and do exactly as he asks. "Anything for you."

"Cheers." He takes the headphones from me and is silent for a long moment. "This is surreal, you know."

I can't help but razz him. "What, us in bed together? Should we torture Frieda by sending her a picture of us?"

He lets out an exhaled chuckle. And then, more seriously, "I—Christ. I feel a little lost, Chloe. Like I'm in over my head."

I fumble in the dark for his hand so I can squeeze it.

"Dad and Erik, they're—this is nothing to them. This is old hat. The same with you. I felt like a bloody alien today when we were at the hospital. A freak. All this—" He waves around in the dark with his free hand. "I'm a fish out of water. Maybe Mum and Dad had a point after all."

"You've been here for less than a day. I know it's got to be a lot to take in. I'm overwhelmed being back, too." I squeeze his hand once more and let go. "But we'll get through this together."

The two of us are silent for a long time, listening to the dueling snores of Cameron and Erik through the door, Nell's deep breathing, and the sounds of life outside the window. In this small bedroom, in this bed, it's like we're in an in-between world of our own. My mistakes, his unknown history—all of it is outside those walls.

"I'm scared," I admit out loud to the both of us.

"You'd be daft not to be." He lets out a long sigh. "I wish I could promise you that it'd turn out okay tomorrow, but I won't lie to you like that. But I will promise that Dad and I will be right here with you, no matter what happens. You're not alone anymore."

Chapter Twenty-Four

I don't think I slept for more than ten minutes the night before. It shows, too—as I stare at myself in the bathroom mirror, I marvel at just how dark the bags under my eyes are and just how fried my hair looks. I briefly debate running out and getting a box of hair color to re-dye it back to its natural state, but if I'm honest with myself, I know I'd only be risking making it look worse. It's best if I just hold tight and find somebody local to fix it for me.

But that leaves me anxious, knowing the first time I see Jonah and Kellan in half a year, they're going to realize, right off the bat, that I purposely tried to hide myself by altering my looks. My colored contacts are gone, true, but there's no way to hide the fact my hair is significantly shorter and white-blonde.

I wonder what they're thinking right now, what they're feeling. If they've slept at all or if they suffered through the night, wondering about all the possibilities of today, too.

I wonder what they'll say.

If they'll forgive me.

If I'll ever forgive myself.

Erik left ten minutes ago, claiming he wants no part of my drama. I totally get it and don't blame him for taking off. Cameron and Will have offered to stay in the apartment and hang out in the back bedrooms where Nell is contained, just in case I need them. Even still, now that it's a few minutes before ten a.m., the urge to run out of the door and not look back is tempting because my heart is hammering down on stubborn nails inside my chest. I briefly debate whether or not to construct a shield, but it's a crutch I can't fall back on. From here on out, no matter where the chips may fall, I've got to be honest not only with myself but with both Jonah and Kellan. It's only fair.

So not only am I nervous as all hell, I'm also terrified and excited and a handful of other nuanced emotions. Nervous I'll hurt them again with my truths. Excited because this'll be the first time I've seen either man in over six months. Terrified that they won't forgive me for what I've done. Overwhelmed by all the changes in my life, even though I've been the architect behind them.

Will calls me over to the small dining room table and holds out a shot of tequila. Only, it's retracted when I go to grab it. "One for courage," he warns. "Just know I refuse to go through any sort of alcohol poisoning shenanigans again."

As much as I wish I could get drunk right now, it'd be the worst thing I could do. I tug the glass out of his hand. "Don't worry. I've learned that lesson."

He picks up his shot, warm laughter filling the space between us. "Cheers to new beginnings." His grin slides into a smirk. "Preferably non-vomit-y ones."

I sigh, but it's loving exasperation. "Just clink already, will you?"

Our glasses come together in a brief chime of hopes and promises and another chorus of cheers. The tequila burns on its way down, but it's warm and fortifying.

He eyes me over the glass. "You look green, and not in one of those Goblin ways." When he purposely takes a giant step backwards, I reach out to swat him.

"It's the tequila, you prat."

His wide grin reforms. "Listen to you. I'll make you an honorary Scot after all."

The doorbell chimes, and I send a plea to the tequila in my belly to start working its magic. Because my heart has redoubled its efforts to hammer a hole straight out of my chest. And, damn Will for being right, I do feel a bit nauseated.

"I've got it," Cameron calls out from the kitchen. Footsteps sound along the dark hardwood floors, and I know, just know, that I'm going to pass out and make an even bigger jackass out of myself.

"Alright. Just one more." Another shot is shoved toward me; I gratefully down it as he follows suit.

I don't know what to do with myself. Where to stand. Should I stand? Sit? Should I go to another room and make an entrance? Should I—

Wait. Cameron steps into the living room, and he's sheet white. If anybody's going to throw up right now, my money's on him. And this does not make sense.

Will removes the shot glass from my fingers and adds it next to his on the table. I nudge his arm and whisper under my breath that something's wrong with his dad. But before he can say anything, in walks Astrid Lotus, followed by her daughter, Callie. And then, with identical expressions that radiate uncertainty, first Jonah, then Kellan appear.

I'm pretty sure my heart bursts straight out of my chest. That handful of emotions I was feeling earlier explodes into a cacophony that I can no longer decipher. He's here, they're here, and—

And I still have no idea what to do. I don't want to start straight off with another round of apologies—even though they're absolutely deserved—because that's all I ever seemed to say to them. But they deserve to hear the truth. It's just, I didn't know it'd be in front of an audience. Which is a selfish thought, because I'm in the wrong, and I've got to be the one to start making amends, whether in front of one of them at a time or the entirety of Annar. If they felt the need to bring along Astrid and Callie, then who am I to complain?

Still, it's hard to really look at either man right now, not like I want to, even though the pulls toward them both are so strong it's a miracle I'm even standing. Because there's confusion there, and oh, gods, hurt, so much hurt and expectations, and all of a sudden, I feel even worse about myself than I did ten minutes ago when I'd only felt like the lousiest girl to ever exist.

Especially since a glance at Jonah's hand shows no sign of his Connection ring.

Cameron motions toward the worn couch and chairs in the room and offers everyone a seat. Callie and Kellan choose to sit; Jonah remains standing, arms crossed, but he's close to the couch. Cameron and Astrid are standing in the midway point between me and Will and her children.

Jonah's hair is a bit longer than when I left. It irrationally bothers me that this happened and I didn't know about it. He's got dark circles under his eyes, too, and I ache for him, for the hell he must have gone through this last week. Our eyes lock together, and he asks a silent question that has my hands twisting together and regret surging through my bloodstream.

He asks me why I did it. And also possibly why my hair is blonde.

All I can think is: oh, sweet gods above, I love this man with everything that makes me me, and this feeling is so strong that it nearly knocks me off my feet.

I take a deep breath and a step forward at the same time, but I skid to a halt when Astrid says, "You took me by surprise. You have to admit, this would be the last place I'd ever expect to see you again."

My eyes fly to her, my stomach sinking. She'd loved me once. Protected me. And I'd failed her just as surely as I failed everyone else when I bolted.

"Yes, well, the same could be said for you," Cameron murmurs, and then my eyes snap straight to him. Huh?

Astrid delicately clears her throat. "How have you been, Cam?

You look well."

I turn to Will, who is now watching his father and Astrid with utter confusion. And then I look back at the man who has become my surrogate father, and the woman who became the twins' surrogate mother.

Because they know each other. And I did not see that one coming.

"*Cam?* Who the fuck calls him Cam?" is what Will says. I think it's angled at me, but as his eyes are riveted on his dad and Astrid, I can't be sure.

They ignore him. "Good," Cameron murmurs to Astrid, tugging at his collar. It's his turn to clear his throat. "And you?"

Astrid smoothes her knotted-up side braid with a trembling hand. "Also good." She motions toward him. "The beard is . . . it's different."

His eyes widen.

"I like it," she hastily adds. "It's just . . . it's been a long time."

"Cheers. You look well. Like you haven't aged a bit. But then, I guess it's always been that way, hasn't it?" I've never seen Cameron appear so uncomfortable.

It's then I notice that Kellan's tugging on the bracelet he always wears as he stares at the woman he considers to be his mother in confusion. It sounds weird, but this little action, the one that lets me know he's uncomfortable with something, makes me want to cry because it's so familiar. Gods, I've missed him.

He must sense these feelings rolling around me, because he looks away from Astrid to where I'm standing. When our eyes finally meet each other, the sharp pull of the Connection between us wicks the air straight out of my lungs. Oh, does he look good. Tired, sad, confused . . . but so, so gorgeous.

I blink and look away first. I need to get control over my feelings for him if I'm ever going to be able to make amends to any of them. Stupidly, even just a half hour ago, I thought it might be . . . not easy, but easier than before, simply because I know what I want now.

But no. All those feelings I had for him before are just as strong as always.

Nearby, Astrid's smile is tremulously fragile as she shifts her attention to where Will and I are standing. "I am so pleased to see you home safe and sound, Chloe." In the next few seconds, I'm surrounded by the best kind of motherly hug I've ever felt. My arms don't know what to do. I loop them around her, but it's like they aren't worthy to hug her back, let alone hear these kind words.

She squeezes me, the scent of violets strong and reassuring before she lets go. "And I am so pleased to see you again, William, although I'm sorry it's been so long."

I know I ought to be focusing on righting my wrongs right now, but I'm sorry. Cameron wins for my immediate attention when he coughs again, shoving his hands into his pockets, looking like he's in the most uncomfortable situation of his life.

Will's dark eyes flash at his father. "Did she just say what I think she just said?"

Astrid frowns, confused, and the WHAT THE HELL IS GOING ON HERE siren is going off at full blast in this room. "He's lovely," she says to Cameron, who apparently doesn't know what to say. "I see so much of the both of you in him."

I briefly catch the confusion on both Callie and Kellan's faces as my eyes make their way to Jonah's. There's another silent question for me. I think it's: *what the hell is going on?*

Which is an excellent question.

"What the hell is going on?" Will wisely demands for all the rest of us in the room.

Cameron and Astrid have a silent, anguished stare-off, graduating what was once the worlds' most awkward moment to the universe's. Something passes between them, and abruptly, all my shit feels pretty insignificant to whatever's going on with these two.

Finally, to me and Will, he says, "Astrid and I . . ." He scratches at his beard. "We go way back."

"What's this?" Callie says from her perch on the couch at the same time Will says, "What the hell?"

The twins remain silent. They're smart. I'm stupid, because I ask, "What does that mean, *go way back?*"

An undecipherable look passes between them before Astrid says, "I grew up with William's mother, Molly. She was my childhood best friend. Our families even immigrated to the Human plane together."

Did not see that one coming, either.

"Technically," Astrid says, her smile nearly breakable, "I'm your godmother, William."

And . . . the surprises keep coming.

"Excuse me?" he asks at the same time Callie barks from the couch, "Excuse me?"

"Wait," Kellan says, wading into this mess, "so you know these nons?"

Ohh, his voice is so good to hear again.

"Yes, this!" Callie juts an accusing finger toward her mother and Cameron.

Will glares over at Kellan and Callie, no doubt irritated by the use of *non*. I swat at him before he can start a fight, though, which earns me a glare. And a further silent question from Jonah.

I let out a frustrated sigh. I so badly just want to grab Jonah's hand and drag him into my bedroom or, hell, even the hallway—Kellan's, too—but in light of what's going on with the people I consider to be family now, that'd only prove my selfishness.

Astrid answers her children, her words soft and sad. "Cameron was married to my best friend. Of course I know him." She pauses. "William is like you, Callie. His Elvin heritage from his mother is Magical. And his father is . . ." She bites her lip, her smile so bittersweet. "Human. Kellan? Don't let me hear you say *non* like that again, like it's an insult. Are we clear?"

Kellan rolls his eyes, which clearly rubs Will the wrong way. He snaps, "*Métis*. We half-breed freaks have a fancy name all to ourselves, or do you not know? Oh, wait. Obviously, by the fucking disgusted tone of your voice, you don't care, right?"

That clearly pisses Kellan off, who's off the couch in a flash. Jonah's there to block him, though.

This cannot be happening. Not now, not like this . . . not after so long. I grab Will's arm and shoot him a meaningful look that tells him to lock down whatever latent anger he's got percolating inside. He has every right to it, but just not in *this* moment. "Stop. He—he's not—Kellan didn't mean anything by that."

Which, I think, pisses Kellan off to hear me say, since I definitely don't have a right to speak for him, but the last thing we need is a fight between all these people I love. Before Kellan can counter me, Will turns to his father. "So, not only did you and Mum keep me in the dark about being a . . . an *Elf*"—he sneers, turning the word into an undeserving curse—"and her being a Magical, but apparently the entire universe knows about it except for me?"

Well, so much for trying to stop the deluge from coming.

Cameron stays silent. Suddenly, both twins, plus Callie, are riveted on what's unfolding around us. Me? For the zillionth time in my life, I wish I could rewind time.

"Plus," Will grinds out, "you also conveniently forgot to tell me that I have a godmother?" He shoves tight fists under his arms. "Do I have a godfather, too?"

Cameron sighs. "Son—"

"Yes." Astrid's regained some of her composure, even though her hands are full on shaking now. "Callie, darling, I didn't mean to hide this from you—"

Callie's off the couch now, too. "Hide *what*? What is going on here?" She looks at me. "I thought—this is Chloe's homecoming! We're here because of her! Because—and now, there's—WHAT IS GOING ON HERE?"

"Astrid, I really don't think this is the time," Cameron says,

A MATTER OF TRUTH

which only infuriates Will further. He fills his shot glass again and downs it in one gulp.

"We have nothing to hide." Although her voice is unsteady, it's clear Astrid is feeling more than a bit defiant. "I've . . ." Her spine straightens. "I've missed you, Cam. And I'm tired of keeping all this in. It's finally time to let it go."

"Fuck. Me," Will groans, grabbing the tequila. I toss out a quiet warning of, "No more," but he throws my hand off. "Luckily for me," he says, glaring now at his father, "I hold my liquor loads better than you, Chloe. It must be the Scottish in me, unless, that's been a lie, too." He chugs the shot. "And as much as I'd like to get plastered so I can erase all of this shite, I highly doubt we'll be doing a replay of your stint in the hospital."

Both Jonah and Kellan's eyebrows shoot high. Heat rushes my cheeks. I so did not need that crack right now.

"William," Cameron warns, his voice sharp. I'm hoping he's referring to both Will's crack and the drinking. In either case, Will pours himself another shot anyway, ignoring us both. I attempt to wrestle the bottle of tequila away, but the look he gives me stops me dead in my tracks.

I remind myself he's hurting, that his world has been turned upside down, so I try a new tactic. "I'm not cleaning up after you," I whisper harshly when he downs the next shot.

"Yes you will. You'll remember how I did the same for you when you spewed all over my truck."

I CANNOT EVEN. I refuse to look over to where Jonah and Kellan are. The silent questions will be far too humiliating. Instead, I snatch the bottle away for good this time and lean in, hissing under my breath, "I know you're upset, but Will—please!"

He closes his eyes and bites his lip hard, like he's centering himself, which has to be hard with all that tequila. And then, eyes once more open and the anger thankfully gone off his face, Will motions to where Callie and Astrid are. "Enough about our drinking ailments. I believe this woman here was about to also blow the lid off of her personal *Parents Hide Shite From Their Kids* box. It's apparently an epidemic. Please feel free to proceed."

Well, I suppose bitter sarcasm is far better than blatant anger.

Callie stares at Will like he's lost his mind. I think she might be right.

"Astrid, you don't need to do this," Cameron says, but Astrid shakes her head.

"No. He's right. I've . . ." Steely resolve flashes in the lavender of her gorgeous eyes. "Callie, your biological father was William's godfather. Molly and I grew up with Ben—that was his name."

Gorgeous, unshakable Callie Lotus's mouth drops open and stays that way.

"When your parents died, I took you in." Astrid's smile is tight, ready to shatter at the smallest word. "Technically, I was your godmother, too. You were Ben's little girl; I could never turn my back on you."

Callie's mouth snaps shuts and then reopens. And then shuts again, before she says, "Were you having an affair with my dad?"

"No." Her answer is firm. "Ben was my friend. He and Molly— they were like my brother and sister."

Now Callie is shaking. "You told me you didn't personally know my parents! That you just knew *of* them!"

"I know," Astrid murmurs. "I'm sorry. I just . . . I thought it would be better. Molly and I knew the difficulties your parents had been going through, so we . . . we thought, in an effort to stave off the problems already associated with your birth, this was the best."

Callie stares at her mother for a long moment. Then she stomps over to where I'm clutching the tequila and yanks it straight out of my hand. Will oh-so-helpfully passes her my shot glass from the table. She waves it off and chugs directly from the bottle.

Oh. My. Gods. I'm standing next to a track in which two trains are heading straight at each other going full steam and the weirdest thing of all is that, for once, I'm not one of said trains.

"Let me guess," Will sneers, swinging the shot glass in between

Cameron and Astrid. "You two are the ones who had an affair."

And the unthinkable happens. Silence is his answer.

This is not happening. This is not—

"Are you bloody serious?!" he growls when the rest of us can't seem to pick our jaws up off the floor. His anger reemerges with a vengeance. "You cheated on my *mum*?"

"No." Cameron takes a step closer to where Will and I are standing. "Astrid and I were over before your mother and I got together."

Holy effing hell. I SO did not see that one coming.

Neither did Callie or Will, who are staring at their parents like they're strangers. And, honestly, I don't blame them one iota.

Finally, voice close to cracking—"This is shite, Dad."

Cameron nods slowly. "I know you're angry, son—"

"Angry doesn't even begin to describe how I feel," Will spits back. To me, he says, "Can you believe this? Who the fuck are these people, Chloe? Why are they here?"

"They're . . ." I try to swallow the lump in my throat, but it's way too big.

"I'm Jonah and Kellan's mother," Astrid supplies, "And Callie and I are here because we wanted to welcome Chloe home and let her know we missed her and love her."

"Their *mother*?" Cameron asks quietly. He's shocked. And . . . angry?

"They're not biologically mine." There's anguish on her face. "But they're mine all the same." She pauses. "They're Lucia's boys."

Hold on. Cameron not only knows (and I guess dated?) Astrid, but knew the twins' mom? I need a notepad to keep track of all of this.

"And Ewan?" he asks, and now, Kellan and Jonah wade into our complex circle that's been intertwined for a long time without anyone knowing it. My fingers itch to touch Jonah when he comes closer, but he and Kellan position themselves across from where I'm standing with Will and Callie.

"He's here in Annar," Astrid is saying while Kellan asks just how Cameron knows their dad. And my eyes meet Jonah's once more, but there isn't a question there. Just sadness.

Cameron sighs. "Molly and I lived in Annar for a very brief time when we first were married. She knew your parents, and I through her."

A pair of tears trickles down Astrid's cheeks. She hastily wipes them away. "Now, you. How did you come to be here with Chloe? Because Cameron, this is . . .." She chuckles quietly. "Talk about a small world."

Kellan gives me a look that basically says: *now* that's *an excellent question*. When he turns and looks at Jonah, I immediately know they're talking their way. And as much as I used to complain about them doing it for years, now I find this action comforting.

I've missed them both so much.

I take a deep breath, trying to recall all the words I've practiced for hours, but Cameron beats me to the punch. "It's ironic, isn't it? You, taking in Ben and Lucia's children—knowing they're your family, even though your blood doesn't run through their veins? It's the same with this hen here." His arm drops across my shoulders, and despite everything that's just gone down, love for this man fills me up. "She's my girl. She's our family. It was clear from day one that she needed us and we needed her. And we're here to give her the support she deserves as well as give Will a go at getting to know his mum's past."

I sniffle and loop my arms around him into a hug. What I see in Jonah's eyes now: *I did NOT see that one coming*. Kellan's expression is identical.

"She's a Dane," Will says quietly, but there's a smirk playing across his lips. "A mix-up in the hospital or something. Look. Our hair even matches." He leans in. Thank the gods, he's joking. This is a good sign. "Oh, wait. Are your roots . . . dark?"

I smack his hand away and laugh. And he laughs that wonderful laugh of his, and suddenly, things don't seem so dire at all. And that's how Karl finds us when he comes into the room, me and the Dane boys laughing, Astrid, too, in a quiet way, with everyone else wondering if they've stepped through the portal to Crazy Town.

"I knocked," Karl says. He's confused and concerned at the same time. "But there was no answer. I almost left, but I heard voices, so . . ."

"No worries, man," Will says. He and Karl knock elbows, and now there's another question from both twins: *they know each other?* "You're always welcome to barge right in, mate. Except, you may want to turn around and leave, as we've currently found ourselves in the midst of parental secrets and lies and general incestuousness. Chances are, one of these stellar, so-called upstanding parents here might have actually either: a) sired you, b) had an affair with one of your parents, or c) claimed you as their own."

I'd best describe Karl as an owl at the moment.

"Will," Cameron sighs. "Enough. Karl, we didn't expect you until later tonight."

Karl greets Cameron, holding up an envelope that must surely be from Zthane. And then he looks to me, concern filling those hazel eyes of his. "Do I even want to know?"

"Why are you here, Karl?" It's the first time Jonah's spoken since coming into the apartment. I want to bottle his words so I can listen to them all the time, especially since I'm pretty sure, the moment he and I finally get to talk, he's the one who's going to want to run away, screaming, because this here? It's a hot mess.

"Right." He clears his throat uncomfortably. "Zthane has sent the paperwork we discussed last night, Chloe." He hands the manila envelope to me. "He's also requesting a meeting with you and Will as soon as possible. He, uh . . . we need to discuss some . . ." He glances quickly at Jonah and then back at me. "Obviously, there are key matters we need to discuss in more detail."

This so does not sit well with either twin, both of whom loathe being kept out of the loop.

Will must see how this stresses me out, because he says lightly, "I refuse to give up my pancake recipe. Zthane will just have to do without." And then, "Honestly, mate. You know we laid ourselves bare last night. You need to tell Nightstorm to back off, give us some space. We'll do our duty, but you know as well as we do that a bit of rest is well deserved, especially after these last two weeks."

Karl rubs at his hair tiredly. "I know. Zthane's just—you must understand that this is a game changer."

Astrid cuts in, her voice quiet yet steady. "Is this something the Council should know?"

"Yes," Karl tells her. "And it'll be brought up shortly, just as soon as Councilwoman Lilywhite is debriefed further."

I can't believe this. First the bomb about Cameron and Astrid, and now this? What else could go wrong right now? I try to keep my frustration at bay, especially at how Karl is busting out my official title. He knows I haven't had time to tell Jonah and Kellan yet. There's a smidge of pity in his eyes, though.

"What is going on right now?" Kellan asks. "What are you guys talking about?"

But Karl doesn't answer him. He glances briefly at the twins and then back to Will and me. "Can I talk to you two privately?"

It's clear this makes both Jonah and Kellan unhappy, Astrid, too, but Will and I reluctantly follow Karl into one of the back bedrooms. Once the door is shut and Nell nearly knocks me over, Karl murmurs, "Things seem to be going well."

"Are you daft? Did you not hear anything I said back there?" Will paces the room; it's not a good sign. Maybe I ought to let him drink more tequila after all.

"I assumed you were joking," Karl says, leaning back against the door.

Will groans. "I wish I were! To briefly recap, these people come in, and it turns out my dad and this woman used to date, and she's my bloody godmother, and that girl out there is my godfather's daughter, and my mum and that woman were best friends. So if you think Chloe's had her say yet, think again. She's been sidelined due to the insanity unfolding in my living room. You can't drag her away until she's had her say. You know this, mate."

"Gods, this is shitty timing," Karl says quietly. "I assumed that you'd at least have had some time with Jonah so far."

I try not to cry. Or think about how incredibly hurt he looks out there.

"How about this—I'll give you an hour leeway to get down to HQ. I know it's not much time, but it's a start, right?" He rubs at his five o'clock shadow. "I've got to take Kellan back with me, though. Something's come up in Los Angeles, and he's needed for a turn-around mission. He should be back in Annar by morning, though."

Great. Just . . . great.

"And . . . Zthane has asked me to personally debrief Kellan during the mission, if there's time. Being the Guard's lead Emotional, we need him involved. I know the timing sucks, but Chloe, over the last week, you've managed to take out three Elders. These things have been trying to kill our kind, not to mention the Métis for too long. We've finally got a way to defeat them." His words are steady yet soft.

"I know," I tell him. The familiar sting of tears threatens to surface, but I force them back. I've got to stay strong. I assure them both that this is fine, that I'll get down to Guard HQ within the hour, but they don't look too sure at my conviction. And rather than being pissed that they doubt me, I'm pleased by their concern.

It's a good thing, having brothers.

It's clear Kellan is torn about having to leave when he argues with Karl about finding a different Emotional to do the mission. There's this anguished look that he allows me to see for just the smallest of moments; I think my own face mirrors his. After half a year, this is the closest we've gotten to each other—only to have him leave before we get to talk at all? But, in the end, he goes, because he knows it's the right thing to do. So when he and Karl head to the door, I muster my courage, trail after them, and pull Kellan aside before he leaves. Thankfully, Karl gives us some space.

"If it's okay with you," I tell him quietly, "I'd really like to talk to you as soon as possible."

An entire array of emotions flash through his beautiful blue eyes—sadness, happiness, anger, worry—before he carefully schools them into the undecipherable gaze I know to be his self-defense mechanism. I watch his right hand pull through his hair, shorter than the last time I saw him, and try my hardest to squelch the wish that nearly knocks me to my knees that it was my hand touching him.

"I'll come over in the morning," he tells me.

I want to hug him, but I don't. I'm too scared. He takes a deep breath, nods his head, and tries to hide the pain in his eyes when he leaves. And it breaks my heart, just like it always has.

"You two really do look alike," Will is saying to Jonah when I get back to the living room; mostly, I think, to cut through the unbearable tension in the room.

"Really?" Callie snaps. "That's amazing. Identical twins typically look nothing alike."

"Callie," her mother admonishes, but Callie glares back and takes a *so-there* chug of tequila.

Will outrights laughs at Callie. It's the wrong thing to do, because her eyes narrow dangerously.

"Don't," Jonah says to Callie. His hand is flexing over and over.

Will's head tilts to the side, his own eyes narrowing now. "Why is it I get the wrong sort of vibe between you two? Has the incestuousness of this lot included something between you?" The press of his hand against my shoulder is filled with pity.

Good lords. This just keeps getting worse. Because, now Jonah's eyes have narrowed and I'm wondering if I ought to turn the lights on so everyone can see without squinting.

"You're an asshole," Callie hisses.

Will's furious. "Cheers. I believe it takes one to know one."

Astrid and Cameron are nearly beside themselves when a full-fledged shouting match breaks out between Callie and Will. And I've never been the best peacekeeper, but these people here are my family, and I can't let any of this devolve any further, especially since I have so little time to talk to Jonah. I shove my body in between Will and Callie, both hands pressing against their chests. "Will? Shut it. Callie? Same to you. Because your anger right now isn't with each other, and screaming isn't going to solve anything."

Will storms away, muttering about the need to find more alcohol since the bitch stole his tequila. Callie's grin is vicious as she purposely chugs another shot-worthy swig from the bottle.

"Look," I say to Cameron and Astrid, "I know I am quite possibly the worst person ever when it comes to dealing with secrets and lies. But I'm thinking you guys need to talk to your kids, either together or separately. They deserve that."

Astrid sniffles again, nodding. Cameron pulls me closer and kisses the top of my head. "Always the smart one, lass," he whispers into my hair. And then, "You'll be okay if Will and I go for a walk?"

The Dane boys had wanted to be here for me when I laid myself bare. I thought that's what I wanted, too—their love and support. But I know I have it, whether or not they're in the room with me or on another plane. They've got my back. They love me, and that's not going to change just because I've made mistakes. And it makes all the difference in the worlds.

I nod, my face pressing into his worn flannel shirt.

"We'll have our phones with us if you need us to come home," Cameron tells me. Something slams into the kitchen, forcing a sigh from him. Another quick kiss is laid against my head. "Love you, hen."

"Love you, too," I whisper. And then he leaves to no doubt drag his son out of the kitchen.

I turn to find Astrid talking quietly to Jonah across the room. I wonder if she's saying the same things to him that Cameron just said to me.

"I'm pissed at you," Callie murmurs. Her shoulder bumps into mine.

"I know," I tell her.

She sighs heavily. "I'm also glad you're finally home."

We hug, and for the first time since coming home, hope seeds within me.

Chapter Twenty-Five

We're sitting across from one another—Jonah on the couch, me in a chair, and there's a coffee table between us. In all the years we've known each other, I've never been more nervous. There's a lot at stake right now. But as unsettled as I feel, I don't hide my emotions from him. Right now, he deserves honesty that's one hundred percent pure, not a diluted, piss-poor version whose purpose is to assuage my guilt rather than my conscience.

I refer to Will as my best friend, but Jonah—he's been my real best friend for the bulk of my life. We've shared more together, both in our dreams and in real life, than most people ever get to experience. So to be as nervous as I am makes me want to laugh, because this man has seen me naked, knows my body as well as his own, and has held my hand through good times and bad. I should not be so nervous—but then, I never should've treated him the way I did, either. So anything that may happen today—my heart being ripped out of my chest, for example—will be the result of my own actions.

I clear my throat and spin my index finger in a circle over my shoulder. "That was crazy, right?"

His hand flexes against the couch arm, even though he's trying to radiate calm and indifference. I wonder if he remembers I'm aware of this tic of his, that I'll always know when he's upset or scared or worried. I'm glad that this, at least, is still true. "I'll admit I didn't see any of that coming," he finally says. Hearing his voice, directed at me, is the best present I've received in a long time.

How could I have ever done this to him? How was I so stupidly blind to realize what I had?

"Right?" I scratch my scalp, but quit when I realize it's a tic of mine, too. He already knows I'm nervous and guilty as all hell. There's no need to shred my scalp while I'm at it. "So." I swallow hard. I wonder if he can feel just how much I love him, too, if he can accept it through everything else running through my body. "I owe you an explanation."

He doesn't say anything. I'm glad he doesn't—and it makes me wonder if maybe he's changed these last six months, too. Because for a long time, Jonah tried too often to take care of my needs before seeing to his own. Old Jonah would be reassuring Old Chloe that there's no need to explain. That he understands, whether or not he really does.

I'm on the edge of my chair, unable to relax. My hands twist in my lap. "More importantly, I owe you an apology. I left last year without a single word to you. That was . . ." I shake my head slowly, refusing to break eye contact with him. Gods, his eyes are gorgeous. "Incredibly selfish of me. Disrespectful. And you didn't deserve that. I know it seems like all I've ever done in the last few years is apologize to you, but Jonah, I am truly sorry for leaving like that."

His right hand stops flexing long enough to rake through his hair. He blows out a hard breath. It's then I notice he's trembling— very faintly, but it's there all the same.

For the first time in a long time, I wish I was an Emotional, so I could know what he's feeling, too.

"I was out shopping with Callie, and I realized I didn't have my phone. I came back to the apartment to get it, and I . . ." I can't seem to swallow the lump in my throat. "I overheard an argument between you and Kellan."

Those cerulean eyes of his, the ones I've lost myself in so many times, widen in surprise and confusion.

"You two were so cruel to each other. None of us were talking anymore, and . . ." I force another gulp. "I was so sick, Jonah. The ulcer kept coming back. All those blinding headaches. I felt like I wasn't able to hold it together anymore. Between the mess due to our Connections and work, I was—"

He's surprised again. "Work?"

Sadness and shame washes over me. I don't want to talk about it, but . . . I need to. Have to. "Before you banished him, Jens Belladonna let me know I killed two nons on one of my assignments."

He's quiet for a long moment. "You realize that I'm responsible for a lot more than two deaths over the last two years, right?"

"I know." I fight back the tears. And this is part of the problem. He's always had a tough time dealing with the fall-out from his actions, and I knew it, and focused instead on my own worries. What does that say about me? Certainly, that I wasn't as supportive to him as he'd been to me. It'd been all about me back then, and I hate that. Here on out, no matter what, that's not who I want to be anymore. "I know. It's just . . ." My hands are folded so tight that I fear I might lose circulation. "I wasn't ready for that yet. I knew someday it'd be the case, but . . . I wasn't *ready*. I was really resentful that I was forced to skip right over all those stages that everyone else gets to go through, the ones that help Magicals ease into their crafts. It felt like the moment I joined the Council, I was thrown into the fire." I sigh. "I know it was the same for you, too. And others. It's not like I was the only one. And I'm not trying to devalue your crafts, but more often than not, it seemed like I was asked to get out there and destroy things rather than create, and it was a heavy burden to bear."

"Why didn't you talk to me about how you were feeling about everything?" He's so sad. "I would have helped you, Chloe."

"I know." I'm crying, and it pisses me off, because I want to stay strong. "I know that now. I wish I had. But at the time, it felt like everything was spiraling out of control, and before I knew it, I was lost and didn't know how to get out of the maze I'd wandered into."

One of his palms presses in between his eyes.

"And . . . the Connections . . ." My voice falls apart, and I'm shaking all over. "It's really hard to have two Connections, Jonah. I know you have two, too, but—it's overwhelming at times." I wipe my nose. "Sometimes, I wondered if everything I did damaged one or both of you. Like, whether me even breathing, *existing*—hurt you. And I hated myself for it. What good was I to anyone if I couldn't even love myself? I couldn't—I didn't know what to do. In the end, it seemed like the only solution was for me to leave. I hoped . . ."

I finally look away. It's becoming increasingly difficult to not just ugly cry, especially since he's looking at me like I've just killed a whole bag full of adorable kittens and puppies right in front of him. "I thought that maybe if I were out of the equation, you two wouldn't be so angry at one another anymore. So I left. I wanted to give you guys a chance at a normal life. I just thought—" Okay. I give in. I'm totally ugly crying now. "I know you probably don't believe me, but I thought I was doing the best thing for you. For Kellan. And, if I'm being honest, for me, too."

Both palms press against his eyes now.

"I was nineteen, Jonah, and all I could see ahead of me was a lifetime of guilt and stress. I know you two felt those things, too. How was that fair?" I wipe my cheeks. And then I take a deep breath. My heart hammers harder than ever. Because I finally tell him what I should have told him a long time ago.

I tell him I cheated on him with his brother, and it happened more than once.

Jonah's quiet for a long time. He leans back against the couch and stares up at the ceiling, his hand clenching in and out, and a million scenarios play out in my mind over what he's finally going to say to me. How it can go so many different ways—in anger, in fury, hysteria, anguish, or sadness. All will further serve to break my heart, because he never deserved what I've done to him, never once.

I desperately want to get a tissue, but I'm too scared to leave my chair. Because what if he leaves while I'm gone, even for a minute? So I wipe my nose and cheeks with my sleeve and sniffle and continue to ugly cry as silently as I can. I wait, even though it kills me to do so. I've made him wait over six months. I'm willing to wait for him for as long as it takes.

He's worth it.

Just when I start worrying I'm going to flood the apartment with my tears, he says, still staring at the ceiling, "I already knew you cheated."

I stop crying long enough to gurgle out, *"What?"*

He laughs quietly, but there is no humor in his pain. "I've known for a long time."

I am the worlds' first person to exist without a beating heart.

He finally looks at me. There is so much hurt in his face that I wonder if coming home was a mistake. He's in anguish, and it's because of *me*. "I know a lot of things. For example, I know you hid your emotions from me for months behind some kind of shield that some hider—Kopano, most likely—taught you how to construct. I never said anything to you about it, because I figured you needed it and would tell me about it when you felt it was time. My father used to use one against us when we used to live together, so I know what one feels and acts like. I knew it had to be difficult to live with an Emotional, and I regretted being so in tune with your feelings all the time, but I also knew there was no way I could ever turn that part of me off—at least, not when it came to you. I knew about the deaths you're talking about, but I didn't know you knew. They were accidental, by the way. Not that that diminishes how you feel, but selfishly, I hoped you'd never know, because I worried it'd gut you. I knew you'd be angry with me if you found out I knew and never told, because you hated being kept in the dark—even though I watched you increasingly keep everyone in your life in the dark, too. Ironic, isn't it, that you hated all the secrets your parents kept over the years and accused me of holding things back and you did just the same." He blows out another hard breath. Runs his hands through his hair, yanking the strands. His point, valid as all hell, is painful. "I know you and Kellan . . . that something happened in Costa Rica. And on that damn yacht he took you out on in Kauai. I knew you were falling apart. I knew that every single one of us was self-destructing—you with your ulcer and depression, him with his efforts to reassign his pain, me—" He looks down at his hands. "The thing is, I knew all of this, but I didn't know how to fix any of it."

I have to search for my voice. Jesus. I'd been so very blind. "How were you self-destructing, Jonah?"

He stares out of the window on the far side of the room, silent for a good twenty seconds that leaves me even more anxious than before. And then—"Did you know that sometimes my brother and I release memories to one another without even realizing it?" When his focus returns to me, it's accompanied with a bittersweet smile. "It happens when we're dreaming. I don't know why, or how, but sometimes he sees my memories and I see his. For Kellan last year, the more he held in what had happened between the two of you, the more it ripped his soul apart and the more frequently I saw it all."

Oh, gods. I'm back to ugly crying. "You . . . you *saw* what happened?"

He nods, his barely-there smile so incredibly sad and rueful.

I have to close my eyes. I have to focus on breathing. In. Out. In. Out. Because he knew, he saw, and suddenly, it all makes sense. He stopped talking to me toward the end because . . . *he knew*. I'd hurt this man, the one I love more than anything in all the worlds, and all I could focus on then was my own pain. And then I left him without a single word, which had probably been an entire ocean's worth of salt on the wound I caused. It would've been absolutely understandable if he believed I'd never truly loved him at all, Connection or not. Or that I didn't love him enough, which is even worse.

"I know it probably means nothing to you now, but I am so sorry," I choke out.

He's silent again, simply watching me with that awful agony in his eyes.

I love him so much that it's ridiculous, but my love is not the kind he deserves. At least, it wasn't then. Maybe one day it will be, though. If I'm lucky enough.

"Jonah—"

"When I found out we had a Connection, I was . . ." He leans forward, his elbows against his knees. "Relieved, I think. Because I knew it would be forever. What I felt for you—what I wanted, what I hoped for—forever seemed like a blessing. But in reality, forever is a really long time when your heart wholly belongs to a person who doesn't reciprocate in kind."

My cheeks are soaked.

"The thing is, logically, I understand. Because you've got a Connection to him, too. But I guess I'm the failure of an Emotional my father warned I'd turn out to be, because in the last six months, I learned that I can't always live logically. I can't pretend, either. You deserted me. I'm not okay with that, even though you thought you were doing the right thing. I know you think that; I feel it in you." He pauses. "I guess I'd thought—hoped—I'd meant more to you than that." Another pause. And then, "I'm not okay with you having a relationship with us both. It's not who I am. It's not what I want. At one point, I wondered if maybe I could, if I could just learn to control my feelings better. If I could just pretend better. Be the better person. Be who you two needed me to be." He shakes his head. "I'm not that guy, Chloe. I'd rather live with the pain. I'm sorry, but . . ."

He stands up. My legs jerk me up, too, but then refuse to move anywhere else. And all I can think is, oh my gods, oh my gods, this is not happening.

Now that I know what I want, *this cannot be happening.*

He closes his eyes and takes a deep breath. His hand must be cramping by now. And then he takes my heart out of my chest. "I can't do this anymore. I'm . . ." He swallows hard, and then, voice barely loud enough to hear, "Done." Louder, "I—I have to go."

The urge to scream, plead, fall to his feet and beg for forgiveness, another chance, anything at all, clamors against my skull and rib cage. But in the end, I simply nod, because if he needs to go, I have to let him. All I've ever done is take from him. It's time to give. If he needs me to let him go, I must do it, even though it's the absolute last thing I want.

When he passes me, he slows down, the pull between us vicious and unforgiving. He must feel the love I have for him. It's impossible to hide any longer. But his feet are better than mine, stronger, too, because they keep moving. Down the hallway, out the front door.

Out of my life.

Will and Cameron, accompanied by Erik, come home from their walk to find me still standing exactly where Jonah left me. I'm not sure if I'm still crying. I don't know how much time has passed. I vaguely hear Erik telling Cameron words like *shock* and *time*, and then Will pushes me toward my bedroom and gets me into bed. He offers to stay with me, but I send him away. I need to be by myself right now.

I lie here for the entire night, awake, thinking about what I've done. I want to fight for Jonah, for us, but if he's done with me, would I be only prolonging the festering wounds I've inflicted upon his soul? They need to heal. All of the injuries we've developed this last year need to heal. Scar tissue needs to develop. But it's hard to give him that room now that I know what I want.

I don't know what to do and it terrifies me. I won't run, though. I'll never run again. I've got to prove to him that I've changed. That I understand things better now. Running doesn't solve anything.

But I'm helpless right now. There's nothing I can create that will fix this. Only time, and time is the most brutal of all solutions, because there is no way to manipulate it in your favor.

Chapter Twenty-Six

Kellan shows up the next morning as I listlessly roam around the apartment. Dark purplish smudges under his eyes tell me right away how his mission went, and old habits die hard, because guilt festers in the bit of my belly for asking him to come over so I can explain why I abandoned him last year when he clearly ought to be resting. Nothing says loving support like breaking someone's heart after a grueling day at work.

We linger at the door for several minutes, him right outside the threshold, me right inside. Our awkward conversation goes like this:

Me: "You look tired."

Him: "I'm fine."

Me: "We can do this tomorrow, if you want to go sleep first."

Him: "I said I'm fine."

Me: "Want to come in?"

Him: "Who the hell owns this place anyway?"

Me: "Cameron. It's—I guess it was his wife's. And his. I mean, they were married, so—"

Him: "I can't believe you're living with these guys. Why are you living here? You have an apartment of you own. It's still there. Everything's still there."

Me: "Oh. I'd wondered. Want to come in?"

Him: "Fine. Whatever."

And now we're in the kitchen, me making him a cup of coffee because I genuinely fear he's going to pass out from exhaustion and him leaning against the counter, watching me.

The thing is, as I study him, I can't help but acknowledge just how much I love him. But now that I'm here—*we're* here—and after everything that went down yesterday, it crushes me to know that, despite everything, despite my feelings for him, his for me, how good we are with one another, and how I still dream at times of a life we could have together, I need his brother more.

And I don't hide it from him. Maybe that makes me a bitch, but I can't do this anymore. I have to be honest. *We* have to be honest.

"I fucked up," is what I tell him first. Thankfully, with him here, with at least this Connection being satisfied by being around its match, I'm no longer the zombie I was just minutes before.

"No shit."

He's got every right to be angry, and I know it. I try not to let it get to me. "I'm sorry I left without saying anything."

Will chooses this moment to come into the kitchen. And, just my luck, he's shirtless, with a towel hanging from his neck. "Chloe, you've got to—" He stops when he sees Kellan. "Oh. Apologies. I didn't know you had company."

Kellan glares at my friend, no doubt remembering the antagonism between them yesterday during the worlds' most awkward Family Secrets Reveal Day.

"Yeah, um," I move a hand between them. "Will, this is Kellan. Kellan, this is Will. You guys didn't get to formally meet yesterday."

At Kellan's name, Will's eyebrows shoot up. He knows how devastated I am with what happened with Jonah. I can see the question in his eyes, and how he wonders if I'm sliding back into bad habits.

And it kind of hurts, coming from him of all people.

But Will sticks his hand out, because he's that kind of guy. I hold my breath, waiting to see if Kellan will reciprocate in kind, and it takes a good three seconds, but he finally does. And I let the breath go, relieved that I'm not going to have to referee a fight between these two today.

"You were saying?" I prompt Will as he pours himself a cup of coffee. Nell comes trotting into the kitchen; it warms my heart to watch Kellan automatically bend down and pet her satiny head.

"Right. I need you to call Frieda when you have a moment and tell her to take her head out of her ass. Obviously you haven't been checking your messages this morning. She's called me a good five times, the last two asking where you are and whether or not I've lost you in Glasgow already."

My eyes slide over to where Kellan is. He's sipping his coffee, watching us curiously, which is admittedly a much better turn of events than searing anger and disappointment. "Frieda is a friend I used to work with in Alaska."

This surprises him. "You had a job?"

His incredulity makes me do one of those breathy exhales of a laugh. Talk about a surreal situation. "Yes, Kellan. How do you think I afforded to buy food? Pay rent?"

Well, okay. I don't quite tell him everything, because I'm holding back that I afforded a lot of things thanks to the money I stole from him and his brother.

Some of the old easiness between us resurfaces, though. "Just what kind of job did you have?"

"She was a waitress," Will supplies. "With a vicious cleaning fetish. We had the cleanest diner in all of Anchorage."

My cheeks burn. Kellan laughs, though—it's quiet and small, but it's a laugh. "I never pictured in my wildest dreams that you would ever be a waitress, let alone one with a cleaning fetish."

My lips tug up at the corners. "Why am I calling Frieda, Will?"

He pulls a box of crackers out of the cupboard. "Paul proposed."

"Shut. UP." My cup slams onto the counter.

"I know this will come as a shock, but Frieda is outraged. I'm tired of her bloody rants. If I have to listen to them one more time, I'll be doing more than telling her to bugger off." Will grabs a jar of Marmite out of the fridge; he'd found a small grocery store last night that actually carried it. "It's your turn."

"Why isn't Ginny dealing with the fallout?"

He points his knife at me. "Our dearest Gin has already planned out the entire wedding. Frieda has disavowed her as a traitor. She somehow thinks you or I will talk sense into Paul. I'll be honest, I sent Paul a text and told him to insist he was joking and find a nice girl who'll appreciate him, but you know Paul. Said he sees loads in her the rest of us are blind to or whatever."

I pass him a plate. "Turn off your phone. It's an easy solution."

And . . . he looks so sad. Lost. Which means only one thing. I snatch the plate back. "Will—"

Now he feigns innocence. "Give me back my plate. Do you want me to starve?"

"Of course not. It's just—"

Will rips the plate out of my fingers and glances at Kellan, who is not hiding his amused interest in this conversation. "This is neither the time nor place for such a conversation. Don't you have a *mea culpa* to commence with?"

I'm a dog with a bone. "Will—"

"Chloe," he mimics in falsetto.

We have a stare-off for a good five seconds before I relent. Finally, "I refuse to apologize for caring."

"I don't expect you to." He nods toward Kellan. "It was good to finally make your proper acquaintance. And now, I'm off to go watch the hockey game I taped, because at least that will be normalcy in this madhouse of family horrors."

When he's gone, Kellan asks, "What was that about?"

"It's a long story." I rub the spot between my eyes, leaning a hip against the counter and trying desperately not to remember in vivid detail us being in another kitchen during another lifetime. "I'm sorry, Kellan. I really am."

He sighs, setting his coffee cup down.

I tell him what I told Jonah—about how I hated hurting them, how I didn't know if I could live with it, about the weight of work, about being sick all the time. And then I tell him I told Jonah about the two of us and what we did behind Jonah's back.

"He knew," is what Kellan finally says.

It's my turn to sigh. Oddly, I'm not on the verge of tears, and I'm not sure if it's because I'm numb or in denial or because if I let myself go, I'm afraid I'll be right back to where I was.

I've only blacked out twice since Jonah walked out yesterday. I figure that's a victory of and in itself. But then again, it's hasn't even been twenty-four hours.

"I realize I didn't ask you ahead of time if I could tell—"

"Chloe." He takes a step closer, and I can finally smell him. It's spicy and warm and sexy and it makes my senses and resolutions go fuzzy. "It's not like you needed my permission to tell him." He swallows. "We already had that discussion months ago." His half smile that I love quirks, but it's sad. "Technically, we fought and nearly tore each other's throats out, but in the end, we talked, and he told me he knew, and I told him the truth."

"Oh." I don't know what else to say. But I force myself to take a step back.

He runs his hands through his hair and steps away, too. There's a space between us now, one that I think we both understand is necessary, if at least for today, even if it's becoming increasingly difficult not to just launch myself into his arms. "I get why you left. It pisses me off you did it, but I understand."

We stand in the kitchen in silence for a long time. A lot of questions circle round my head, but I don't know if I have a right to ask any of them. I don't know where I stand with Kellan at the moment. He's my Connection, yes. I still love him, yes. But I abandoned him and hurt him and have decided, once and for all, that I want to spend my life with his brother, even if his brother wants nothing to do with me.

And if he's reading my emotions, he must know that. Right?

"When I was gone," I finally say. "Did you two . . . were you close again?"

He's twisting the cuff on his wrist. "We live under the same roof nowadays, if that's what you're asking."

I don't know how to feel about that. I'm glad that they're together again, but . . . it also means that Jonah's no longer living in our old home. And yet, my apartment is apparently still there waiting for me if I want it.

"Are you . . ." I wonder if I even have a right to ask. "How are you?"

He looks over my shoulder. "Part of me wants to not tell you. Walk right through the door and leave you wondering like you left me for months. I knew you weren't dead—being the son of somebody who lost his Connection due to death, I know what that can do to a person—but I didn't *know*. And that's messed up, Chloe."

"I know," I whisper.

"It's also fucked up because, during those times in which I was so angry I wanted to break everything in my apartment, I also eventually came to the realization it's exactly what I did to you, too. I may not have run away without a word, but for eight months, I left you in the dark."

I stretch out a hand—not to touch him, which I ache to, but because I need him to stop this. "Do not turn this around on yourself. If anyone is apologizing today, it's me."

"You tore me apart when you left," he says. "It wasn't the first time. I doubt it'll be the last. But here's the thing. I've learned to live without you in my life over the last few years. You and I, we've done this dance far too often. I hold you at an arm's length, we come together, and vice versa. It's . . ." He shakes his head sadly. "I think if we ever went to see a shrink, they'd say we're completely dysfunctional."

I focus on my breathing. In. Out. In. Out.

"You tore me apart," he continues, "but you absolutely gutted my brother."

The tears that minutes before I thought were gone forever find their way home after all.

"I'm not saying that to shame you, because I think we all know that you carry more guilt in you than most people could ever bear." He passes me a paper towel so I can mop up my face and blow my nose. "I'm telling you this because I think you need to know."

Will breathing ever be an easy task again? I tell Kellan, "He's done with me."

I try not to disintegrate when Kellan doesn't disagree.

"Earth to Chloe."

I flinch from Will's snapping fingers. He sighs and drops down next to me. "You need to eat."

"Not hungry," I say, eyes dropping back to the dossier on my lap, the one Zthane passed over this afternoon after Kellan left. He forgave me for not coming in last night, but says we—the both of us—are going out on a mission soon. Tomorrow, as a matter of fact. I need to be all about the mission. Find Elders. Kill Elders. Stop Elders from killing more Magicals, both loved and stranger alike.

I've just gotten off the phone with Caleb. It was weird, calling my former Conscience on the phone, but I figured I owed him an apology for shutting him out like I did. He was . . . livid. Yelled at me for a good ten minutes straight before finally relenting and admitting he missed me. And then we talked, really talked. I told him all about my reasons and my choices, and the funny thing is, Caleb understood where I was coming from. Before we hung up, he promised to come and visit me within the week. He also told me that, once the link between a Conscience and its ward is broken, it's forever broken. From here on out, we're nothing more than friends.

It was yet another hurt to add to my growing list of *How Chloe Royally Fucked Up This Time.*

Will slides the folder away, flipping it shut. "Believe it or not, Dad is on the phone with that woman—Astrid? They're *chatting*. My father is on the *phone*, and he's *chatting* with a woman. I cannot be out there listening to this any longer." He eyes me warily. "Have you called him?"

I blink and try to focus on Will's face. How had I never seen the Elvin features in him before? Was it just because I didn't want to? "Your dad?"

He rolls his eyes. "No. You know I mean Jonah."

Something inside me breaks again. I shake my head slowly. "He doesn't want me to call. He made it clear that he's done with me."

Will's dubious. "You two have a Connection."

"We also apparently have free will. Jonah,"—each syllable of his name is a jagged shard of glass against the tender yet still beating muscle in my chest—"exercised his right to choose whether or not he wants to be with me."

He sighs heavily through his nose. "I don't think that's the case. I think it's more—you hurt him. He's reacting."

"I don't want to talk about this. Not today, at least. We should be overlooking the mission specs." I snatch the folder back from him.

"Out of curiosity, why aren't you with Kellan?"

The folder turns heavy in my hand. "What?"

"When you first told me about these guys, and how you cheated on Jonah with his brother, I've gotta be honest, I assumed you were with Jonah out of a misplaced sense of obligation and habit. It was Kellan I thought you really loved. But . . ." His hand falls on top of mine. "Here you are, single. He's single. I saw you guys earlier. He's so in love with you that it's amazing he can even stand upright. You're pretty keen on him, too. Isn't this the perfect opportunity to at least *try* to see what things would be like with him?"

Ah. Which is what I think Kellan hopes for, too. Or at least, it's what I saw in his eyes when he left, even though he must have sensed how I felt about him, about his brother. We didn't hug—it would've been too much, too soon. But that sharp tug between Connections was there, strong as ever, and when he walked out of my door, the instinct to go after him and kiss him senseless nearly smothered me.

"I love Jonah," I tell Will. My voice is hollow, which makes sense, as it's how I'm feeling right now. But it's okay. Because I'm going to go out and kick some ass and kill some Elders and I'll find ways to fill up that hole. I have to.

Chapter Twenty-Seven

Most of the team is already waiting at an airstrip in Novosibirsk, Siberia. A Cyclone I don't know (apparently Raul is on an extended vacation) will be piloting us to the remote region the Elders have been spotted in. Two Shamans I don't know too well are there (Zthane wasn't taking any chances), as well as a pair of Blazes (Brock and Vance?) and a female Elemental I don't know. Outside of Karl, Will, and myself, the last member of the team is Kellan, which does not make me happy in the least. I argued for a good ten minutes with Zthane and Karl over his participation, but outside of me claiming I worried my Connection could get hurt, I had no real ground to stand on when it came to dismissing him from the team.

"Emotionals have always been successful controlling the Elders," Zthane reasoned repeatedly. "You know me. Besides, Kellan's the best we have on the Guard. Of course he's coming." The thing is, I understood where Zthane was coming from, and agreed even, but the thought of Kellan getting hurt made me want to destroy things.

I caved in the end and agreed to his addition to the team, but it's definitely left me on edge. This, coupled with the sharp pain of losing Jonah once more has me antsy and admittedly far too bitchy. Will and Karl bear the brunt of my constant snapping fairly serenely as we exit the airport, inside of which the portal is conveniently hidden, and onto the tarmac, but I guess I step on one too many toes because Will finally says, "Time to sheath the claws, Chloe, lest you want the entire team to think you're on your period."

"That is incredibly sexist of you, Will," I snarl in return.

Karl laughs, but I don't. Just what if today goes badly? Lee's told us there are four Elders in the region, and with a team this large, the odds are stacked in our favor. But I can't help but worry that something will go wrong, that somehow those things will get the best of me and take me out, leaving the rest of the team defenseless out in the wilderness of Siberia.

Must. Stay. Focused.

Which means, of course, I wonder what Jonah is doing right now, where he is, how he's dealing with everything. I laid down the law with Zthane last night that, while I was caving and allowing Kellan to come, there was no way in hell I'd approve both Whitecombs on the mission. He tried for it, of course he did—the twins have proved to be highly effective together against the Elders in the past. But if I had to contend with attempting to protect both of them and Jonah's snubbing all at the same time while trying my best to kill these monsters, I don't know if I could do it. It's bad enough Will's here, being so perilously fragile in his non-Magical state (not that I'd ever admit that out loud to him, though) but Zthane figured that, after being so effective against the Elders in the last two fights, Will should come because he has experience against these monsters that nobody else on the team, save me and Karl, have.

"According to Erik, there's a small Métis colony about two hundred miles south," Karl tells me as we approach the military plane the Guards has absconded for the mission. "So I don't think we can term this Elder sighting as random."

"Shite," Will mutters. He adjusts his sunglasses in the bright morning light. "How many?"

"Colonists or Elders?" When Will indicates the Métis, Karl continues, "Four families—like I said, small, but no number is small enough when you have these things gunning for them."

"There was an attack, wasn't there?" Will asks quietly.

Karl sighs heavily, his mouth a bleak line. And then he nods.

My stomach heaves. "Anybody hurt?"

Karl readjusts the straps of his backpack and stares straight ahead. "Three-year-old twins and their mother were in the car that the Elders targeted. Only the little girl made it—her brother and mom are dead thanks to these monsters, not to mention a family of four that were nons in a nearby car."

"Christ," Will whispers.

"They were first generation Métis," Karl tells us as he waves at the pilot in the distance. "Erik says the Métis governing bodies believe that the closer the bloodlines are to Magicals, the more likely they become targets. These kids—" He shakes his head swiftly. "Their mom left Annar about a decade ago for their dad. She was a lower level Elemental. And now there's a little girl who doesn't have her mom or her twin."

I can't even wrap my mind around such a tragedy. This needs to stop. People—Magicals, Métis, and nons alike—should be safe from these monsters. And I'm reminded of a promise I made long ago, to Earle Locust-tree, who'd lost his husband to the Elders and then was attacked by them himself. And now he's gone, along with the rest of the team that fought to protect me, and I'm left with the promise that I wouldn't give up trying to stop these monsters.

I hope to do him proud today.

Maybe it's because I've been removed from Annar for awhile, and maybe it's because, other than with Callie Lotus, I haven't really been around such a situation before, but I'm shocked at the level of hostility and distrust coming from the team inside the plane that's angled toward Will. Well—not from Kellan, who isn't here yet, since he's en route directly from another mission nearby, but from the rest of the team, yes. They're regarding Will with wary eyes, whispering to one another like his presence is unwanted and unnecessary. Every so often I catch snatches of what they're saying; ugly words about how he's a non, a freak, how his presence is most likely some kind of appeasement offering toward me, float throughout the belly of the plane.

It's infuriating, not to mention insulting. I would never have been able to do what I've done without Will's help and guidance.

For his part, Will pretends to ignore them, although I know it's got to be driving him crazy. He sits in the web seat next to me, settling the sword I've made him in between his legs so he can swing it around in a wide arc as we chat about our friends back in Alaska.

I try to follow his lead, but when I hear some kind of innuendo about how he must surely be some kind of toy I picked up while out "sowing my wild oats," I can't hold my fury back any longer. "What the hell are your problems?" I shout.

The plane goes deathly quiet. Karl and the Cyclone (I think his name is Flip?) stick their heads out of the cockpit, from where they'd been discussing the flight plan.

Will's hand finds my arm. His voice is flat when he says, "Don't bother."

"What's going on?" Karl demands. But he knows. I can tell by the look on his face he already knows what has me pissed off.

I don't care what Will thinks. How they're acting, what they're saying—it's *wrong*. "This is the team you guys picked for me?" I'm practically seething as Karl and Flip fully enter the body of the plane. "These are the people you think I can trust?"

"Who does this little girl think she is?" snarls the Elemental I don't know.

Before Karl can say anything, I stand up, pressing a hand against the side of the plane. "I'm the person who will get your sorry ass demoted to some desolate city to work on thunderstorms for the rest of your life if you don't watch your mouth."

She stands up, too, clearly pissed off. "I don't answer to you."

"Lola, sit down." Karl's tone leaves no room for bargaining on her end.

It's at that moment that Kellan boards the plane, his hair messy from the wind and dark circles ringing his eyes from what was no doubt precious little sleep in his effort to make it here on time. "Sorry I'm—" The tug between us is sharp and sudden. His focus lands on me, those gorgeous blue eyes of his widening in surprise. And then they narrow as they turn to Karl. "What is Chloe doing here?"

"This is my question," Lola snarls. She's got full-on bitch face going. "Because this Council princess thinks she can—"

Kellan's eyes flash with anger. "Don't even think of finishing that sentence, Lola."

Shocked, Lola finally does as Karl says and sits down.

But I'm done with this. How is this going to play if they're going to be fighting me and Will the whole way? "If this is how it's going to be," I say to Karl, "then get me Zthane on the phone right now so I can tell him to send this group of jackasses straight back to Annar. I don't need them." A quick glance at Will has me correcting that. "*We* don't need them."

Karl rubs at his hair. I know he's in a difficult position, but my nerves, so freshly raw from the return to Annar, won't let this go. "You know having a team gives us our best shot."

"Really?" I let out an ugly laugh. "That's funny, because Will and I did just fine on our own."

Will groans in frustration, but before he can say anything, Kellan steps in between us. "Can we all just calm down a minute so we can figure out what's going on here? Chloe, what are you talking about?"

The Electric sitting next to Lola—Vance, I think—says in this awful, condescending tone, "Dude. She brought a *non* on the mission."

Will's finally had enough, because he finally wades in. "Wow. Karl, I'm going to concur with Chloe. Bigoted prats will not help us no matter how good you say they are."

"Not. Another. Word," Karl snaps at Vance. And then, to the

rest of the team, "The next person who speaks out of turn will be physically removed from this plane, mission, and most likely the Guard. Councilwoman Lilywhite was absolutely right in her statement that she can have any of your sorry asses demoted at any point. I'm sorry that we did not make it clear prior, due to security reasons, but Councilwoman Lilywhite runs this mission. What she says, goes. You have a problem? There's the door."

That gets their attention.

"You were informed that this was an Elders mission—that much is true," Karl continues. "Four hostiles were spotted in the region as early as twelve hours prior by Lee Acacia. However, you were not given the true mission specs. This is not merely recon." Flip slips out from behind him and sits down on the other side of Will, which is relief. If he shows he has no problem with Will being here, then maybe the rest of the team will take pause.

Karl crosses his arms, his tone completely no-nonsense now. "Before we discuss them, there's something that needs to be made clear. This is a top-secret assignment. No details of any part of what transpires today may be revealed to any person outside of this aircraft." He lifts his chin briefly toward Kellan, tapping his forehead. "No one else is cleared for this. *No one.* Understood?"

Kellan's eyes widen again in surprise. Karl's ordering him to not even tell Jonah, not even their way, in their heads. But he nods and offers his assent, just as every other person on the plane does, but it's me he chooses to focus on.

I try not to squirm in my seat under his intense gaze, because with this group, I need to stay strong. The Guard will annihilate the feeblest members of their teams, because to them, weakness is not an option in the field.

"Another thing that needs to be made clear," Karl is saying, "is that you, in no way, will spew any more of that prejudiced crap toward Will Dane. His participation in this mission is vital, and it has nothing to do with Councilwoman Lilywhite's wishes. Both Nightstorm and I have determined that his expertise in this arena is critical toward our success today." He pauses, then delivers the next line with deft precision. "I have never been as ashamed of any team of mine as I am at this moment."

I try not to laugh at the panicked horror that flashes across nearly every face in the plane. As for me, I'm nearly bursting with pride that Karl is the stand-up man I always thought he was.

The Blaze, Brock, asks in a quiet, low voice tinged with a Southern accent, "Pardon me, sir, but what kind of expertise can a non lend us on an Elders recon?"

But it's Kellan that answers first. "He's not a non." A ghost of a smile graces his lips. "Will Dane is a Métis, which means he's part Magical. He's also Molly Hellebore's son, so he deserves your respect."

Will stiffens next to me as a collective gasp pings off the metal walls. And then he asks, voice low and carefully controlled to sound bored, "And you know that, how?"

Kellan's amused. "Did you really think, after everything that's gone down, I wouldn't dig up every last piece of dirt on you I could?"

Oh. My. Gods. Seriously? I hiss, "Kellan!"

He's totally unapologetic, though.

Vance clears his throat. "Hellebore was a wicked good Smith. What's she up to nowadays?"

Will's stare is stony. "She's dead."

"Oh, man—I'm sorry," Vance says quietly. It's obvious he's grossly uncomfortable, but after what's just gone down, I have no pity for him.

"We were discussing the mission that Councilwoman Lilywhite is leading us on," Kellan says to Karl. It's impossible to miss the annoyance lacing his words, especially as he offers up my official title. Last year, when I served as bait on an Elders mission, he'd begged me not to go. Tried to blackmail me. In the end, I went, but if today's anything like then, he's just as pissed off I'm here as I am with his presence.

Even after everything that's happened since then, old habits die hard.

"Right." Karl moves toward where I'm standing. "While Councilwoman Lilywhite was on recon in Alaska during a secret, Guard sanctioned mission—"

Wait. What? He's—is he lying to the team about where I've been and what I've done? I really should have read Zthane's report more carefully.

"She and Dane were repeatedly attacked by the Elders."

"You were *what*?" The anger in Kellan's voice nearly knocks me back into my seat.

Okay? I thought Karl told him about what went down already! I turn toward the Quake, who offers no apologies. "Not finished yet, Whitecomb," he says evenly. But now that he knows that Kellan's my Connection, too, he's most likely sympathetic to what Kellan must be feeling right now. And I get it—I do, because had I just found out that Kellan was running around, being attacked by these things, I might be close to losing a gasket, too.

Still, it would have been nice not to blindside Kellan in front of a whole team. Had I known, I would've told him yesterday when he was at the apartment. Wait—"I thought you were going to debrief Kellan yesterday," I say to Karl.

"Yes, well," Karl leans against the wall, "things came up and it didn't happen."

"Which is fine, since you and I are going to discuss this ourselves," Kellan says to me, like we're not in the middle of Karl's briefing.

"Later," Karl insists. Bless him. "Because right now, you all need to hear the real reason why we're here. During these attacks, Councilwoman Lilywhite and Dane realized something. There is, in fact, a way to destroy the Elders."

This bomb goes off exactly as Karl predicted it would. Everyone, even Kellan, suck in their surprise and stare at me and Will like we're . . . not freaks, exactly, but like we've done the impossible. Which I guess we have.

Karl's grin is grim. "Three Elders no longer exist thanks to these two."

"You say it was just us, but I think you're forgetting yourself." Will taps the floor with the tip of his sword. "I seem to remember quite vividly a certain Quake helping out with two of those beasties."

Karl shrugs this off like his role was nothing, which is so typically Karl.

"How . . . how is that possible?" Brock asks.

Kellan sits down in the web seat across from me. If I were a betting woman, I'd say he's a torn between fury and pride over what he's just learned.

Karl nods in encouragement at me. So I take a deep breath and address the team. "I willed them out of existence. I'm a Destroyer, too, remember." I glance over at Will, who is back to playing with his sword. "It just took someone reminding me of what I can do."

Will rolls his eyes. It's obvious he hates that there's so much attention on him here. But, he's got to suck it up, because I don't think I could have done it without him.

"The thing is," I continue, "it appears I need to be touching them in order to do so." My lips twist ruefully. "You should know they can make themselves look a little more like people now. And they can talk. And they can be touched, bleed, and turn their limbs into weapons."

Will mutters, "Creepy as fuck is what they are."

"Yeah, they are." Karl shudders, then, as if he's annoyed he showed his true feelings toward what we saw, he scowls.

No one seems to know how to take this. Karl, admitting that he's scared, too? It's almost too much for them. But, despite my own fear over what we're about to face today, I force myself to sound cool and in control. I need to get them to focus on what's going to go down, so nobody freaks out once we're confronted. "If after what you see in a couple of minutes, you still decide to continue on with the mission, you need to understand there's an excellent chance you're going to get hurt. The Elders need to be incapacitated for me to be able to work my craft on them, and they won't go down without a fight."

"Chloe." Kellan is trying so hard not to show his true feelings in front of everyone on the plane, but as he's twisting his cuff around at an alarming speed, I know he's struggling. "Please tell me you weren't hurt fighting these things."

He'll know if I lie. I search for the right words to describe the hell I'd gone through, but none of them seem soft enough.

So Will answers for me. "The first time we fought one of these beasties, it cut us up like we were paper dolls. Broke some bones. We didn't have any of your fancy healers with us, so we were simply stitched up afterwards and given some extra blood to replace what we'd lost. The second time . . ." He glances at Karl, and then me. "There were four against the three of us." He pauses. "We were able to take down two, but the others fled."

There are too many emotions to handle raging in Kellan's eyes, so I look away, back toward the team. Their horror is much more manageable.

"What Will isn't telling you is that we were lucky to make it back to Annar when we did," Karl says flatly. "We had a very talented Métis who took care of our injuries, but the truth was, they nearly killed us. And that might very well happen today." He pauses, looks around the airplane. "For this mission, we will give Councilwoman Lilywhite every chance possible to take out these bastards. This team is built of people who've been found capable of incapacitating the Elders, one way or another. That is what we will do. We will do our best to stun them long enough for Chloe to do her job. If you don't think you can do this, then you need to let us know right now. You'll be free to leave after Whitecomb ensures your silence."

Nobody gets up. Not even the bitchy girl who called me a princess and insinuated Will wasn't worth her time.

Karl nods just once. "It's important you know they adapt to our crafts. The first time I knocked one out, it lasted ten seconds. Then, within minutes, it went down to eight." He scratches at the back of his neck. "Chloe, are you ready to show them what they'll be up against?"

No, I want to whisper. Not with Kellan sitting here across from me. But I create a screen in between the body and cockpit of the plane, just like Zthane requested me to do. And then I throw my memories up for all to see.

The team watches in tense silence as I first show them what happened with Cailleache, and then when Karl, Will, and I fought in the warehouse. It's brutal viewing it again, seeing just how badly we were all cut up in the end. I look even worse up on that screen than I remember being—the last shots I show them, where I'm laying in the dirt, bleeding out, seem more like something that happened to somebody else rather than me.

But I let them see it all, even Erik stabbing me in the ass with a tranquilizer while I groaned like a dying, beached whale, because it's best they know what to expect. I'm all about choices nowadays. If they want to leave, they should have the right to.

Oh, gods. Jonah left.

I force myself to focus. Can't think of that right now. Not today, not when so much is at stake.

When it's finished, and I've done away with the screen, Lola murmurs, "Well, damn."

One of the Shamans titters nervously. "What she said."

There's a tense spat of laughter from everyone but Kellan. He simply stands up and says, "We need to talk. Now."

I go to argue, but Karl tells us we have five minutes. When Kellan stalks out of the plane, I turn to Will and ask quietly, so none of the other team can hear me as they discuss what they've just seen, "You okay?"

Exasperation sighs out of him. "Don't baby me, Chloe. I don't need you fighting my battles for me. I can do nicely all on my own. Didn't you see me up there? I'm quite the badass with a sword."

That's the problem, though. I saw too much. I saw Will, cut up and hurting, wielding that sword like it was his own arm, and it scares me, knowing this daredevil is willing to go out and fight with me simply because he loves me. So I give him a winning smile. "Fat chance of getting me to stop."

He rolls his eyes, but I know it pleases him.

Outside of the plane, Kellan's hands are in his hair as he stares into the foggy distance. My heart aches, because I've thrown so much at him in the last couple of days. I reappear after bailing for half a year, I break down when his brother dumps me, and then I inform him that I'd nearly died while fighting the Elders.

If the situation was reversed, I'd be worse than a wreck. But Kellan—his voice is low and level when he asks, "Are you out of your *mind?*"

I come over to stand near him. The impulse to touch him, hold him is so strong that I force my fingers to curl into fists that I stuff under my arms. "I'm finally thinking quite clearly, thank you very much."

His eyes close for a brief moment before finding me. He knows my words carry multiple meanings. "Those things nearly killed you."

I can't sugarcoat it—not to him, not anymore. "That's true. But they didn't. And I'm hoping today, if you're going to be on the team—"

"Like I'm going to leave you here on your own," he mutters. "Did you lose your mind on your walkabout, too? Oh, wait. Are we now calling it a 'secret Guard sanctioned mission'?"

I hide my smile, even though he sounds so bitter. Also, now's not the time for us to wade into all that mess. "What I was saying was, I'm hoping my chances at survival are even better today, now that you're here with me."

His head tilts to the side as he studies me. "And yet, you don't want me here."

I'm honest. "I don't relish the idea of you getting hurt, no."

A small exhale of a laugh lifts into the misty sky above us. "There's no way to convince you to not do this, is there?"

I shake my head slowly.

"Well, then, obviously I'm coming." He stuffs his hands into his coat's pockets. "If Jonah—"

I . . . I just can't. "Don't," I whisper. I blink back the sting threatening my eyes. "I need to focus today. It's going to be hard enough with you there. Just . . . he . . ." I swallow and turn my head away.

Gods. Right now it would be so easy to just let Kellan hold me like he wants. Like *I* want. But Kellan has made it quite clear to me over the years that if anything's going to happen between us, it's going to be because I choose him. Choose us.

And I haven't.

And I won't, as incredibly tempting as it is. And I can see it in his eyes right now—he wants me to, almost desperately so. As much as it kills me to have to deny him this, it slays me even more so, because all of that love I have for him is still just as potent as before.

Late last night, in sheer despair, I actually considered calling him and begging him to give me—us—the chance we'd always been denied. Knowing Jonah doesn't want me anymore . . . it's crushing. Will keeps saying it's not the case, that Jonah's reacting to what I did and rightfully so, but part of me wondered if he was right, that this was my chance to finally see what things would be like with Kellan. I love him, after all. I cheated on Jonah with him several times, thereby destroying the integrity of the relationship I had. My feelings toward him—and his brother—tore me apart. Part of me wants to see where this will go. Part of me wants it so badly that I nearly threw out all of my resolutions and resolves away.

I won't lie to myself. I'll always want this with him. I'll always want *him*.

But then my heart reminded me of its truth. There's love for Kellan, yes—boundless, everlasting love of the very best kind. But the truth of the matter is, it needs Jonah more. And I need to do whatever I can to fix that, even if it means giving him the space he needs until another chance for me to make amends rolls around.

Somebody from inside the plane calls for us. Kellan's head tilts down toward mine. "Are you sure about this, C?"

I'm not sure which sure he's referring to. Either way, I tell him, my voice soft in the mist, "Yes."

And then we go back into the plane.

Chapter Twenty-Eight

The turbulence as we head north, following the Ob river, is brutal. Kellan is kind enough to make us all less air-sick, but my teeth rattle in my head with every bump met of this metal bird we fly in. As always, Will remains unflappable, even dozing for a few minutes before a particularly strong jolt wakes him up.

"You suck." I have to yell at him, since the propellers are so loud.

"Occasionally," he tells me in return. "It's a shame you'll never know just how well."

I burst out laughing. "You're awful!"

His smile is crookedly charming. "That's not what she said."

I roll my eyes, the corners of my lips tilting upwards, and it's then I notice Kellan watching us, his face devoid of any emotion. He's sitting in the web seat directly in front of us, next to the Blaze, Brock. Since we boarded the plane, he's been very quiet, and I don't know if I ought to draw him into our conversations or leave him alone.

Will makes the decision for me. He yells out, "So. Kellan. Chloe tells me you're an ace surfer. I've been considering taking lessons—"

Liar. He's never once mentioned this to me in the half year I've

220

known him. But I love him for it anyway.

"—and was wondering if you had any pointers for an uncoordinated bloke like myself."

Another lie. Will is one of the last people I would ever call uncoordinated.

Kellan studies Will for a second or two, but then a hint of a smile curves his lips. "Well, for one, I'd advise you to live near the beach."

"Already done that, mate. In case your geography skills aren't as ace as your surfing skills, let me assure you that Anchorage is indeed a coastal town." He turns to me. "You Annar people are horrendous with geography."

I laugh, remembering his teasing me back in his kitchen in Alaska.

Kellan actually chuckles, too. "I know where Anchorage is. I meant you ought to be closer to a spot where there are decent waves, like Yakutat. That's if you plan on heading back to Alaska any time soon." That half-smile of his that I adore quirks for a brief moment. "Of course, if you stay in Annar, then it won't be a problem, as you'll be able to go to whatever break you like whenever."

Will's long legs spread out in the tiny aisle in between the rows of web seats. His eyebrows lift upward. "You know of Yakutat?"

Kellan's eyes meet mine. "I do."

I clear my throat and then force my voice to carry across the aisle. "Have you surfed there before?"

"Once, when I was fifteen. Joey thought it would help develop 'character.' Personally, I think all it did was help incite hypothermia." His smile ticks up a teeny notch. "Too bad I didn't have a Creator with me at the time to make me a special wetsuit. I guess I wasn't lucky enough at the time to know you then, so I'll just have to make up for it now and convince you to give me what I need."

I'm going to pass out, because surely we are too high in the air and there isn't any oxygen anymore and—

"If you like," he says to Will, like he can't tell he's affected me, "I can take you out and give you some pointers sometime in the next week or so. Chloe can tag along and we can make fun of her when she attempts to stand up."

The other Guard have stopped talking with one another and are now listening to Kellan. And my heart swells, because right here, right now—Kellan is publically declaring his approval of Will.

"I'd like that," Will is saying. "Plus, I'm always game to pick on my favorite blonde. Oh wait, my mistake—you're only a fake blonde."

Feeling like a total mush toward Kellan in more ways than one, I know I need to redirect this conversation back to something safe. I say to them, "Har-har. Pick on Chloe and her inadequacies, why don't you?"

"It's ridiculously easy to do," is how Will responds.

But Kellan? He refuses to do as I want, because he says, "As there are precious few inadequacies I can find in you, as you call them, I have to make do when I do find one." The corner of one side of his mouth lifts higher. "But for all of your perfections, you truly do suck at surfing."

Butterflies explode into a full-fledged frenzy in my chest. Damn him for being so sweet. And hot. And desirable. And also, for knowing he's getting to me, because there's a spark of victory in his eyes the moment my heart decides to sprint even faster than it was just moments before.

How am I going to do this? How am I ever going to resist this man?

"Are we talking about the same girl here?" Will asks. "Because, mate, let me assure you that her bowling game is the worst you'll ever see. She's bloody wretched, which in a way makes her handy to have around, as you know you'll always beat her."

Thank the gods for Will. "You suck," I say lovingly once more.

"Again," he repeats, "it's a pity you'll never know just how well."

Before we land, I make everyone what I hope are the Elders equivalent of bulletproof vests, only I make sleek, fitted black long-sleeved shirts and pants that are hopefully flexible and lightweight and yet warm in the chilly forest we'll be heading into. Karl provides sophisticated earpieces he commandeered from the Guard HQ so attacks can be coordinated and members accounted for. When the team is finished gearing up, we look like some kind of Black Ops mission, which I think that several of the Guard rather like."This is the photo we ought to take for Frieda," I tell Will once we're on the ground. Most of the rest of the team is off to one side, making sure their bags are packed properly. "Totally screw with her mind, make her believe we ran off to join the CIA or something."

From behind his dark sunglasses, an eyebrow lifts. "And you call me devious." But his lips curl upwards. "Let's do it. It'll be proper punishment after all those bloody texts she tormented us with."

"Are you serious? I was kidding!"

"And yet you weren't. C'mon now. Pass the phone over."

"I'll take it," Kellan says, holding his hand out. I stare up at him, but as he's behind dark sunglasses, too, I can't tell what he's feeling about all of this.

"Right. Thanks, mate." Will passes over his phone. "Chloe, hold out that bad-ass bow of yours. I shan't hold my sword, because that will simply confuse her, so we'll just make do with what you have."

I can't stop cracking up. "You're crazy!"

"Very possibly true. I'm here today with you, hunting beasties, aren't I? The lone Métis amongst the mighty Guard?" He says this lightly, but I get what he's letting me know. He's here because of me, and what I mean to him, and because he's the kind of good guy who heard people were getting hurt and didn't think twice about jumping into the fray.

I lean into him, curving my arm around his waist. His loops around my shoulders, pulling me even closer into the lines of his body. As Kellan steps forward, Will's phone facing us, I look up at my friend, my heart feeling like it might burst because I adore him so very much.

"Thank you," I whisper.

He leans down and presses a lingering kiss against my cheek. I hear the phone click, signaling the photo is done, and then Will's arms are gone and he's already half way between me and Kellan.

"Aw, brilliant, mate. Just brilliant. Chloe, look here—we actually look like we're shagging like bloody rabbits, don't we?" He chortles, clearly delighted, as he takes the phone back from Kellan. The screen is held up for me to see, but I'm staring at Kellan.

And . . . I'm astonished, because Kellan is smiling, too. A real smile—not one of the ones I know he can put on like an actor taking the stage.

As Will moves away, already sending the photo to Frieda, I find myself saying to Kellan, "That was . . . surprising."

Kellan adjusts the straps of his bag on his shoulder. "I would've thought that his propensity towards pranks would be something you knew about him."

"Not that." I slide my sunglasses from the top of my head down to my eyes. "I meant . . ." An exhaled laugh escapes me. "Maccon Lightningriver kissed my cheek once, and you nearly ripped off his head."

"The difference is," Kellan says, stepping closer, "Mac was interested in you."

I scoff. "He was not."

"He most certainly was." Kellan's lips twitch. "I'm an Emotional, or have you forgotten? Lust is a pretty easy emotion to pinpoint in people, since it's so strong."

Huh. That's . . . I never saw that one. Mac and I were friends, good friends. I knew he was a player, but never once did he try to hit on me. As this is a bit of a sore subject between us, I switch tactics and tease, "You don't think Will feels the same?"

There's that half-smile I love. Damn him—butterflies explode once more in my chest, making it so hard to be clear about what I know I want nowadays. "I know he doesn't. I knew it the moment I stepped into his apartment the other day. He loves you—probably more than anyone else in all the worlds other than his dad—but he thinks of you like his sister, not the girl he wants to scream his name in bed."

My cheeks blaze; and then, like I have no control over it at all, an image of me doing just that in Kellan's bed flashes through my mind. I force myself to count to ten and will my heart to slow down, but as I'm not hiding behind any shields anymore, I know he feels all of these confusing, conflicting feelings racing around me. So, even though he's completely aware of how he's affecting me, I fake outrage. "Are you telling me you surged with him without his permission, in addition to whatever other checking up on him you did?"

"Hell yeah, I did." He takes my bow from me and pretends to check it over. "This is nice work."

"Kellan!" I hiss under my breath. "Why would you do that?"

"Complement your work? I wouldn't think that would piss you off so much."

I glance over and spot Will and Karl talking about thirty feet away. I snatch the bow back and snap quietly, "I'm talking about you surging with him!"

"I think the better question is, why wouldn't I?" Our booted toes touch, we're standing so close to one another. "The love of my life disappears for half a year. She shows back up with some guy who radiates overprotectiveness and love. Damn right, I'm going to surge with him and figure out who he is to you."

I'm buzzing at the proximity. Kellan is one of the most dangerous drugs I think that's ever been created. His name falling from my mouth is a cross between a plea and a curse. Please, I think to him, please do not do this. Not now.

I watch him take a deep breath, like he's steadying himself.

I swallow and try another tactic. Forcing scorn and irritation in my voice, I say, "He's my *friend*."

"I know that now." His head bends down, so that my whole vision is his gorgeous face. And, oh, for the love of all that's good in these worlds, let me hold strong in this moment, because it's taking all my willpower not to just grab him and kiss him. How is this going to work? Am I ever going to get a grip, even when I'm sure? "It's why I haven't killed him, Chloe. Because . . . I think if I'd found out you two were something more, I just might have tried."

I try not to breathe deeply, because good lords, does he smell good. So I hold still until he rights himself. But he knows. Of course he knows what he just did to me—and it wasn't because of his mojo. It was all him.

As I have far too many times in the past, I resent myself once more for being weak.

The screaming comes in bursts, like bullets out of a gun, exploding into the dense silence long enough to rattle snow off branches and dead leaves off trees before disappearing once more. And I nearly jump out of my skin, like I always do, because even now, even after everything that's happened lately, those sounds are some of the most terrifying I've ever heard.

I asked Kellan a little while earlier if he'd make it so I didn't feel any fear, but he refused, claiming fear was important in situations like this. Fear would help keep me alive. And yet, I wish I didn't have this fear in me right now, that I could just charge head first into the fight I'm picking today. But it's here, and I am scared, more so than I think before because now I know one of my Connections is with me and the stakes are all that much higher.

When the bursts of screams grow louder, Karl motions for the team to fan out. He, Will, and I will maintain the middle formation like before, with one exception—Kellan refused to stay on the edges to work like everyone else.

Karl didn't bother arguing with him. I tried to, but Kellan wasn't having any of it. So here he is, right in the line of fire, and my nervousness kicks up to a whole new level. "Still four?" Will asks Karl quietly.

Karl's quiet for a moment, a finger pressed against his earpiece before nodding.

A scream shoots at us from the near north. I pull an arrow out of my quiver. "Four's nothing, right?" I whisper to Will. "With this many on our team?"

He smiles easily. "Child's play."

"You should go back to the plane. Stay where it's safe."

"This shite again?" He clucks quietly. "I'm here, Chloe. Okay? I'm staying right where I am."

Kellan's hand on my arm sends such a strong shock through me, my knees nearly buckle. "Chloe," he murmurs, but my fingers go to his lips, stopping the words I want to say, too. Words I won't say, not even now.

The Elders attack simultaneously, surprising us with two extras that somehow eluded Lee. If I'd thought their forms were creepy before, they're beyond terrifying now. More humanoid than ever, with more developed weapons jutting from their limbs, these monsters are the epitome of boogeymen. Both Blazes instantly go on the offense, sending streaks of fire at the shape shifters, and Lola yanks lightning down from the sky while Flip twists thin tornadoes from the clouds to herd our prey, but the deft movements of these killers leave them unscathed.

I'm shooting arrows as fast as my fingers allow me. Kellan has one of the Elders cowering before him moments after it hurls itself at me. As Karl sets off another round of sonic booms and Will's sword flashes before shrieking nearly strips the trees bare, I launch myself at the Elder Kellan's got subdued. It swings its dagger like arm right at me, driving deep into my recently repaired shoulder, but I manage to will it out of existence fairly quickly.

Too quickly, because once more my chin hits the ground. When will I learn? Even still, I got this one down within a matter of minutes.

Kellan's immediately at my side, hauling me up and stripping the pain from my arm. There's no time to thank him, though, as another sonic boom nearly sends us sprawling. I scramble over toward the downed shape shifter; Karl bellows from nearby, "Five seconds, Chloe!" And five seconds is longer than I have, because the Elder rouses and immediately charges me. I fumble for my bow, but it's on me before I can slide the arrow out of the quiver. A pair of quick slashes to my right arm knocks my breath right out of my chest and my bow right out of my fingers. Dammit! I messed up the Elder-proof suits again! And then the Elder is squealing, twisting in agony as it writhes before me. I thank my lucky stars that Kellan is behind me, even as another sonic boom sounds. My hand slams down against the Elder, and within a split second, I'm once more diving toward the dirt.

Or not, because Kellan catches me this time right before I hit the ground. "Will's got one staked nearby," he tells me, and before I know it, we're darting across the clearing as fast as we can. Fire blazes in and out of our path as the four remaining Elders lead the team on a grim chase. Lightning strikes the ground fast and hard, but nobody other than Karl and Will are making sufficient enough contact to be useful.

Only Kellan has been able to get to them from a distance.

One of the Elders hits Will from behind, sending him sprawling. I yell at Kellan to cover Will as I collapse over the pinned shape shifter. It gnashes what looks like smoke fangs at me, and I recoil just long enough for it to stake my leg to the ground.

OH MY EFFING GODS DOES THIS HURT.

I slam my fist against its quasi-solid body, but the pain in me is so intense that I can't—I can't—

Stars dance before my eyes. I've lost the ability to breathe.

Worse yet, I think the screaming I'm hearing is coming from me.

And then Kellan is there, my face in his hands, as the Elder is swinging its free arm at him, and he's saying—he's saying—look at

228

him, I think. He wants me to look at him. Listen to him. And the pain, it subsides enough that the moment I see the monster below us make contact with his arm, I'm able to make it disappear.

Shrieking so ear piercing it leaves my ears bleeding surrounds us, and then the remaining Elders disappear.

"You're bleeding," I tell Kellan. My voice shakes just as hard as my limbs do.

He closes his eyes and drops his head against mine. "I'm going to make you sleep now, okay?" he whispers so quietly that surely nobody else can hear him, not when our ears are bleeding like they are. "You're going to sleep until I get you to the Shamans back at the plane."

I don't argue with him.

Chapter Twenty-Nine

Surprisingly, Zthane deems the mission a success even though I only managed to take out three Elders. The entire plane ride back, the team was fairly subdued. I think the Blazes and Elemental knew that they'd not even come close to helping contain our enemy. A non with a sword proved more effective, and that must've smarted, although nobody had the balls to say it out loud around us. Kellan was on edge the entire time, this time sitting on the other side of me rather than across. To make matters worse, Jonah called him not ten minutes before we landed in Novosibirsk.

I tried not to listen to the call. I really did. But it basically came down to Jonah knowing that Kellan was freaking out, and he wanted to know why and if it was about me. I guess Kellan had been pretty successful at blocking his brother for the most part of the mission, but when I was pinned to the ground and nearly killed (or so Will said, when claiming the Elder's other sword-arm came perilously close to going straight through the top of my skull before Kellan subdued it), he lost any control he had over shielding the situation from Jonah. So I got to listen to Kellan argue with Jonah about why he was blocking his memories, thanks to the promise Karl extracted earlier, and then flat out lie, claiming it had nothing to do with me.

Relief had nearly melted me straight to the floor of the plane. Jonah was worried—Jonah was calling! Angry as he is, hurt as he is, after everything I've done . . . it was a good sign, right?

I tried to hold onto this during the debriefing back in Annar, even when my eyes threatened to shut me out of coherent conversation. Even after having the thrill of seeing my good friend Etienne Miscanthus again, who came to help share Elders histories with Zthane. It was a success, the head of the Guard kept saying to all of us. The Council can't know yet (outside of the members in this room, he clarified). The Council will never sanction having their Creator go out and repeatedly get cut up, risking her life. Kellan argued the validity of this point, sounding much like his brother, but in the end, Karl and I overrode him, siding with Zthane, and agreed to meet in a few days to set up the next round.

"It's good to see you, peacock," Etienne murmurs when he hugs me goodbye. "Let's have tea soon?"

I tighten my arms around him. I've missed him. "Of course. Tell Mac he must come, too."

Etienne pulls away, his hand going to my cheek. "We wouldn't have it any other way. See you soon, pumpernickel." And then he goes over to where Zthane is so they can discuss the situation further.

"I should get you home," Will's saying as we exit through the HQ doors. "Dad's probably out of his mind with worry. At least this time, he won't have to worry about patching us up."

I laugh, but Kellan doesn't find this humorous at all.

I'm just about to do something incredibly stupid, like ask him to come back and maybe have dinner with us because I can't resist him and the feelings I have for him one second longer, when Sophie Greenfield materializes. And I stand there, shock coursing through every vein, every nerve when she leans forward and presses a kiss against Kellan's cheek.

Is it my imagination that he flinches when her lips touch his skin? That his entire body shrinks away from hers in visible disgust? Or is that wishful thinking?

"There you are!" she says, and I swear, an ugly sense of triumph

is what curves her mouth and softens her voice. "I was hoping you'd
be free for dinner."

Before Kellan can say anything, she turns to me and Will.
"Look who's crawled back to Annar. And is this the non that
everyone's talking about? The one you dumped Jonah for?"

"Who the fuck is this?" Will practically barks at Kellan.

But me, I don't even know what to say. Think. So I do the only
thing I can do in this excruciatingly awkward, torturous moment—I
turn around and walk away without another word. Kellan's voice,
raised and angry, fills the background, but I close my ears to the
particulars.

It's none of my business, I tell myself with every step. He's free
to do whatever he likes with whomever. And then—I need to get the
hell out of here before I fall entirely apart.

I resent that thought, resent that even after everything I've gone
through, everything I've decided, Fate still shows how it can screw
with me by manipulating my heart this way.

"Who was that?" Will asks, jogging the last few steps to catch
up with me.

"Sophie," I say tersely, because anything else would be too
much.

"You realize that helps me in no way."

I focus on the sidewalk in front of me.

He sighs, knowing I won't—or perhaps can't—elaborate any
further. "Well, whoever she is, she just got her ass ripped off and
handed to her by your boy there. It was rather embarrassing for her,
although I'm not sure it fazed her one bit."

I smash the fierce pleasure that comes with this back into the
box it came from.

"Chloe, wait." It's Kellan's turn to jog to where we are. He
reaches out to grab my arm, but I deftly move it away from his hand.
There is no good in our touching in this moment. None at all. Not if
I'm going to stay strong in the moment and do the right thing for
both of us. But if he can't get through to me physically, he plants

himself in front of me and attempts to stop me with his words. "Please—just . . . let me explain."

I force a bright smile upon my face as I finally stop. "There's no need for an explanation." Because there isn't, I tell myself, even though it hurts like hell knowing it to be true.

It's Will's cue to dismiss himself, telling me, "I'll meet you at home, yeah?"

Before Kellan can say anything further, I dig deep and cut him off at the pass. "Look. If you haven't forgotten, I abandoned you—I abandoned everyone. I left Annar and moved away for over half a year. It is completely reasonable that during that time period, you . . ." I force myself to say it, even though it's shards of glass coming up through my throat, "That you would do whatever you like, with whomever you like, including Sophie."

All of his panic transitions to fury. "There is *nothing* between me and Sophie, Chloe."

Two fists reach inside my chest and grip my lungs so hard I can barely get out, "The point is still the same, Kellan."

"Why, hello," his heart says to my dagger that slides so easily into it. "Fancy meeting you here."

I can't escape his touch now as he angles us to a nearby alcove. Oh, gods . . . tingles zip up and down my spine, my arms, my chest, my legs—everywhere, everywhere, and it's like a drug, and I have to yank my arm away lest I relapse in ways I may never recover from. "Why are you doing this?"

To let you go, I think, even though it breaks my own heart into tiny pieces. And the thing is, Kellan Whitecomb—not so much his actions, but what he means to me, how I feel about him—has always had the ability to render me senseless. I can't let this be how it is anymore. No matter what, I need to get a grip and act fairly.

Even still, this moment here hurts more than I can articulate, but I need to do it. He's nobody's second best. Not even mine. He's too wonderful for that.

And because I'm not hiding anything from him, he must feel

this, since he snaps, "Fine. You can think you're being noble,"—
ouch—"or self-sacrificing or whatever the hell you think you're
doing, but I *know* you. And I need you to understand right now that .
. . yes, while you were gone, I found ways to deal with the pain of
your loss." He steps closer to me, viciously twisting the leather band
around his wrist. "Gods. She's relentless. Whatever happened with
her, I regret that more than anything. There is nothing between her
and me, no matter what she thinks. Nothing. She's—you can ask
Jonah. She's . . . unbalanced."

I'm not surprised to hear he's slept with other women during my
absence. It's an agony I'm quite familiar with. But the one that hits
me out of left field, the one that has me leaning back against the
wall, is the thought that maybe Jonah did the same.

And Kellan must know I'm feeling this way because the hurt in
his eyes nearly sends me back to Alaska.

I whisper words so familiar to the both of us, words that have
defined way too much of our relationship together. I tell him I'm
sorry.

He walks me home in silence. I do not offer to have him stay for
dinner.

Chapter Thirty

In the last week, other than talking to Zthane and key members of the Guard, as well as the surprisingly sympathetic pair of Etienne and Mac over tea, I have yet to answer for my actions over the last half-year. A brief phone call from Astrid informed me that the Council is well aware of my return and that they've been in contact with the Guard concerning the debriefing I gave upon re-entry. Apparently Karl wasn't kidding when he said that Zthane was claiming I'd been on a top-secret Elders recon mission in Alaska. So, during one of our daily meetings at Guard HQ, I confront Zthane about this.

"I'm not afraid to take responsibility for my actions," I tell him, even though it's a lie, because of course I'm scared. I'm tired of living in fear, though, tired of always worrying about making the wrong step. If I have to take the hit because I did something wrong, so be it. "And, honestly, it will be all the worse if you're caught lying about what I've done. The Council—"

"Knows the truth already." Zthane sighs deeply and leans back in his chair, his fingers tented in front of him. When my eyebrows lift up, he clarifies, "Well, certain people within the Council know—those specifically on the Elders Subcommittee." His dark eyes flick over to where both Karl and Kellan are sitting. "There was a meeting two nights ago to discuss some of the more relevant aspects of the situation."

Huh. Mac mentioned this Subcommittee at tea yesterday, saying he was part of it. But he never mentioned anything else, including that he'd been discussing my case with his—our—peers.

Giuliana comes into the room, setting a tray of coffee down on the conference table before handing Zthane a dossier.

I wait until the Elemental's seated to ask, "Meaning?"

He pops off the lid to his coffee and pours in a pack of sugar. "Meaning I told them about you and Dane's escapades in Anchorage, and of the contact you made with the Métis colony. The Subcommittee was quite interested in these aspects and wishes to explore them further." He recaps the coffee. "Punishing you for the foibles of youth or the whatnot will only distract the Council from the issues at hand. And Chloe, this is not the time for that."

I find myself laughing at that. Is this the equivalent of a hand smacking? "*Foibles of youth? Is that what we're calling it?*"

"Is there another term for it?" He re-tents his fingers, the tips pressing up against his lips. "Frankly, you are not the first Magical to do what you've done, and most certainly will not be the last."

I nearly choke on my own coffee. "Excuse me?"

"Do you think you are the first of our kind to run screaming for the hills? Or, for that matter, the first Creator?" His smile is tight. "While not every Creator has done so, it's not an entirely uncommon occurrence. Despite what you think, the Council and Guard are keenly aware of the pressures you are under concerning your craft, not to mention your—and I say this with all the love in my heart—age and lack of experience."

I pretty much only blink at him in return.

"Please do not feel as if I'm excusing your actions," he says, voice cool in the warm afternoon. "Nor are you free to take this as the Guard or Subcommittee I reported to as giving you a free pass, but it will serve all of our purposes far better if we focus on the tasks at hand. That, my dear, is to deal with the Elders, as well as form diplomatic ties with the Métis. I believe you are currently residing with several representatives of the Anchorage colony."

I can't help but look over at Karl. He's got his poker face on, as does Kellan, who I've found out, is now in the upper echelon of Guard management.

I turn back toward Zthane. "What kind of diplomatic ties?"

His smile loosens just a tiny bit. "The kind that will begin the long road to recovery between our populations."

Will cracks my bedroom door open. "You decent?"

I shut the file that Zthane sent home with me. "What's up?"

He leans against the doorframe and says quietly, "Your mother is here to see you."

I sit up on the bed and stare at him, slack jawed. Surely he didn't just say that my mother was here. My mother told me nearly a year ago that she was siding with my father, that there was to be no more contact between us until I relented and got Jonah to lift the ban he placed on Jens Belladonna. Since I'd rather cut off my legs at the kneecaps than do such a thing, radio silence had filled the space between us.

I clear my throat. "Astrid?"

Will frowns. "You mean Dad's phone buddy? I'm afraid not. This woman introduced herself as Abigail Lilywhite." He shuts the door behind him and joins me on the bed. "She's sitting out there with Dad right now, but if you want me to tell her to go to hell, I'll be glad to do so. But . . . I've got to be honest with you—she looks really nervous and a wee bit glum. It's up to you, though. Tell me what you want, and I'll make it happen."

My mother is here.

I have no idea how she got here, how she even knew where I was staying, but my mother—Abigail Lilywhite—is here.

My knees wobble when I stand up. "No. I'll . . . I'll go talk to her. It's not your problem."

He lays a hand on my shoulder; it's steady and warm and oh-sobrotherly. "Do you want me and Dad to stay out there with you guys? I'd offer up Erik, too, but he's down at Guard HQ talking with Zthane. Official Métis business now and all."

I tell him no, that I need to do this on my own. But this only has Will reminding me that they'll be here for me in any way I need them.

My heart kind of grows twenty sizes in this moment.

Sitting on the edge of the couch in the living room, holding a cup of tea and petting my dog, is my mother. She looks exactly as I remember her—beautiful and tall, her face devoid of most expressive emotions. When I come into the room, though, she sets the cup down and slowly stands up. Cameron, who's been sitting across from her, does the same.

"Hello, Chloe," my mother says.

All the moisture in my mouth miraculously disappears. "Mom," I croak in return.

Cameron quietly tells my mother it was nice to meet her and excuses himself; on his way out of the room, he pulls me in for a quick hug and kiss, whispering words his son told me just minutes before. And then I'm alone with my mother for the first time in nearly a year.

"You look thin," she says, and it's enough to make me want to laugh bitterly, because it's what she said during our last meeting, too.

I uproot my feet and somehow make it across the room to sit down in the space previously occupied by Cameron. She sits down, too, and we let the familiar silence that has defined our relationship for so long fill the space between us.

I can't take it, though. Not after everything that's happened. I break first. "What are you doing here?"

Her eyes do not stray from the cup of tea she's reclaimed. "Is it really that surprising that I would want to come and see if my daughter, who has been missing for half a year, is okay?"

I think prior to today, I might have accepted this comment from her. Built up hope to go with it. I might have let it slide by without much argument. But that girl . . . I left that girl behind. "Actually, yes, considering you and Dad basically disowned me."

She winces, and it's enough to startle me back into my chair. "Chloe . . ." She lets out a long, melancholy sigh and sets the cup back down, untouched. "Hindsight is always twenty-twenty. I know it will not mean much to you, but if I could go back and relive that day, I might do it differently."

My unattractive gaping lets her know just how I feel about the sincerity of such a statement.

She fingers the edge of her blazer as she coolly regards me. "Your hair is different. It's . . . I think I preferred the brown. This blonde is too brittle for someone like you."

"Seriously? That's what you have to say to me? Just—*oh, my bad for treating you, my only daughter, like crap, and by the way your hair sucks*?"

"Rome wasn't built in a day," she practically whispers. And it hits me, really hits me, that my mother is sitting in this living room with me and my father is not. My mother, my cold fish of a mother, just actually admitted she'd made a mistake. What did I do in return?

I acted like a bratty child.

"I'm sorry," I tell her. "That was unfair of me."

She sucks in a breath and shakes her head before letting it out. "You and I . . ." A wan smile fills out her thin lips. "We are not good at communicating with one another. We never have been. It will take some time to learn how to do it."

Is she . . . is she saying what I think she's saying?

"These people you're living with—these nons—"

I stop this nonsense immediately. "Cameron was married to Molliaria Hellebore; thus, Will is a Métis. No matter what they are or aren't, I won't stand for you saying anything bad about them."

Her smile tightens. "I was not disparaging them. I was merely saying that I'm glad you are somewhere with people who seem to have your best interest at heart."

Oh. My. Gods. Am I asleep? Is this really happening?

"I will admit I know very little about the situation, but from the small discussion I had with Cameron, his affections toward you were obvious. The same with . . . Will, you said?"

"I love them," I tell her. "They took me in and loved me and accepted me." My voice shakes. "Cameron Dane has been more of a father to me than Noel Lilywhite ever has."

I can't tell if this hurts her or not, as she merely nods her head in acquiescence.

It hurt to even ask, but I do it anyway. "Where is Dad?"

"He chose not to come today. He is . . ." She sighs again and smoothes imaginary wrinkles on her slacks. "Your father is who he is. That said, he is aware of where I am. He is also aware that, if he does not approve of my actions and choices, that is his choice, not mine."

My mouth drops open.

"I never had the warmest of relationships with my own mother. It is very probable that I do not have it in me to ever be the mother that you want. But . . ." She leans forward, the ice in her green eyes softening, if even just a teeny fraction. "But I would like the chance to see if I ever could be. I have squandered too many years being selfish rather than being a mother. You're twenty years old; I can never reclaim that time. I can only ask that, from this moment forth, you give me a chance to try to get to know you, and for you to get to know me. It should never take a mother nearly losing her child to make her realize just how precious that person is to them."

I pull my hair back and study her. Really study her. She seems . . . sincere.

Rome wasn't built in a day.

I blink tears that threaten to overwhelm me back. "No promises."

She lets hers fall—just a few, but it's enough to crack the ice around my heart. "That's good enough for me."

When she leaves a quarter of an hour later, we hug. It's

awkward as all hell and short, but it's a hug. And then I ask her a question that's been on my mind since I first found out she was sitting in my living room. I ask her how she knew where I was.

She grips the doorknobs, twisting it open. "Jonah told me when I called him inquiring about you, but only after he let me know what he thought of me as a parent."

Had she reached in and plucked out my heart, I don't think I could have been more stunned.

In the next few seconds, she and her surprises are gone in a swish of perfume. I lean back against the door, attempting to piece together what just happened. As confused as I am, as much as my heart aches, I know one thing to be true.

My mother just laid down the first brick in what I can only hope will be our foundation.

Chapter Thirty-One

The sun is bright and warm this morning as I relax on the wide patio outside of the Dane's apartment with Nell at my feet, and I have to admit, after months of living where cold, snow, and darkness were the norm, it's a welcome change. I lean my face back and let the warmth seep over my skin.

I've just tried calling Cora for what seems to be the tenth time since coming back to Annar, only to reach her voicemail. My path to reaching out to my friends has been riddled with roadblocks, although I've talked to a few of them by phone so far. Lizzie and Graham are currently on a break; she claims that the physical distance between them has begun to take its toll on their relationship. Meg and Alex got a dog, or—as she called it—a starter baby. He seemed annoyed by the whole thing, which I could totally get because Meg apparently dresses the dog up in clothes. But as nice as these conversations have been so far, the distance between all of us—once so close—has grown. And I'm fully aware that's on me.

"You remind me of a cat we had when I was little, one who liked to lay in front of windows and doors so it could soak up the rays."

I open my eyes and find Callie standing in the doorway. I can't hide my smile; it's good to see her. "At least you didn't liken me to a lizard on a rock or something."

She sits down in the chair across from me and passes over a shopping bag. But I'm not interested in what she's brought me to wear; I'm more interested in my friend and how, despite the months in between the last time we hung out, it feels like time has barely moved at all.

At least this relationship has not deteriorated for the worse.

"Cal—"

"You know," she says, as if I haven't spoken at all, "Annar in the spring is really beautiful. Don't you think?"

I know she doesn't want to talk about spring, though. "I missed you," I tell her.

She leans back in the chair and studies me, her green eyes narrowing. Nell trots over and licks her hand. "Good gods, girl. Why is it still this trashy blonde?"

"I guess I haven't gotten around to finding a good hair stylist to do it." I tug on the ends, now scraping my shoulders. "I didn't want to risk doing a poor job at home. Any recommendations?"

She pulls out her phone. "Is today too early?"

I can't help but laugh. So many things have changed, but not Callie Lotus—and for that I am so grateful. I sit back as she calls in a favor to get me into her hair stylist.

When she's done, she shoves her phone back into her purse before leaning back in the chair. "What you did was really shitty, Chloe."

I totally deserve that.

She drums her fingers across her stomach. "I mean—you bailed on me that day. Left me to the wolves when I couldn't produce you afterward. So, I'm kind of torn here. Part of me wants to kick your ass for what you put us all through, and the other just wants to hug you because I've been worried as all hell."

I think I already know, but I ask anyways. "Wolves?"

"What do you know so far of what went down once you left?"

I scrub my face. Gods. Facing up to one's actions is no easy task. "I have bits and pieces. Mind filling me in?"

As she has done in the past, Callie doesn't soft shoe around the bitter truth. She tells me how, once Jonah came home and found my purse and phone left behind, he immediately called her. And then, when she couldn't produce me, he called Kellan and from there, they went to every single one of their houses to search for me. Days went by, no news came, and the Guard became involved. Jonah proceeded to tear apart my apartment, and when he found my ring, the shit truly hit the fan. People were scared that I'd been attacked by the Elders, but she says that Jonah and Kellan always knew differently. From the moment he found my ring, Callie says Jonah knew what I'd done.

My heart breaks when I hear her tell me, in a clinical voice, of how he desperately tried to hold it together for work. That Astrid constantly worried about him, how she tried to get him to move in with her but he balked, claimed he didn't want to inconvenience anyone any further than he already had. Of how they finally convinced the twins to at least move in together, since Kellan was having a hard time, too—although, according to Callie, it wasn't as intense as what Jonah was going through because Kellan already knew what it was like to live without his Connection.

She steps on the pieces of my heart so freshly cracked and grinds them into dust below me when she tells me how Jonah basically slid into some kind of robo-mode and threw himself into work. She tried to talk to him about it, Astrid, too—even Kellan, but two months into my absence, he simply stopped talking about me in any capacity other than directives toward the Guard's search to find me.

As for Kellan—Kellan did what Kellan has always done when dealing with his pain.

When she's done, I tell her, "I love him."

Her eyebrows lift up.

"Jonah, I mean." I'm well aware my smile is brittle, and that I'm declaring this to another person who lost their heart to him at a young age, one that even today may still feel that way. "I realized it in Alaska. Realized . . . no matter what I feel for Kellan—who I still and always will love desperately, make no mistake about that—it's nothing compared to the need I have for Jonah. My life is crazy, and I know it sounds weird, but he's been the only true consistency my entire life. He's my rock when everything else is upside down . . . and . . . I love him, Cal. I came home, ready to tell him that, but now he wants nothing to do with me." I lean my head back against the couch and stare up into the puffy white clouds in a pale blue sky. "Which, in a way, is exactly what I deserve after what I've done."

I hear rather than see her sigh.

Tentatively, hopefully—"How is he now? Do you know?"

"The same. A work-a-holic. He's on the Elders Subcommittee, you know."

My head snaps forward so I can stare at her. I really should get a roster of the damn committee already.

She rolls her eyes. "Yes, it means what you think it means. Obviously, he's completely aware of everything that went down in Alaska and Russia now that Zthane finally spilled the beans. And before you ask how I know, obviously my mom is on the Subcommittee, too."

My whispered question about whether or not there's still hope barely voices against the sounds of the city behind us.

"Here's my two cents on the issue—which ought to come with a disclaimer, since he's not actually speaking to me about you or anything. But . . . you threw J for a loop, Chloe. Big time. He's had a lot of loss in his life, what with his mom and Uncle Joey—even, to some extent, Hannah; it's in his nature to withdraw into himself, especially since his father was always on him and Kel to not embarrass the family by acting overemotional." She grimaces and adds, "*Unprofessional*. Can you believe it?" She shakes her head. "But let's not talk about Ewan Whitecomb and his idiotic notions on how his children ought to act. We're talking about how he lost his mom and then Joey, two of the most important people in his life, and how he lost *you*, only to have you come back looking like a whole different person. I honestly don't think J knows how to deal with it. Not like Kel, anyway, who's long learned how to deal with life without you. Jonah's hurting right now. I mean—it's obvious to us all he's thinking about you, and trying in his own way to . . . I don't know . . . *help* you via the Subcommittee the best he can, but . . ." She leans forward. "You need to give him some time."

Dammit. I've started to cry. Gods, I've made such a mess of everything.

"What's going on out here?"

Will's standing in the open French doors, holding an open cardboard box. Nell jumps up in an effort to get to the box.

I wipe my eyes. "Nothing. Just . . ." I quickly glance at Callie, who is staring at Will. Like . . . really staring, and I can't tell if it's because she's annoyed he's here, fascinated with him, disgusted he's carrying food, or finds him extremely hot. "A reality check, I guess." I motion toward Callie. "You remember Callie Lotus?"

"How could I forget," he says flatly, dropping the box on the glass table in front of me. He gently pushes his dog away from the table. "Adopted daughter of my Godmother, biological offspring of my Godfather," he waves a hand between them, "fellow Métis, etc . . . etc . . ."

Callie's frown deepens, but her eyes do not leave him.

He sinks down on the couch next to me and drags the box closer. "Do you know how long it took me to find this bloody hot dog cart of yours? And then how long I had to wait in line to buy these things?"

I press a hand lovingly against his cheek—bless this boy for both the hot dogs and for trying to change the subject to something less painful—and then reach for one of my special treats. Good lords, have I missed the Gnomish hot dog cart by the entrance to Annar's central plaza. "Thank you for braving the big city for me."

"Here to steal more of my tequila?" he says to Callie.

She's sucking on a lemon when she says, "As a matter of fact, I'm here to invite you all to dinner Friday night. Mom thinks it would be . . ."—she goes to roll her eyes, but thinks better of it—"a good idea to reacquaint"—her face pinches even tighter—"herself with you and your father, although I have no idea why." She flips the end of her long, silvery ponytail up to inspect non-existent split ends. "And of course, see you, Chloe. Mom's missed you, too."

"Reacquainted," Will snorts. "You do know that they've been chatting on the phone together, right? I think Dad even went and had lunch with your mum one day."

Callie and Will stare at each other so long and hard I actually start feeling uncomfortable. I slowly unwrap one of the hot dogs. "Is this like one of your family dinners?"

All the weirdness (hostility? I still can't tell) she'd just shown Will melts into pity. "If you're asking if J will be there, then no. He's off on a mission to South Africa in the morning. Kel will be, though. He'll be coming back from Oklahoma City just in time."

I remember how desperate I used to be to spend time with Kellan, how, if I'm being honest with myself, I still am, but right now? I'd give anything and everything to even have five minutes alone with Jonah. Or, hell, even just be in the same room as him.

It would be so easy right now to just give in to the Connection I have with Kellan. Just . . . embrace the love I feel for him and see what we would be like together. But the more I've thought about it over the last few days, and despite the temptation it truly taunts me with, the more I know it wouldn't be right. Because, even if Kellan and I were together, I'd be thinking about Jonah. Worrying about him. Loving him. Wanting him. Needing him.

And as mercenary as it sounds, that's the key. I love them both, but I need—*want*—Jonah in my life more.

As much as it terrifies me, I know it's time Kellan and I finally have a talk.

Chapter Thirty-Two

Kellan murmurs, "You fixed your hair," but he's not looking at me. He's staring out at the gorgeous vista in front of us, a magnificent city skyline blending into a pink and orange sherbet horizon.

I slide my legs in between the railing and sit down, leaving a good two feet in between us. I'm dangling next to him on the thin, bronze strip separating empty space and the top of the Dane's apartment building, wondering how in the hell I got to this place. How it all came to this.

How I can even make it through the next five minutes, let alone day, week, month, or the rest of my life.

I lean my arms against the ornate railing and drop my chin on them. "It almost feels like we're floating up here."

He doesn't say anything, just keeps staring out at the beauty in front of us. Karnach at sunset is one of the worlds' most awe-inspiring sights—the quartz in the marble glints and flashes golden and pink in the blazing light, making it glow.

I want to scoot closer, revel in the comfort and warmth of his perfect body against mine. But falling into old habits does neither of us any good. "Kellan . . ."

"You don't need to tell me," he says quietly. "I already feel it in you." He finally turns to face me. "I felt it the very moment I saw you after you got back from Alaska. Gods. The overwhelming love that consumed you the moment you saw my brother—it was like a tsunami." He sighs into the void below us. "You've always gone back to him, you know. No matter what you've ever felt for me, no matter what we've done, it's always been Jonah for you." His bitter laugh is barely voiced. "I guess I always hoped that somehow, someway . . . maybe it would change. I even thought . . . when we were in Hawaii, it had changed. If anything, what you feel for him has only intensified, even though you fear you've lost him for good."

I bite my lip and study him. He looks so tired, so . . . resigned. So heartbroken that my own heart crumbles right along with his.

"I love you," I tell him, letting him feel the truth of how that love permeates every cell in my body. "That will never change."

A sad, quiet sigh escapes his beautiful lips. "Just not enough."

I don't know if I can do this. How I can even contemplate hurting him—hurting me—like this. But all night, all day, all I could think of was how this was better than dragging along the pain until it defined us, tainted everything we feel for one another. I'll never be able to let go of him. Fate won't let me. But I can choose right now to do everything I can to begin the long road home toward hope. "Kellan. You know that's not true. I tore apart my life because I love you so much." I close my eyes and mentally curse myself. "That came out wrong. You certainly had nothing to do with my actions this year. I and I alone chose to do what I did. What I meant was, my feelings for you are so strong, so . . . powerful, that I found myself doubting all the decisions I'd made for myself—at least, the ones concerning *this*." I press my fist against my heart.

His forehead drops against the railing, his eyes drifting toward the people filling the streets below—people going about their daily lives, blissfully unaware that above them two people are breaking their hearts apart.

"I wish I could be the girl you deserve," I tell him as those pieces surge up into my throat, threatening to strangle me. "Gods, I wish that so very much, because you are . . . ." I nearly choke as I say this, desperate to keep myself from shattering. How does a person let go of a future with somebody critical to his or her existence? How do they survive? "You are one of most important people to me in all the worlds. I am so blessed that I have gotten to know you, love you . . . be loved by you . . . It's a gift. One of the best gifts I could ever receive."

He lets out a shuddery breath; my own collapses inside me.

I lean my head against the railing and watch him, silent tremors wracking my body. So much of me is screaming that I'm making a mistake, that I should tell him I was wrong, to forgive me, hold me. Kiss me. Make love to me. I'm terrified of losing him, beyond scared of what giving him up like this might mean to the both of us. But I can't let Fate dictate this moment. I can't let this Connection between us be what defines our relationship.

He deserves better. So very much better.

The lovely half smile of his that I love appears after I doubt myself for the ninetieth time in less than five minutes, even if just slightly. "You and I never would've worked in the long run, you know. We're too alike."

A gurgly laugh escapes me. *"What?"*

His voice, as light as he's trying to make it, shakes just as much as mine. "We're all adrenaline, Chloe. It'd be all raging and fighting and hot make-up sex."

He's lying. Well, not about the hot sex, which I'm pretty sure would be spot-on since so many of our make-out sessions were nuclear, but definitely about the fighting. When we dated in high school, we were a dream together. In Costa Rica? The same. He and I are ridiculously compatible. But I play his game. "Plus, we'd always be chasing after one another. I don't know if you notice or not, but we both have a tendency to run away from our problems."

Another soft laugh escapes him, because he knows I'm right. "It's a problem for the both of us, isn't it? We'd have to put preemptive tracking devices on one another in case of an argument or misunderstanding."

This is probably the most gut-wrenching thing I've ever had to do. So much sadness twists through me, compounding the urge to double over and gasp, yet it's not a new feeling. I've felt this way over Kellan too many times in the past. No doubt I'll feel it countless times in the future. But the difference is this time, as I sit next to him while the sun slips behind Karnach, I finally know what it is I want.

Like he knows I worry he's going to stand up and leave and never look back, Kellan holds out his hand and I take it, watching his long fingers curve around mine before a gentle kiss brushes my knuckles. Lovely, delicious tingles sparkle through my body. What if this is the last time we touch? Hold hands? Can I—even as sure as I am—ever live without this again? Do I really even want to? "Except, I'm done running. I'm not going anywhere this time."

"Me either," I whisper. And I mean it.

"Good." A gentle squeeze, and then we are no longer touching; I've begun my mourning in earnest now. "You asked me once, a long time ago, to promise you that we would be something important to one another. I'm finally ready to make that promise to you."

I know my smile is bittersweet and more than a wee bit teary. He's giving me another gift right now, one I don't know if I deserve. But because I love him so very much, and because, at heart, I will always be selfish when it comes to him, I gratefully take what he offers.

Because I will gladly take anything he has to offer me if it means I still get to have him in my life.

"I promise that I will always be here for you when you need me. I promise to be your friend, your confidant, and the person you can always count on. I promise you that you have my heart and my loyalty. I promise you that you will always have my love." He leans his face against his arms, head tilted toward me, and I swear, his smile is just as bittersweet as my own.

There's a fist in my chest, and it's squeezing the crap out of my heart. Because I love him. I do. I love him so much, it's ridiculous. He is an amazing person, so smart and warm and loving, and anybody, *anybody*, would be lucky to call him friend, let alone lover. To let him go tears me apart. I doubt I'll ever get over it. I know I'll never get over him. But it's not fair, keeping him and me in limbo when I finally know that it's Jonah who I want and need. In a way, Kellan was right. He and I have been intensity personified this last year and a half, tortured by high highs and low lows. He's all about the rush—whether it be sweeping me off my feet or jumping out of a helicopter. And it's not all because of me. That's just who Kellan Whitecomb is. He's a risk taker. And that's all well and good, but what with the stress of being a Creator with crappy parents who have written her off, I need—no, crave my feet firmly on the ground, at least most of the time, anyway. Even still, if he'd told me we could never see one another again, I don't know what I would've done. So I tell him, since saying anything more would just exacerbate the constriction against my heart, "Ditto."

Because to promise him anything less would be a lie.

Chapter Thirty-Three

"I see you're back to your natural color."

I look up from the peaches I've been examining to find Sophie Greenfield leaning against a nearby table. Will and I are at Annar's farmers market buying food for tonight's dinner at the Lotus'. Initially, it had been suggested we go out to a restaurant, but once everyone took a moment to remember what happened the last time we were all together, we compromised and decided to eat at Astrid's. That said, Will was pretty forthright about wanting to cook for everyone, even if it wasn't his own kitchen.

So here we are, buying fruit and veggies, and I'm confronted by what appears to be a pissed off ex-girlfriend of Kellan's.

I slip a pair of peaches in a bag. "Thanks."

"It wasn't a compliment." She takes a few steps closer, her dark sunglasses glinting in the late morning sunlight. "We need to talk."

Yeah, that's not going to happen. Of everybody in Annar I need to talk to, Sophie Greenfield is not even on the list. I may be in the middle of the painful process of letting any future I have with Kellan go, but I'll be damned if I ever play nice with this woman. I add the bag of fruit to my basket. "Look, Sophie—I don't know what it is you want, but I'm on a pretty tight schedule here—"

"What I want is for you to go right back to the Transit Station and re-lose yourself."

I blink at her from behind my own sunglasses, taken aback by the sheer vehemence radiating from her.

"Don't think that just because you've been gone, I've forgotten what you've done."

Is she for real? I glance around, wondering if I'm somehow dreaming, because surely she's not still . . . I don't know, angry or resentful for whatever happened between her and Kellan nearly a year ago. Can she? "Actually," I tell her, "I haven't thought about you at all and will continue to not do so."

She flips her gorgeous red hair over her shoulders so it cascades down her lithe back. "I don't know what it is about you that seems to turn Kellan into an idiot, but just know I'm not going to be putting up with it anymore. He and I have worked hard to rebuild our relationship."

Anger and confusion root me to the spot I'm standing in.

"I can't believe I was able to find everything on the list," Will says, reappearing from wherever he took off to five minutes before. He shakes his basket. "And then some." It's then he notices Sophie; there's no doubt he recognizes her from earlier in the week, since the Muse is such a siren it'd take amnesia to forget such a face. A glance is thrown between us ladies. "Right, then. We need to get moving; no time for crazies. I've got a sauce to whip up."

Let me count all the ways I love Will, starting with this one.

Sophie draws in a sharp breath. I nearly laugh, because, outside of the twins, it's rare for any man to not immediately fall to his knees in obsession. "Excuse me?"

But then, Will probably matches her in terms of physical attractiveness, so he's used to ignoring irrational ogling with the best of them. "That's funny. I'm quite sure I was clear in words and meaning."

Her glasses are shoved to the top of her head; blue eyes blaze in return. "You don't know the first thing about me."

"Actually, I believe I know more than I'd ever like to."

Interesting. Will isn't lying when he says this, but as I wasn't the one to spill the beans on our shared sordid past, does this mean he talked to Kellan about it? I know they've become friendly with one another lately; it's almost humorous that Kellan would talk to Will about his dating problems.

By the looks of it, I'd say Sophie wants to tear Will's head clean off and throw it as far as she can after this comment.

Which doesn't faze Will in the least. "Are you ready?" he asks me.

I nod, but as we approach the cashier, I turn back to Sophie. "I know it doesn't mean much, coming from me, but maybe it's time to move on."

She turns on her heels and leaves; even in anger, she appears as if she's gliding.

"She's a wee bit terrifying, isn't she?" Will asks as we pay for our food.

Yes, but not necessarily for why he thinks. She's terrifying because her anger today was tenfold to what it was after her breakup with Kellan, when it ought to have finally diminished into acceptance and regret.

And that understanding leaves me uneasy, to say the least.

Astrid's expansive kitchen is a dream come true to Will. As Cameron and Astrid awkwardly, yet adorably catch up in the sitting room, drinking a wine that Callie sourly admitted came out of Astrid's special, private reserve, I hang out with Will, helping him prep dinner.

"I thought you worked in a diner."

Will looks up from his pot, frowning at Callie's comment. "So?"

My friend looks gorgeous tonight, wearing a silky silver dress that matches her hair yet leaves her appearing out of place in the kitchen. "I guess I'm surprised that you're not making . . . I don't know. Diner food."

What surely must be a sharp retort is cut off by Will's cell phone going off. It's Becca's special ringtone; I watch the muscles of his shoulders tighten, almost like somebody slapped a whip against his back.

I think Callie sees this, too, because her eyes widen in confusion.

But then Will pulls out his phone and sends the call straight to voicemail. "Sorry to disappoint you, princess. Were you hoping for diner fare, then?"

Callie leans against the counter, sighing loudly through her nose. Will shoots me a pointed look from where he's sautéing onions.

As he's done for me in the past, I change the subject. "I still can't believe that Cameron and Astrid used to date each other."

And . . . maybe that wasn't the topic to choose, because Callie practically snarls, "What I can't believe is how they're out there sitting on the couch next to each other. It's gross."

Will rolls his eyes and says flatly, "The bloody nerve, sitting on a couch together. Jesus. What's this world coming to?"

Callie comes closer to where he's standing by the stove. "You think this is a joke."

He sets the wooden spoon in a cradle nearby. "Not at all. First of all, I don't see what the big deal about two adults sitting on a couch together is. If you and I sat on a couch together, would that mean we were . . . shagging? That's what you're insinuating, isn't it?"

For the first time in my presence, cool-as-a-cucumber Callie Lotus flushes bright red.

"Unless this is a Magical custom that I am yet unfamiliar with. Chloe?" I start when Will says my name. "Have you forgotten to fill me in on this? All these times we've ever sat together somewhere, were you secretly planning on us shagging? Because if that's the case, I apologize for leaving you unfulfilled."

It's completely unattractive, but I let out a cross between a snort and a laugh.

"You know that's not what I meant. It's just . . . ." She pushes stray hairs off her cheek. "They're acting happy about all of this."

The nod Will gives is facetious at best. "Ah. Now I see what you're getting at. You're upset that your esteemed, blueblood of a Magical mother is friends with a peasant like my non of a father."

I didn't think it was possible, but Callie's even more red now. "That is not what I meant, either!" She grits her teeth. "Especially since my biological mother was a non, too."

He dumps a small bowl of crushed garlic into the pan. "I know it seems like a antiquated, bizarre idea and all, but I like the idea of my father being happy. If catching up with your mum happens to make him so, then I don't see what the problem is."

This surprises Callie. "They used to *date*." Her palm presses flat against the counter, propping her up. "I would have thought, of anybody here tonight, you would understand this."

A small smile tugs at his lips.

She switches her attention to me. "Chloe. Explain this to him."

Yeah, right. "No thank you," I tell her sweetly.

"Let me explain something to you, then, Callie." Will adds some rosemary and salt. "I am well aware of what this could mean, if, indeed, it means anything at all. See, I've done some prying of my own. Your mum and my dad were quite serious once upon a time for teenagers. After they broke up, my dad nursed a broken heart until dating my mum." She opens her mouth, no doubt ready to counter his accusation, but he keeps going. "My parents had a fantastic marriage that seems pretty fucking impossible to replicate. They were *happy*. Not put-on-a-show for the neighbors happy, but genuinely happy. But she died, and he didn't, and the last thing she'd ever want is for him to pass by a chance to experience happiness again, even if it's with her former friend. Even if it's merely as *friends*."

"Callie, why is this so upsetting to you?" I ask, cutting a French loaf into thick wedges. "It's not like they're dating or anything. Plus, your mom admitted Cameron was her first love, too."

"Exactly." She swipes the butter dish away from me and begins to add chopped bits of garlic and seasoning. "This guy was her first love. When she told him she couldn't have kids, he ditched her for her best friend. And now that his wife is dead—"

Will is flat-out glaring.

"Sorry. I don't mean that as an insult or anything. Now that he's *single*, it's like she's some kind of back up. Second choice. Mom should never be second choice to anyone."

"That is most certainly not what happened," Will snaps.

Kellan chooses this moment to walk into the kitchen, and I'm instantly a thousand times happier than I was just a minute before. He trades the bottle of wine in his hand for a piece of bread I've just sliced. "Whoa. Why all the hostility?"

As he pops a large piece in his mouth, I say tartly, "That's for dinner. Also, they're arguing over whether or not they ought to be pleased their parents are becoming reacquainted."

"I don't like how he can do that," Will mutters, and then Callie surprises me by voicing her opinion that Emotionals are true pains in the ass, too.

Interesting.

Kellan's amused, too. He eggs Callie on with, "Is that what we're calling it? *Reacquainting?*"

Oh, boy. It's Callie's turn to glare.

"You can put on your bitch goggles all you like," he informs her, serene as can be, "but just remember, I'm impervious to your vitriol." To me, he says, "Personally, I think it's great."

"Really?" I grin up at him. Happiness of my own floods my senses at how easy things are between us despite our talk yesterday. Maybe we can do this after all. "Me, too."

"Traitors," Callie mutters. She pulls over the bread so she can butter the slices.

Kellan leans down and whispers in my ear, "Wanna know a secret?"

Must. Not. Focus. On his breath. On my skin. I suck in a deep breath, which is a stupid thing to do, because now I've got a lungful of his yummy scent. We're friends. We decided to be the very best, very closest of friends. Oh gods. He smells so good.

One day at a time, Chloe.

Except, the urge to kiss him right now nearly renders me speechless. So I end up saying, oh-so-eloquently, "Urgh?"

I can practically feel his grin growing against my earlobe. Delicious shivers wrack my spine. "Forget about what's happening out there with Astrid and Cameron. It's these two you ought to be paying attention to since they're incredibly attracted to one another. Did you know that?"

He pulls away and I'm frozen for a moment before bursting out in laughter. He's got to be kidding. Astrid and Cameron, okay, I can maybe see that. They have been talking a lot lately and used to date. But Will and Callie? No. No way. They've done nothing but argue since the moment they met. Callie's hung up on Jonah and Will's unfortunately still stuck on Becca. "Are you *serious*?"

"Yep." His grin is adorably naughty as he helps himself to another piece of bread.

"*Serious*, serious?"

Two fingers are held up. "Scouts honor."

My sides hurt, I'm cracking up so hard.

Both Callie and Will ask what Kellan's just told me, but we're too busy laughing to answer. "Screw you two," Callie finally snaps, and when Will agrees, I reach the point where tears leak out of the corners of my eyes. It feels good to laugh this hard. It feels better to do it with Kellan. Like the promises we made each other last night will be kept. And that we can do this.

Dinner is highly entertaining for once. Every so often, Kellan nudges me with his foot when either Callie or Will slide furtive glances toward one another in between insults and debates. They think they're being so sly, staring at each other when they think the other isn't looking. How had I not noticed this before? I try not to giggle at the table since, while they're watching each other, Kellan and I are watching them. And Astrid and Cameron? Forget it. They're in their own little world where they're only noticing each other. They're not doing anything other than talking, but they're totally enraptured with each other.

Afterwards, the unbelievable happens—Astrid and Cameron encourage us *kids* to go get ice cream. I'm not kidding. They said *ice cream* in unison and passed over money to us twenty-somethings, which forced another round of tear-worthy laughter from me and Kellan and confusion and annoyance on behalf of Will and Callie.

Halfway down the block, as we trail behind the constantly bickering pair, Kellan says to me, "Astrid is really glad to have Cameron back in her life."

Which makes me so very glad. Nothing inappropriate had happened tonight—I don't think I saw them touch once, but the joy I saw in both Astrid and Cameron's eyes when they spoke to one another was so sweet. "They're cute, don't you think?"

"Like puppies." He fails at keeping his face straight. "Actually, they are. Ridiculously so. FYI, Cameron is pretty happy, too. I tried not to pry too much into their feelings, though. I mean, Astrid's my mom. I may be twenty years old, but I still don't want to know if my mother is digging on some guy or not, you know?"

I kick at a stray rock on the sidewalk. "Isn't it weird though? I run all the way to Alaska, and I end up hooking up with Astrid's old boyfriend of all people."

Kellan lifts up an eyebrow, his lips curving in a smirk. I burst out in another round of laughter and swat at his arm. Which . . . was a mistake, because touching leads to longing and . . . no. Don't go there, Chloe. "Gods, no! EW! Not *hooking up*, you skeevy perv."

"You're the one who said it. Not me."

"You know what I meant."

He shoves his hands in his pockets and gives me that half smile of his. Will I ever become immune to it? "It is pretty crazy, though."

What's crazier yet is that we're going to go get ice cream, and we're laughing and joking and things feel so easy between us. And it makes me feel like anything is possible.

"You realize," he says, "that if these two hook up, we will officially win the prize for most incestuous family ever."

I can't stop laughing with him tonight.

He taps his chin playfully, pretending to be deep in thought. "Let's see. My mom—well, you know what I mean—and your dad (again, you know what I mean) are hooking up. Pardon me. I mean, getting reacquainted, although I'd lay money down that they go on an official date within the next few months. It'll take them awhile, you know. There are a lot of strong feelings in their history, some very hurtful ones, too. A lot of water under their bridges that they need to cross. Yet I digress. J and Callie dated, even though they were, in essence, brother and sister (at least that's how Astrid sees us, anyway). Cal is lusting after her mom's old boyfriend's son, who is virtually your brother, although she'd rather stab him than admit that out loud. He's pretty hot for her, too. You dated both me and J."

My lips twitch. "Anything between you and Callie to admit?"

"Believe it or not," he says slyly, "we made out once. And I can attest it was like kissing my sister. How Jonah managed it for years is beyond me. I had to gargle with mouthwash afterwards."

I resist the urge to ask if he ever felt like he was kissing his sister when his mouth was on mine. And then I have to resist the flood of memories of kisses we shared that were so hot I nearly lost my mind. "What about you and Will? C'mon, C. You can tell me the truth. It'll make the incestuousness complete. Did you two hook up in Alaska?"

He's calling me C again, which warms my heart considerably. "Nope. Not a single kiss. Not once."

He's skeptical, but jokingly so.

"I mean, he's kissed me on the head or cheek before, but that's hardly romantic." I clear my throat. "You and Callie actually kissed? When was this?"

He wags a finger at me and tsk-tsks, purposely ignoring my

question. "I'm disappointed in you. You've let me down here. Our circle is incomplete. You must go up to Will right now and lay a big, wet one right on his lips."

Yeah, right. I kiss Will in front of Kellan, and there's no doubt a fight would break out, even though they've begun to be friends. Just like I think would happen with Callie if I ever witness another kiss between her and either Jonah or Kellan, even though I love her. Still, I find myself shaking my head, grinning like I'm drunk or something.

This is what Kellan does to me.

"How about Cal, then?" He motions towards our friends, clearly arguing, yet walking mere inches away from one another. "Willing to go kiss her?"

"Ha! You wish."

The light in his eyes is impish. "I do, actually. It would be incredibly hot; the memory might just get me through many a lonely night."

"Oh my gods. *Kellan.*"

He breaks down in boyish giggles, and I swear, I once thought Will's laughter was pure, addictive happiness. I was wrong. Kellan's is, and there's no comparison.

Chapter Thirty-Four

Exhausted from the third Elders mission I've been on since coming back to Annar, I practically collapse onto my bed. Ever since Russia, we've failed to take any of the Elders out; it's like, once these Magical ancestors see I'm there, they disappear without a trace. After today's failure, Zthane put a temporary halt to our missions until the Elders Subcommittee can reconvene to discuss the situation. Until then, the Guard's attention has switched to implementing protective measures for the identified Métis colonies on the various planes.

Erik and Cameron are down at Guard Headquarters nearly every day discussing the situation. A new Council Subcommittee is currently forming to help build and strengthen diplomatic ties. It's a slow start—there is unfortunately deep-rooted bias on both sides, but conversations are taking place. It certainly helps that Karl has thrown his full support behind Zthane and Erik's initiatives.

I've offered my support, too, but as I'm still on an unofficial time out from the Council, it doesn't mean much yet. Every day I work toward changing that. I may not be going to Council meetings yet, but I faithfully read the minutes (even when they nearly put me to sleep). I vote, even though it's via computer. And I strategize with Zthane and the rest of the Guard about the best ways I can be used to get the Elder problem under control.

As for right now, I'm almost too tired to even change into my pajamas. I debate even leaving my muddy shoes on as my eyes drift shut. It's much nicer to lay here, reminiscing about this one time Jonah and I went hiking on the outskirts on Annar and I ended up wimping out halfway up the trail because, no matter what I like to think about myself, I am not a natural hiker nor am I inclined toward outdoor sports. We ended up resting near a really beautiful waterfall, and we'd really talked about our future that day—not the future he saw for us, or the one that I imagined, but the one we wanted together. It wasn't an exciting day, nor an overly romantic one in our history as a couple, but I hold on to it now because of its simplicity. How it made me feel normal, like I was just a girl and he was a boy, and we were in love and it all just was, rather than us being Council members who dabbled in the worlds' affairs when we were still teenagers.

The ache I feel for him is so tangible that I am positive I can stick my finger in it and swirl it around until my chest constricts once more.

I roll onto my back and stare up at the ceiling, sleep no longer claiming me as its own. Now it's just sadness that presses me against the sheets—sadness and a knowledge that I and I alone am responsible for messing up what I had with the best guy I've ever known.

Sometimes, a girl doesn't need a bad boy like so many stories tell her she does. She doesn't need to redeem him, and he doesn't need to redeem her. Sometimes a girl doesn't need a tortured artist or the recovering playboy, but somebody who helps balance her out, someone who makes sure her feet stay on the ground when life is tough and lift up into the air when her lips find his. She needs somebody smart and funny and comfortable and exciting all at the same time. She needs somebody to go to sleep with who makes her feel secure enough not to care that she snores or drools, and somebody to wake up with who won't judge her when her hair sticks up and pillowcase lines crease her face. Sometimes a girl needs somebody who she's content talking about deep things with, or small talk, or sometimes nothing at all.

Sometimes a girl just needs a partner who will help her grow rather than explode.

I had that. I had that and now I kick myself over and over again because I was stupid enough to let it go.

My phone beeps to let me know a text message awaits me. I sigh heavily, debating whether or not to leave it be until morning. It's probably Zthane or Karl with yet another idea about why we're striking out so much with our missions lately. Or maybe Caleb, checking in with me to see if I contacted the University of Alaska about online classes yet. But ignoring it would be the Old Chloe thing to do. Even still, I'm annoyed when I roll over to grab my phone.

And then a pair of hummingbirds take flight in my chest. Because the text isn't from Zthane, Karl, or Caleb. It's not even from Kellan, whose texts I practically live for when we're not talking on the phone or hanging out with one another.

It's from Jonah.

It's been nearly a month since he walked out of this apartment. Three weeks, four days, ten hours, seventeen minutes, and . . . well, I'm not too good with seconds. But he's been gone that long, and we've had radio silence, and now, there's a text, and it's from him.

It says: **You called me from Alaska on your birthday and hung up. Yes or no?**

I'm laughing maniacally, muddy boots streaking my comforter as I surge up on my knees. Three weeks of separation, and this is what he chooses to say when he finally reaches out? And seriously—how does he even remember? It was a teeny call that had him saying hello twice and me hanging up immediately. A standard wrong number type call that devastated me but should have meant absolutely nothing to him.

There's no way he could know about it. I didn't tell Kellan or Callie—the only people who know about that call and the idiotic aftereffects are Will and Cameron, and they would never break confidence.

My hands shake hard when I type back: **Yes.**

Ten agonizing minutes pass. **Why?**

I retype my message back at least a dozen times. **I missed you and needed to hear your voice so I could get through the day.**

Another five minutes pass. I'm going to die. Just die right here on my bed. But then: **Did you call my brother, too?**

I'm clutching the phone like it's the embodiment of our Connection. No—not our Connection. Our past. Our bond that we forged together, Connection or no. **No. Just you.**

Three minutes this time. **Why?**

I don't hesitate. **Because I missed YOU.**

He's faster with his replies now. **Why did you hang up?**

I was afraid. It's honest.

He doesn't text back, but when I fall asleep hours later, hope has officially found its way back into my soul.

Over the next week, I get sporadic texts from Jonah. Sometimes it'll be in the middle of the night, and say something like: **Why a diner?** Or while I'm in one of the never-ending meetings at Guard HQ, and I'll stop paying attention to Zthane so I can read: **Who's Frieda and why is she turning down Paul? (also, who's Paul?)** One came in during a dinner out with Cameron and Will, and Will ripped the phone out of my hand and read aloud: **Why blonde?** Which made Will tease me mercilessly about how he first thought I was a stereotypical California girl for being all blonde and blue-eyed.

None of the texts are personal—at least, not in concern to Jonah and his feelings—but all are questions about my life in Alaska. Why Cameron? Why Will? What's up with the pancake thing? Why blue contacts? Where did I live before Cameron's house? Did I have a car? Friends? Did I really bowl? (I have no idea where he learned that bit). Most the time, he doesn't reply further after I answer the question. But the hope in me has continued to grow, because if he were well and truly done with me, he wouldn't be texting. He wouldn't care about these things.

At least, that's what I'm choosing to hold onto.

I slam my phone down on the coffee table. "I cannot get ahold of Cora. It's been weeks and . . . nada."

Callie looks at me over the rim of her cup of tea. "You're kidding me, right?"

I dramatically flop onto the couch. "No! I try calling her every day, but—"

She sets her cup down. "Nobody's talked to you about Cora yet? None of those people you call Cousins?"

I'm alarmed. "No! Is she okay?"

She sighs. "Cora and Raul got married two days before you came back to Annar. They're on their honeymoon—a month long safari in Africa. One of her stipulations was to go technology free. She didn't want the Guard calling Raul in for a mission."

It feels like I've been punched in the gut. Cora's *married*? And nobody thought to *tell* me?

"It was a nice wedding," she says calmly, like she hasn't just dropped a bomb on my existence. "Big, too, in Madrid. Cora wanted it here, but Raul's mom was pretty insistent he do it at their local cathedral. I was supposed to go as Kellan's date, but as you well know, he was in Kuergal at the time. So I was Mom's wingman. Speaking of—where's Will?"

I blink a few times. "Um . . ."

"I came home last night and found Cameron over. He and Mom were drinking wine and laughing." A beat passes before she stands up and clenches her fists. Then she shoves both hands into her hair, a strangling groan coming out of her pursed lips, before she drops back down into the chair. "Okay. Here's the deal. Shit. I can't believe I'm even going to—" She slides down in the chair, all askew yet dressed impeccably. "Fine. FINE. What's the deal with Will, Chloe?"

I try not to show my amusement. "You mean between him and me? Because—"

"No. *Gods*. I already know there's nothing between the two of you. Kellan would have torn him apart with his bare hands had he sensed anything between you guys; you know this. No, I'm asking what . . ." She sighs through her nose. "I can't get a good bead on him, Chloe, and it's driving me insane."

"Well, if you're asking if he's some kind of sketchy guy, then—"

Her glare nearly cuts me in half. "You're going to make me say it, aren't you?"

I cut her some slack. "Kellan already told me how you have the hots for Will."

Her skin goes from porcelain to cherry red in approximately one second. "That *asshole*." She pounds a fist against her palm. I do not envy the phone call Kellan will be getting shortly.

"So if you're asking me whether or not he's dating anybody right now," I say, "then I can answer that one. He's single."

Her mouth opens then snaps shut.

"That said," I say, making sure to tread carefully, "Will's situation is . . . complicated."

She covers her eyes with a hand. "Of course it is, because apparently I am only attracted to complicated men. Is he gay?"

I assure her that he's not, but then I apologize for not being able to go further, since I do not want to break his confidence. She stews moodily about this until the man in question comes through the front door, appearing as if he's been on a thirty-six hour bender.

I want to ask him if he's okay, because I know this must stem from a Becca call, but from the look he gives me, I hold the question in. Instead, I say, "I thought you and Kellan were going to go surfing today?"

True to his word, Kellan has taken Will out a few times to show him the ropes. I haven't tagged along, though. I've had enough shame on a surfboard, thank you very much.

"Yeah, yeah," he says, running a hand across the stubble decorating his chin. "We went this morning. I don't think I'll ever get used to travel by portals. Seems too surreal, you know?" He drops onto the couch next to me; a whiff of saltwater nearly undoes me. I love that smell. I particularly love that smell on a certain person whose text messages from last night have been read and dissected probably a hundred times now.

Will nudges me. "Guess who came along?"

My breath catches in my throat.

"I have to admit," he says casually, "that I rather like your Jonah. He seems like a good bloke. Quiet, but we got on well."

"Well, well," Callie murmurs. "Color me shocked that J crawled out of his hole to socialize. Surfing lately has been a solitary thing for him."

It takes just about every last ounce in me not to inquire whether or not Jonah asked about me.

But then Will hands me a gift, wrapped up shiny and pretty with a ribbon when he says, "Thought you might like to know that while we were waiting for Kellan to come in, he asked me how you were doing."

I'm speechless. Hopeful and ecstatic and speechless all at the same time.

"What did you tell him?" Callie asks.

Will ruffles my hair. "I told him the truth, that you're busy with work and keeping your head down."

As if on cue, my phone beeps. My heart flies into my mouth as I reach for it. Sure enough, it's Jonah.

You should talk to Will. I think he needs you today.

I didn't think it was possible to love Jonah any more than I already do. I was wrong. Him caring about my best friend like this only makes me love him all the more.

One week, four days of texts, and I finally get something other than a question from Jonah. I'm out jogging through the park in central Annar, dripping sweat and cursing my need to get fit so I can take down the Elders, when my phone beeps in my sock. I immediately come to a halt, breathing hard, and search for a nearby rock to collapse onto.

I've missed you, too.

A thousand flowers erupt from the mossy carpet surrounding the rock I'm sitting on. I'm no Nymph, and plants aren't my thing, but damn, if I haven't just forced life to spring anew all around me. I squeal and clap and reread the text dozens of times. I'll never delete it. Never.

He misses me. And I couldn't be more hopeful if I tried.

It takes me two glorious yet anxious minutes before I answer him. I want to say the right thing. No pressure, but the truth. Always the truth from here on out, no matter what happens. **I never stopped missing you. I miss you now.**

He doesn't answer, but I spend the rest of the day in a deliriously happy fog. I greet every person I come into contact with the biggest smile that's stretched across my lips in a long time. I hug more people in the span of three hours than I have in over a year. People probably think I've lost my mind, but I. Don't. Care. Jonah Whitecomb misses me. I treat Will and Cameron to a four star restaurant dinner and order sparkling cider rather than wine. Because I need my wits, and there'll be no more drunk, morose Chloe. I offer up cheers to at least a dozen things—blue skies, successful missions, them living in Annar with me, Will's pancakes, Cameron finally shaving off his beard (not that I didn't like the beard—I make sure to include that, too), Cameron relenting and giving me a flannel shirt of his that I love. I'm into recognizing the little things. Love and appreciation, I'm discovering, doesn't have to be big and bold. They're best served in the ordinary joys of daily life.

I've officially become a text-a-holic. Jonah is sending me at least three messages a day now, and each one sends me into a tizzy of happy delight. Some even sprout into conversations. He hasn't called, and I haven't seen him yet, but we've gotten now to a point where we're communicating.

Just now, he sent me: **Astrid really seems taken by Cameron Dane.**

It sounds ridiculous, but this text melts my insides like butter. He's sharing something about his mom to me. Granted, it's about my—well, my pseudo-dad, but still. And I've already been a front row witness to the mush these two are generating, plus there's the whole bit with Kellan where we love to dish on the relationships developing between the parents and children. Still, I answer: **Cameron is the same. I wonder what their story is?**

It's a bit disingenuous, as I already know in pretty good detail what their history is, but I've got to keep this texting bit going.

He hasn't told you?

I'm grinning. **Well, I know about the past. I meant the present?**

Ah. Obviously, I don't have details. I just know how she feels when she thinks about him.

Now I'm laughing. I decide to be bold. **We should play detectives and get to the bottom of the Astrid-Cameron relationship. If there is one, I mean.**

And then my breath is shallow, because I'm scared I went too far with my use of *we*. But he writes back: **Sounds like a plan.**

The hummingbirds in my chest refuse to leave. It's okay. I've begun to like them sticking around.

"I AM SO FURIOUS WITH YOU!"

I shrink at Cora's outburst, but within the next two seconds, she'd got her arms around me and she's flat-out crying and cursing at me. It's all I can do to throw my arms around her, too, and tell her how much I love her and missed her. Raul hovers awkwardly in the background, like he isn't sure if he ought to be yelling at me, too, or prying his wife away from me.

Wife. He and Cora are married. My Cousin is married, and I wasn't there for the wedding, and the regret that fills me up for that is immense.

For the next hour, Cora pulls my story out of me, and in the end, she's hugging me again. "I missed you," she tells me. "You are never allowed to do such a stupid thing again. Did you hear a word I said when you took off to Hawaii that one time? You're not alone, Chloe. No matter what awful shit is going on, you have people who are here for you." She takes my face between her hands. "You. Are. Not. Alone."

Gods, I've missed her, too.

Chapter Thirty-Five

Minutes after I hang up from another cathartic phone call with Caleb, I climb into bed, the minutes from this past week's Council meeting waiting to be read on my iPad (and, if I'm being honest, lull me to sleep). But then my phone beeps, and I'm instantly awake. Jonah asks: **What are you doing right now?**

Hope explodes through my veins. I try to play it cool, though. **Reading up on this week's mtg. FUN. You?**

Minutes go by, and the hope so sparkling and fresh begins to fizz out. Finally, just as I pick my iPad back up: **Where are you?**

I pull in a sharp breath. My hands begin to shake. I think my palms are sweating, too, which is so gross but it is how it is. **Home. You?**

Almost five weeks after I returned to Annar and Jonah walked out of my apartment, he sends me the following text: **I'm outside your building.**

Obviously, I'm out of bed and at the window immediately, peering out into the darkness. I can't find him. He's not there. Is he lying? Wait. I smack my forehead. My window faces the back of the building.

I throw a sweatshirt on and find my flip-flops. And then I'm out of my room, running through the apartment, and Will and Cameron are yelling at me, asking what I'm doing, and I tell them I'll be back, but I've got to go. I don't bother with the elevator; I run the entire length of the stairs, and then I skid through the lobby to the front door.

I throw them open and nearly knock down Erik. "Oh! Sorry!" I murmur, grabbing his arm before he hits the pavement.

"Jesus, Chloe," he says, readjusting the bags filled with groceries in his hands. "Is the building on fire or something?"

But then I see Jonah, standing, about twenty-five feet down the sidewalk, holding his phone in one hand and tugging at his long hair with the other. He looks shocked that I'm standing in the open doorway, my hair in a sloppy pony tail, face scrubbed clean with no make-up, dressed in pajama shorts and a sweatshirt and wearing flip-flops.

"Chloe?" Erik asks.

I'm dazed. Grinning and dazed and all I can say is that I'll see him later and if I'm lucky to not wait up for me.

Once the door is closed behind me, I take a deep breath and walk over to where Jonah's standing. He is so ridiculously gorgeous that I feel like writing all that silly poetry Will once accused me of. "Hi," slides out of me, all giddy, lovely joy that's made up of two letters. I hope he can hear me over the beating of my heart. It's got to be drowning everything out here on the street out.

"Hi," he says in return. He's not quite grinning, not like me, but he's not frowning, either. I'll take it. And I'll gladly drink in the sight of him, because nothing has ever been so welcome or beautiful to me before.

Like the poet I just imagined to be, I say, "Hi!"

My idiocy doesn't faze him in the slightest. "You—wow. Did you run down here or something?"

I laugh. Is it so obvious? "Yes. As a matter of fact, I did."

He shoves his phone in his pocket and reaches out a hand. I go still and pray that I don't pass out from excitement when he lightly fingers a loose strand of hair. "It's nice to see it's back to brown."

"I was a lousy blonde," I admit. I'm thankful I'm wearing a

sweatshirt, because I've just totally broken out in goose bumps. And I think my skin now envies my hair.

He laughs under his breath, and this bubble of joy burbles up my chest. He thought something I said was funny! I inspired something other than hurt and anger! I'm making progress!

"So," I say, keeping my voice light. "Were you out for a stroll or something?"

He closes his eyes for a brief moment, and I kick myself for counting my eggs before they are hatched. But then, he opens them back up, and I lose myself in the cerulean that I couldn't replicate anywhere even if I tried. "If by stroll, you mean I walked directly here from my place, with several detours back home and then back this way, then yes. I'm on a stroll."

I can barely contain my giddiness. "Do you want to come in?"

He looks up, like he can see the window to our apartment above. "No, but—can we take a walk? Would you be up for that?"

I blurt out my assent before he can even finish speaking.

We walk side-by-side, not touching like I want, but close enough to be considered a victory to me. For several minutes, nothing is said, but it's okay. This is enough.

Even still, I eventually break the ice by saying, "Did you ever get Astrid to tell you what's going on with her and Cameron?"

He chuckles under his breath. Oh, lords, do I love this sound. "No. Not yet. But I do know she still has strong feelings for him, is conflicted and sad over what's gone down between them, yet is ecstatic about what's happening now. She's glad to have her friend back."

"Hmm." I keep my focus on the road ahead of us. It's hard, because I want to totally stare at him, which sounds creepy but when you've gone without looking at the face of the person you love the most, sometimes you get a bit desperate. "I'm no Emotional, but I think I can say that Cameron is the same. He loved his wife a lot, but I think that spark with Astrid might still there. If you know what I mean."

He's quiet for several minutes. "Have you seen your parents?"

"My mom," I admit. "She came over once, and we've sent some emails back and forth. My dad—I guess now he's upset with me because of what I did. Which I get." I let out an exasperated puff. "It's funny; for a long time, I suppose I never really understood the relationship between you and Astrid. How you considered her to be your mom when you *had* a mom. I get it now." I give in and look at him now; I'm rewarded because he's staring at me, too. Enough to cause him to blush when I catch him. I bite back my grin. "My own mom is . . . I won't say coming around, but she's trying, though. Whether or not we ever get to a place where she and I are close, I think I'm finally okay with it." The grin escapes anyway. "Sometimes family is more than blood. Sometimes a family is built on love."

He stops on the sidewalk. "I'm glad you found that with Cameron and Will. I really am."

"Yeah. Me too." Oh, I'd give every last cent I have to touch him right now. "I'm glad you found that with Astrid."

He bites his lip, and my heart kicks into triple time. "Look, Chloe . . ."

I hold my breath. It's ridiculous, but I literally hold my breath. My name never sounds better than when coming from his lips.

He takes a step closer. I'm lightheaded as I stare up at him. "I'm not saying I'm over what happened."

Reality crashes down upon me like an Acme piano from three stories up.

"But," he takes another step closer, his hand lifting to touch my cheek, "the truth is, I miss you."

I lean into his touch. Thank the gods, we're finally touching after months and months of not doing so. Tingles zip up and down my body. I swear, if he keeps this up, I just might have an orgasm right here on a public sidewalk in the middle of Annar. "I miss you, too."

His eyes pin me to the sidewalk where I stand. "You're not with

Kellan."

I want to laugh, but know it'd send the wrong message. "No."

"Why?"

I let the emotions slamming around my heart spill out so he can feel them. And then I lay it all out for him like I wanted to the day I came back from Anchorage. "Because I want to be with you, Jonah. Even if you don't want to be with me anymore, I know my truth. And I've learned the hard way that a person has to be true to themself if they want a chance at happiness in life."

I think he's holding his breath, too.

"I love you." I reach up and touch his face, too. "I'm not saying it because I expect you to say it back. I'm saying it because it's one of my truths. When I was in Alaska, pretending to be somebody I'm not, I realized something. I love you, I've always loved you, and I always will. My life is crazy. I'm going to be asked to do awful, terrifying, exciting things, and sometimes it scares the crap out of me. I have two Connections, which seems impossible at times to comprehend. I'm obviously immature and don't know how to deal with all this stuff at all times, but I'm finally trying to get a grip on everything. There are these sick and twisted creatures trying to kill me all the time, and I'm having to deal with that. But when I was working at a diner, serving pancakes, wondering what it was I wanted in my life, who I wanted to be, and where I wanted to be, I realized that one of those things was you."

It hurts to see the skepticism in his eyes—it's small, but still there. But I know it's there because I put it there. And even though he must feel all this in me, sometimes emotions, even from an Emotional, aren't rational.

"Here's the thing. I love your brother. I do. I always will, thanks to the Connection. He's one of my best friends. I hope he always will be. And . . ." I swallow. I have to get this right. This may be my last chance. "And the truth is, if there was no you, there'd be no doubt in my mind that I'd be with him. But there is a you." Our feet overlap, we're standing so close. I stare up into his eyes, so much love filling me up right now that it's amazing I haven't exploded in a shower of glitter and flowers. "Jonah . . . you're more to me than just my Connection. You're the person I'd want to be with even if there were no Connection."

It's out there now. I've said it. I want him, I've chosen him. There will be no more indecision. I'll struggle with my feelings toward Kellan the rest of my life, there's no doubt about it. But I've finally chosen and Jonah now knows it.

He doesn't say anything, which makes me anxious, but I remind myself this is a lot to throw on somebody who's still smarting from desertion. I can't expect him to just roll over and say, "Well, okay. Let's get married tonight." Although, come to think of it, it'd be really great if he did.

Finally, in what I can best describe as hushed awe: "You actually mean that."

Before I can assure him of this truth, both hands are on my face and then his lips are on mine and I am finally, after wandering for so long that I got lost, exactly where I want to be.

I am deliriously, wildly, fantastically, ecstatically, giddily in the throes of bliss due to love. I cannot even begin to hold back my joy, even when faced with a moody Will and a pair of groggy, middle-aged men who haven't had their coffee yet early the next morning.

I'd spent a good, long time kissing Jonah last night before he walked me home. Like I'd done in high school, I'd made him promise to come over bright and early in the morning so we could have breakfast and then talk. So here I am, banging pans around as I attempt to make said breakfast, while the men I live with watch with amusement.

"For Christ's sake, let me cook," Will eventually says when I apparently do not crack an egg properly. "We don't want him running away due to food poisoning or anything."

I gratefully relinquish control so I can set the table.

"Hen, it does my heart good to see you so cheerful," Cameron says, pressing a quick kiss against my head.

Erik grunts and pours himself a cup of coffee. "So this is why you were acting like you'd lost your mind last night. I should have figured it had to do with a boy."

I sigh happily, thinking of my boy. He should be here in less than a half hour. "You guys don't mind him joining us for breakfast?"

"You'll have to do without me," Erik says. "I'm to go to Anchorage for a couple of days to talk with colony representatives."

"Of course we don't mind," Cameron assures me. "I'm quite looking forward to finally getting to know this Jonah of yours."

"Dad, you say this like you haven't ever met the bloke," Will calls out.

My eyes widen; Cameron chuckles quietly. "Fair enough, son. Yes, I've briefly met Jonah a few times whilst visiting Astrid. And he's been at a few of the meetings Erik and I have had with the Council concerning Métis matters. But I am looking forward to getting to know the person you've given your heart to, hen."

I can't help but give him a huge hug.

We say goodbye to Erik; minutes later, a knock on the door tells me that Jonah's here. Cameron insists on getting it, so I wait nervously in the living room, practically bouncing on the balls of my feet until I hear Jonah's voice in the hallway.

And then there he is. And I melt all over again.

I check the impulse to tackle him in front of Cameron and instead allow a ridiculous grin to overtake my face. It's beautiful to see that it's mirrored on his face, too. Good lords, do I love Jonah Whitecomb's smiles. He's got this adorable dimple that appears that I just want to lick.

Cameron winks at me, not doubt amused by how I've been rendered nearly speechless by the sight of our guest. "I think I'll go and check on Will's progress with the baked French toast he's making."

I wait until he's gone to say, ever-so-eloquently, "Hi!"

He laughs and runs a hand through his wonderfully messy hair; the silver ring on his thumb glints in the early morning light. I missed that ring. I've missed his laugh. I've missed that dimple. "Hi," he says in return.

It's the perfect come-on line, because I can't help myself. I take three steps forward; he meets me with the same. And then my hand goes to the back of his head, my fingers curling in his lovely black hair, and I'm tugging his mouth down to mine. His arms go around me, which is a good thing, because once his tongue touches mine, my knees give out.

I think I could kiss this man all day long and never get tired of it.

We've obviously got a lot of work to do. Just because we're here kissing, doesn't mean everything that's happened in the past two years is swept under the rug. I don't want it to be ignored. I want us to deal with it once and for all. There are discussions still to be had, decisions to be made, more apologies to be spoken. But those can wait until after breakfast. For now, it's heaven just to be able to kiss Jonah once more.

Minutes later, Will calls us in for breakfast. Smart boy for not coming in and interrupting. I don't bother blushing, because there is no part of me right now embarrassed to be with Jonah.

Today is a good day. Today is all about new beginnings.

In the small dining room off the kitchen, Cameron motions to the table. "Come have a seat, you two."

"Will's a great cook," I tell Jonah as we sit down. My voice is shaking again. The hummingbirds are back, clamoring in a panicked frenzy against my ribs. My mouth goes dry. He's here. He's really here with me, having breakfast. "His pancakes are the best. You'll love them."

Will sets a casserole dish down in the middle of the table. "Baked French toast, remember?"

Okay. Now I blush.

"Do you like to cook?" Will asks as he sits down on the other side of Jonah. "Because we all know how rubbish Chloe is at it. Five months at a diner, and she's ace with coffee but can't cook a meal to save her life."

I worry that all this instant familiarity with Will and Cameron will rub Jonah the wrong way, that he'll look at them and our shared history as yet another representation of my mistakes and choices. But he's all ease when he says, "Astrid's been teaching me recently."

I cut a wedge of French toast out; it smells divine. "Really?"

He nods, his grin so adorable I melt into a blissful puddle once more. Before I completely become a useless lump of contentment, he turns back to Will. "I wouldn't say I'm any good at it yet, though."

"Unlike surfing." Will leans back in his chair and chuckles. "I don't think I've ever felt quite as inept at something as I did surfing next to you and your brother."

"Were you awful?" I ask Will.

"Actually," Jonah says, "he's a natural. Surprised both me and Kel quite a bit."

Will grins lazily at me.

"I went surfing a few times when I was a lad." Cameron sets his coffee cup down. "Nothing exciting, just small waves, and I was shite at it, but I can definitely see its allure."

Will's intrigued. "When was this?"

"Oh, let's see. I went on holiday to Cornwall with some schoolmates shortly before I enlisted in the RAF. Borrowed some boards and tried to impress some of the local lasses." He chuckles, dark eyes sparkling. "Tried being the operative word. Crashed more than I stood, that's the truth."

Will laughs heartily. "Did it work?"

Cameron matches his laughter. Father and son sound so much alike. "I didn't try too hard, son. You mum was waiting for me back home, and she would've skinned me alive had I done anything other than look."

"Was this before or after Astrid?" I ask slyly.

As Cameron studies me, I school my face to radiate innocence. He eventually chuckles. "Obviously after."

Will passes his father the syrup. "And look at you now, coming full circle."

Cameron groans and throws his hands up.

"You and Astrid have lunch an awful lot lately, don't you, Dad?" Will winks at me. "And send the kids out to get ice cream when you do. Chloe? Don't you get the feeling *ice cream* is code for something?"

I smother my laughter and look over at Jonah. He's focused on Cameron. I wonder what he feels in him. Cameron always comes across as so strong, so together, despite the blows he's been dealt.

Cameron tugs at his collar. "William, I love you, but you are an arsehole."

Will and I laugh and laugh. It's easy to laugh now, with Jonah sitting here next to me. My laughter feels free.

Just as Cameron is about to take his first bit of French toast, Jonah says, "You should ask Astrid on a date."

A good three seconds of stunned silence fills the room. Cameron doesn't even put the fork in his mouth. Then Will and I crack up all over again.

"Or even," Will says, "ask her out for *ice cream*."

I've got tears now. Cameron sighs heavily, even though it's obvious he's amused with us.

Will points his knife at his father. "I'm just saying, if her own son—an Emotional, no less—says it's a good idea, maybe you ought to just do it already."

Cameron pours himself another cup of coffee. "I believe we were talking about surfing, not my love life." He realizes his slip of a word with a massive groan, and Will and I are relentless with our teasing.

Once we've calmed down, I say to Will, "I have to admit that I'm surprised that you're okay with all of this."

He angles his eye roll toward Jonah, as if to say, *can you believe her?* "I'm not a total boor. Besides, won't it be fun to see how Callie reacts to it?"

At Callie's name, Jonah's eyebrows lift. I try not to giggle. "Maybe you two ought to go get some *ice cream*, too."

A true miracle happens: Will Dane turns bright red. Now I have to resist the urge to cackle outright.

"What's this?" Cameron asks gleefully, no doubt thrilled at the idea of his son taking an interest in anybody who is not Becca.

"Yes, Will," I say innocently, "what *is* this?"

"I haven't the slightest idea of what you're talking about," he tells me coolly. But he's attacking his French toast like there's no tomorrow, so I know he's all riled up. "That girl is insufferable. She's practically a princess."

Amazingly, Jonah's eyebrows lift even higher as he turns to me. There's a question in his eyes—apparently, Kellan never shared this information with him.

I pop a piece of syrup-soaked toast in my mouth and mumble, "Yep."

He turns back toward Will, the corners of his lips tugging upward.

Will glares at me. I smile serenely in return. It's Cameron's turn to laugh. But then Will's phone rings, and the moment is broken.

He chooses to silence it rather than answer.

I chew on my lip, deciding how best to approach what I'm about to suggest. It's something I've been considering a lot lately, especially now that Cora's back in town. I eventually just say it. "I can fix this, you know."

"Fix what, hen?" Cameron asks quietly.

"I can call in a favor." My voice is steady and sure when I address Will, but I reach under the table for Jonah's hand. Gods, I hope this doesn't backfire on me. "I can send a Shaman to Glasgow and I can fix this for you."

Will simply stares at me.

"Technically, we're not supposed to meddle in these sorts of circumstances," I continue, "but I will do it for you." I take a deep breath. "Cora will do it for me. She'll go to Glasgow and heal Becca. She'll—all the damage from the accident will be healed. Or at least most it. A lot of time has passed, so. . ." I swallow. "I mean, she can't bring back the baby or Grant, but Becca shouldn't be a problem."

I love that Jonah squeezes my hand. He doesn't have the slightest clue what's going on right now, but he's showing me he'll support me in this.

"Meaning . . .?" Will's voice is so low I barely heart it.

But mine is steady. Confident. Loving. "Meaning you can finally have the closure you so desperately deserve."

Cameron puts a hand on his son's shoulder. "Is this true, hen?"

"I haven't talked to Cora about it yet, but I'm fairly confident she'll do this for me."

Will leans back in his chair, rocking it back on two legs, eyes on the ceiling for a long moment. Just when I think he's going to tell me to go to hell, the chair drops to the ground.

"Okay," he tells me.

"Yeah?"

"Yeah," he says.

Chapter Thirty-Six

Today is, without a doubt, one of the best days I've had in a long time, and the funny thing is, I have nothing of real significance to show for it. I haven't gone anywhere exciting, didn't experience anything new, didn't even do something as sublimely romantic as watch the sun go down. I simply spend it with Jonah, talking. After breakfast, Cameron and Will give us some space, so we sit in the living room and talk. We're completely honest with one another, finally opening up about things that should've been conveyed a long time ago. Granted, neither of us reopens the can of worms that was my affair with his brother, but everything else is fair game. I lay myself bare about work, family, and the strain of two Connections. And then, to my surprise, he admits he'd also been breaking apart due to work and the Connections, yet held back from telling me because he knew I was struggling under the strain of my own nightmares.

"The day I came back," I say, taking his hand in mine, "you mentioned something about how none of us were dealing well with our situation—me getting sick and running away,"—I swallow—"Kellan and his adrenaline highs . . ." I press a kiss against the back of his hand. "Jonah, how were you self-destructing?"

He takes me in his arms and leans us back into the couch; the strain—or is it fear?—of times past bunches the muscles under my cheek, but, as he gently strokes my hair, he says, "It's embarrassing to admit, but when I wasn't with you and worrying about getting you to eat, I'd forgot to do the same because too many other things were on my mind. Slept too little, out of fear of seeing whatever my brother was dreaming about or the atrocities that my actions set into motion during missions. Ran too much, in hopes of finding that groove where I didn't have to think about anything, only to . . ." His chest rises and falls slowly in the silence that surrounds us.

I blink back my tears and whisper, "Tell me."

"You know that lame excuse celebrities always give when they're hospitalized? Dehydration and exhaustion?" His scoff smacks strongly of self-reproach. "That was me way too many times during the last year, sitting in Kate Blackthorn's office, being lectured about how I once more pushed my body to the brink of dehydration and exhaustion, and how one day I was going to collapse where others saw me instead of her office and then I'd really have to explain to everyone what was going on."

And I had no idea, because around me, Jonah only ever presented himself as someone completely in control of himself. Kellan and I, we wore our agony on our sleeves, yet Jonah hid his behind long sleeves of responsibility. Still, that's no excuse—none at all for somebody who lived with him, slept in the same bed as him. I should have known.

I tell him this, tell him how sorry I am for failing him so completely. I'm being ridiculous, he counters—how was I supposed to see what he didn't want me to? But it doesn't matter. I hate that blind, oblivious, selfish girl. "Did Kellan know?"

Pieces of my hair curl around his fingers. "Yes."

"Did Astrid? Or Callie?"

His head drops down to meet mine; our hair skims across each other as he silently tells me they didn't.

So. Just Kellan, because they're Magical twins and have a hard time hiding things from one another, and Kate, who's his Shaman. I don't bother asking about his dad; Ewan Whitecomb has been ignorant of his sons' lives for years.

My fingers twist in his t-shirt. "No more hiding things from one another. From this day out, no matter what happens, we need to trust each other enough to be completely honest, to be ourselves, warts and all. To know that we're not alone. That, no matter what happens with the Council or missions or whatever the rest of the worlds throw at us, we'll always have each other to lean on." I disentangle myself so I can face him. "If that's what you want, I mean. I realize that maybe I'm jumping the gun here . . ." I take his face in my hands. "But I want to be this person for you. I want to be more than just your Connection or your lover—I want to be your *partner*, if that makes sense."

He tugs me closer so he can brush his lips across mine. Tremors of bliss shudder throughout my body—how can he do this to me with such a light touch?

"I love you, Chloe." His words are soft and hot against my mouth, the last said for a good amount of time.

"Exciting, isn't it?"

Jonah bends down and peers at a photo stuck in the corner of my vanity mirror. It's the Moose gang at our bowling alley back in Anchorage and everyone is smiling wide, our arms around each other. Well, I'm fake smiling, because I couldn't really smile then, but it was a good night and an even better memory.

I really miss those people.

He taps at the bottom of the photo. "Those shoes are hideous."

I laugh and pull a box out of my closet. "Voila! The world's tackiest yet most awesome pair of bowling shoes." I dangle one purple and turquoise shoe on the end of my index finger.

He takes it from me and eyes the Z on the back. "For *Zoe*?"

"Shut up." I snatch the shoe back and try my best to look stern, but I really want to break down in giggles. "I fully realize I suck at aliases."

"You really do." His dimple deepens, and I go all melty inside. "It's amazing you managed to elude the Guard as long as you did."

"Yes, well. It wasn't like I was thinking clearly when I made all my paperwork." I box the shoes back up. "Also, I have another confession I've just realized I haven't made yet."

He sits on the edge of my bed, alarmed, which I get, considering how much we've shared already today. "Should I be worried?"

"Weelll . . ." My cheeks heat up. "Technically, you funded my trip."

All these cute, scrunchy lines form on his forehead.

I sit down next to him, lacing our fingers together. "Kellan told me once that you guys hide money in all your houses. When I left, I went to one and found the secret box you had there. I didn't take everything in it, but . . . I took a lot. Okay, most of it. Obviously you haven't discovered that, right?" I twist my head to study him, looking up through my eyelashes.

He's shocked. "Which house?"

I take a deep breath. "Rome."

I worry when he's quiet for a long time, because Rome is a sacred place for us, but then he laughs. Really laughs. I'm bewildered, because I thought for sure he'd be pissed. I had to tell him, though. There can't be any more secrets.

"You aren't mad?"

"Maybe if I'd learned that four months ago I would be." His dimple taunts me. "Today, it's just . . . wow. It just figures that that's how it was." And then, more serious, "I have one last confession, too."

I brace myself. This could be the moment he decides to tell me that, when I was gone, he met somebody. Did things that—no. I refuse to think about it. And if he tells me this is what happened, I'm just going to have to deal.

"Maybe you running away was the best thing to ever happened to us."

Ohhh. I'd only thought I was melty before. Now I know I am.

"Yeah?"

His hand curves around the back of my head, and he leans in, the smell of him, all spice and mint, flooding my senses until I go lightheaded. This is love. This is true love. This isn't Connection love, or Fate love, or anything other than an old fashioned case of being hopeless, deliriously in love. I know the difference now. "You know what you want, right?"

Gods, yes. Him. Preferably naked right now, and in me, on me, and around me, but I'll take a kiss, too.

I nod slowly.

"I used to think I did, too," he says, his breath warm against my mouth. "I was wrong. I only thought I knew what I wanted."

"Do you now?"

"Yeah, I think I finally do."

It's becoming increasingly hard to breathe, but not because I'm crying or upset. He's stealing my breath away. "What do you want, Jonah?"

His lips are so, so gentle against mine, yet every last nerve in my body flares to life. "Everything you mentioned earlier. I want to be able to come home and lean on you. Know that you've got my back. I want to be the same for you. I want us to be lovers. Best friends. Partners. Because, it's *you* I want. Not my Connection, not a Creator, but just Chloe Lilywhite."

You have me, I want to say. You'll always have me. But I don't think I could get a word out right now if I tried. I'm pretty sure it'd just sound like a moan.

"This you," he continues, lips flutter soft against the corner of my mouth. A finger traces down my neck, down my chest until it's over my overworking heart. "The one who finally knows what *she* wants."

What I want is for him to kiss me. So, I grab his face in both hands and crash my lips into his, and all of those nerves that just lit up with a tiny kiss burn white-hot when his tongue enters my mouth.

I have never, in my entire life, been so turned on and in so much need as I am in this moment. I want him. I want him so much that it's hard to think of anything else. I get up, my lips still on his, my tongue still swirling around his, and rotate so I'm straddling him on the bed. Gods, he tastes so good.

If it's the last thing I do, I'm going to seduce this man. We no longer are bound by any stupid proclamation from my father insisting we wait until marriage to have sex. That said, I am painfully aware of what Kellan told me once, of how when they lose control physically during love making that they can feel one another. Kellan knows that I've chosen Jonah, but I refuse to pour salt into the wound we share. So I decide to build a shield around us, one much like the one I used to use to mask my emotions from the twins, one that hopefully will keep the link he has with his brother out.

He breaks away, trailing his tongue and mouth down my neck. I arch into him, heat spreading through all of my limbs until I'm trembling. When he gets to where my shoulder and neck curve together, his teeth graze my hot skin, sending shivers skittering down my spine. My fingers dig into his shoulders, curving around until there's no way I'll let go of him again.

Our mouths meet once more, not gently, and I marvel at the intensity of what his kiss alone can do to me. I'm on fire, soaring, diving, exploding, suffocating, and it's beautiful. *He's* beautiful. I suck his bottom lip in my mouth, and he gasps. It's possibly one of the best sounds I've ever heard. I swallow this sound, wanting to keep it in me forever.

It's my turn to gasp as his fingers dance down my sides until reaching the bottom of my t-shirt. I let go of his shoulders and raise my arms high so he can slide my shirt, oh so slowly, off me. I shiver when the cotton grazes my fingertips on its way to the floor.

"Cold?" he whispers into my ear before gently biting the lobe, which prompts another shiver.

All I do is laugh quietly, because cold is the last thing I am right now. Besides, turnabout is only fair. I slide my own fingers down his hard chest to grab the bottom of his shirt and pull it off.

Here's the thing. I've seen Jonah Whitecomb in various stages of undress countless times before. It's not like I haven't ever seen him naked or ogled him prior to this moment. But tonight, marveling at how handsome he is, how perfect his chest looks, I can't help but think I never truly *saw* him before. I want to tell him, but again, no words come. I simply stare in his eyes, my heart thumping painfully against my ribs.

Memories flash brightly through my mind, of the first time I saw him in my dreams. Of our first kiss. The first time I cried and he wiped away my tears. Finding both of our Connection rings. The first time we merged. Skinny-dipping in Tahiti. Out of order, all important, big or small, and I'm trembling because I was a fool to ever think that this person here wasn't the one for me.

His hands curve around my waist and slide upwards, twisting until they cup my breasts. Even through the thin fabric of my bra, his fingers scorch deliciously into my sensitive skin. "You're so beautiful," he murmurs.

What I am is yours, I want to say. Instead, I kiss him again, putting everything I'm feeling into this tango between our mouths. When he unclasps my bra, it's my turn to sigh into his mouth. He swallows my sound just like I did his; I like how we are keeping these pieces of each other. Making them part of us.

My bra joins my shirt on the floor, and I shiver again because his eyes have darkened as they travel slowly from my face to chest. I arch closer, needing him to touch me. And the moment his mouth finds one of my breasts, and his teeth graze my nipple, I very nearly collapse. Every part of me burns blue like a newborn star.

Suddenly, he's flipping us around on the bed so I'm lying down and he's over me. My hands go to the buttons on his shorts. If somebody knocks on my door or calls, I will kill them. Literally kill them with my bare hands. But I'm so shaky that he needs to take over, the dimple teasing me even though his smile is gentle. I prop myself up on my elbows and watch him remove his shorts and then his boxers, and I swear to everything good and holy in all the worlds, it's the most erotic sight I've ever seen.

Gods, he's gorgeous.

He climbs back onto the bed and I lift my hips so he can slide my skirt off. It's torturously slow, even worse when he takes his extra-sweet time with my panties. I've gone from trembling straight to quivering—there's no doubt from this moment out that I'm putty in his hands.

He stares down at me with hooded eyes for an eternity. I lean up higher, ready to grab him and drag his mouth back to mine, but he gently pushes back my arm. "There's no rush." His husky voice is like an auditory shot of lust. I'm molten now.

His mouth lingers on my navel, his warm tongue tracing a path south and then back up to my breasts. I collapse back against the bed, my fists curling in the sheets as Jonah slowly explores every inch of my willing body. Stars explode in my eyelids, each heartbeat close to his ear telling him *wantneedwant.*

He gives me what I crave when his hand slides down my body and swirls between my legs. I ought to be embarrassed by how wet I already am for him, but I'm not, not even when he presses a lingering kiss right above the spot where his fingers are torturing me in the best of ways. Instead, I moan; the sound brings his mouth back up to mine, and we're kissing, hotter than before, and the intensity of it all is too much, because my body supernovas underneath his hands and touch.

But it's not enough. Even as my body shudders out in waves, I snake my hand down between our bodies until I find him, hard and ready. Despite the urge to take him in my mouth, I need him in me right now more. I need this connection between us. I need us to finally be one, even though he's so big I worry we won't fit. He gasps at my touch, making me smile. I run my fingertips lightly up and down the length, delighting in how he's the one shuddering now.

His hand replaces mine and he looks down at me, eyes serious. He's asking me if I'm ready for this.

I nod slowly but surely. The desire in his eyes intensifies, which only magnifies my own yearnings.

"You don't happen to have . . ." His laugh is husky, a cross between and plea and a moan as he presses his forehead to mine.

I know what he's asking for. I let go of him and hold up a shiny, silver square in my fingers that I've just created for a brief second before ripping it open. And then I revel in putting the condom on him, drinking in the quiet hiss of pleasure that precedes his body shuddering under my fingers.

He kisses me, lips light and teasing against mine. My hips buck up, brushing against him, and oh, good lords, I need him right now. Need him so bad. Slowly, gently, he pushes into me, our eyes locked together the entire time. It stings for the briefest of seconds, but I embrace the sensation.

Because this, here, with him—it's real.

He stops moving and presses his forehead against mine. "Is this okay?" he whispers, voice strained.

Is he kidding? This is better than okay. I've waited for years to know what it feels like to have Jonah Whitecomb inside me. And it was worth the wait, although I wish I could've had this experience a million times already. I lift my hips again, driving him in deeper, and the control he'd been so desperate to hold onto breaks. We come together in a frenzy of sweaty bodies, kisses, and friction, and pressure mounts stronger than before in me.

This is bliss. This is love. This is better, a thousand, million, trillion times better than I ever thought it could be. This is—

My body supernovas once more, and the room explodes in a shower of rainbowed light that matches how I feel. Jonah thrusts into me one last time, my name falling from his lips, and I lean up to kiss it away so I can hold it in me, too. Because the way he just said my name, as his *wantneedwant* fills me up, is seriously the best sound I've ever heard.

Chapter Thirty-Seven

When I wake up, it's in a panic. My hand shoots out, fumbling until it hits warm, bare skin.

He's here. I'm not dreaming. This is real.

Jonah shifts in his sleep, his arm snaking out to pull me closer until we're pressed up against one another. My bones and muscles sink back into the bed I've called my own since coming back to Annar in relief. As my heartbeat slows, I can't help but watch him, reliving what happened last night in exquisite detail until my own skin turns warm.

We finally, finally made love. And then we did it again. And, okay, a third time, too.

I'm achy and low on sleep and yet more content than I've been in forever. It'd been beautiful, so blissfully wonderful that I don't think poets or songwriters ever knew what they were talking about when they attempted to describe what it's like when two people become one. Because what I felt last night—what I feel now, safe and secure in his arms, is better than anything anyone ever described before.

There's no way I ever let it go again.

"I called Cora," I tell Will as we fight over the last buffalo wing on the plate.

He looks away from the hockey game on the television set, his dark eyes undecipherable.

"She's agreed to go to Glasgow and meet Becca." I shove the tasty wing his way; news like this shouldn't come alongside giving up the last snack during a game. "I guess the question now is whether or not you want to go with her."

He wipes his hands on a napkin before running them down his face. "Christ. Ask the easy questions, why don't you?"

I mute the television. It's just him and me in the apartment; Jonah had to go into work for awhile, and Cameron is out grocery shopping.

"How much damage is this Cora going to reverse? How does it work?"

"I'm not a Shaman, so I can't really answer that," I say, "but I would assume Becca's spine would be fixed and she'd no longer be paralyzed. She'd probably be off the ventilator, too."

"And . . . her mind?"

"Cora can probably repair any brain damage associated with the crash," I tell him quietly.

"What about memories?"

"Okay, that Cora will have no control over. She deals in physiology. I have a friend who is a Dreamer that deals with stuff like that. Sometimes Emotionals do, too." I lay a hand against his knee. "We don't have to do anything if you don't want to, Will. I offered simply because I'm tired of seeing you trapped in this endless loop. It's not fair that you haven't had closure."

He looks away.

"Two people you loved betrayed your trust." I'm fully aware of the irony of me eschewing the unfairness of this situation to him, but I plow on anyway. "Your girlfriend cheated on you with your best friend. She was going to have his baby. He died before you could ever confront him about what he did. She . . . for all intents and purposes, the girl you knew died that day, too—except her ghost comes back to haunt you way too often, reminding you of what you guys had. Any confrontation you have with her, any chance you have at making a clean break is lost when her mind scatters once more." I lean my cheek against his shoulder briefly. "You deserve a chance to move on one way or another."

After slipping an arm around me, he's silent for nearly a minute. "Is it bloody awful that I'm terrified she's going to want to pick up where we last left?"

"That can only happen if it's what you want, too." I, of all people, know this lesson too well, so I don't push him any further today.

"Chloe . . . if you're not ready, I can go back to my office and call in to the meeting today."

I tear my eyes from the glimmering glare of glass on the front door to Guard HQ approximately twenty feet away. Jonah's been quiet for most of the walk from my apartment to where we're supposed to have a meeting in fifteen minutes. "What? Don't be silly. Why would you do that?"

He sighs and runs a hand through his dark hair. "You know why."

He's right. Today the Guard and the Elders Subcommittee are convening; it's the first meeting we'll both be in attendance for since getting back together several days ago. At least forty-to-fifty members of both the Guard and Council will be present, plus several Métis who came back with Erik just for the occasion. While this is daunting enough, we're not worried about any of them.

It's Kellan's presence that has my stomach in knots.

For the moment, Jonah is still living with Kellan in his apartment, and from what he's told me, a conversation occurred between the brothers after Jonah and I decided to give our relationship another try. It went . . . badly, which is both surprising and predictable all at the same time. Jonah tried to talk me off the ledge I quickly placed myself on when I heard they nearly came to blows, explaining that, rationally, they both understand the situation; it's just, Connections aren't always reasonable. If they were, I would never have run away, nor would have Kellan. Jonah wouldn't have shut down. Kellan, Jonah assured me, meant everything that he had promised that night on the roof. It's just . . . it's going to take some time.

Everything always takes time—the one thing we are forced to suffer through with no hopes of fast-forward or rewind. Like a cruel mistress, time marches forward with no regard to feelings. All we can do is follow and pray that each second we live through gets easier like promised.

Before we get to the door, I whisper, "I don't want to hurt him." And myself. And Jonah.

Jonah sighs and gently steers me toward the wall. "He knows that." I can't see his eyes behind the dark plastic of his glasses, but I'm positive they're filled with just as much guilt as mine are.

I lean my head back against the textured stones of the grandiose building behind us. "Is he aware we'll both be here?"

"Yeah." Jonah's just as hushed as I am.

I ask what's pressing heavily against my heart. "Will there ever be a day in which we won't have to worry about hurting him? Or hurting ourselves?" Or me not wanting his brother so much that it clouds my judgment?

He gently touches my cheek. "I don't know, honey."

I bite my lip and look up. The sky is hard to see here in this part of Annar, where all the building reach high and lean toward Karnach. "I tried to break the Connection to him once in Alaska. Right after I called you."

His intake of air is sharp.

"I was . . . gods. Miserable. Freaking out. It occurred to me that maybe I could will away Connections if I tried." My smile is bittersweet. "It killed me to try it, but . . . all I could think was how I couldn't tie either of you down to me any longer. How it wasn't fair to you guys, that you deserved a better life. I had a few shots of whiskey and then tried to break the one to him first."

His head tilts away, like he's peering into one of the windows nearby. "And . . .?"

I shove wispy strands of hair freed by the light breeze caressing Annar back behind my ear. "And . . . I felt even worse than before. Like I punched myself in the heart. I had another shot and tried again, but all I ended up doing was making myself so miserable I ended up drowning in whiskey."

He's unbearably quiet when he asks, "Did you try ours?"

It hurts like hell to do it, but I tell him the truth. "Had it worked with Kellan, I would have."

Twelve breaths pulled in and out of my chest occur before he speaks. "We tried to influence each other when you were gone. Make it so the other didn't feel the Connection's pain, so we didn't care you were gone, or that we even loved you at all. Or perhaps even convince ourselves that we could move on, love somebody else."

Gods, that hurts to hear. I'd hoped for something like that, of course, but it doesn't stop the pain of the knife to the chest any less.

"Did it work?" I barely whisper.

He shakes his head slowly, his hand clenching repeatedly by his side. It's the first time since reuniting that I've seen him do that.

"You two coming?"

We turn to find Will, sipping a cup of coffee. Jonah takes a step back from me and shoves his hands into his pockets. "Yeah," I tell him. I clear my throat. "Are Cameron and Erik already up there?"

"I believe so. They wanted to bring in the Métis reps early to meet Zthane. They're bullying me to join their merry little party, you know. Become official and whatnot." He takes off his mirrored sunglasses and squints at us. "Everything okay? You two look like somebody died or something."

I bark out a quiet laugh. "Just admitting more of my sins."

Will's eyebrow shoot up, the paper cup halfway to his lips.

"Chloe," Jonah says, reaching out and grabbing my hand, "it's water under the bridge. Don't beat yourself up for this, not when we tried the same."

I let him pull me closer. "Is it, though?"

Somehow when he tells me it is, I believe him.

Chapter Thirty-Eight

Kellan's deep in conversation with Karl and Giuliana, but the moment I cross the threshold of the doorway of the conference room, the tug between us flares to life. He must feel it, too, because he quickly apologizes to Giules for cutting her off, and then heads our way.

Will quickly dismisses himself to go over to where Cameron and Erik are talking with Zthane and Astrid. I don't blame him for wanting to get the hell away from the complicated mess created by our Connections. And although somebody calls his name from across the room, Jonah stays by my side. My heart thumps hard with every step Kellan takes toward us. I don't know how to do this. I still love him. I love them both. I don't know how to—

"Hey," he says casually, but there is a genuine gleam of concern reflecting back at me in the blue of his eyes. "Was worried you guys were going to spend the entire meeting downstairs or something."

The oh-so-familiar prick of tears attacks me without notice. He's trying so hard right now to act normal, like I haven't basically cut out his heart and flaunted it in front of him. Like I'm not standing here with his brother after telling him that, despite our shared Connection, I need Jonah more.

Kellan sighs and takes a step closer to where we're standing. "Chloe . . . don't . . . ." He sighs again. "It's okay. It's going to be okay."

He can't promise me that. How can he? How can any of us ever think it'll be okay? Because I've chosen, and I mean it, and yet . . . the tug between me and Kellan is just as strong, and I love him, and I love Jonah and—

Jonah's name is called again; as he leans toward me, his hand goes to my lower back. "I'm going to leave you two to talk. Just remember, we're all on the same page here, honey. No more secrets, remember?"

I nod and then he goes over to where several members of the Subcommittee are, huddled around an iPad.

The smile Kellan gives me doesn't reach his eyes. "He's right, you know."

I want to collapse into the safety of his arms, but I hold back. Maybe some day we'll be able to do that again, but right now is too soon for any of us involved. "How are you?"

He ducks his head to run his hand through his hair, the action eerily reminiscent of Jonah's just ten minutes before. And then he leads me out into the empty hallway. "I don't want you to take this the wrong way, C . . . but I need you to try your best not to focus on me in the coming weeks, starting right about now."

I also need to try my best not to break down sobbing right now, too.

"I know it's going to be hard. I know you're freaking out right now, and you're worried, and confused, and there's all this toxic guilt building back up in you." He holds a hand out, but I think it's more for him than me. "The three of us are going to find a way to deal with this. It can't be right now, because we've got to turn our focus on the Elders situation. But we will find a way to make all this work. For now, you've got to let me find a way that works for me to deal with everything that's gone down, and I can't do it when I'm worried about you worrying about me."

Panic blooms in my chest, faster than before.

"I meant what I told you," he says quietly. "I'm not going to abandon you. I won't do that to my brother, either. You two . . . you're the most important people in my life. You always will be. But right now, I need to take a step back and look at ways I can personally deal with this. And you two need to be focusing on how to repair everything that's gone down between you in the last few years."

I want to cry so bad right now. Just break down and ugly cry over the unfairness of it all.

Why did Fate do this to me? Us?

"Please believe me when I tell you that, despite what I feel for you, C—what I'll always feel for you, and what I *know* you feel for me—I will never wish for anything other than your happiness. Jonah's, either. I may be jealous as all hell over . . ." He swallows hard. "Let's just say that I will always want and fight for the best for the two people I love most in the worlds. If this is what makes you happy, if this is what makes him the same, I will never stand in the way of that. I almost lost both of you guys over this. I'm not willing to risk that again."

"What about your happiness?" I choke out. Because right now, I'm pretty sure I'd give everything I have to ensure that.

Somebody calls out that the meeting will start in two minutes; it's enough to drive Kellan several steps back away from me.

Tiny pieces of my heart chip off with each step he takes.

"They need us in there," he says quietly. "Let's let that be our focus today, okay?"

I do as he asks, even though it hurts to do so. For the next three hours, everyone in the conference room focuses on the Elders problem. Two more Métis colonies on two separate planes were attacked in the last week; three people are in intensive care, two others dead. It sounds horrible to admit it, but I was incredibly relieved neither colony was Anchorage. Several Magicals were attacked over the same time period, resulting in one death on the Goblin plane. All accounts have the monsters constantly evolving into more humanoid figures. People are scared, and rightly so.

I'd foolishly thought that, once I discovered I could kill the Elders, the problem was basically solved. Nothing could be further from the truth. As we'd discovered on the last two missions I was sent out on, the Elders are careful not to come anywhere near me.

"Councilwoman Lilywhite," the head of the Subcommittee, a Gnomish Informer named Johann Baldurrsson, asks in the aftermath of another round of futile arguing over what we should do to counteract this line of evasion, "are you certain you must be touching the beasts to eradicate them?"

All eyes are on me. "I'm afraid so."

Baldurrsson strokes his snowy beard. "There's no chance you're mistaken?"

I feel like I'm letting them all down. "I wish I were. I tried it, only to fail. I have to be touching them."

"And yet, with each touch, you risk your own life," he murmurs. "Which leaves us at quite the quagmire. How do we send in our assassin when, chances are, her life is just as at risk as theirs?"

I want to argue that it's my risk to take, that it's my responsibility to go out there and at least try, but I see the point he's making. If I die, not only with Magical-kind be thrown into a tailspin, but so will the worlds we govern. My death is nothing but chaos for all involved. That said . . .

"I don't think they want to kill me," I admit. "Cailleache made it seem like they want me in particular taken alive."

"That frightens me every more," Astrid says. So far, she's spent the majority of the meeting quiet, taking notes. Here she is, though, and there's no hiding the worry in her lyrical voice. "Our history with the Elders shows they are thirsty to eradicate anybody with Magical blood—everyone, that is, but a Creator."

Uneasy silence follows these words.

Will's the first to break it. "Chloe told me a story once, of how some early Creator stripped these beasties of their bodies and whatnot. What if they think a different one will reverse what's been done?"

I'm aghast. "They could *never* make me do that."

"Ah, but that's the thing." Zthane taps his pencil against the table. "They're constantly evolving. We don't know what they're capable of, Chloe—except their ability to kill powerful members of our kind. The possibility that they *could* make you do that is something we cannot discredit."

"So what's our option here?" Maccon Lightningriver asks. "Because from where I'm sitting, it's sounding like you are all claiming we don't have any viable options right now other than to sit on our hands. People are dying—Magicals and Métis alike. What's to say the Elders will stop with our kinds? What happens when they spill into the general populations?"

Baldurrsson says quietly, "We cannot risk the Creator. Until we can absolutely guarantee her safety during such confrontations, we shall not sanction any such missions. Until then, we will simply have to play defense the best we can." He turns to the Métis members sitting nearby. "What are the chances that we can convince your colonies to relocate to Annar? Our boundaries are secure."

Erik is the one to answer. "Although there are those who are heartened by recent attempts by Annar to mend past wrongs, there are still many Métis who fear and distrust Magicals. I'd say . . ." He turns to his bleak-faced colleagues. "Maybe twenty, thirty percent could be easily persuaded. Others will need to be swayed, while pockets of Métis will never agree to such measures."

Baldurrsson rubs his forehead; the long hairs of his eyebrows go askew. "Some are better than none. Nightstorm, we sanction the process of bringing Métis families into Annar as soon as possible." His weary eyes flick my way. "Councilwoman Lilywhite, your immediate task is to expand the boundaries of Annar to create room for an influx of citizens, as well as new housing."

"Is that what the Métis will be?" a representative of the Russian colony asks, his accent harsh. "Will they be considered equals or simply poor refugees who must line up for handouts from the mighty Magicals?"

Astrid is the one to answer. "The Council meets tonight to discuss just this matter. This Subcommittee has been tasked to decide whether or not diplomatic ties with your colonies are within the best interest of Annar."

The Russian frowns. "And?"

"And," Baldurrsson says, "it is our recommendation that anyone with Magical blood, no matter the percentage, be afforded full citizenship."

"What about the discrimination we have been subjected to?" a representative from one of the Dwarven colonies asks. "What is to stop Magicals from devaluing our kind, as they have always done before?"

"For one thing, you need to stop thinking of this as an us verses them situation," Jonah says. It isn't the first time he's voiced his opinion today, but he's been selective about what he argues about. I love that he doesn't go crazy like some of the other people, high on emotions with precious little logic. He's been levelheaded the entire time. Focused. I could not be more proud of him. "That only exacerbates the problem. Why should any of the Métis want to come here when their own leaders propagate their differences? You have to remind them that they belong here, too. That, just because they can't practice Magic, it doesn't mean Magical blood doesn't run in their veins."

The Dwarven representative grunts, but in the end, it's decided.

Annar will open its arms wide to its lost children.

Chapter Thirty-Nine

"Think I should call him? See if he's okay?"

Jonah looks up from the sauce he's stirring on the stove. Watching him cook us dinner is incredibly sexy. "I know you mean well, but you heard what Will said. He needs to do this on his own."

I lean against the smooth granite countertop next to the stove. At first, I'd been really hesitant to come over to Kellan and Jonah's shared apartment, since I'd only ever been here before with just Kellan, but I couldn't avoid it forever. So here I am, ogling Jonah as he cooks, choosing to focus all of my fretting on Will rather than Kellan for once.

Who am I kidding. Of course I'm concerned about Kellan, too. Jonah knows I'm worrying, too—so he's tried his best to be transparent, as best he can and with Kellan's permission, about assuring me that his brother is fine.

I miss him, though. I'm wildly, happily, fantastically in love with Jonah right now and I'm thrilled with how things are going with us and yet . . . Kellan's absence cuts me like a knife.

I guess something never changes.

"At least I'm not the only one he didn't allow to come," I finally say to Jonah. Cameron didn't go to Scotland, either; only, he didn't seem to take it as personally as I did.

Jonah sets the wooden spoon down. "I probably shouldn't tell you that Kellan did, though."

I push myself up. "Why would he go?"

"I think he's going to work in tandem with Cora on Becca's recovery."

I'd told Jonah the gist of Will and Becca's history (with Will's permission, of course) so he'd be up to speed on what I was asking Cora to do. "Huh." I sneak a few pieces of uncooked pasta to munch on. It's probably best I don't spin this conversation back toward Kellan, because then I'll probably cry and ruin the evening. So I decide to talk about yet another person that leaves me emotional. "My mom called me again today."

He reaches over and tucks stray hairs behind my ear. I love how his fingers afterward continue to slide gently downward as they trace the curve of my neck. "When was this?"

"When I was out to lunch with Caleb." I break a piece of spaghetti in half. "She wanted to know if we could have lunch soon. Or coffee, if lunch was too much for me."

"How do you feel about that?"

I like that he asks me this even though he already knows how I feel, as if he knows I need to practice letting all this stuff out rather than bottling it like before. "I'm conflicted. Hopeful. Nervous. Wary. I keep waiting for the other shoe to drop. Or, maybe since they've already dropped, my mother to simply chuck them off a balcony."

He smiles wryly. "If it's any consolation, I've felt her remorse over the relationship you two have."

Remorse I share, for as much as I wanted a relationship with her, I never really pushed for one, either.

I sneak another piece of dried spaghetti. "Callie likes Will, you know."

He chuckles as he checks on the bread in the oven. "I thought we were talking about your mom."

"We're talking about Will and Callie now. Kellan told me before that Will's attracted to Cal, too. Is this true?"

"Have you asked him about it?"

"Gods, yes. He told me to mind my own business."

Jonah chuckles again before leaning over to kiss me. "Yes. He's attracted to her. That said, he wouldn't act upon it until whatever it is he has with Becca is resolved. He feels really conflicted about all of this. Guilty, I guess."

It's as I figured. Now that Jonah's brought up the importance of resolutions, that leads me to . . . "I've been thinking."

"Uh oh." He looks up from dumping cooked pasta into a colander in the sink. "I hope you're not planning on matchmaking. I can tell you right now that both Will and Callie are the sort to like to figure this stuff out on their own."

My lips curve upwards; I can't stop sighing over how adorable he is when he does mundane things like cooking. Maybe adorable isn't the right word; maybe gorgeous is, in an unaffected, obvious way. He's wearing an old, thin red t-shirt and well-loved jeans that hug his lean runner's muscles in all the right places, but the effect the sight of him on me is the same as if he'd been standing before me in a pristine tuxedo.

Or in nothing at all.

"You were saying? Or rather, thinking?"

I force my eyes back up to his face. He's amused, no doubt by the equal parts of nervousness and desire raging around my body. "Oh. Right. I was thinking—"

Wait. Can I do this? Just ask? Just . . . say it? Let him know what's been on my mind for days now?

We've travelled this road before, were engaged for over a year, only for me to cry off not once, but twice. Okay, to be fair, he'd postponed once himself. Those postponements, upon reflection, had been for the best. The state of mind I'd been in, the confusion and despair . . . despite our Connection, we would've been doomed to unhappiness.

Things are different now. I'm sure now. Even though I love his brother, and that'll never change—*I'm sure.*

So I take a deep breath and count to ten to give myself enough time to change my mind. But I don't. If anything, each second makes me want this all the more. "Will you marry me?"

It's clearly not what he was expecting, because he goes very still, steam coming up from the hot noodles in the colander in his hands. For the tiniest moment, I wonder if I've just made yet another colossal mistake when it comes to us as a couple—we're in a good place, and I don't want to do anything to threaten that between us, but on the other hand, I can't very well pretend that this isn't what I want. So, no. No matter what, this isn't a mistake. This is my truth, and I've got to put it out there whether or not it goes south for me.

Since he's not speaking, I continue, "I know this may seem sudden, since we've only technically been back together a really short time, but I've learned recently that life is too short to be without the person you love. Even a life that spans two centuries, if we're lucky." I take the colander away from him and set it to the side. He takes a dish towel I pass over, eyes on me the entire time, like he's trying to figure out if I'm serious or not, despite what his craft must be telling him.

He's still not saying anything. So I add what's been percolating around my head since the moment I gave him both my body and soul. "I want to live with you. I miss that so much. I want to wake up to your face, go to sleep with it being the last thing I see. Fight with you over which television show or movie to watch. Eat dinner together when we're both at home. Share our successes and defeats. Encourage each other to chase the dreams we want. Know that we are free to be who we are and that the other person accepts us as is. Spend our holidays together, and share our families so they becomes *ours,* not just yours or mine." I reach out and claim his hands so I can lace my fingers through his. "I want our last names to be the same. I want us, when we're ready, to add to our family, and for that baby to know that he or she is so incredibly loved by both parents. I want us to grow old together, so that when we're nearing the end of our existences, we can look back and think, 'Wow, we were the luckiest and strongest because we had each other.'" I take a measured, deep breath. "I actually do wish I had the power to break our Connection so I could show you that, even without it and Fate and everything else out there, I would still choose you, Jonah. You're who I want. You're who I need."

He's still not saying anything with his mouth, but it's okay, his eyes are doing all the talking I need to hear. They're filled with awe—but more importantly, they're filled with love.

I take one of his hands and press it against my heart. The muscle in my chest isn't racing for once. It's slow and steady. It's sure. "I love you, Jonah Whitecomb. More than you can ever imagine. Will you marry me?"

He steps into me, so that our feet overlap one another and our chests press together. Both hands cup my face and he stares down at me with those beautiful, beautiful eyes that I've lost myself in too many times to count over my lifetime. My heart finally kick starts, because sometimes, even though a girl can be one hundred percent positive about what she wants, when a boy you love looks at you the way mine is looking at me, you have no control over your body at all.

I've known him for sixteen years, and it occurs to me that I fall in love with him a bit more every single day.

One of his thumbs slowly traces my lower lip. His head dips so that not only do I feel his thumb on my mouth, but his breath, too. I love him, I love him, and—

"Yes."

I can't help the blissful smile that overtakes my face. And then my mouth meets his, claiming sweet victory.

Dinner is totally not going to happen. Both of our shirts are somewhere in the kitchen. My skirt is in the hallway, I think. His shorts are in the doorway to his bedroom. I'm on his bed, my knees digging into the soft sheets as I rise up to meet him. My heart's thumping a staccato that the entirety of Annar must hear, and I'm lightheaded and yet more grounded than I have felt in years.

His knees brush against the end of the bed. "That thing you do," he murmurs, hands falling soft against the comforter. "Where you block your feelings from me—"

"Never again," I say quietly, the vow filling the space between us.

He smiles, the dimple gentle yet lips mischievous. "I wasn't going to ask you to hide yourself from me tonight. Because," one knee, then two bring him up onto the bed, "I want to know exactly how you feel when I make love to you."

Ohh, things in me go molten pretty damn fast. "Yeah?"

"Because when I get to feel what you're feeling when I'm in you," he continues, and heavens above is this man sexy, "it's the most fucking amazing sensation in the entire universe."

Oh, sweet heavens above, he just set my entire body on fire, and he did it with just words. My butt drops to hit my heels, my palms go flat against the bunched up sheets below me just to prop me up, because I'm pretty sure my muscles just turned to jelly.

"You—you were saying?" My words come out as tiny gasps.

I love how his lips curve up on one side as he slowly crawls towards me. "Right. I was asking if you think it's possible to shield me."

It's rapidly become more difficult to breathe. My hands slide backwards, my spine arching as it instinctively angles towards him. He's moving too slowly, and I need him *now*. "You mean, like a condom?"

He chuckles quietly. "That, too, although I come prepared this time." He reaches over to the nightstand and produces a small, silver square. "I meant an actual shield, like the one you used to block your emotions from me last year. Because, this is about you. And me. And us." His eyes, so vivid blue despite the dim light from the lamp next to his bed, darken with something I desperately want to hold onto forever. "And I don't want to have to worry about holding myself back. I hate that I didn't think about doing it before, but . . ."

His grin is rueful. "It's kind of hard to think clearly when the girl you love more than anything else in the worlds is touching you."

He's so close that I can feel the heat radiating off his body. Smell the mint on his breath, the spiciness leftover from his body wash. And it makes me hot, hotter than I've ever been before in my entire life. I want to melt right into him until we're one.

I'm hoarse when I say, "I've already been doing it."

There's relief in his beautiful eyes, and a whole lot of desire that sends a sharp spike of longing through me.

I bite my lip, trying desperately not to moan, as my butt hits the bed and I lean back on my forearms. His body lifts over mine, his strong arms finding ground on either side of me. I grab his shirt and tug him closer. I want this. I want him. I want us. I want all of this more than I've wanted anything else in my life. I try to bring our mouths together, but he holds back, our lips barely brushing, as his forehead comes to lie against mine.

My heart attempts to escape out of my chest.

His breath is heavy against my lips, and I ache, just *ache* everywhere. I wrap the shield around us like a hug, its strength fortified by the love I feel for him consuming every last atom that makes me me.

He licks his lips slowly, the edge of his tongue just barely grazing my mouth. All that jelly in my arms now liquefies. They tremble so hard I don't know if I'll be able to keep myself propped up.

I mimic his movement, and he shudders in response. There's a heartbeat between us before his mouth finally meets mine. From that moment on, everything is magnified between us, every touch, every kiss, every motion of brushing, sliding, grazing, worshiping skin against skin. Thousands of tiny nerves flare to life all over my body so that I am all feeling, no . . . no thinking. Worrying. Right now, this here, with this man . . . this is everything.

As turnabout is fair play, I take my sweet time exploring his body, kissing so very many places, licking others just so I can hear him groan and feel just how strongly his body reacts to me and my touch. Just like I'd wanted to do days before, I take him in my mouth, sucking him until I know he's perilously close to shattering. When the torture becomes too much for him, he pulls me up and flips me over so he's now over me, his mouth reclaiming mine for long, scorching minutes that leave me panting. And then he traces pulse lines down my neck with his lips and tongue until he finds my heart and then one, then the other breast. I arch up into him, all the cells in my body sparkling in fizzy, combustible, achy heat that threatens to tear me apart.

I need him to feel this, too.

I trail a hand down in between our bodies and stroke him. I delight in the sharp intake of breath, how his body now jerks and curves toward mine. With my other hand, I bring his face back up to mine and kiss him until starbursts bloom in my closed eyelids. "I need you," I whisper against his mouth, my nails grazing him until he quakes against me again, "in me."

His lovely, shuddery sigh nearly undoes me right then and there. "I need that, too. Gods, I love you so much, Chloe."

Nothing has ever sounded so beautiful to me before. These words, they're a gift. So is this man. Even though I don't know if I deserve him or his love, I'm going to hold onto them with both hands.

"I want . . . can we try something?" he murmurs against my neck as he positions himself above me.

I reach down and grab his buttocks, angling him so he slides into me. I gasp; he's so big, I'm so tight, but oh the sweet gods above, does this feel like heaven. "Anything."

He's so deep inside me, I can feel him all the way to my inner core. My eyes nearly roll right back into my head, I'm so very wonderfully filled. But then he pulls up so he's nearly all the way out. "Before you come . . ." And then he's back in me; I buck my hips up to meet his. "I want us to . . ."—another thrust that nearly disintegrates me—"merge."

The thought of this has me precariously close to coming already. But I don't want this moment to be over so soon, so I refuse to let my body have its release just yet. Kiss to kiss, caress to caress, thrust to thrust, we move together in perfect synchronicity. And then, just as I no longer have any more control over holding myself back, I surge into his mind, he into mine.

Before today, whenever we merged, I would have laid down money that it was better than any kind of orgasm that rocks a body, because it's born from souls. We've even done something very similar to this before, although never during actual intercourse and only ever with one person climaxing at a time due to oral sex or the like. It was phenomenal. But tonight, though? Tonight I learn the real truth—when merging souls and physical orgasms collide during actual intercourse, a person's being becomes nothing but stardust in the vastness of time and space. We are no longer just lovers separated by bodies.

We are one.

We are nothing.

We are everything.

Chapter Forty

My apartment—well, my old apartment—is exactly how I left it down to the placement of my purse and keys on the counter and my pajamas on the floor near my bed. There are magazines open on the coffee table and dishes in the sink. When I open the refrigerator, there's even a bottle of half-year-old orange juice.

I've just stepped right into my past.

"Callie said you tore this place apart," I say to Jonah when we're in my bedroom.

He leans against the doorframe, hands in his pockets. "I did."

I glance around my room. It's . . . not clean, by any means, but it's the kind of messy I would have left behind, not the kind made by a desperate man searching for answers.

"I straightened up afterward," he says quietly. "Just in case you came back. I didn't want you to have to deal with my . . ." His smile is bittersweet. "Rage, I guess. Or desperation."

I come over to where he's standing. "I'm so sorry I put you through that. I will regret that every day until I die."

He pulls me flush against his body. "I don't want your regret, Chloe. I think that we've had enough of that from both of us to last more than a lifetime." A leisurely kiss precedes, "Let's just focus on all the good things we've got going right now. Stepping back into old habits in which we drown ourselves in guilt doesn't do either of us any good."

I press another kiss against his mouth. "One day at a time?"

The dimple appears, even if just barely. "One day at a time."

I lean my head against his chest. "What about your stuff? Is it still next door, too?"

My face rises and falls with his sigh. "No. It's all either in storage or at Kellan's."

Next to my bed is a candid picture of the two of us taken maybe a year or so ago. To almost anyone looking at it, all they'd see are two people content in love. I'm kissing his cheek and he's smiling and looking away from the camera. I loved this picture for so long, but now, as I look at it, I realize it was just as fake as we had been. To move on, we need to let these pieces go and build ourselves new ones.

"I don't want to move back in here," I tell him.

He's quiet for a long moment. "I bought the apartment above Kellan's a few months ago. It's being remodeled, so . . ."

I pull away from him and stare up in shock.

He tugs on his hair. "I didn't mention it before now because I wasn't sure what I was going to do with it."

I shake my head in amazement, a wry smile tugging at my lips. "You and your real estate ventures. When will you ever learn to just tell me about them in the first place?"

He pulls me back to him. "I'm sorry—"

I reach up and lay my hand against his cheek. "I thought you basically just forbid that word. If I can't say it, you shouldn't be able to, either."

"Touché." He kisses my palm. "We can go look at it today, if you like."

We head back out into the living room, our hands entwined. "What made you buy an apartment?"

"Honestly, partially because it was one of those things that I did to prove to everyone I was moving on. Maybe even try to prove it to myself, too."

I pick up my purse and phone. "Partially? Also, why the one above Kellan's?"

His lips purse together as he considers how to answer me. Finally—"The building Kellan lives in doesn't have a lot of movement in terms of sales, but one came up while you were gone. Sophie Greenfield had put a bid on it, and . . ." His head tilts so his dark hair spills into his eyes. "After everything that happened this winter, there was no way in hell either of us were going to let her own that apartment. Buying it seemed to kill several birds with one stone."

I keep my voice light even though everything in me goes taut like a thread ready to snap. "What happened with Sophie?"

He picks up a shirt of his off of one of the chairs in the living room, one that he must have left behind. "Are you sure you want to know?"

I consider this carefully. "I've had a few run-ins with her since coming back. She's . . . still angry at me, I guess. And possibly deluded, because she thinks . . ." I try not to choke on the words, "that she and Kellan are a couple again or something."

Jonah tosses the shirt back down and sits on the couch. "Well," he says carefully, like he's afraid to set me off, "some of that may have to do with the fact that he had sex with her several times while you were gone and may have given her the impression that they were back together."

I drop like a stone in the chair across from him. *"Whaaaat?"*

The smile he gives me isn't much of one at all. "Everyone was very sympathetic to me when you disappeared, Chloe. I know they all meant well, but . . . personally, it was too much. I didn't want their sympathy. I didn't want . . . I didn't want that kind of focus on me. I wanted to be left alone in my misery, and eventually, people got the message. Kellan was forced into his isolation over the situation, though. Nobody but Astrid and Callie knew how hard your disappearance affected him. He was just as destroyed as me, since his Connection was gone, too, and he had to put on the act he always does, where nobody knows about the link between you two. So he acted out, lapsed back into behaviors he knew would mask his pain."

Even though I knew he'd done this, had guessed it the whole time I was in Alaska, I still feel sick to my stomach.

Kellan acted like this because of me. He hurt her—again—because of *me*.

"Sophie was relentless after you disappeared. She figured it was her shot to win him back or something. He refused to even acknowledge her at first, but she tracked him down at some bar one night when he was really . . ." Jonah won't meet my eyes. "Upset, for lack of a better word. He ended up going home with her. He regretted it immediately, but the damage was done. Out of guilt, he gave it a half-hearted try for a few weeks, but then he dumped her again."

Oh, gods.

"She basically stalked him after that. Called him constantly, showed up at work and the apartment without notice. Confronted him in public numerous times, even once hysterically claimed she was pregnant with his baby in front of an entire restaurant we were in." He finally looks at me. "I found her in our apartment more than once. One time she was in the tub in Kellan's bathroom, all flowers and bubbles and champagne. Another time, she was . . ." He's grossly uncomfortable telling me this. "Um, waiting for me, naked in my room. She . . . uh . . . thought, I don't know, she could make him jealous by hitting on me. It was . . ." He tugs on his hair. "Anyway, there was also one time Kel woke up to her standing over his bed, watching him sleep."

My nails dig into my palms. Did something happen between Jonah and Sophie, too—like she threatened so long ago? My anger threatens to consume me, but he gets up and comes over to where I'm sitting.

He takes my hands. "You have nothing to worry about, at least on my end, Chloe. Because, as hurt as I was, as much as I missed you . . ." He kisses the backs of my hands. "I couldn't stand the thought of being with anyone other than you."

And I believe him. I just do.

He kisses my cheek and sits down on the coffee table in front of me. "We've changed our locks several times since those break-ins. We couldn't figure out how she got ahold of a key, since no part of the door was damaged. The doorman is on notice that she's never allowed in the building anymore." He looks down at his hands. "I think she's mentally ill."

And by think, he means know, since he obviously understanding feelings better than most.

"She feels . . . off," he continues. "I don't know how to explain it. She genuinely believes she loves him, Chloe—although I would term it more obsession than true love. But to her, it's true love. She's even convinced that they have a Connection that the Seers keep missing. Kellan doesn't know what to do about it. He knows he fucked up by messing with her like he did. He also knows he never should have slept with her again the second time or humored any of her talks of a future between them."

Okay. Okay. Must think about this logically. Several pieces of furniture nearby are shuddering with my fury. I force myself to take several deep breaths, counting to twenty before I speak. Thankfully, the room calms. "You two are Emotionals. Have you not thought of influencing her to stay away?"

"Yes. Of course we have." Jonah's bleak. "But we were warned we'd be punished if we did."

Excuse me? Jonah is second tier Council and extremely influential. Kellan is highly ranked within the Guard; his mentor runs it now. Who in the worlds could ever tell the Whitecomb twins that they are forbidden from using their crafts on some psycho bitch that is stalking them? "Who told you that?"

"The first time Kellan called the Guard about her breaking into our apartment—it's when we realized this was a real problem—Sophie's parents petitioned the Council within a half hour, claiming they were fearful that we would retaliate and break the law by making their daughter a zombie. No matter what I argued, I was forcibly reminded that I could not influence another Magical simply because she was having,"—he flashes air quotes—"romantic difficulties with my brother. Nor was he allowed to influence her simply because he was tired of her." A frustrated sigh fills the room.

This just doesn't make sense. "Law? What law?"

"The one forbidding Emotionals from influencing other Magicals in matters such as love and hate without written permission beforehand."

What? This is the first I've ever heard of such a thing, which I guess just goes to show how little I really paid attention to my Council duties before. Shit. What else am I blindly ignorant to? I clear my throat. "Do you guys ever do that, though? Work on people without them knowing?"

"Most things are okay. Like, making hysterical people calmer. Or, those who are suicidal, we give them hope once more. But we never work on anybody without permission when it comes to matters of the heart." He leans forward. "Chloe, nobody wants to find out that they're in love with somebody because an Emotional made them be—or find out they loathe someone for the same reason. I get why there's a rule. I agree with it in principal, actually."

A frustrated sigh escape me, too. This is my fault. All of this is my fault. "What can we do?"

"Nothing we haven't already done."

"Maybe . . . I could talk to her?"

"Since I happen to know she hates you, I'm going to ask if you can make every attempt not to talk to her again."

I blink.

"What she feels toward you . . . it makes me uneasy," he says.

"Should I be worried?"

He pulls no punches. "I think we all should be worried."

Later that night, Jonah shows me his new apartment. Sawdust

and plastic tarps litter the floor, walls are half painted, but behind all this, I can see something infinitely dear to me: a home. More importantly, a home with him.

I nudge a paint can with my foot. "You know how much I've always wanted a gray living room."

I delight in watching his cheeks turn pink under his golden tan as he realizes I caught him subconsciously (or even consciously?) choosing colors that I would've picked for a home.

"It's okay." I loop my arms around his waist, twisting my fingers in his belt loops. "Apparently, I recreated your pea coat in Alaska. Karl called me out on it. I was looking for you, too."

He nuzzles my neck; my knees go weak. "Yeah?"

"I dreamed about you a lot, too," I admit. My voice is all breathy as his hands move underneath the hem of my shirt, skimming the line of skin right about my skirt.

His voice is soft against my sensitive skin. "Good dreams?"

I tell him that, while some dreams helped me relive good times between us, others had me losing him over and over again, only for me to destroy whatever place we were in in my desperation to find him. Anxiety crawls the walls of my stomach as I think of these nightmares and how they tortured me for months.

"I'm here," he tells me, cupping my face with both hands. "You haven't lost me."

I nearly choke on my regret. "I almost did."

The kiss he gives me is gentle, soothing. "I have something for you."

"Other than an apartment?"

He grins as he pulls away. "Do you like it then? If you don't, we can rent it out and find a place more to your liking."

"Are you kidding?" I glance around. "I love it." I lean up on my tiptoes so I can kiss the corner of his mouth. "You have excellent taste, Mr. Whitecomb."

He laughs, and I delight in how he blushes once more. I'm told that, while the renovations are almost done, if I want to switch out any of the paints, I'm free to do that. None of the appliances in the kitchen have been bought yet, nor has any of the furniture other than what we already own, so we can go shopping for them as soon as I want.

"Is that my gift?" I tease as I throw open the closet door in the master suite. I'm faced with what looks like a whole other room— not just a closet, but an entire room dedicated to clothes, shoes, and the like.

Whoa. I don't even have one-fourth of the amount of clothes needed to fill such a space.

"No." He pulls me away from the closet. "Nor is that." I'm led over to a huge bay window that has a bench built in right in front of it. I sit down, but he drops down to a knee. The hummingbirds in my chest take flight as I drink the sight of him in the beautiful moonlight spilling into the room.

"I proposed to you, remember?" Despite my teasing, my voice trembles.

I love how deep his dimple is right now. "You didn't give me a ring, though."

"But . . ." I motion to his hand, except . . . the ring we'd found isn't there anymore. It hasn't been there for awhile, not since he took it off the moment he found mine in the secret box. And now it lies next to the one that had hugged my finger back in the apartment we left behind a few hours ago.

He shakes his head slowly. "I loved those rings, Chloe. Part of me still does. I have a lot of happy memories associated with them. It's just . . ." He blows out a breath that sends the hairs around his face floating. "Fate picked those rings out for us. We didn't have a say in them."

For a moment, I don't know what to say. Jonah . . . he feels that way, too? Resentful of how Fate has manipulated us so much?

"This one, though," he says softly, pulling something out of one of his pockets, "I think . . . it would mean a lot to me if you wore it." His palm opens to reveal one of the most beautiful diamond rings I have ever seen. It's still rose gold, like our others, but constellations of small diamonds surround a beautiful square one in the middle. Wait—there's one small blue stone near the center diamond. Maybe a sapphire? "This is the one I've always wanted to propose to you with. This is the one I've always seen on your finger when I dream about our future. This is the one I wanted to pick."

My breath catches in my throat. It's gorgeous. Just absolutely gorgeous.

"It's been in my family for generations. My mom wore it last. It would mean the worlds to me if you wore it, too, as a symbol of how much I love you." He's uncharacteristically nervous, which I would find adorable if I didn't actually feel like bursting into tears brought on from sublime happiness right now. He wants me to wear his mother's ring?

My voice shakes with emotion when I tell him, "I love it."

He holds the ring up so the blue stone faces me. "This one . . . this sapphire is from Astrid." His smile is so very sweet. "Because I've been lucky enough to have not one, but two wonderful women to raise me. Maybe someday, when we pass this ring down to our son or daughter, you can substitute one of the stones for something that represents you, too."

Okay. I officially burst into those noisy, happy tears. I stick my hand out and the moment he slides it on my finger, this feeling of overwhelming contentment overcomes me. He gave me his mother's ring. Somehow, after everything that's happened over the last few years, he trusts and loves me enough right now to hand over one of the few possessions of hers he still has.

I pull him up so I can throw my arms around his neck. "I love you so, so much, Jonah Whitecomb. Nothing would make me happier than to wear this ring."

Later, as we lay naked on the ground on top a blanket I made us, sated in each other's arms after an intense yet beautiful round of lovemaking, I marvel at how right this ring looks on my finger.

I will never take this one off.

Chapter Forty-One

"I'm gone for like a week, and you get engaged?" Will nearly slams his coffee cup down on the table. "Plus you're moving out already?" He glares at his father. "Dad! Is this not moving a wee bit too fast? Didn't you lecture us just a few months back about how the two of us are way too young to even contemplate marriage?"

Cameron sighs and sets the newspaper he'd been reading down. "Son, you know as well as I do that love doesn't always move on the timetables we'd like it to."

"I'm not moving out today," I assure him. "The apartment isn't even done yet. Plus, it's a ten minute walk away, so chances are, I'll be over here everyday anyway."

Will arrived in Annar less than an hour before—he'd been ready to go to his room and pass out when he noticed the ring on my hand. From that point on, rather than telling us what happened in Glasgow, he drilled me on the particulars of everything that happened in the last few days.

Cameron and I exchange a worried glance. If Will is acting this upset over me moving out, it's because something bad happened in Scotland.

"How is Becca?" Cameron asks quietly.

He's silent for so long I actually start believing he's not going to tell us. Just as Cameron gets up to head into the kitchen, Will finally says, "Cora came through. Becca's . . . she's fine. Miraculous recovery and all. Her family nearly shattered the record for hysterical sobbing over how the doctors didn't know shite." He sighs and drops his chin in a propped up hand. "She doesn't remember anything about the accident. Broke down when she learned that Grant was dead." He scrubs his hair with his free hand. "Had to be tranquilized or some shite when she learned she lost the baby."

"Oh, son," Cameron murmurs, reaching out to lay a hand on Will's forearm.

"Kellan came in quite handy then. Got her . . . to a point, I guess, where she wasn't bloody hysterical all the time. Then she called me. Begged me to come see her. Jesus. It was brutal."

My heart goes out to him.

"She . . . she wants another chance. Says she misses me, that we've lost too much time already. Told me she was sorry for what she did, so very bloody sorry that she shagged my best mate and was going to have his baby."

"How do you feel about that?" I ask softly.

"Like she fucking punched me right in the balls." He stands up. "I'm going to go to bed. Chloe, if you dare to get married while I'm napping, I'll never speak to you again."

I stand up and hug him tightly. "Understood."

When he's gone, Cameron says, "I worry about him, hen."

Me, too.

After much going back and forth on how to handle the situation, Jonah and I finally decide it'd be best if he talked to Kellan about our decision to get engaged again. Initially, I'd wanted to be there, but in the end, I realized there was a good chance I'd just flat-out make things worse by sobbing outright, wracked by guilt, which would have done neither man any good.

Even still, I'm a nervous wreck tonight, knowing that Jonah is having that discussion with Kellan while I'm to have one with

Callie.

Jonah's ex-girlfriend shows up at my apartment, board game in hand for what she believes to be a leisurely night in. But Cal's always had keen eyesight, so the moment I attempt to hug her, arms outstretched, she stops me with a look that is an agonizing cross between resignation, surprise, and flat-out pain.

My stomach plummets three stories down. She's been telling me for some time that she's over Jonah. Hell, she's made it clear numerous times lately that she's more than interested in Will (although, if I tell him, she warns, she'll cut me out of her life forever). So knowing that seeing the ring on my finger crushes her is a blow I wasn't quite prepared for.

Within seconds, though, she pulls out a smile and hugs me anyway, murmuring congratulations in that husky voice of hers.

"Callie—"

She pulls herself upright. "Don't you dare apologize, Chloe. I can see that's what you want to do. I'm just—I'm being stupidly sentimental. That ring . . ." She shakes her head, sending silvery strands floating around her shoulders before letting out a throaty, sad chuckle. "I used to dream about that ring on my finger."

I can't help but ask, "Do you still?"

"No." And then, more firmly, "No. Not anymore."

Will comes out from his room, hair adorably mussed. "Chloe, have you—" His feet come to a halt the moment he spies Cal. "Oh. Hello, Callie."

They stare at each other so long that I've become the awkward third wheel.

I take the board game from Cal. "Do you want to join us?" I ask Will. "I ordered a pizza and—"

"Why do you look like that?" Callie asks quietly.

She's not talking to me, though. One of Will's hands goes to his hair. "Like what?"

"Like you've . . ." She flushes, waves her hand around. "Like that."

I've got to admit, I'm just as confused as he is about what she's talking about. Other than looking like he just got out of bed, he looks just like Will. Incredibly gorgeous, yes, but it's not like she hasn't ever seen him before.

"Oh, well." He ducks his head. "Right, then."

Is it wrong to admit I'm amused by how dorky they're acting right now?

"Is that a yes?" I ask him.

He blinks, like he's just remembered I'm in the room. "Um . . . yeah. Of course. Let me—I guess . . ." He runs his hands down his wrinkly t-shirt and then blushes himself. "I'll be right back."

After he leaves, I turn to Callie. "Smooth moves there."

She snatches the board game back. "Shut up." And then, more gently, "Is he okay?"

I wish I could answer that one myself.

According to Jonah, things did not go too well when he talked to Kellan about our re-engagement. There was no fighting this time, nor arguing—just Kellan shutting down right before his eyes before leaving to go do who knows what. He hadn't come back by the next morning, but Jonah assured me that he was in contact with Kellan their way and his brother was asking for some space to wrap his head around everything.

It was hard not to go running after him. I bite my lip, wanting to keep the words inside, but I eventually murmur, "Maybe we should have waited to tell him?"

We're looking at furniture today, despite me being able to make us pretty much anything we want; while I'd been so excited to do this very normal, couple-y thing just an hour earlier, now I feel the weights of our actions pressing down against me once more.

Jonah pulls me close and kisses the side of my head. "He appreciated me telling him right away. He asked me to tell you he doesn't want you to feel guilty about any of this."

"How can I not?" I whisper softly.

He leans his head down against mine. "One day at a time, honey. And if that's too hard—one step at a time. One breath. One heartbeat. I'm not promising that someday we'll all look back at this time and laugh at how we agonized over our situation, but I do think there will come a time in which we'll all have learned how to deal with it better."

I swallow. "Will he be coming tonight?"

We'd decided to announce our good news to our loved ones at a dinner party at one of Astrid's favorite restaurants. There will be no big wedding planned this time; in fact, we're leaning toward doing it down at Karnach in the next month or so with just our closest friends and family present. Nothing fussy. Small is the way to go, we figure, when trying to lessen the devastating impact this blissful yet bittersweet occasion will bring to the other most important person in our lives.

"No." He kisses my hair once more and pulls away. "I told him about it, though. I left the choice up to him on how he wants to handle all of this. He thinks it'll be best for everyone involved if he stays at home tonight. But he wants you—us—to know, he's done running."

It is so incredibly selfish of me, but I'm glad Kellan won't be coming. The entire time, I'd be so stressed worrying about him, wondering how he was feeling, that I'd probably make myself sick. That would only stress Jonah out and then Kellan, too; eventually they would do that dumb thing they do where they bend over backwards to try to make things right for me. In the end, it would be a miserable experience for all of us.

One heartbeat. One breath. I pull another in, count to ten. To twenty. I force myself to look at the beautiful ring on my finger, remember how I came to the choice I did. The happiness that fills me at such thoughts will always be bittersweet.

In this triangle, someone is always going to be hurting, and I hate that thought so much it makes me want to blow up everything in sight.

I force myself to focus on picking our furniture for the next hour. After we'd found some pieces we like, we head over to the sales counter. As Jonah schedules delivery times and pays for our items, I stare out the large glass windows at the front of the story. It's the perfect sort of day in Annar, with soft white clouds gracing cool blue skies and gentle breezes tempering warm sunlight.

Just before I turn back to Jonah, a flash of bright, white hair in the group of people waiting at a stoplight across the street catches both my attention and my breath. A man stands there, one whose accusatory words have caused too many nightmares to count over the last year.

I blink, but he's still there. Tall. Elegant. Grizzled goatee. White hair. Paler than I remember, wearing a long, black coat on a day when everyone else is packing away his or her outerwear. He's standing across the street, an undecipherable smile on his thin lips as he stares right at me.

"Jonah," I say quietly, tugging on his sleeve. "I know I'm out of the loop and all, but is Jens Belladonna back in Annar?"

The sales clerk hands him our paperwork. "No. He's still classified as missing. Why?"

I turn back toward the window, but the man is no longer there.

I jog out of the store, ignoring Jonah's concern. Once I'm out on the street, I search in every direction. That was Jens. I'm positive of it. Where could he have gone?

"Chloe, what's going on?" Jonah asks when he joins me.

"I just saw Jens Belladonna." I point across the street. "Right there. He was watching us."

Jonah's forehead furrows. "Maybe you just thought you saw somebody that looked like him?"

I go to argue, but as Fate would have it, another ghost from my past blocks our path. Which is just . . . fabulous.

"Well, look at this." Sophie Greenfield's smile is so cat-ate-the-canary smug. "Slumming again, Jonah?"

He closes his eyes briefly, but not before I see the anger he's attempting to hide. "Sophie, we really don't have time for this right now."

She actually has the audacity to reach out, like she's going to trail her horribly lovely fingers across his cheek. Unable to help myself, I slap her hand away. But this only exacerbates the haughty smile. "Did Jonah man up and tell you about what happened between us while you were gone?"

Jonah refuses to play her game, though. "We're leaving now, Sophie. I advise you stay away from the both of us."

"Did you know I was naked in his bed?" Sophie's voice carries across the sidewalk as we walk away. "And that I loved it when he put his hands on me?"

I swing back around, furious. How dare she manipulate what happened like this—and in public no less! Just as I'm about to put her in her place, Jonah grabs my arms and says quietly, "Don't engage her. It only makes it worse."

"But—"

"Believe me when I tell you that Kellan and I have made this mistake far too often. It only ends up antagonizing her to act out more. Our best line of recourse is to walk away right now. You do not need her parents petitioning the Council, claiming you've been unfairly attacking their daughter in public. Not now, when you're just reassuming your duties."

I stare at him in amazement. Over his shoulder, Sophie mouths, "You know I'm telling the truth."

My fists clench tightly, but I let Jonah steer me away.

Chapter Forty-Two

When my mother walks into the private room Astrid reserved for us at her favorite Elvin restaurant, my stomach decides we're on a roller coaster. She looks around the loud room, clutching her handbag close.

She came. My mother came to my engagement dinner. And I have no idea how I feel about it.

I'm rooted to the spot below me, Jonah's hand on my back as he laughs at something Moira Graystone has just said. I've got my goddaughter Emily in my arms and all I can do is simply stare at the woman I grew up with but hardly know .

Abigail Lilywhite finally spies me and winds her way through the room until she reaches us. She clears her throat and nearly forces herself to smile. "Hello, Chloe. You're looking good this evening."

No . . . no comment about being too thin? My hair not being right?

Jonah nudges me and I blink hard. "Um . . . hi, Mom."

Karl and Moira know how things are between me and my parents, so our awkward greeting doesn't faze anymore. Moira simply reclaims her daughter and, after saying hi to my mom, too, she and her husband wander over to where Zthane and Giuliana are talking to Cora and Raul.

"I'm glad you could come tonight," Jonah tells her.

It's then I notice her smile is brittle, like she's completely afraid to do the wrong thing. Say the wrong thing. So I step forward and hug my mother. "Me, too," I whisper in her ear.

Her thin body trembles, like she's holding in too much emotion. "As am I."

Tonight, we'll add more bricks to our foundation together.

Dinner is wonderful. Everyone is so happy for us, even though we get teased for getting engaged more times than most couples. Astrid and Cameron are so cute together (despite their vehement protests that they are, in fact, not a couple), as are Cora and Raul. Will and Callie spend the entire time bickering and it's so adorable I just want to pinch their cheeks. I get at least twenty hugs from Emily, and the sweetest picture of me and Jonah she drew. Caleb takes care of my mother. Outside of Kellan, everyone I love most is in this room tonight.

Speaking of . . . "I love you," I tell Jonah.

He kisses me, prompting lots of glasses to clink. We laugh and for once, everything is perfect. Incandescent. Free. Like we have a right to this bliss. Like . . . maybe everything is going to work out after all.

Midway through dessert, I excuse myself to go to the small ladies' room across the restaurant. I practically glide across the floor, the biggest, goofiest grin filling my face.

I am in love and I don't care who knows it.

It isn't until I'm washing my hands that I become aware of someone standing behind me. "You're a tough one to get alone," he says, voice distorted and wheezy. "So many people looking out for you. Even here, in this place of gluttony."

I stare at him for a moment in the mirror before turning around slowly. I don't even allow myself to feel vindicated in this moment. I'm . . . freaked out, to be honest.

"Hello, Jens," I say.

His thin lips curl into a smile. It is, in no way, pleasant. "Hello, little Creator. How lovely you look today."

I quickly survey my surroundings. There is no one else in the bathroom. A singular window is off to the side, propped open, no doubt, by Jens. A door leading back to the restaurant opposite the window. It is not an ideal place to launch at attack, but it is doable. Collateral damage will be minimal.

"Come now." He's close enough now to drag his fingers across my arm. "Let us talk together for a few moments, you and I."

Shivers of disgust flare up and down my arms. His skin, it's . . . dry, papery. Tiny white flakes remain where his fingers have lain.

I have to fight my nausea back.

The moment my hand moves, his swipes out and grabs it. He's strong, almost unnaturally so. Within less than a second, the bones in my fingers break like tiny twigs under a giant's feet.

The pain is blinding. All I can do is gasp, because it's more than a punch to the gut. It's a godsdamn cannon ball and I can't even make a sound out of shock.

"I have always liked this about you." His eyes are beetles, flat and black. Lifeless. "How you are so willing to take risks. An entire restaurant filled with sentient life, including those that you cohabitate with and have feelings for, and yet you are willing to blow me and this room up without a second thought."

My other hand angles, but he catches that one, too, crunching more small bones like they're nothing. OH MY GODS OH MY GODS. Searing pain tears through every nerve ending in my body. He slams me back against the sink, the hard porcelain unforgiving against my hipbones.

This time the urge to scream out in agony consumes me, but before I can, one of his papery, disgusting hands clamps over my mouth.

"Can you do it, little Creator? Can you simply think of a change, and make it so?"

Why is . . . why . . . how . . . I shake my head desperately, but it's hard, so hard to think of anything else but the pain raging through me. I need . . . must . . . cage? No—will him out—

Gods, I can't *think*.

Jens clamps down harder the fragile fragments left intact in one of my hands. Darkness swarms my vision. "We cannot converse if you keep trying to attack me. Be a good girl and show some respect."

He removes his hand from my mouth slowly. Tiny white flakes rain down between us. "Jens . . . why . . .?" Even to me, my voice is slurred.

"Do you really not know?" he asks, amused. "Can you not feel it?"

Any attempt at coherent thought is countered with various pressure adjustments against my still trapped hand.

"Oh, little Creator. I'm worse than disappointed. You should know that appearances are *always* deceptive."

I'm teetering on the edge of blackness. "Who . . . not . . . Jens?"

He closes in on me; a putrid smell threatens to overwhelm the remaining, functional senses I've got going for me. He taps my forehand with a long finger. "Think, little Creator. Think. You can figure it out. You're a bright girl." That ugly smile of his curves upward once more. "Shall I let you in on a secret?"

I actually throw up now. Between the pain and the smell, I can't stop myself.

If Jens, or whoever this is, is bothered by the rancid remains of my recently consumed dinner all over his shirt, he doesn't let on. "We have been in the midst of a game together for some time now. It has been droll, this game of cat and mouse we play. In the spirit of our burgeoning relationship, tonight will be all about riddles. You have asked me a question, and I was gracious enough to give you a clue. Now, it is my turn. Tell me, little Creator. Which one is out there right now? What is the name it goes by?"

I struggle to focus, but all I want to do is to let myself fall into darkness. What . . . what is he talking about?

Surprisingly, the pressure on my ruined hand relents momentarily. Jens leans forward, his ashy lips too close to my ear.

Nausea rushes back like a tsunami. "I have to admit, I cannot tell those two apart." The hairs on the back of my neck stand at attention. "All I can see is that they are two halves of a whole."

Is he . . . Jonah? He's asking about Jonah? I struggle, panicked, but lights flash before my eyes as my hand is refolded tightly into his.

"Abominations." And now his lips do make contact, on the space right before my ear; bile surges once more up my throat. "Fate should not have allowed that. *I* would not have allowed that. Once, such perversions would have become tributes. Offerings of appeasement."

My eyes, already unfocused and swinging wildly, land for a brief moment on his hand, still holding mine in a vise-like grip. There's a signet ring on the pinky. This is Jens' ring. Every single time I've ever seen him, he's been wearing this ring.

This is Jens, and yet it is not. Because Jens . . . Jens knew the difference between Jonah and Kellan.

I wish Caleb were still in my head, to tell me what to do. Tell me who is here with me. I close my eyes, let myself sink into the abyss threatening to take me, but a sharp crack against my face forces me back up once more. "My patience wears thin," the Jens person says.

I think he might have shattered my cheekbone, too. "I'll die . . . before I . . ." I pull in a shuddery breath.

Jens smiles, and then laughs. It is not Jens' laugh. It is sly, old, filled with countless atrocities and immeasurable power. "Oh, no, little Creator. There will be no death allowed for you, not for some time now. I cannot guarantee that for those nearby, though."

My concentration, on the verge of coherency, is shattered once more as he clamps down on both of my hands. I gasp, "Don't . . . please . . . don't hurt them . . ."

"It is beneath you to try to protect those who are inferior, and yet you still try. You are a Creator; every life is beneath you. Dealing death is not to be feared. It is to be revered."

I start to cry. Flat out cry.

He leans close again. "I can smell how much you wish to destroy me. It is intoxicating. Exhilarating." He caresses my cheek with his lips. The shudder wracking my body turns epileptic. "I will look forward to encouraging you to give into that side of yourself."

I try to speak, to tell him to fuck off, but he squeezes even harder. Blurry lights invade the darkness in my vision. "Did you know that pain can help? You just have not learned this lesson yet." His nose traces my neck as he pulls in a long, deep breath. "You are trying so hard right now to overcome me. You are vibrating with power, so much so, and yet . . . it is still contained by such a fragile vessel. I wish I could be inside you right now, feel what you are feeling. It would be almost humbling. Exciting." He pauses, licks my neck, as if he is tasting something new.

My knees nearly give out. Bile resurges in the back of my throat.

"Can you feel my excitement?" he wheezes softly.

I fight. As hard as I can. I kick and will everything in me to crash against him, but it's no use. The pain is blocking me from doing anything with my powers.

I'm nothing but a rag doll in his hands.

"Soon enough," he murmurs, licking once more from the base of my neck all the way to my forehead. "Soon enough, little one."

He releases my hands so suddenly I nearly crash to the floor. In desperation, I attempt to yank the stall doors off their hinges to use as weapons against him, but he wraps a hand around my throat and presses the other against my forehead. A loud squealing sound roars through my mind and then my entire being. I've never heard anything like it before.

It's deafening.

The doors before me suspend in mid-air. Jens yanks me off my feet so my toes dangle limply against the ground. Just as I begin to lose consciousness, I watch the doors slide back into position, as if they'd never been yanked off in the first place.

How . . . how is this possible?

"Tonight is not our night. Until it's time, sweet dreams," he murmurs.

The sound in my mind ratchets up a thousand decibels until I am pain personified. I shatter over and over again until, thankfully, everything fades to blessed black.

Acknowledgments

While writing is a very solitary process, a book cannot be successful without a team. To my editor, Natasha Tomic, my agent, Pam van Hylckama Vlieg, and my publicist, KP Simmon, I'm lucky to have such a strong team behind me. Thanks for believing in me and for everything you do for me and my stories. It makes all the difference. While I'm at it . . . Carly Stevens, this cover? I'm still sighing and swooning over it. And Julie Titus? Your formatting skills make me so happy. *Grazie* to you all, ladies—you're simply the best around.

Fact: I have some of the best critique partners and beta readers around. Tracy Cooper, Andrea Johnston, Vilma Gonzalez, Megan O'Connell, and Cherisse Nadal, I cannot thank you guys enough for all the time, love, suggestions, feedback, and encouragements you've given this book and these characters. All the love to you guys.

I also have an amazing street team—guys, I pinch myself every day because I am so very lucky to have such dedicated, wonderful fans. Thank you for everything you all do for me. Please know that I'm eternally grateful for each and every one of you. I also feel incredibly lucky to have so many book bloggers championing the Fate series—thank you all so much. There are a few I'd like to send specific shout-outs to, who have really made this journey special: Natasha at Natasha is a Book Junkie, Vilma at Vilma's Book Blog,

Cristina at Cristina's Book Reviews, Ana at The Book Hookup, Megan at Paperbook Princess, Jessica at Lovin' Los Libros, Caitlin at The Road is You, Chelsea at Starbucks & Books Obsession, Meredith at Pandora's Books, and Kathryn and Shelley at TSK TSK What to Read. Ladies, your tireless support and pimping of my books means so very, very much to me.

To my three boys and husband, I love you guys more than all the cupcakes in the world. Thanks for putting up with all my crazy writing hours. Mom and Dad? Thanks for always believing in me as a writer. To my friends and family who reach out and support me as I chase my dreams, I adore you all.

Last, but certainly not least, to you, dear readers . . . all the thanks to you from the bottom of my heart.

For information about Heather Lyons and her books, visit:

Facebook
https://www.facebook.com/heatherlyonsbooks

Website
http://www.heatherlyons.net/

Twitter
https://twitter.com/hymheather

Goodreads
http://www.goodreads.com/author/show/6552446.Heather_Lyons

Blog
http://www.haveyoumetheather.blogspot.com/

About the Author

Heather Lyons has always had a thing for words–She's been writing stories since she was a kid. In addition to writing, she's also been an archaeologist and a teacher. Heather is a rabid music fan, as evidenced by her (mostly) music-centric blog, and she's married to an even larger music snob. They're happily raising three kids who are mini music fiends who love to read and be read to.

Other Titles by Heather Lyons:

A Matter of Fate (Book 1)
Beyond Fate (Book 1.5)
A Matter of Heart (Book 2)

Made in United States
Troutdale, OR
05/02/2024

19541028R00196